THE YEAR
AFTER

THE YEAR
AFTER

THE YEAR AFTER

Martin Davies

WINDSOR
PARAGON

First published 2011
by Hodder & Stoughton
This Large Print edition published 2012
by AudioGO Ltd
by arrangement with
Hodder & Stoughton Ltd

Hardcover   ISBN: 978 1 445 89419 5
Softcover   ISBN: 978 1 445 89420 1

British Library Cataloguing in Publication Data available

Printed and bound in Great Britain by
MPG Books Group Limited

No year has been like this that has just gone by;
It may be that what Father says is true,
If things are so it does not matter why:
But everything has burned and not quite through.

Charlotte Mew, *The Quiet House*

A woman drowned in the River Hanna when the men were away. She was found in the dark pool below Hannesford Court, not far from the place where the river gurgles from the moor. No stone was placed in the churchyard and the grass grows quickly there, so few remember. Memory is an uncertain witness.

Visitors to Hannesford who find their way down to the old donkey bridge seldom pay much attention to the turbulent pool where she was discovered. Their eyes are caught by the honey-coloured stone of the great house, the high chimneys that lead the eye to the moor beyond. Later they recall Hannesford's lawns stretching out in the sunshine, the scented gardens, the little blue and white summerhouse hidden in the trees. Never the swirling water.

1

London in 1919 was a city of shadows. I arrived late in the evening, my uniform still grimy with Flanders dust, and took a room at the Mecklenburg, reluctant to face the emptiness of my own rooms in Rudolph Square. It had been a solitary journey, the boat quiet and the train nearly empty, and I felt subdued. I'd gone to war in the company of friends, people I knew well. I was returning alone, to a city where I felt a stranger.

Three days before Christmas the winter season should have been at its height, but London struck me as drab and strangely muted. The big houses would once have been ablaze with lights, and the streets around them jammed with motor cars. Even at the height of the carnage the city had always retained a certain restless gaiety, a desperate determination to make the most of the moment. I'd seen hollow-cheeked officers home on leave transformed in a matter of hours into the dashing young blades their friends remembered, dining at Mimosa's, dancing at the Clarion, surely never a fellow to match them with a girl or a glass. Only the shadows in their eyes betrayed them, and only to those who had learned where to look. But times had changed since then. Now the future stretched to more distant horizons, and few had the heart to celebrate as they once had. So the big houses stood in darkness, solemn memorials to the lost, and I dined alone off a modest cutlet in the

1

Mecklenburg's splendid, half-empty dining rooms.

I should have come back sooner. Looking around at the pale, unfamiliar faces of my fellow diners I knew I'd missed something. Had I returned as soon as the fighting stopped, when the city was still ecstatic, I would have been greeted by cheers and klaxons and a nation in frenzy, by streetlamps and unshuttered windows blazing in the darkness, and church clocks chiming every hour of the night in defiance of the grounded Zeppelins. There would have been shouting and excitement, and the hubbub might have helped me to understand that all was truly over.

But in the days that followed the Armistice, unsettled by the silence of the battlefields, trying to remember who I really was, I'd not been in the mood for celebration. The dead, it seemed, remained dead, even when the guns were quiet; I'd no idea why I was not among them. And then the influenza had reached camp and there'd been a shortage of officers, and those who remained in France all seemed possessed of wives and children. I would watch them write their letters home and feel guilty. Most of them were not long in uniform. I knew them less well than I knew men still lying in the fields. But after so much time, what were a few more months to me? Without thinking too much about it, I let it be known that I for one was in no particular hurry to cross the Channel.

No one seemed too disturbed by the delay. My sister in England knew me too well to be either hurt or surprised. She wrote assiduously: kind, fond letters with news of my nephews and the promise of a warm welcome in Derbyshire when the army let me go. And my mother, serenely settled in the

2

south of France with her secretary and her writing and her views of Cap Martin, wrote letters about her postman and her publisher and the magnificent *fruits de mer* from the bay beneath her house, all as if nothing in the world had ever changed. I would go to visit both as soon as I got out, I resolved, and after that I'd find some better rooms in London, somewhere with a view of the park, where I could decide what to do with my unexpected future.

But at night in the mess, when other officers spoke of England, I found myself thinking of the moors above Hannesford. When they talked of being home for Christmas, I'd remember the holly around the fireplace at Hannesford Court. And when a jovial fellow with a ticket out of France mentioned that he had people in Devon, I thought of the Stansbury family. For me, Devon would always mean the Stansburys.

And then there was the letter from Freddie Masters which found me near Dieppe, late in 1919, still waiting to be demobbed. A peculiar letter about the death of Professor Schmidt. The professor had been a guest at Hannesford in those last months before the war, when being German in Britain was not yet a crime; a gentle man interested in moths and English country churches, who had died of a heart attack while the famous Rose Ball was at its height. Masters asked in the most casual possible way if I'd ever felt any disquiet about the manner of the professor's death. It was an absurd and rather bizarre question. There had been no mystery about it. His heart had given out. I'd seen him die.

Masters was a prattling fool.

And yet as I stood on deck, that winter of 1919,

3

watching the coast of Belgium say its farewell in an ironic blaze of sunlight, I was still uncertain of my plans. My mother, according to a postcard from Cap Martin, was beginning another novel. My sister was in Perthshire, spending Christmas with her husband's family, and would be busy with children and visits and in-laws. And in two or three days, after five years in uniform, I would no longer be in the army. It was an oddly unsettling thought.

So I decided the best thing to do was to get up to London and have a decent dinner and a very, very long bath. And when I arrived in town—after sending for my things and bathing luxuriously at the Mecklenburg—I found three letters waiting for me: crisp, neat envelopes addressed in different hands. One of them, I saw at once, was from Margot Stansbury. Although my fingertips hovered over it, it was not the one I opened first. Instead I waited until I was settled in the green leather fastness of the hotel library, then turned to the envelope I'd been expecting, a note from Lady Stansbury on stiff, cream-coloured paper, inviting me to spend Christmas at Hannesford Court. Since first meeting the Stansburys I'd received just such a note every year, until the exodus of young men had put a stop to such things. The same handwriting, the same notepaper, even the same, very faint, scent of violets.

Dear Tom,
We do so hope you will join us . . .

It was over five years since I'd last been there. Since then, even if I'd wanted to go, the Byzantine subtleties of the military machine had made such a journey impossible. Either my leave had fallen when the Stansburys were away, or the opportunities to visit them had been too fleeting. Yet before that, before the hostilities, I'd rarely missed the opportunity of seeing in the New Year in the company of Margot Stansbury and her siblings.

Margot. Her letter lay on the side of my armchair while a very elderly waiter fussed over a glass of the Mecklenburg's brandy. *No, nothing else, thank you. Yes, France. Yes, it had been bad. Yes, perhaps things would get better now . . .* I waited until the old man shuffled away before turning to Margot's letter.

Was I disappointed? Perhaps, although I don't really know what I'd been expecting. In style it was laconic, slightly amused, slightly irreverent. Very like Margot.

> *Do come, Tom. Mother insists tradition must be maintained, and you are practically part of the tradition now, aren't you? Besides, there's Harry's memorial service to get through, so we'll all need cheering up. It will be <u>bloody</u> if you don't make it . . .*

There was no reference to any event in the past, nothing of the last time we met. That too was very like Margot.

The third letter was far more surprising. In my reply to Freddie Masters's note I'd made it clear I felt no disquiet whatsoever about the manner of Professor Schmidt's death; but for some reason Masters had seen fit to write again. This persistence was perplexing, for Masters had never struck me as a persevering sort of fellow. We'd met often at

5

Hannesford Court, but we'd never been close; even by the standards of Harry Stansbury's crowd, Masters had been a colourful, rather ridiculous figure. He'd had a safe post in one of the ministries when the war broke out, and I'd been rather taken aback a couple of years later to run into him on the Strand and find him commissioned in an infantry regiment. That meeting had been cordial enough but Masters had shown no inclination to treat me as a confidant. Which is perhaps why the contents of this new letter piqued my curiosity.

Thanks so much for your reply, old man. All very reassuring. Even so, if you're home in time for Christmas, do try to make it down to Hannesford. I shall be there for the duration— yea, even until the champagne corks fall silent —and there's something I want to talk to you about. It's rather delicate—God forbid, possibly even unsavoury—so I'd be obliged if you didn't mention it to Sir Robert and his good lady, or any of the clan. Don't want to say too much about it now, old boy, but it does relate to that fellow Schmidt. If I remember rightly he was a friend of yours . . .

And it was true. In our own way, I suppose we had been friends. But there was no denying that in those last few days, with Hannesford Court so full of distractions, I hadn't been as attentive to the professor as a friend should have been.

Memory is a contrary thing. I've seen the tiniest shard of hot steel shatter it the way shells shatter a church, leaving parts of it in pieces, others mysteriously untouched. But it can be tenacious too, like the grasses on those Flanders plains, creeping slowly back into the sunlight long after the bombardment has rolled away. I could still remember, in vivid fragments, the night of the professor's death: the darkness on the terrace, the heat, the heavy scent of roses; the velvet shadows where I stood, brimming with self-pity; indoors, the band blithely playing the 'Fairy Waltz'. And the slightly absurd figure of the professor, treading slowly up the steps from the lawn, then crumpling, clutching at his chest. I remembered that Anne Gregory had reached him before I did. There had been tears in her eyes.

The night of the professor's death had been my last at Hannesford. It was the night I vowed that I'd never willingly set eyes on Margot Stansbury again.

They were cutting holly in the woods below Hannesford when word arrived that he was coming home. I heard the rumour from the vicar. It was one of those brilliant December mornings when the ground is hard and the sky is very clear, when every branch and bush and spider's web holds the pattern of the frost.

It had been a good year for berries—the hedges were full of them—and the spiked boughs that would appear in such profusion at Hannesford Court on Christmas Eve were glorious with scarlet. The trees had thrived on neglect, but now they were being cut again. After a succession of bitter, silent winters, the Stansbury family had decided that Christmas was once again to be embraced.

'They say Tom Allen's about to be demobbed,' the vicar told me on his return to the vicarage. 'I heard the news from Lady Stansbury who had it from someone at the ministry. Such a mercy that he's come through it all, eh?' His tone was jovial. Not many from Hannesford had come through it. 'It will be wonderful to see him again. You might even bump into him when you go up to London, Anne. Or perhaps we'll be seeing him down here. He always used to make it down for Christmas, didn't he?'

'Yes, he did.' I'd put down my sewing to welcome him and for a moment I was able to busy myself with his coat and hat, with placing his gloves very carefully on the edge of the hall table. 'But that was before. So much has changed. Who knows what he'll want to do now?'

At the time, I'd been in no doubt. I wasn't going back. It would have been easy enough to keep away: a summer abroad, a Christmas with my sister, a polite disentangling of ties formed almost by accident. I would have seen the Stansburys in town, of course; the world was too small to avoid that. But they moved in much more elevated circles than I did: our encounters wouldn't be too frequent.

In France, I thought I had put it all behind me. I'd thought my memories of Hannesford pulverised by the guns. But that first morning in London, blinking in the pale sunlight, nothing seemed quite as it had done. Once upon a time my days in town had filled themselves without effort. Every call led to an invitation. There were dinners, there was dancing, the theatre, always evenings in company. But this time my calls were of a different nature. *So good of you to see me . . . So great a loss . . . Terribly missed by all of us who knew him . . .* At some of the houses I visited there was no one at home. I found them shut up, deserted by families anxious to avoid a season in town.

So after a morning pacing the cold, grey pavements I felt disenchanted and a little lonely and was ready to be gone. And Hannesford had its appeal. It was true I'd vowed to keep my distance, but everything that had happened to me before the fighting now seemed oddly indistinct. Besides, I had a great urge to stride out on to the moors again, to fill my lungs with Devon air. And there would be company at Hannesford—music and noise and bustle. Surely a few days in the country would do me good? Time enough to plan for the future

9

after that.

And so I did as the letters had urged me and wired the appropriate replies, and by early afternoon I was once again at Paddington Station seeking out the Hannesford train. At first the familiarity of it all was unnerving. The station seemed unaltered, as if I had stepped back to a time before the trenches. The same high roof and hissing locomotives, the same fraught struggles with parcels and train doors; the same unmistakable sounds of departure. The crowds unchanged, collars up, hats pulled down, the same biting cold. Hardly anyone in uniform.

But when I looked again, I noticed that there were differences. The place was bigger, surely? And somehow shabbier. And the faces . . . Were they the same? Were they any harder or leaner or sadder than before? I couldn't tell. It was a foolish game to play. Shivering, I went in search of cigarettes.

It happened to me like that quite often, like a recurring dizziness, a fleeting sense that somehow nothing had altered. But those moments never lasted; something always broke the spell. This time it was the match-seller beneath the station clock, propped up on crutches, pale with cold. When I approached he straightened and attempted a salute.

'There's not so many still in uniform this last month or so, sir,' he said, eyeing me with approval. 'Back to a nation of shopkeepers now, you see. France, was it, sir?'

The familiar question.

'Mostly.' I nodded. 'Yourself?'

'The same, sir. But not for long. My battery took a hit at Loos.'

'Bad luck.'

10

A cigarette lighter lost in the mud, a broken watch, a leg torn off at the knee. *Bad luck, old man, bad luck.* The world had turned to chaos but somehow the language stayed the same, forged in an era where misfortune was a dropped catch or a bad bounce on the tennis court. A world where match-sellers were young boys possessed of all their limbs.

'It *is* hard, sir,' the man was continuing, replying to a question I hadn't asked. 'But I'm quite handy with these things now, and at the end of the day my wife comes and gives me a hand. Or my boy. He's a fine lad. Do you have any young 'uns yourself, sir?'

I shook my head. 'I'm afraid I don't. I'm not married.'

The man smiled. His lack of self-pity seemed genuine and rather humbling. 'Plenty of time for that now, sir, now you've come through it.'

He took the coin I offered him and slipped it beneath his coat, then tried to come to attention again. When I turned at the ticket barrier and looked back at him, trade seemed brisk. But it struck me that few of those who paused to make a purchase did so long enough to meet the seller's eye.

*   *   *

The train that left Paddington that December afternoon was far from full, and I found a first-class carriage with only one other occupant, an elderly lady who nodded me a curt greeting and then returned to her book. For the first twenty minutes of the journey we sat in silence and, lulled by the motion of the train, I'd fallen into something of a

11

reverie when she startled me by addressing me by name.

'I'm sure you will forgive me for intruding, but I feel sure we have met before. Captain Allen, is it not?'

I'd been twisted away from her, towards the rushing fields and hedgerows, but now I turned politely and straightened. Her face rang no bells.

'Yes, Tom Allen. You must forgive me. I was daydreaming most shamefully. And I'm afraid . . . So bad with faces . . .'

'Not at all.' She spoke briskly and waved the apology aside. 'I'm Miss Westerley, Lieutenant Farrell's aunt. We were introduced once, very briefly, at the Savoy. I wouldn't for a moment expect you to remember it. It was three years ago now, and, of course, a great deal has happened since . . .'

I tried to cast my mind back to a place and time that already seemed unimaginably far away.

'Why, yes, of course I remember . . .' And it was true that I did have a dim recollection of a night out with Farrell, of introductions being made.

'I probably remember the occasion a great deal more clearly than you do,' Miss Westerley continued. 'You see, it was the last time I saw James. I think of it often.' She allowed herself the briefest of pauses before carrying on. 'You were not a captain then, I recall. I should congratulate you on your promotion.'

I shrugged, embarrassed, and mumbled something about my good fortune, about what a fine man Farrell had been, until she silenced me with another slightly testy wave of her hand.

'I'm sure you have earned your good fortune,

12

Captain. Tell me, are you going far?'

'To Hannesford,' I replied. 'In Devon.'

'Yes, yes, I know Hannesford. Are you a friend of the Stansburys?'

'I've known them for a while now, although it's a long time since I was last there. I met them a few summers before the war, when my mother took a house nearby. The Stansbury children were about my age.'

'Ah, yes!' A look almost like amusement passed across her face. 'Harry and Margot, the famous Stansbury children. Although I believe there were others, were there not?'

'Five in all. But Harry and Margot were the ones everyone noticed.'

'Indeed.' She spoke rather drily, as though unconvinced this attention was deserved. 'I remember a time when everyone was talking about them. They quite took London by storm. Tell me, were they really as remarkable as people made out?'

Not for the first time, I found myself unsure how to answer the question, how to describe the pair who had once so beguiled fashionable society. For all the times I'd been asked, I was still no better at framing a reply.

'It's hard for me to say,' I explained, hoping for safety in evasion. 'They were certainly both greatly admired.'

Miss Westerley shook her head sadly. 'So many of our brightest and best . . .' she murmured, in a sentence that needed no completion. 'Such a bad business. So, is your mother still in Hannesford, Captain Allen?'

I explained that she had taken herself off to the

south of France before the war. Miss Westerley nodded, then narrowed her eyes.

'Tell me, Captain, as you are still in uniform, do I take it that you mean to make a career of the army?'

'Far from it.' The alarm must have shown in my face, for she smiled. 'I'm on final leave. I should be out officially any day now.'

'You have been in long?'

'Since November '14. I knew someone who managed to swing me a commission in the Dorsets when it all started.'

'Then I am surprised you were not home long before this.'

I shrugged. I rather liked her brusque, peremptory manner. 'It's my own fault. I somehow contrived to put myself to the back of the queue.'

'So I assume you are not a married man, Captain. But perhaps there is someone waiting for you at Hannesford . . . ?'

'No,' I told her firmly. 'No one waiting.'

She nodded to herself, then peered at me over her spectacles.

'You've been away a long time, Captain. You will find things have changed a good deal since you left.'

After that, there was a short pause. When she spoke again, it was of the plays popular in London that season, and of the prospect of snow should the weather turn colder.

* * *

It was already dark when the train reached the station at Hannesford. It lay in gloom, much darker than I remembered, lit by a single lamp that cast

14

an insipid glow along the platform, jaundicing the smoke from the locomotive with a rather sickly light. The platform seemed deserted and the only other passenger to alight was descending from a second-class carriage at the far end of the platform, where the gloom was deepest. I had to look twice before I realised the figure was a familiar one.

'Anne!' I called. 'Miss Gregory!' And I hurried towards her, leaving my bags where they'd fallen.

At the sound of my voice she turned so that the light fell on her face, and I thought for a ghastly second I was in error. But to my relief she smiled back.

'Hello, Tom!' Her voice was warm, but there was no great surprise in it. 'I wondered if you might be on the same train.'

'So it *is* you, Anne! I barely recognised you.'

And it was true. I'd always considered Lady Stansbury's companion a young woman. Her face had been as fresh and as unlined as my own.

'Am I to be flattered, Tom?' She looked amused. 'After all this time any change is unlikely to be for the better, you know.'

I felt myself flushing. 'Not at all. You look well. Changed for the better, of course ...' I paused, aware of my own confusion, relieved to see she was still smiling. 'Confound it, Anne, it's wonderful to see you. How long has it been?'

'Five years, I think. Five years last summer. A long time.'

Looking at her more closely, I realised that my mumbled apology had not perhaps been so very far from the truth after all. Yes, her face looked narrower than I remembered, and her figure slighter, but there was still the same pleasing openness in her expression. How old had she been when we last met? Twenty-five? Twenty-six? About my own age, probably. Back then I'd thought of her as young, but she must already have been approaching that age at which a woman's prospects of marriage began to falter. And now she had lost the youthful softness I remembered in her. Without it she was plainer. Yet when we reached the spot where I'd dropped my cases there was something striking in the way she stood and looked at me in that smoky yellow light. In a way I couldn't really define, she seemed to have more presence.

From somewhere behind me the stationmaster had appeared out of the darkness and the train was making ready to depart. Anne pulled a face as the din engulfed us.

'You look different too, Tom,' she went on when it subsided. 'How did you get so thin? And it's odd to see you in uniform. You were always the least militaristic of them all.'

For years I'd barely thought about Anne Gregory, but now I felt immensely cheered at seeing her again. Some of the solitude I'd felt in London began to disperse.

'And what about you, Anne? I heard you'd gone for a VAD.'

'Gone for a *nurse*,' she corrected me. 'Remember, I'd been a nurse before my life at Hannesford. And a jolly good thing too. Some of the sisters were horrible to the poor old VADs. I felt quite sorry for them. Are you expecting a car?'

'In the lane as usual, I should think. I wired Lady Stansbury the time of the train.'

'Good,' she replied brightly. 'That saves me a walk. You can drop me at the vicarage.'

16

That was a surprise.

'The vicarage? You're not at Hannesford Court?'

'Times have changed.' She smiled up at me. 'I'm at the vicarage now, looking after Mrs Uttley. She's really very poorly, I'm afraid.'

But my question was only half answered.

'How did that come about, Anne? I would have thought Lady Stansbury was desperate to get you back.'

My astonishment was genuine. I really couldn't imagine Hannesford Court without Anne Gregory's quiet presence somewhere in the background.

'She certainly wrote me a very nice letter. But I didn't want to go back. Come on, there's the driver.'

As our bags were stowed into the familiar Hannesford car by a chauffeur neither of us recognised, I listened to a concise, bloodless account of Anne's wartime service, a series of dates and place names, London, Folkestone, Belgium, France. It was, I realised, a speech she had given before, a set of practised lines sterilised by repetition. It told me everything and said nothing. And in that respect it was strangely familiar. I had my own well-worn litany of events and dates. In Anne's crisp reticence there was a glimpse of something shared.

When she finished she didn't ask me to reciprocate. We fell instead into observations about London and the details of our journeys. I told her how dirty I'd found the boat train, she complained about the shortage and unreliability of London's motor buses. It never occurred to me to ask the reason she'd been in town, and it was not until we were almost at the vicarage that we spoke of Hannesford Court. At the first glimpse of its chimneys above the hedges we had both fallen silent.

'Do you remember?' I mused. 'When I was last at Hannesford I told you I was never coming back.'

'Yes, I remember.' She was watching the dark hedges slipping past the window. 'And when I signed up for war work, I thought the same. Yet here we both are.'

'But why the vicarage, Anne? You still haven't explained.'

We were entering the village now and could see the church ahead of us, shadowy against a sky not yet entirely dark. She didn't reply at first, but kept her face turned towards the night.

'It's funny, isn't it, Tom? When Lady Stansbury first brought me to Hannesford it was to rescue me from being a nurse. She thought it a scandal that the daughter of her old friend should have sunk so low. So I came to Hannesford and made myself useful. Almost one of the family, but always the last into dinner. Then, somewhere a long way away, some shots were fired, and suddenly all those perfect, elegant young ladies who used to visit were falling over themselves to become nurses. What a strange world it is!'

She turned and looked at me.

'Lady Stansbury truly believed that bringing someone here was the greatest gift she could bestow. But out there in France, working in the hospitals, I knew I couldn't go back to the way things were.'

There was such calm certainty in her voice that I almost envied her.

'But what will you do instead?' I asked.

18

She smiled a smile that was full of ghosts.

'Nurses are in demand, Tom. There are still a lot of young men who need nursing. If not here, perhaps overseas. But first there's Mrs Uttley. She was always very good to me, all the time I was at Hannesford, and she was in such a state when she wrote to me, poor dear. And I suppose I knew that saying yes . . . Well, that it won't be for so very long.' The car was drawing to a halt. 'Is there time for you to come in? I know they'd both love to see you.'

I promised to call on the vicar and his wife the following day. In many ways Anne and I had been two unrelated planets, separately orbiting the fiery star of the Stansburys. That night, as I watched her disappear into the shadow of the vicarage, I found myself wondering how many other things at Hannesford I would find so altered.

From the village, the road to Hannesford Court is not direct. A footpath through the woods is the shortest route between the two, but motor vehicles must go round by the new bridge that crosses the River Hanna near the water meadows. The professor and I used to walk in those meadows quite often; he liked to look for butterflies there. But that night, as the headlights of the Daimler picked out the familiar driveway, I was thinking only of what lay ahead. I don't think I really thought of the professor at all.

There was thunder in the air the day I first arrived at Hannesford. I could feel it in the uneasy heat that pressed upon me as I stepped from the train. No one else alighted when I did. A chauffeur had been sent to meet me and the porter was quick with the bags; as they fussed towards the car I was left alone on the platform, still some way from the village, taking in the undulating fields and the blue distance of the moors.

That was the day the colours changed. I'd left behind a world of drab parlours and damp shrubberies, places where the brightest hopes paled quickly into carefulness and prudence and thrift. But at Hannesford nothing was grey. It was a world bathed in brilliance. Even the storm clouds were dramatic, ink black and vertiginous, gashed with indigo and violet. Below them the fields were a sulphurous yellow, the wheat tinged with a sullen glow.

By the time the car turned away from them, on to the long drive of Hannesford Court, that glow had darkened to mutinous amber and the storm was already breaking. My first glimpse of the old house was startling. Beyond the towering chimneys the high slopes of the moor flashed white with lightning. And with every new surge of the storm, my spirits lifted. Here was energy and colour and open space, life on a scale I'd never known. This was my future, where my life began, the place where I would find adventure.

When I was ushered indoors—hunched beneath the butler's umbrella, my skirts already wet from the storm—the scent of flowers almost overwhelmed me. From somewhere unseen there was a breath of orange blossom, and around me, in every bowl on every surface, there were roses.

2

'Tom! How smart you look! Welcome back to Hannesford. It is *inexcusable* that you have been away so long.'

Lady Stansbury greeted me in the Great Hall, the oldest part of Hannesford Court and the most impressive, a huge vaulted room with exposed timbers and an enormous fireplace. From the shadows at the rear a Tudor staircase rose to a gallery landing. There, as tradition dictated, a suitably dark and mysterious Christmas tree was already in place, waiting to be decorated.

My hostess's voice was exactly as I remembered it, light and musical, a voice to smooth ruffled feathers and to charm stuffy drawing rooms. But I saw at once that in other ways Lady Stansbury was much altered. I had written to her more than once since my last visit, polite letters with details of my postings or, later, those letters of condolence about mutual friends at which we had all become so adept. But her replies had not suggested any change in her. Without fail they maintained her tone of benevolent condescension, as though nothing that occurred could weaken even for a second the fortress of her self-possession.

Now, however, standing in her presence, I could see the suffering written in her face. She appeared much older than before, spare and fragile, as if the process of ageing had come to her suddenly, and had been both precipitous and punishing. Her cheeks had disappeared beneath her cheekbones and her hair seemed thinner, leaving the shape of her skull suddenly more pronounced. The suggestion of pampered timelessness that had once characterised her appearance was vanished entirely.

But something else had changed too. For all the time I'd known her, Lady Stansbury had moved through the world as if gloriously and elegantly unaware of the tedious practicalities supporting her existence; but the woman who greeted me that evening seemed altogether more purposeful. It was as if, instead of reeling beneath the blows of fate, she had found from somewhere the unexpected strength to face them. I'd seen similar things occur in the trenches. New officers arrived all the time. There was never any guessing who would shrink and who would grow.

'You must promise not to desert us again, Tom,' she continued. 'Especially now, given all that's happened. We are all so happy to have you back.'

She waved away a housemaid and steered me towards the fire.

'The others are dressing, but they will be down soon. We have a full house, quite like the old days.' She hesitated. 'There was something I wanted to ask, Tom. I know you won't be offended. I would be so grateful if you could change before Sir Robert sees you in uniform. It's quite wrong, I know, but this last year the sight of young men in uniform rather upsets him. It's so clear they've *come through it*, if you see what I mean. I'm sure you understand ... Now we haven't put you in your usual room. We thought, with it being so close to Harry's ... But the Blue Room is lovely, and Evans will be helping you. You remember him? He has agreed to come back to help us. Quite the old school, Evans, and such a good example to the others . . .'

Lady Stansbury, of course, had never been less than charming, but I hadn't always warmed to her. That night I was surprised by a pang of sympathy. When I looked down from the gallery and saw her below me in the Great Hall adjusting an arrangement of flowers, I was struck for the first time by how very small she seemed amid the grandeur of her surroundings.

Upstairs, the house felt cooler. The Blue Room proved both more spacious and more anodyne than the room I was used to, as if over the years the footfalls of constantly changing guests had gradually trampled out its character, leaving it a pale space waiting to be filled. But I was grateful to find myself in a different bedroom. I had spent too many restless nights in the other, too many pointless hours looking at the ceiling, berating myself for my own foolishness. The Blue Room suited me nicely. I had bathed and changed and had successfully fended off the attentions of old Evans when I heard a tap at the door.

I'd often wondered how it would be when I next saw Margot Stansbury. Even though I'd vowed to stay away, there could be no question of avoiding her for ever. In such a small world our paths were bound to cross, and I'd imagined the meeting in many ways. In each one I was utterly changed from the man she'd once known: wiser or more worldly, or famously successful in some unspecified field. Later I began to imagine it differently. I was disfigured, perhaps, or maimed, or blind. But always I imagined Margot as she'd been when I last saw her: fresh and flawless, her golden lustre unaltered and undimmed. The thought that she too might change never occurred to me. Margot would always be Margot.

But the woman who stood before me that night *had* changed, just as Anne Gregory had changed, in ways that were both striking yet difficult to define.

'What's the matter, Tom? Seen a ghost?' She closed the door behind her and studied me with amusement. Blue eyes, dark lashes, the corners of her mouth rising in that teasing half-smile.

'Margot...'

'Yes, Tom, I know. It's been a long time. Don't be a bore and make me go through all that. The point is that you're here.'

She was looking me up and down with undisguised curiosity. 'Mama's right, you *are* thinner. Wait till Cook sees you. She'll consider it a personal affront.'

'Mrs Adkins? Is she still here?'

'Oh, yes. Mrs Adkins battles on. She's still a treasure. Unfortunately nowadays she has a list of things she refuses to cook because someone told her they were the Kaiser's favourites. Mother says it makes planning meals confoundedly difficult.'

We both laughed and the tension was broken. Margot stepped further into the room.

'You know, Tom, I can hardly believe you're back. We'd come to believe that no one we cared for would ever come through it. Harry, Julian, Oliver ... Even the sort of people you could never imagine anything out of the ordinary happening to, like the Everson boys or Tippy Hibbert. All those dreadful, dreadful telegrams. But here you are. It seems incredible.'

She came forward then and pressed her cheek to mine, the familiar greeting that had always

24

unsettled me, although I had seen her do the same to small boys and ageing colonels.

'And what about me, Tom? Have I changed?'

'Of course not.' This time I'd learned my lesson; and in truth I found myself in two minds. So much about her was exactly as I remembered it. Her features were still exquisite, her skin still flawless, the blue of her eyes no less bright. Every time I'd ever been away from Margot there had been this same moment on my return, the point when the image in my memory collided with the real thing and was found pale and wanting. Nothing ever prepared me for the reality of Margot.

And yet she *was* changed. If not in her looks, perhaps something in her manner, in the freedom with which she carried herself. It was as if an element of caution or restraint that had always been there was now removed. Whatever it was, I found the difference a little disconcerting. It reminded me that for five years, unseen by me, the rest of the world had been turning. I felt a little lurch at the thought—the shock of the swimmer reaching for the bottom who finds nothing solid, only deeper water.

'Don't look so glum, Tom.' Margot was still watching me, a smile on her lips. 'It's not very flattering. You might pretend to be pleased to see me.'

'Well, naturally ...' I pulled myself together. 'Margot, I *am* pleased. I really am. It's wonderful to see you. But strange, too. Being back at Hannesford is a little hard to believe.'

She nodded and stepped closer to straighten my tie.

'Of course. Everything's a bit strange now, isn't

it? We were all so busy longing for the war to be over that we never stopped to think how things would be when it was.'

She stepped back to admire her work.

'I'm so sorry about Julian,' I said.

There. It was out, the thing I knew I had to say.

She nodded and stepped forward again, busying herself with a further adjustment.

'Yes. It was simply bloody for him. He was the last person who should have been helpless like that. It would have been so much better if he'd been killed outright. All that talk of dying for King and Country. But dying isn't always the worst thing, is it, Tom? That last year was terrible for him.'

'And terrible for you.' I said it as gently as I could but she shook her head.

'Rather worse for him, wouldn't you think? Now, come on down and meet the others. Mama's invited some dreadful dullards, I'm afraid. You must come and see for yourself . . .'

*   *   *

I don't think I'd ever liked Julian Trevelyan. At first he was just one of the many new acquaintances I was making at Hannesford, and I felt it less strongly. But as time went on I began to form much clearer opinions about Harry Stansbury's friends. Oliver Eastwell, for instance, was bluff and hearty and rather slow of thought. Freddie Masters was a buffoon. Tippy Hibbert was set to become a country squire straight out of the pages of Thackeray.

In Julian I detected a superciliousness that good manners couldn't entirely disguise, and sometimes, in his teasing of others, I thought him rather cruel.

26

And then there was that air he had, as though he believed all the finest things in life were his by right; and that Margot, even Margot, was simply another one of those things.

Yet he was considered good-looking and I could just about see why. He was powerfully built and I suppose he had a certain surly, square-jawed handsomeness. I seldom saw him dance, but once or twice I followed his eyes when the music was playing and found him observing one or other of the ladies present. A rather hungry look, I thought. No, there was no doubt that Julian Trevelyan had his passions; and he would not have lacked for female company when he desired it.

That last summer, when Margot's inclination towards Julian became clearer and clearer, there was no denying the pleasure he took in her company. But to me it resembled the pleasure of the collector rather than the lover, and I told her so. That was on the night of the Rose Ball, and I hadn't seen Margot since. It was remarkable to think those had been the last words we'd exchanged.

*   *   *

The Great Hall was already thronged with guests when Margot led me down to join them. It made for a pleasant scene. The lamps filled the old room with a welcoming glow and the huge fire hissed and crackled with pagan ferocity. Against that background, the groomed neatness of the company was oddly comforting, the crisp, black outlines of the men softened by the looser lines and pastels of the women. It wasn't until after the fighting that I began to appreciate properly the reassuring

27

certainties of evening dress.

In terms of numbers the party seemed as extensive as it had always been, although once upon a time I'd have expected to recognise every guest. Now, letting Margot drift away, I hung back to survey the scene, trying to put names to faces. The London banker and his wife talking to old Colonel Rolleston were people I'd seen at Hannesford before, but not frequently, and surely never before at Christmas. Most probably two of Margot's dullards. Next to them were the Finch-Taylors, who were regular guests. Laura Finch-Taylor was my age, her husband a good deal older, a contemporary of Sir Robert's, and he seemed to have doubled in size since I'd seen him last. The Finch-Taylors were in conversation with a good-looking man of about forty, someone I didn't recognise. When Margot appeared near them, all three turned to watch her. It was the effect Margot always had. That, at least, had not changed.

In the centre of the room Lady Stansbury was holding court next to a tall young man of eighteen or nineteen. On catching sight of me he detached himself from the group and made his way over.

'Hello, Tom!' he began affably. 'Remember me?'

'Bill!' The youngest of the Stansbury children had been about thirteen when I was last at Hannesford. 'Goodness, how you've grown. I'd never have guessed it was you.'

And that was true. Bill Stansbury had been rather an inconspicuous child, slightly in awe of his older brothers and sisters, and a little pallid, as though somehow deprived of light in their shadow. As I remembered it, he'd been much given to silent adoration of Harry.

28

'We're all so glad you could make it, Tom. Freddie Masters says you're on final leave. Is that true?'

'It does look that way.' I'd long ago grown cautious of making definitive statements about the future.

The young man grinned affectionately. 'I expect it's true if Freddie says so. He's generally right. I dare say you'll miss army life a great deal when it's over, Tom. I should warn you, it's awfully dull back on Civvy Street.'

Only then did it dawn on me that Bill Stansbury was old enough to have been in uniform himself. The thought was rather shocking.

'I should think it must be,' I replied gravely. 'Remind me, Bill, what was your regiment?'

'I was with the Devonshires, like Harry. Of course, I didn't get overseas myself before it was all over, which was rather galling really. It was the same for Denny Houghton over there. He missed out too. It feels terrible not to have done our bit.' He lowered his voice a little and leaned closer. 'But, of course, after what happened to Harry and Reggie, well, the mater was in a terrible state about me going. And Father ... Well, you know how much he loved Harry. We all did. But it's rather knocked the stuffing out of the old man, I'm afraid.'

'And Reggie?' I looked around. 'I heard from someone he was recovering well.'

'Oh, yes, tremendously! You know what a fighter Reggie's always been.' But there was something a little uneasy in the young man's manner as he said it. 'He's not here this evening,' he went on. 'Doesn't feel up to company just yet. Wants to stay on at the sanatorium in Cullingford for a little longer. It's

29

a frightfully good place, of course, and there are lots of officers like Reggie there. The doctors and nurses are simply the best.' He leaned closer still. 'To be perfectly honest, Tom, I rather think Mother would like a word with you about Reggie . . .'

But instead of saying more he straightened and stepped back, as if a difficult topic had been adequately dealt with, leaving him free to move on to more congenial subjects.

'I say, Tom, did you hear about Freddie? They've given him the DSO, you know. Isn't that marvellous?'

Freddie Masters, war hero. The world was a peculiar place.

'Yes, I heard about that. Is he here? He wanted to talk to me about something.'

'He's had to motor over to Crowmarsh to see his aunt.' Bill grinned. 'Freddie says she's the richest maiden aunt in Europe and that her wishes are law. But he'll be back by bedtime. Mother gave him a day pass.'

Bill Stansbury seemed delighted to have me with him as he circulated, making introductions and occasionally adding little comments of his own beneath his breath. And if his admiration was a little disconcerting, at least there was in the young man's enthusiasm something of the gaiety and excitement I'd missed so sorely the previous day.

'Let's see, Tom, who's next . . . I'll spare you Denny Houghton for now. Splendid fellow—I was at school with him—but he's really only here for the shooting. Mama insisted he should come because she's so short of young men . . . The Finch-Taylors you know, of course. They say the war's made old Horatio richer than ever. And doesn't Laura look splendid?' Bill blushed a little. 'She says she can see a lot of Harry in me, which is jolly decent of her, isn't it?'

Laura Finch-Taylor chose that moment to look across at us and her eyes darted from me to Bill and back again with a quick, slightly feline smile. Then, before either of us could respond, she'd turned back to her husband, as calm and as aloof as before. In a land full of widows, Laura Finch-Taylor's choice of husband had begun to smack less of oddity, more of remarkable foresight. But her smile remained as unfathomable as the Sphinx; I'd never really known what went on behind those dark eyes of hers.

'Over there, talking to my mother, that's Violet Eccleston,' Bill went on. 'She's the daughter of an old friend of Father's. Father fell out with him a few years ago but they made up when Harry died. Eccleston wrote him a very decent letter. But I'm afraid Violet is rather heavy going. She's very *modern*. She lives in a flat all by herself and studies economics in the British Library.' He spoke the word as though referring to a slightly distasteful ailment. 'Father can't bear her, I'm afraid, but she had to be invited for fear of reopening the breach. And Mama says there are going to be too many young women at the New Year Ball as it is. She's terribly worried about the dancing.'

'What about Susan,' I asked. 'I haven't seen her yet.' Susan was Margot's younger sister.

'Coming down tomorrow,' Bill replied cheerfully. 'She hasn't been very well lately. Just over-tired, the doctors say. Of course, losing Oliver so soon was pretty beastly for her. Mother thinks she should come back and live here, but Susan won't hear of

31

it. She's staying on in Oliver's house in Huntingdon Square . . .'

Susan Stansbury had married Oliver Eastwell only a few months before he was killed. Oliver had been one of Harry's inner circle, a good-natured fellow, rich and eager to please, but always at least one step behind the quick wits of the Stansburys. His engagement to Susan had surprised me and I'd wondered how on earth Susan would survive being married to Oliver for the rest of her life. It was a sentiment I felt more than guilty about now that the question wasn't going to arise.

'And Margot?' I asked casually, resuming my study of the assembled company. 'How has she been?'

'Well, you know Margot!' Bill waved his hand airily. 'Always the same. Of course it was wretched for her losing Julian like that. Everyone always said they were destined for each other. And of course with him hanging on for all those months, well, it was an awful time. In the end it was a bit of a shock, him dying so suddenly, but a blessing too, for him as well as Margot. She was awfully cut up about the whole thing, but terribly brave about it.'

And as if to emphasise her resilience, from the far side of the room came a little ripple of laughter. Margot Stansbury, although robbed of a fiancé, was clearly *bearing up*.

*   *   *

The good-looking man I'd noticed earlier turned out to be an American named Neil Maclean, described rather vaguely by Bill as an industrialist. At close quarters he looked older than I'd realised:

32

late forties, perhaps even fifty, but with the energy of someone much younger. His face, slightly tanned by the elements, was alert, and his eyes searching. He greeted me with a crisp nod of the head.

'Very pleased to meet you, Captain Allen,' he began, holding out his hand. 'Margot tells me you saw a lot of the show in France.' His voice was low and barely accented. 'So what does the future hold for you now?'

I shrugged. Having a future at all was still an unfamiliar idea.

'To be honest, I haven't given it much thought. I'll be here until New Year. After that, who knows?'

'Time to think about it, Captain.' His tone matched mine for lightness, but his eyes were serious. 'After everything you've been through, I should think a man needs something to occupy his time.'

And in that he was probably right. Even if he wasn't, his advice was at least a change from the usual platitudes: *I expect you'll want a good rest now, old man*, as if war was a particularly arduous round of golf.

'Have you known the Stansburys long?' I asked him.

'A couple of years. We met at the Van Troosts'. What about you? I believe you're an old friend of the family.'

Was I? It didn't seem long since I'd been the newcomer, arriving at Hannesford by foot across the fields, hot and a bit uncomfortable, wishing I'd never agreed to come. But perhaps I *was* an old friend now, if only by default. Survive long enough and you're everyone's oldest friend.

'I've known them a while. My mother took a

33

house near here one summer, four or five years before the war.'

Put like that, it seemed neat and rather conventional, and not at all like my mother, who wrote novels and kept parakeets and revelled in her own eccentricity. My father had been a quiet, sober man of private means, comfortable rather than affluent, with an interest in Greek literature. Shortly after his death my mother had acquired a secretary called Winifred whose company suited her a good deal better, and her life became increasingly picaresque as she moved Winifred and the parakeets between London and Paris and back again with increasing frequency. Her books, she used to declare, were the sort of works neither her husband nor her father had ever let her read, and they sold accordingly. When I visited her in Hannesford that summer I'd done so cautiously, and with the intention of staying no longer than a week.

But I had reckoned without the Stansburys. Harry and Margot gloried in company, and it was not uncommon for strays such as myself to be drawn into their circle. I'd accepted their first invitation without enthusiasm, at the insistence of my mother. The Stansburys were a very grand family and the prospect of picnicking with them seemed both dull and daunting. I expected stiffness and good manners and very polite condescension.

However the path through the meadows had soothed me. From among the buttercups you could look out, across the river, to the purple and green uplands of the moor. And the Stansbury children were not at all what I'd expected. Harry was blond and high-spirited and, in a subtle way, flirtatious with the young ladies around him; Margot was frivolous and funny and clearly accustomed to admiration. There'd been a moment when she'd looked across at me with bright, smiling eyes, and I'd understood why.

By the time my mother decided that Winifred and the parakeets would benefit from summers on the Mediterranean, filial duty had long ceased to be the reason I visited Hannesford. The Stansburys had extended their hands to me, and I, partly flattered, partly amused, partly thinking of Margot's eyes, had allowed myself to be clasped.

*   *   *

It was not until just before dinner that I spoke to my host at any length. I'd always found Sir Robert a rather imposing individual who, when not out with the guns, was invariably busy with his plans for the renewal of Hannesford Court. But this time I found his handshake loose, almost apathetic.

'Ah, Tom, Tom. Good to have you back. I was just talking to old Rolleston here about the drawings for the memorial. Have you seen them yet? They're very fine, I think, very fine indeed . . . But we need to get our skates on. The memorial in Cullingford is already taking shape. I'm hoping Freddie Masters and yourself will join me after dinner to let me know what you think . . .'

After five years away it seemed a rather peculiar welcome, as if I'd just strolled in from a walk in the gardens. And as we talked it struck me that Sir Robert's gaze, which had once seemed so stern and commanding, now rarely lingered in one place for more than a few seconds at a time.

'He leaves a great deal to Mama nowadays,' Bill Stansbury explained when at length the company was summoned to dinner. 'Just the opposite of how things used to be. When we heard that Harry had been killed, well, he just seemed to *collapse*. He's actually much better now than he was. But it would be wonderful if you could help him with his plans. And just to warn you about the memorial service for Harry, I rather think Father is hoping you'll say a few words . . .'

It was said so casually that it took me a moment to grasp the meaning. Lady Stansbury had mentioned in her letter that a service in her son's memory was planned for New Year's Eve, but she hadn't indicated that I'd be expected to speak. It was a troubling thought. Perhaps it was fortunate that, before I could respond, Bill had managed to find something equally surprising to throw into the conversation.

'I'm afraid you'll be between Lucy Flinders and the Eccleston girl at dinner, Tom,' he went on. 'That's because Mama thinks you reliable. I've got Laura Finch-Taylor and the doctor's daughter, which isn't too bad. As for Margot, she'll probably be next to Neil, the American. Mama's frightfully keen on her marrying him.'

*   *   *

I remember quite clearly my first sight of American troops, somewhere behind the lines in the darkest days of 1918. It had been a terrible month. Our lines were shattered and we were falling back past landmarks familiar from years before; places won inch by inch at terrible cost, gone in the course of

36

an afternoon. I was at a dressing station when I saw them, and even from a distance they stood out. There was something about the way they marched, a straightness and a sense of purpose that I hadn't seen anywhere for what seemed like years. The nurses cheered them out of sight, and they left behind them a faint but undeniable scent of hope. But I hadn't cheered. Something about their freshness made me sad. They reminded me of another, younger version of myself, one long since missing in action.

Professor Schmidt had always said that the future of the world lay not in Germany's hands, nor in the hands of the British Empire, but across the Atlantic. America, he said, was an empire with no history to deflect it from its path. His opinion had infuriated some of the company at Hannesford. In the summer of 1914, it did not do for a foreigner to question the future of the Empire.

Was it Harry Stansbury who had lost his temper with the professor over his opinions? If so it was unusual, because Harry was not easily riled. My memory of the incident was hazy, but I know it was the week before the Rose Ball because the gardeners were busy putting up the awnings. It was the end of a golden afternoon, hot, with shadows just beginning to lengthen. I had been looking for Margot by the lake and was heading back to the house through the old herb garden. Before reaching the terrace, still hidden from view, I heard voices: one raised, one low, but very earnest. One of the Stansbury boys, I thought, falling out with someone. Wary of interrupting, I paused until I heard a set of footsteps stamp away into the house. Then, when I rounded the corner, I found

37

the professor alone, flopped awkwardly on a seat. He looked shaken, dabbing at his brow with his handkerchief. On seeing me he had tried to rise.

'It is nothing, Tom. Quite nothing,' he had insisted. 'Just a little political disagreement, that is all. These are troubled times.'

How hard it must have been for him in those last days, a German who loved England. And yet back then German things were familiar to us: German *lieder*, German governesses, German waiters in cafés; German dogs, German hock, German nobles in the royal party at Ascot.

We knew much less about Americans, and mothers in Lady Stansbury's circle did not think of them as husbands for their daughters. But of course by the end of the war London was a different place. By then America was all the rage: American soldiers, American music, American loans. If I hadn't previously understood how profound the change had been, I understood it that night, in the Great Hall at Hannesford Court.

*   *   *

Before we went into dinner, Lady Stansbury drew me to one side.

'Tom, dear, before we go in, I just wanted to have a quick word. It may be difficult to find the opportunity later on.'

I could see from her manner that she was not completely at ease, so I mumbled something about Sir Robert and the memorial service.

'Oh, yes, of course. We'd be so grateful. Sir Robert wants it to be one of Harry's fellow officers who speaks, and you are so good at knowing the

38

right things to say . . .' She tailed off, taking my agreement for granted. 'But to tell the truth, Tom, it was actually Reggie I was hoping to speak to you about. It's so hard for me to talk to Sir Robert about him. It upsets him terribly. You have *heard* about Reggie, haven't you?'

There was an earnestness in her voice as she asked the question that I'd never heard there before. The old Lady Stansbury who drifted through life in a state of benign detachment had always spoken in a voice tinged with aristocratic *ennui*.

'I heard it was bad. But I understood he was making a good recovery.'

She greeted this with a quick, slightly impatient nod.

'Recovery. Yes.' Her eyes met mine. 'Reggie has lost both his legs, Tom. And there are . . . scars. On his face. He looks . . .'

Her voice wavered, and for the first time ever I felt I was being offered a glimpse behind the façade. But almost immediately she was in control again, crisp and slightly brusque.

'Tom, I'm afraid, to those not used to them, his injuries appear rather monstrous. The shell took away part of his face.'

As she spoke, I was aware again of that unworthy dismay I always felt in the company of men who had once been whole and now were not. After my first year in the throes of the storm, I'd no longer feared dying. I'd expected to die. But whenever I looked down on some stretchered wretch who had *not* died and saw the terrible ways in which the human form could be bent or broken . . . In those moments, I would feel a different, more debilitating

39

form of fear creep across my skin. And I felt the horror again, that night, when Lady Stansbury spoke of Reggie.

But of course I didn't let it show.

'Poor chap. It must be ghastly for him.' What was it Bill had called me? *Reliable*.

'You see, Tom, I'm afraid Reggie isn't taking it well. He is not—has never been—a stoic. He always lacked self-control. There are so many young men around him making the best of things, but Reggie, well, he's so *angry*, Tom. Angry all the time. He'll barely agree to see us. And now he's written to say he won't be coming back to Hannesford for Christmas.'

She paused and I could see genuine bewilderment in her face.

'Why would he say that, Tom? We could do everything for him here. And I've told him again and again that we want him to come home. We'd make up a bedroom for him on the ground floor, and we'd get a nurse, of course. But when I try to speak to Reggie about it he just flies into one of his rages and says he wants nothing to do with Hannesford or with any of us, ever again. To use his words, he says he's not prepared to come back here to be our . . . our freak show.'

There was no mistaking her distress now. I felt an impulse to take her hand, but such an intimacy lay well beyond us. Instead I tried to find some words that were both comforting and not entirely false.

'I'm sure in time it will get easier,' I assured her. 'For Reggie and for all of us.'

Was that true? Easier for Reggie? Or just easier for those around him, gradually growing

40

accustomed to the horror?

But Lady Stansbury looked grateful. 'Let us hope so, Tom. I wondered, would you talk to him? I know you've only just arrived, but I thought perhaps if you were to go and visit . . . Cullingford isn't very far, and Wilkes could drive you over tomorrow.'

Of course I had no choice. I'd never been particularly close to Reggie Stansbury and had no great confidence in my ability as a go-between. In fact, as far as I could recall, Reggie and I had mostly avoided one another. We'd had little in common, so it hadn't been hard. Reggie's passion was shooting. I rarely touched a gun.

'Of course Reggie never really enjoyed New Year here,' Lady Stansbury went on. 'I know that. I think he used to dread all our big occasions. But I hate to think of us celebrating here at Hannesford while he sits alone in that sanatorium. Besides, if he isn't here, everyone will be asking why. I know they'll think that we're ashamed of him. And then there's the memorial service. Can he really intend to miss that? It's simply too awful to contemplate . . .'

She took a deep breath, and when she spoke again her voice was softer.

'Dear Tom, I've often wondered what you must think of us all. You've known us for a long time now. You must have noticed . . . Well, it must have been apparent that I have not always found Reggie easy. I don't deny it, Tom. Sometimes I have found Reggie very difficult to love. He was always so *different* from Harry and Margot, so very hard to understand. But I have always tried, Tom, I promise you. And now this ghastly thing has

41

happened. If there is anything at all we can do for Reggie... Anything...'

She paused, and I found myself turning to where her guests were gathering, affable and jovial, looking forward to an excellent dinner.

'I shall go to Cullingford first thing,' I promised.

I had little idea what to expect when I first arrived at Hannesford. I was still in the Great Hall, still gazing in wonder at its profusion of roses, only half listening to the messages of apology being relayed by the butler, when a movement above me caught my eye. And there she was on the stairs, Margot in a pale summer dress, so fair and fresh and calm that suddenly the roses were garish.

As she came down to welcome me she was already apologising for her mother's absence, for the lack of a proper welcome, for the storm that had led the house party to take precautionary shelter at a neighbouring house when they should have been hurrying home. Her features were bright with vitality and there was laughter in her voice. I had read about society beauties, and had seen their pictures in the popular magazines. I'd imagined them as they appeared in their portraits, stiff and unreal, their beauty as carefully chiselled as the features of Greek statues. Not real people at all. But Margot was real. She was warm and alive and pressing her cheek to mine.

'Harry's here somewhere,' she was saying. 'I'm sure he'll be out in a moment. We're so pleased you've agreed to come, Anne. Mama desperately needs someone to help her with things. I'm afraid I'm quite useless that way . . .'

A young man emerged from a door at the back of the Great Hall. I saw he was fair like his sister and a little older, with the same blue eyes. He was immaculately dressed too, and the hand he held out to me was warm and firm in its grip.

Nothing Lady Stansbury had written in her letters could have properly prepared me for the Stansbury children.

43

Dinner at Hannesford that night was a polite and pleasant affair, yet it left me vaguely dissatisfied.

Certainly in terms of setting, no fault could be found: the grand dining room was unchanged, still sultry in red and green, slightly overwhelming in its declaration of opulence. The rituals of dining, the little Hannesford ways, were all the same, too. I'd been told the country was in the throes of a servant crisis, that the families who had once driven their male servants so enthusiastically into the arms of the recruiting officers now found it impossible to induce them to return. But if there was a crisis of staffing at Hannesford, for that evening at least Lady Stansbury had contrived to conceal it. Courses came and went with practised ease, glasses were recharged swiftly and unobtrusively, and the Hannesford machine seemed in every way as smooth as ever. And yet for all the familiarity, I found it all utterly different.

Hannesford dinners had always been *memorable*. With Harry and Margot as the lure, there was never an evening when there were not new and intriguing people to encounter. When I first dined there I'd never before witnessed so many good-looking young people at one table. And even if I felt a little outside it all, I couldn't help but feel that I was witnessing something rather special. Much of the brilliance was ephemeral, of course, and what passed for wit was often no more than clever timing. In many cases the beauty that made such an impression on me must have owed a great deal to both time and money. But the laughter was spontaneous and the exhilaration in those bright eyes genuine, and sometimes the atmosphere tingled with excitement.

But that had been five years ago. Now, where Harry Stansbury once sat, young Bill Stansbury was making slightly awkward conversation with the doctor's daughter, while next to him Laura Finch-Taylor smiled her secretive smile and listened intently to Mapperley, the banker, who was explaining that financiers such as himself may have great rewards but had *great responsibilities too*. Margot was a distance away, positioned near her mother and Neil Maclean, making modest and seemly conversation. And I, who had once loved to remonstrate with her about the iniquities of her behaviour at the dinner table, found myself listening instead to the polite opinions on fashions of the young girl on my right.

Lucy Flinders, it emerged, was barely seventeen. It was strange, in that room of all places, to be seated beside someone to whom Harry Stansbury was little more than a name. Yet she struck me as vaguely familiar. I'd known two of her cousins from my early days at Hannesford, and had expected to find them present on my return. But one, it transpired, had married a wounded Canadian officer, and the other, who'd been engaged to a man killed near Ypres, had accompanied her sister to Vancouver. I remembered them as friendly, slightly foolish young women. It was hard to imagine real tragedy entering either of their lives.

And now it was their young cousin who sat at dinner and seemed oddly untainted by suffering. Her smile hid no secrets, her trivialities were

45

unforced; her laughter was simply laughter. Lucy Flinders had been twelve years old when the first shots were fired in Belgium: men like Harry meant nothing to her, and she had no brothers. It was as if somehow the carnage had never quite touched her.

On my other side, Violet Eccleston spent much of the early part of the meal directing a peroration about trades unions towards Neil Maclean. Only when that was done did she turn rather abruptly and fix me with a quizzical stare.

'All this must ring very false to you, Captain Allen,' she declared, in a manner that did not invite contradiction. She had a rather deep voice and the habit when speaking of thrusting her chin forward as if every sentence was a challenge. She accompanied her statement with a jerky wave of her hand at the room in general. 'After everything you've experienced in the last five years, to return to a world that persists in these tired old forms must make you despair of progress.'

It occurred to me that Violet Eccleston seemed as comfortable among the tired old forms as anyone else, but I let it pass. 'Certainly it's strange to find some things so unaltered, Miss Eccleston,' I remarked cautiously.

'Oh, but it *must* be. I mean, you have seen for yourself the way the war marked the end of a whole chapter in mankind's development. And it is not to governments that we must look for guidance in the future, but to our intellectuals and our scientists. Would you not agree?'

To my great relief, Neil Maclean intervened. Despite the earnestness in his voice, I realised the American was smiling.

'Miss Eccleston believes the dominant force in the coming years will be international socialism,' he explained, 'and predicts that establishments such as Hannesford are destined one day to end up in the ownership of the people.'

I allowed myself a quick look around the dining room. At the head of the table Sir Robert was eating pheasant beneath a portrait of one of his ancestors. Neither seemed particularly concerned by the imminent threat.

Shortly after dinner, while the gentlemen were still at the table, Freddie Masters returned to Hannesford. Rather than join the ladies, he headed straight for the dining room.

'Ah, Sir Robert! My aunt has accepted my parole and has released me in time for the Hannesford port, of which she knows me to be extraordinarily fond. Will you allow me to join you? No, gentlemen, please don't disturb yourselves. I shall take the seat of one of the departed lovelies. Which, in your opinion, would least resent the impertinence?'

'You can sit where the devil you like,' Sir Robert growled, and signalled for a glass to be brought. But there was no hostility in his voice, only a certain gruff tenderness. Freddie, as the jester at Harry's court, had always been a favourite.

With a bow to the assembled company, the newcomer took a seat and surveyed his audience.

'Ah, Allen! Splendid! Back from directing traffic around the ports of Belgium, I see? Good, good! Now, sir . . .' He raised an eyebrow in the direction of the elderly gentleman to his right. 'On the subject of port . . .'

It was not until much later, at the very end of

47

the evening, that I was able to speak to Freddie Masters about the matter touched upon in his letters. Before that Sir Robert insisted we should both accompany him to his study to examine his plans for a memorial to Hannesford's fallen.

There was an awkward symmetry to this summons. Sir Robert had once been in the habit of rounding up stragglers after dinner to show them his plans for the aggrandisement of Hannesford Court, for the bold new wing that was to be his legacy to his heir. Over the years, countless plans and drawings had been laid before them. But when news of Harry's death reached Hannesford, Sir Robert had rolled up the plans and had never returned to them. I found them still in the corner where they had always been, great cumbrous columns of paper, some leaning, some toppled on their sides, like the pillars of ruined temples.

It was a different drawing that Sir Robert spread out across his desk that night, the outline of a stone cross upon a pedestal. Compared to the elaborate architectural confections he had once favoured, there was something impressive in its simplicity.

'This is what we have settled on, Tom. None of the curlicues and what-not that we were offered at first—lions and angels and all sorts.' He studied it for a few seconds and nodded contentedly, his great visions now reduced to this one plain edifice. 'I think Harry would approve,' he added, 'even if the vicar does not.'

This last was said with feeling, and I looked across at Freddie Masters for an explanation.

'The vicar is proving rather obstinate on the subject of memorials, old man. He and Sir Robert have crossed swords.'

'The vicar is talking a lot of nonsense, Tom. He doesn't want Hannesford to have its own memorial to the fallen.' Sir Robert's scorn was apparent. 'The village has given up two dozen young men of the finest sort and it's our duty to remember them properly. I don't care what the vicar says. We must make sure they are *never* forgotten. Never.'

Freddie Masters looked across at me again and I thought I detected a glint of irony in his eye.

'The vicar wants to spend the money on the village school,' he explained. 'You know the sort of thing. *Education for the children of heroes.*'

I nodded my understanding, but Sir Robert was still eager to make his point. His tone was persuasive. I was being signed up to a cause.

'So what do you say, Tom? You were there. You saw the sort of men the country lost. Men like Harry, men like Julian Trevelyan and young Oliver Eastwell. Our very best. You would not grudge them a lasting memorial?'

No, I would not grudge them that. Although I wasn't sure they would find much comfort in it.

But Sir Robert was still shaking his head. 'Those young men in uniform today . . . They are only alive because better men took the field when the call first came. The cream of our youth, who rallied to the flag and died for it.'

The cream of our youth. The flower of a generation. Our best and finest. Already the phrases had a familiar ring to them. For many, it seemed, only the fallen were truly noble, only the dead purified by sacrifice. By failing to die beside them, the rest of us had demonstrated a very culpable lack of ambition.

Meanwhile Sir Robert was looking self-conscious.

'Of course, I don't mean you, Masters,' he added hastily, peering at Freddie. 'I know you'd have been out there much earlier if you hadn't been needed at the ministry. Even as it is, you still put in a good year at the front. And you, Tom, you were over there almost as quickly as Harry . . .'

Without warning Sir Robert's voice began to waver and Freddie Masters made a great show of turning his attention to the drawing on the desk.

'I believe, sir, it was the wording, not the design, that you wished to discuss tonight?'

And so I listened politely while Sir Robert leafed through his papers and read out the various suggestions.

To the Glory of God and in memory of the men of this village who gave their lives for freedom . . . for truth and justice . . . for King and Country . . .

Who, when the call came, thought not of themselves but of the greater good . . . of their fellow men . . . of duty and honour . . .

Who have laid down their lives for the love of God . . . for the defeat of tyranny . . . in the cause of righteousness . . .

So many different reasons. They couldn't all be true. I thought of those pinched, pale faces below the parapet, waiting in silence for the whistle that would send them forward. What single phrase could possibly be found to gather together all those separate truths?

In memory of those who didn't want to let anyone down.

In memory of those who were told they had to go, and did, and died.

And then there were those like Harry Stansbury.

50

Was there, I wondered, in any corner of the country, a memorial stating the truth about Harry?

In memory of someone who said too loudly and too often that he couldn't wait to have a go at the Hun . . .

*   *   *

Drowsy after dinner, lulled by the blazing fire, the company did not linger in the drawing room. In ones and twos they drifted away until, at an hour when Harry and Margot's old circle would just have been coming alive, there remained only a core of old men, brandy glasses in hand, clustered around Sir Robert. The talk was of tariffs and strikes and the iniquities of Lloyd George. When Masters plucked at my sleeve, there seemed little reason to stay.

'Come on, old man,' he urged. 'If you haven't heard it all before, you soon will have. Let's slope off and have a smoke.'

He led me across the Great Hall to the room known as the reading room, a place of leather armchairs and deep carpets, well stocked with newspapers and sporting periodicals and boxes of cigarettes. The fire there had burned low, and a pair of lamps cast a soft, somnolent glow. I settled myself into an armchair near the fire while Masters spent some moments locating a particular brand of Turkish cigarette.

'Ah, here we go! Hard to get hold of these nowadays. Do you know why?'

I shook my head and selected a cigarette. I never much cared what I smoked.

'Well, partly patriotism, of course.' The way

Masters said the word suggested it was not one he particularly liked. 'After the carnage in the Dardanelles it wasn't done to be seen smoking Johnny Turk's tobacco. But you'd have thought things might be back to normal by now, wouldn't you?'

He paused and helped me to a light, then settled down opposite, shaking his head as he did so.

'But it turns out things aren't quite that simple. Take these cigarettes. The Armenian fellow who makes them has shut up shop. Or has had his shop shut for him. It's all turning rather ugly on the shores of the Bosphorus, you see. *Civil upheaval* is the phrase the diplomats are using, which means they don't know what's going on but they know it's a bloody mess.' He looked at me. 'Does that worry you?'

'Should it?' After so long dodging machine-gun fire in France, I felt reasonably confident I could survive a shortage of Turkish cigarettes.

'Well, you see, old man, it isn't just Turkey. It's Germany too. If you kick a man when he's down, and then keep on kicking him, you're likely to make an unholy mess, you know.' Freddie pursed his lips. 'Have you spoken to the Eccleston girl yet?'

'To Violet Eccleston?' This unexpected conversational lurch caught me off guard. 'A little. Tonight, at dinner.'

'She's rather beyond the pale as a conversationalist, isn't she, old man? I suspect Sir Robert would gladly fight another war if it were to rid the world of people like Violet Eccleston. But strangely enough, dear boy, she's right about a lot of things.' He took a long draw at his cigarette then let the smoke out slowly, shutting his eyes as if in

52

bliss. 'Her problem is that she sits there spouting all sorts of theories and it doesn't really matter how much sense there is in any of them because everyone simply wishes she'd shut up and go away. It makes me understand why the Trojans never listened to Cassandra. Annihilation by the Greeks must have seemed infinitely preferable.'

I settled deeper into my chair. I was seeing a new side to Freddie Masters and it was an improvement. Perhaps, away from Harry and the others, Freddie had not always been quite such a buffoon.

'You mentioned in your note something about Professor Schmidt,' I reminded him.

'Ah, yes.' Masters leaned back and peered at me through a veil of bluish smoke. 'Very curious. That week at Hannesford, the last time we were all together, how well do you remember it?'

I considered the question. 'I suppose I have a fair recollection of what went on. Given the way it ended, it rather stays in the mind, doesn't it?'

'Yes, I suppose it does. It was so damnably hot for one thing . . .'

Watching Masters smoke, I was surprised by the seriousness in his eyes.

'It's funny, isn't it, Tom? How many men have we seen die since then? How many hundreds? We've seen so much death we almost stopped noticing it. And yet for some reason we both remember that one.'

I thought of the hard flagstones beneath my knees, a hand in mine so cold it made me shiver, although the night was hot. Anne Gregory, very close to me, tugging at the fallen man's collar. Then, without warning, those cold fingers tightening in a succession of fierce, desperate spasms. Then nothing. Yes, I certainly remembered it.

'Death was new to us then,' I said.

'And still very terrible.' Masters paused for another long draw on his cigarette. 'Now it no longer comes as a surprise. I don't know about you, but it's being alive that tends to surprise me.'

And I knew what he meant. Towards the end, I'd no longer mourned the dead: they were still there, all around me, inhabitants of the same country. I could still feel the ties that bound us. No, it was the living who were foreign to me then, the people at home, the people with a future. And it was the life I'd left behind that I could no longer imagine.

But I said none of that to Freddie Masters, with his high spirits and his DSO and his couple of years spent safely in Whitehall. I still wasn't sure who Masters really was. So I simply shrugged, and leaned forward to knock the ash from my cigarette.

'That summer at Hannesford . . .' I prompted.

'Ah, yes.' Masters waved away the smoke with one hand. 'There was a rather strange atmosphere that week, wasn't there, old man? It all felt slightly feverish and rather intense. Or am I imagining that?'

I don't think he was. There *had* been something peculiar about the gaiety at Hannesford that summer, as if the high spirits were just a little too high and the laughter a fraction louder and longer than it should have been. Easy to think afterwards that a dark presentiment must have weighed upon us all. But we were simply a group of people too often and too closely together, our tempers made volatile by the heat. Certainly the fates of nations had not weighed heavily upon my shoulders that

54

summer. I'd been thinking only of Margot.

'Of course,' Masters went on, 'had the Kaiser backed down, there'd have been a terrible sense of anticlimax. It's hard to credit now how even quite sane people had come to believe we needed a war to clear the air.'

He shook his head, marvelling at the madness.

'Now, as I remember, Professor Schmidt had been invited down here to sort out the butterfly collection, had he not? He seemed a placid sort of fellow,' Masters added. 'Not greatly given to flights of fancy, I should think.'

The fire had burned very low and its light cast strange shadows over his face, accentuating its hollows, making him look older and more tired.

'And then, my friend, in the early hours of the morning, right slap in the middle of the Rose Ball, he dropped dead on the terrace. Verdict, heart failure. I dug out the records recently and had a quick look at them. It all sounds very straightforward.'

I studied his face for a second or two. 'You've been to some trouble over this, Freddie. Are you going to tell me why?'

In reply, Masters's voice was soothing. 'To be frank, old man, I don't really know. None of it is of any importance now. Look, there's whisky in that decanter. Why don't we have a dash or two of that and I'll tell you about a funny thing that happened to me after the shooting stopped. Then we can both forget all about it and go to bed.'

I waited, intrigued, while Masters filled the glasses.

'You see, old man, last year, before I was demobbed, I spent some time in Cologne. Part of

55

the occupying army, don't you know? You were there for a bit too, I think. So you know what it was like.' He handed me a glass and sank back into his chair. 'Here comes the interesting part. While I was there, I was paid a visit by someone who said he was old Schmidt's son.'

I could dimly remember the professor speaking of a son, someone living abroad in the German colonies, a son with tastes very different from his father's. Even when the professor died I hadn't given him a great deal of thought. I certainly hadn't expected him to turn up in conversation at Hannesford.

Masters told the story of his encounter in Cologne with his usual lavish flourishes, but he told it well. As he talked, I found myself recalling my own memories of that city in those first, unreal days of peace: the population bewildered, still stunned by the realities of defeat; the shops empty, the citizens too proud to beg from their conquerors; the winter advancing from the east; so little coal that in the big houses beyond Kanalstrasse there were stories of the magnificent furniture being broken up for firewood. And the occupying soldiers, well, they too had seemed dazed, ill-prepared for peace. They were—in a way hard to explain—suspicious of their own survival. No triumphalism, at least not among the fighting men. That had come later, when the peace tourists dribbled in.

It was in this monochrome setting that Freddie Masters had been visited by Johann Schmidt, a man of forty or more, brown-skinned and creased by the sun, still limping from shrapnel wounds. He told Masters he'd been in Swakopmund in German South-West Africa when he heard of his father's death, and shortly afterwards, when war broke out, had returned to Germany to fight. Because of this, a letter from his father sent shortly before he died had taken some months to reach him. And when it had, there had been little time for him to dwell on its contents.

But now the fighting was over, and he had recognised the name of Captain Frederick Masters. Was he perhaps the same Frederick Masters who had once been known to his father at Hannesford Court? If so, he wished to ask about that last letter. Could Captain Masters perhaps explain what his father had been referring to? It was a little thing, but for a son mourning a parent such things could be important. Perhaps, if all was explained to him, he would be better able to say a final farewell to his father . . .

The letter itself had been in German, a language it turned out Freddie Masters was proficient in. ('Too much Goethe as a youth,' he explained in a stage whisper, sensing my surprise.) For the most part, the contents had consisted of questions to his son, descriptions of various English churches and an outline of the party assembled at Hannesford Court.

'He was rather nice about you, old man,' Masters told me with a smile, 'and quite sporting about me too, really. Said I probably wasn't as great a fool as everyone supposed, which is a compliment of sorts, don't you think? And then came the paragraph that the younger Schmidt had been fretting about. I jotted down some notes at the time and wrote them up afterwards. The translation is mine, old chap, but I think I got the gist well enough.'

He produced a piece of paper from his jacket.

57

The handwriting was rushed and sloping.

*Int. w <u>Johann Schmidt,</u> Köln, 12 Feb. 1919
SW Afrika 1908. Hamburg 1914. Wounded
Chemin des Dames 1917*

*End of letter from Prof. S. Schmidt,
Hannesford Crt, dated June 1914*

*'27th June: Two days since I wrote my last
remarks and I am writing today in a state of great
perturbation. Something horrible has happened
here. I cannot bring myself to say more. I am
greatly shaken. Shaken and shocked. A crime. A
terrible thing. I am unsure how to proceed or in
whom to confide. But I must do something. My
dear Johann, I say again, I am severely shaken. I
sign off now and shall write more anon.'*

I looked up from the paper. 'And that was all?'

Masters nodded. 'Yes. Not much, is it? Which
is why I wanted to ask if you could throw any light
on the matter. Those sentences were written three
days before the Rose Ball. Three days before the
old man died.'

But I could only shake my head in genuine
mystification. 'Something horrible? I've no idea.
Really. There were all sorts of things going on, of
course. Any number of indiscretions, I've no doubt.
But surely nothing the professor would consider a
crime.'

I paused, struck once again by just how far away
that other time seemed. Five years, yet hazy, like
distant childhood.

'I must say,' Masters mused, 'I find it rather

uncomfortable to think of something unpalatable going on here under our noses.'

'Are you sure he meant an *actual* crime?' I asked. 'Or just something he found shocking?'

'Someone cheating at cards or bouncing a cheque, you mean? I wondered about that.' Masters took the note and looked it over again. 'But it all seems a bit extreme for that, doesn't it? A bit of an over-reaction.'

I hesitated. 'A man emerging from the bedroom of a woman who was not his wife? I dare say he might have witnessed that.'

Masters nodded. 'There are any number of things he could have seen that might be considered scandalous or caddish or morally dubious. But *horrible*? That doesn't sound like passing the port the wrong way, does it, old chap? And in case you think it's my ropey German, I should tell you that Schmidt the younger also had the impression that his father meant something criminal, rather than any sort of unsettling social gaffe.'

'So what did you tell him?'

Masters held up his whisky tumbler and swilled the liquid gently around the glass. The glow from the fire turned it the colour of burned gold.

'I told him I'd no idea what his father was referring to and that I was not aware of any shocking act, criminal or otherwise, perpetrated at Hannesford that summer. But I also told him I'd ask you about it, in case there was anything I'd missed.'

'Me? Why me?' It seemed surprising that I should have been the person Freddie Masters thought of.

In reply, Masters stopped playing with his drink

59

and looked at me, one eyebrow raised.

'Because off the top of my head, old man, you were the only other fellow I could think of from that summer who was still alive.'

We were both silent for a little after that.

'Those were strange, heady times,' I ventured at last, 'but I honestly can't imagine what the professor might have been referring to.'

Masters sighed theatrically. 'Nor can I. After all, those were our days of wine and roses, weren't they, old fellow? Remember? Never a cloud, never a thorn, never an evening spent drinking rather too much poor claret. Or at least that's how some people seem to recall it. Here's to short memories.' He raised his glass and drained it in one motion. 'Very well. I'll write to Herr Schmidt and tell him that your recollection confirms my own. Then I think we can consider the matter closed.'

He moved forward to the edge of his seat as though about to rise, but paused and looked pensive.

'There was one other thing, though. Something I didn't tell the professor's son. It quite disturbed me at the time, but of course events conspired to put it out of my mind quickly enough.'

There was no flourish now, not a trace of flamboyance. If anything, Masters looked troubled.

'You see, my friend, on the night of the Rose Ball, three days after he wrote that note, I saw the professor down on the footbridge in the woods. The old donkey bridge, you know the one. It was some time around midnight, I should think. I'd slipped out for some air and ended up on the far side of the stream, up on the top of the slope. I was just heading back when I saw him.'

Masters broke off to light another cigarette then leaned back and let out the smoke in a slow, deliberate column.

'He wasn't alone. There was someone with him and they were arguing. I couldn't tell who it was because the trees were in the way, but it was definitely the professor. He was rather a distinctive shape, if you remember, and he was standing where I could see him. Of course, now I wish I'd carried on down the path, but at the time I wasn't much in the mood for company. Besides, no one's ever grateful if you interrupt an argument. So I just stepped aside into the trees and lit a cigarette and waited.'

I looked at him. 'And what were they arguing about?' I asked.

'No idea,' Masters replied airily. 'They were a long way below me, remember. I could just hear raised voices, that was all. No shouting, but you could tell they were angry. Once I'd stepped off the path, I couldn't see the bridge at all. But I did make out one thing. I heard the professor say quite distinctly, *"I shall take the whole affair to Sir Robert."* Perhaps not those exact words, but something like that.'

'And then?'

He hesitated. Beneath his easy manner there seemed to lurk a very real distaste.

'That's when it turned rather unpleasant, old man. Something I hadn't expected. The other fellow hit him. I heard the blow. First an oath, which I didn't catch, then *crack*. A slap, not a punch. But hard. Really hard.' He studied the tip of his cigarette. 'Well, obviously, that flushed me out all right. I got myself back to the path as

61

quickly as I could. But all I could see from the top was the professor on his knees, groping around on the ground. For his spectacles, I suppose. Pretty sickening, it was. An old man being treated like that.'

He broke off again and I waited, watching him smoke.

'I think I must have called out, but on that path you lose sight of the bridge as soon as you start coming down. By the time I got there, the professor had gone. I think he must have hurried away when he heard me coming. Must have been humiliating for him to have been seen like that. So I didn't try to catch him up. I stayed down there another ten minutes or so, I should think, smoking, calming myself down. Thought I'd sort it all out when I got back to the house. But when I did get there, he was already dead.'

Masters slid the piece of notepaper back into his pocket with an air of finality. 'It's ironic given everything that's happened since, but thinking about it still makes me feel rather ghastly. There was something about the way he was left on the ground like that which sticks in my craw.' He stubbed out his cigarette. 'Anyway, Allen, old man, I'll probably write to Germany tomorrow. So have a think about the good old days, and if you come up with anything, do let me know, there's a sport.'

Left alone, I sat up for quite a long time, watching the fire die its slow, orange death. My thoughts were not particularly pleasant. God knows, I'd seen enough brutality since my last stay at Hannesford, enough to make me impervious to all sorts of horror. Why should the thought of an old man slapped in the face discomfort me? But war was war. Hannesford was different. And the professor had been a friend of mine. A decent man. Someone I'd neglected over the last few days of his life.

Perhaps coming back had not been such a good idea, after all.

The storm that greeted my arrival had been a momentous one—three inches of rain in as many hours, and the river had risen dangerously, flooding the water meadows, turning the dark pool below the donkey bridge into an angry, turbulent cauldron. Two of the lower farms had been flooded, for the first time in anyone's memory.

But after that the sun shone. Bright day followed bright day as if by decree, and I was introduced to Hannesford at its most beautiful. It was that lull in the Season that preceded the Stansburys' summer ball, a brief period of calm when by tradition the Stansbury family abandoned polite society and gathered in the country. It says a good deal for the status of the Stansburys that quite a lot of polite society chose to follow them.

I quickly realised that I had much to be thankful for. Sir Robert was gracious and his wife touchingly quick to rely on me in all sorts of ways. The Stansbury children, for all their flamboyance, never condescended to me. Margot was particularly kind in those first days, before the guests began to arrive, paying me a good deal of attention, showing me around the grounds, introducing me to the village. She made sure that the Stansburys' dependants all knew me by both name and face.

I saw much less of Harry, whose friends were already beginning to roll in. By day he was punctilious in his manners, and never less than charming when it fell to him to escort me on an errand or make conversation over tea. I appreciated these efforts because on such occasions I could see he really wanted to be away with the other young men, doing something boisterous. Oliver Eastwell, Julian Trevelyan, Freddie Masters—at first they were no more to me than flannelled ornaments on the tennis court or boatered oarsmen churning up the lake. At night, from my little room at the top of the house, I could follow the sound of their revelry.

Lady Stansbury's other children made less immediate impressions upon me. Susan Stansbury was slim and dark and reserved, and seemed well disposed to me, but her manner was more guarded than Margot's and I found her far more difficult to read. Young Bill Stansbury was still a child and shy at first, although within three weeks of my arrival he seemed to have accepted my presence as though I'd always been there.

Reggie was more difficult. He seemed the only one of the Stansbury children to have a sullen streak. I quickly saw that his interests were things that took him away from the company of his siblings, and he seemed to consider me another member of the household he was happier to avoid. Sometimes there would be arguments behind closed doors, Reggie's temper boiling over, raging at his brother over some perceived slight. Harry's voice in reply was always calm and courteous, perhaps very slightly patronising.

Had those quiet days continued unchanged my first year at Hannesford might have been one of unalloyed pleasure. But there were not many occasions in the year when the family was alone. Company was the natural state of things, and with the arrival of others everything changed. I was, after all, simply Lady Stansbury's companion, an object of little interest to the sort of society who frequented

Hannesford Court. When guests were present Harry and Margot became the centre of everything while I disappeared into the background.

Before coming to Hannesford, I'd never thought myself lonely or in need of pity. My mother had died too young for me to remember her, and life with my father had been characterised by the quiet rhythms of genteel poverty. It was a manner of living I'd grown up with and understood. Lady Stansbury, finding me unmarried, must have assumed that it was a combination of poverty and plainness that had condemned me to spinsterhood, but in fact I'd not been without suitors, acquaintances of my father who found me good-natured and neat and efficient, and who had never once thought to wonder who I really was. I was merely my father's quiet daughter, a suitable, unexceptional young thing, experienced at keeping house, who would be grateful for an offer. But I knew they offered me nothing—no hope of change or escape—only a continuation of the life I already knew; more years of competence and carefulness and frugality, in the company of someone I pitied rather than loved.

And through it all, I harboured dreams. Dreams I barely confessed even to myself, of a life more colourful, more surprising. Somehow those dreams survived the first flush of my youth, even while I mocked myself for my folly. They survived my father's death and my work as a nurse, and they were still not quite extinguished when Lady Stansbury's letter arrived summoning me to Hannesford Court. Through all the privations of my previous existence I had retained at least some shreds of self-belief.

But at Hannesford there were occasions in the

presence of guests when I found myself invisible. Introductions were made, politenesses exchanged, but then the eyes of newcomers would glide past me, already unseeing, intent on other, more significant social conquests. And the sense of loneliness that sprang up inside me on those occasions was more profound and more distressing than anything I'd ever felt during my empty nights in lodgings after my father's death.

After six months I'd even considered leaving Hannesford. For a time, I exchanged letters with an acquaintance of mine, a nursing sister I'd worked closely with, about the possibility of employment in Australia. But gradually the rhythms of life at Hannesford began to soothe me. Spring brought with it a sense of dark days survived, and soon the countryside was whispering with life. To my surprise, I felt a part of it, glad to see the winter jasmine blossom and the snow retreat from the moors, at home in the landscape in a way I'd never been before. With summer came the Season, and time in London, but I was back at Hannesford long before the Rose Ball, helping with plans, writing letters, caught up despite myself in the growing excitement. And at the end of the summer, when the quiet returned to Hannesford, I felt myself breathing calmer, gentler air. I had time to sit and read and be myself again, and to watch the turning of the leaves. I liked the way Hannesford Court seemed more itself when the visitors were gone. I felt in sympathy with the place, as though it too was able to relax a little and resume its quiet, contemplative habits.

Lulled by Hannesford's calm, I hesitated. Perhaps I could find peace in such a place after all. Perhaps the tranquillity I felt when I walked out to the edge of the moor was enough. But with every house party, with every new set of guests who came and smiled and were charming without seeing me, my confidence ebbed; a little more of me was eroded.

And then the following summer Tom Allen appeared. Another hot day, another picnic. After that, things were different.

4

On Christmas Eve the shooting parties were always out early, while the woods were still dark. They would fuel themselves for the day ahead with prodigious quantities of breakfast, helping themselves from silver chafing dishes in the bright, clattering breakfast room, before Sir Robert led them out into a world newly pale, the sky still flecked with fragments of the dawn. Winter mornings found Hannesford at its most magical; and yet I was rarely moved to join them.

For those who remained behind, the day had a different tempo. After breakfast there might be riding or a walk, usually to the Shepherds, three ancient standing stones that lay beyond Hannesford village. Or for those reluctant to venture abroad there was a morning of letters and newspapers and comfortable idling by fires that never seemed to flag. In the afternoon there would be tea in the drawing room and games of cards at tables that looked out over the frost-striped countryside.

Then, when the light began to fade, the shooting parties would return, calling for poached eggs and beer, and the younger guests would be led by Margot to the gallery for the dressing of the Christmas tree, to be admired in all its glory when the party gathered before dinner. Sherry was always served in the Great Hall, the first occasion of the day when everyone came together, although tradition held that when snow was falling hot brandy punch was served instead. And at the very end of the evening, after dinner and coffee, after

69

singing at the piano, perhaps, by the brave or the foolhardy, guests would retire to their rooms to find by their beds small posies of holly and white lilies, the latter conjured magically from Hannesford's glasshouses. No one could remember the significance of this pairing, if indeed it ever had any. It was simply a Hannesford tradition. Because of it, even at the very height of summer, the scent of lilies always made me think of winter on the edge of the moors.

That morning I was awake long before the guns departed, long before the dawn pressed its pale fingers against the window. The silence of the countryside unnerved me. In London, the rumble of buses and the steady clip of horses' hooves had helped me sleep. But at Hannesford there was no background noise to soothe and distract me, so instead I lay awake trying not to think, waiting for the first movements of the servants and the patient rituals that summoned the house to life.

After that came the stirring of the sportsmen, ponderous and a little grumpy. Once at that hour I would have heard Harry's voice ringing out louder than the others; might even have recognised Reggie Stansbury's impatient step outside my room. But now the sounds were different, more muffled, the stir of activity less distinct; and when at last they stepped outside, the modest crunch of their footsteps on the gravel suggested that the shooting party was much reduced in numbers.

After that the hot water arrived, and fearful of the attentions of old Evans, I made haste to wash and dress and to take myself downstairs.

Often in the past, emerging after the shooting party had departed, I would be the only male at

70

breakfast. Certainly the only male under sixty. At Hannesford young men were expected to shoot, and most did so with enthusiasm. But that year things had changed. It was as if an ancient chain had broken, as if the party Lady Stansbury had assembled was not sufficiently steeped in Hannesford's traditions to understand what was expected of them. Already Mapperley the banker and Horatio Finch-Taylor were comfortably ensconced at the table, talking of financial matters as serenely as if they were breakfasting in the City. At the sideboard, Neil Maclean was peering under one of the silver covers.

'It's quite a spread,' he observed as I joined him. He was eyeing with dismay a tray of smoked haddock in a sea of butter. 'How is it that only the British think fish is good for breakfast?'

Rather spitefully, I helped myself to a large plateful of kedgeree. 'You're not shooting today, Mr Maclean?'

'Not today. I'm not a great one for the guns. Margot has talked me into motoring to Tenmouth later on. I've never seen the place. Margot says it's picturesque and has a good bookshop.'

'It certainly used to have a good bookshop,' I confirmed, although I wasn't at all sure that Margot had ever been inside.

When we took our places at the table neither of the two financiers looked up.

'Who's out with Sir Robert?' I asked.

'Only young Bill Stansbury and Denny Houghton, and old Colonel Rolleston, I think. I'm afraid Sir Robert was put out that it was so few.'

'It used to be just about everyone,' I explained. 'What about Freddie Masters?'

71

Maclean waved his fork at something on his plate. 'Are these kidneys?' he asked suspiciously. 'Yes, I think Masters may have joined them, just to keep Sir Robert happy. And you, Captain? Margot says you never shoot. Why is that?'

I shrugged and reached for the butter. 'I never took to it. As a child I was always a little afraid of guns.'

'And yet you were one of the first to join up.' The American studied me with undisguised curiosity. 'That's very courageous for a boy who didn't like guns.'

'You get used to them.' I continued to concentrate on my breakfast. I rather wanted to dislike Maclean.

'Apologies if I ask too many questions, Captain. But staying here with Sir Robert, hearing about all those young men ... Young Harry Stansbury, for instance. From what I hear he sounds like quite a loss. I believe you're going to be making the address at his memorial service?'

It would have been easy to snub him then, to come up with something frigidly polite that would put an end to the conversation. But when I looked into the American's face there was nothing crass or insensitive in it, nothing but honest enquiry. So I simply nodded.

'Yes,' I replied. 'Everybody loved Harry.'

'And a good many followed his example. What made you so keen to join up, Captain Allen?'

Because I thought I was in love with Margot? Because Margot was marrying someone else? Because I thought that if I died it would somehow serve her right?

'Sense of duty, I suppose. What sort of books are

72

you interested in, Mr Maclean?'

Presently we were joined by Violet Eccleston and Lucy Flinders, then a few minutes later by Margot herself, with a message from Lady Stansbury.

'Tom, darling, Mama says Father has promised the car to Mrs Rolleston this morning so she can pay a few calls. She asks would it be all right if you didn't set off for Cullingford till eleven? Which is a frightful bore, because Neil was going to take Lucy and me into Tenmouth this morning in *his* car, and we thought you might join us . . .'

With that the conversation turned to the pleasures of the proposed outing. I finished my breakfast and slipped quietly away.

*   *   *

The footpath to Hannesford village lay through the woods. I knew the path well and liked it. In the summer there were woodpeckers and small orange butterflies; in the winter, woodsmoke and the crunch of frozen mud beneath my feet. That morning was clear but very cold, and on the north side of Hannesford Court the frost was still hard on the ground. But the air felt fresh on my skin. I felt, if not young, perhaps a little less old.

Only when Hannesford Court was out of sight did my mood begin to change. At first, with a blackbird singing close by, I hardly realised how quiet it was. But then the blackbird flew off and I sensed all around me the silence of the woods. A year earlier I would have panicked. Only a few months before, I'd been dining alone in a busy restaurant in France when one of those inexplicable silences had spread across the room, as if every speaker had paused for breath at precisely the same instant. At first everyone began to look around, and then a cheery French captain broke the hush by whistling a sharp note between his fingers. There had been cheers and laughter, followed by more noise than before. But I had not cheered. At the sound of the whistle I'd found my jaw clenched and my knuckles white, and my hand trembled so much that I splashed my wine on to the tablecloth.

For me the roar of the barrage had never been as bad as the silence that followed it. Silence, then the whistle. Even now, even in cities, there was no escaping the silence. But I'd been learning to keep the panic at bay, learning to breathe deeply and ignore the sweat that pricked my skin, to think only of the next moment, the next breath, my next footstep . . . Even so, it was not without relief that I left the woods that morning and crossed the stile into Hannesford village.

Mr Uttley, the vicar of Hannesford, had once been a classical scholar of some distinction, and had accepted the living at Hannesford thirty years before. Since then he and his wife had become as much a part of the village as the Stansbury Arms or the village pond. When I rang the bell that morning, he answered the door himself.

'Yes? Yes? Why, Tom Allen! My boy! Come in, come in. Anne told us you were back. Such wonderful news. Do come in. No maid today, I'm afraid, and Anne is out running errands. Come in. We are sadly unused to homecomings in Hannesford, I fear, so very practised at valedictions.'

I followed him into the front parlour where Mrs Uttley lay wrapped in blankets on a day bed. A

74

small fire burned in the grate but the ceilings were high and the room had the chill feel of one that has not been properly warm for a considerable time.

'Mary, dear, it's Tom Allen come to see us. You remember Tom.'

Although Anne had warned me that Mrs Uttley was frail, I was still taken by surprise. I remembered a neat, sprightly woman, enormously active despite her complaints of rheumatism, someone who had been at the heart of Hannesford village, knowing everybody, knowing everything; visiting cottages, walking in the woods, dispensing advice and pots of jam with unfailing good nature. Now I found myself in the presence of a waif in cap and shawl whose tiny body took up only a fraction of the bed on which she lay. The hand she reached out to me was mottled and swollen at the joints.

'Dear Tom,' she chirped, 'how good of you to come.' And instantly on hearing her voice I recognised the woman I remembered—her warmth and her vivacity, both unchanged. 'So good of you to bring Anne home last night. The vicar had hoped to be at the station, but you know how it is. Such a busy time of year for him. It's *so* maddening not being able to get about as I used to. But how wonderful to have you back for Christmas.'

I stayed with them for half an hour, listening to their news of the village, of births and marriages and young men lost or wounded, of the farmers struggling for want of labour. More than one farm labourer, they told me, having survived the front, had been unable to settle and had quit Hannesford for the city.

'It's hard for them. Remember Albert Hall? One of the first to volunteer. To escape the jokes about his name, we used to say. He's come through it all, like you, Tom. The Somme, the Salient, everything. Now he won't work. He goes into Hanbury every day to drink. Mrs Collins saw him there, blind drunk in the afternoon.'

The vicar shook his head. 'Such a nice young man, too.'

'He's not the only one content to take the dole, Tom,' Mrs Uttley went on. 'Abraham Giles at Top Farm sent home all his girls when the fighting stopped, but come the next harvest he had to take them back again. Couldn't find men to do the work, you see.'

'But at least we were spared the worst of the influenza here,' the vicar pointed out brightly. 'Such a blessing. Although Mrs Turnbull's boy was one of those taken by it, poor lad. He was in a camp in Plymouth, waiting to be posted.'

Only when I was about to leave did I think to touch upon the subject that Freddie Masters had raised the previous evening. The vicar and his wife had been on friendly terms with Professor Schmidt and on more than one occasion had invited him to the vicarage. When I mentioned the professor's name, both their faces brightened.

'Such a good-hearted fellow,' the vicar exclaimed. 'Wasn't he, my dear? We always found him very good company. People nowadays tend to forget that the German people weren't always our enemies. And his knowledge of English ecclesiastical architecture was really very extensive.'

I nodded my agreement, wondering how to phrase my question.

'I was talking about him last night with Freddie Masters,' I told them. 'Masters was under the

76

impression that there'd been something troubling him in the days before he died. I do hope that wasn't the case...'

'I sincerely hope not,' the vicar declared. 'But of course, I expect his health was a concern. His heart must have been a worry to him for some time. And in those last months he would have felt his position most acutely. If you remember, there was already a lot of anti-German sentiment around, even then.'

His wife looked at her husband thoughtfully. 'You overheard that argument, didn't you, dear? Between the professor and Reggie Stansbury. It quite upset you.'

'That's right, I did, though it seems an awfully long time ago now. Patriotism can so easily turn to prejudice, can it not? And it was only a few days before the professor's death—I remember the gardeners were busy with the flowers for the Rose Ball. I'd taken a shortcut through the park, you see, and I heard them arguing by the walled garden. Reggie was saying some terribly anti-German things, I'm afraid, but of course Reggie's temper was notorious. Such a troubled young man! And you say you'll be visiting him later on? I do hope you will give him our best wishes. What's happened to him is a terrible thing. A terrible, terrible thing...'

When I left them they were still sitting hand in hand, pondering the unkindness of war.

With the low sun bright on its roofs, Hannesford village appeared timeless and serene. It was familiar to me in a way I hadn't expected: the church, the village pub, the cottages littered about them at unlikely angles. A single dog trotted down the street with a sturdy sense of purpose.

77

And around it all was the welcoming smell of woodsmoke. Sometimes you have to leave a place to see it properly.

Was it significant that Reggie Stansbury had argued with the professor? I didn't really think so. Reggie had shouted at everyone in his time; he had a temper that flared up violently and unexpectedly. But there was a great distance between angry words and a cowardly blow in the face. Besides, if I was really worried about it, I could simply ask Reggie for myself. At the thought of my impending visit, I shivered a little and pulled my coat closer around me.

Had I stayed longer at the vicarage, I would have bumped into Anne Gregory again. When I looked back from the stile at the edge of the village I saw her at the vicarage gate, a basket on her arm. No sooner had I noticed her than she turned and looked in my direction, shielding her eyes against the low sun. Feeling I'd been caught watching her, I raised my arm and waved. Slowly, a little uncertainly, the figure at the gate waved back, and I continued on my way, my thoughts returning to the task that lay ahead of me. I couldn't be sure if she'd recognised me.

I was sitting by the river bank the first time I saw him. It was late morning, and the heat was still gathering its strength. Beyond the river, the view of the moor was a jumbled palette of purples and pinks and greens. Around me Margot's friends were playing at picnicking, squabbling cheerfully over plates and glasses, while the young men jostled each other and planned games to play. Down by the water Margot balanced on a rock on the river's edge and splashed water at Julian Trevelyan.

No one knew anything about Tom Allen then, only that he was newly arrived in the village and that he might be interested in Hannesford's old darkroom. No one was even sure if he was coming or whether he'd be able to find us, hidden as we were in a distant crook of the river where the trees cast welcome shadows.

But he had found us, stepping over the low fence with a good-natured smile. There was something about that smile I liked. Perhaps it was an absence of cynicism. His face was oddly free of shadows. In the Stansburys' circle at that time, the affectation of world weariness was almost *de rigueur*.

Amid the noise and excitement of his arrival, the introductions were poorly done. Harry, over-eager, like a schoolboy with a new puppy, dragged him forward, firing a string of names and nicknames at him—Buttercup and Daisy, Margot and Susie, Julian, Tippy, Oliver. No one could possibly have remembered them all. I was kneeling by the hamper, my hands full of napkins, and had been forgotten— not from malice or deliberate thoughtlessness, I knew, but because Harry was like that: charming

79

and slapdash and desperate to get on with things.

But the newcomer had noticed the omission, and when the others moved away he came forward and introduced himself. I liked his handshake, the honesty in his face. Later, as the shadows began to stretch across the fields and the party made its way homewards, he walked next to me and we talked amiably, for no reason I can remember, about the British love of roses.

That night, alone in my room at the top of the house, I remembered his eyes, the warmth in them, the crow's feet that crinkled when he smiled. And when, not many summers later, the casualty lists began to grow and grow, I thought of him then too—though I told myself it was only the alphabet that made me search for his name first.

The sanatorium at Cullingford had been built as the country retreat of a successful tea merchant and was converted to its later use when the flood of casualties from France made the demand for such places starkly evident. It was a handsome building in brown stone, with ivy around the door and striking chimneys. As I approached it, the only indication that it was not a comfortable country residence was a single crutch, abandoned apparently by accident against the front doorpost. At the back, I discovered later, a single-storey extension rather marred the attractive Victorian lines—hastily added when it had become obvious that a good many of the officers coming there for rehabilitation would never again climb a flight of stairs.

I'd visited such places before. Somehow, whatever measures had been taken to make them welcoming and cheerful, to disguise them as the well-appointed homes of gentlemen, they always stirred in me a guilty sense of dread. No amount of dressing up could disguise their purpose. And had things been different, had it been me who'd stopped a bullet or caught a piece of shrapnel . . . It wasn't a thought I cared to pursue.

That morning, as I stepped out of the car, I was welcomed by a brisk nursing sister who asked if Lieutenant Stansbury was expecting me. When I replied in the negative, she raised an eyebrow.

'A friend of his, Mr . . . ?'

'Captain,' I replied, sensing a military rank might help. 'Captain Allen. I'm a friend of the family.'

She led me across a wood-panelled hall into a large drawing room.

'I should warn you that he may not see you,

Captain. Lieutenant Stansbury isn't keen on visitors. That happens, you know. Many of our patients feel more comfortable among their own.'

'Their own, sister?'

I saw her flush slightly. 'I mean among fellow wounded officers, of course. Please, take a seat. There are cigarettes on the table.'

Looking around, the room struck me as strangely under-furnished. The sister must have followed my gaze.

'Yes, it's a bit spartan, isn't it? We remove a lot of the usual furniture, you see, so that there's more space to move around. With so many men on crutches or in chairs, well, I'm afraid the modern household contains far too much *clutter*. That will have to change. If we care about our wounded, we must insist that it does.'

'Yes, of course.' I thought of the rooms at Hannesford with their lamps and their exquisite little tables and their countless stands for plants.

'Now, if you will excuse me, I shall send word to Lieutenant Stansbury that you're here.'

I waited by the window, still standing, wondering if Reggie would agree to see me. If roles were reversed, would a visit from Reggie give me any pleasure? I shuddered at the thought. Outside, at the foot of the lawn, a solitary figure in civilian dress was making his way across the grass, swinging himself along between two crutches. Progress was slow and ungainly, but there was a doggedness about the way the fellow went about the task that made his effort admirable. Without warning I felt a lump rise in my throat.

Embarrassed, I turned back to the room and was startled by my reflection in the mirror above the mantelpiece. Anne Gregory was right, I *did* look thin. And pale. Nothing at all like the man who'd walked across the fields to Hannesford all those years ago. Preoccupied, I didn't hear Reggie approach.

'Hello, Allen. Come to see the freak show?'

Reggie Stansbury was propped up in a wicker chair, his gloved hands resting on its wheels. He was dressed smartly in tweed jacket and tie, and a blanket on his lap covered the place where his legs had been. But it was not those details that caught the eye, not even the missing legs. As Lady Stansbury had warned, Reggie's face was grotesquely, shockingly misshapen. Its left side must have taken the main force of the explosion and seemed to have been torn away completely. What remained had collapsed in on itself, and the skin that had re-formed was mottled and taut like a mask. From one temple, where there should have been hair, a lump protruded which partially closed his left eye, so that he looked at me with his head slightly angled. It was hard to imagine how any human frame could have survived such damage.

But, dreadful though it was, I had seen worse. The one thing I hadn't expected was the hair. Reggie's hair had always been a luxuriant chestnut brown. Now, where it remained, it was silver-grey, as if his very youth had been withered by the blast.

'For God's sake, take a seat.' Reggie rolled himself forward, into the room, and pointed me to a chair in the window. 'I'd heard rumours that you'd come through it all. Didn't believe them though. Seemed impossible. Cigarette?'

I took one from the case Reggie offered me, and he gave a low, dry chuckle.

'It's funny that you should be the one who went through the whole show, Tom. To be honest, I never thought you'd make much of a soldier.'

I shrugged. 'I don't suppose I did. I was lucky, that's all.'

Reggie had produced a lighter, and as I lowered my head to it I found his eyes meeting mine. It felt like a test. I lit my cigarette and straightened, never taking my eyes from his. After a few moments, Reggie's mouth twisted into a smile.

'You know, Tom, back then I used to think you were a pretty poor fish. Too placid. A bit spineless. Always hanging around the edge of Harry's group. I suppose I owe you an apology. What on earth are you here for?'

I exhaled slowly. Reggie and I had never been particularly comfortable in each other's company. 'Your mother sent me. She's worried about you.'

'No, she's not. She's worried I won't be there for the New Year Ball. She's afraid of losing face.' His contempt was withering. 'There's cachet in cripples now, you know, Tom. All the best families have one. The more deformed the better. My mother needs to show the neighbours how bravely she bears her burdens. You know, Tom . . .' He turned to face the lawn. 'She can't even bring herself to look at me.'

He was silent for a second or two. When he spoke again, his tone had changed.

'So tell me, what would you do if you were me? What if you were the one who'd come back from France with no face?'

'You mean about the New Year Ball?'

Reggie snorted. 'Damn the New Year Ball! I mean after that. For the rest of your life? What

84

happens now to the King's monstrous regiment of cripples?'

Oddly, although the words were bitter, there was a tone of genuine enquiry in his voice. But I could only shake my head.

'You're asking the wrong person. I can't even answer that for myself.'

Reggie had opened his mouth as if ready with some retort, but hesitated in surprise. Then he laughed out loud.

'You know, Tom, I believe you mean that. A bit at a loss, eh? And you're probably not the only one. It rather raises the question of what we'd all have done if there hadn't been a war. Sat around on our arses, I suppose. I sit here and curse Fate, but I'm damned if I know what I was going to do with my future anyway. Killed a lot of game, I suppose. And eventually I'd have married someone and made her miserable. Fecklessness—isn't that the curse of the younger son?'

He gave that dry laugh again. 'But of course I'm not a younger son any more, am I? That's the irony. With Harry gone, Hannesford comes to me. The best Tudor staircase in the country, to a man with no legs.'

He snorted again, and tossed the end of his cigarette towards a potted plant.

'You know the really sick joke, Tom? I might even be a better marriage prospect now than I was then. There are plenty of women who'd marry any sort of ghoul if he were the Stansbury heir, don't you think? Position, money and as many lovers as she wants. After all, I'd be in no position to complain, would I? And I'd never creep upstairs unexpectedly.' Reggie laughed coarsely. 'What about you, Tom? You've got your father's money. You must be pretty well off.'

I nodded, embarrassed. 'Comfortable enough, I suppose.'

'Money, unmarried and in one piece. You'll be able to take your pick, you know. But then why rush into it? Think of all those pretty little wives you'll meet whose husbands are damaged goods . . .'

Reggie must have divined my distaste because suddenly he slammed his hand hard upon the windowsill.

'Damn it, Allen! Don't give me that aloof, above-it-all act.' As always with Reggie, the anger seemed to blow up from nowhere. Behind the mask of discoloured skin, the eyes flashed with the same, dangerous fury. 'Do you know just how bloody lucky you are? Do you? How bloody, *bloody* lucky! Name anyone else you know who came through the whole thing like you did. Can you? Can you? I know I can't. It's as if there was one prize ticket in the raffle and somehow you pulled it out. How does that feel, Tom? How does it feel to be the only one who dusts himself down and walks away?'

He was shouting now, his voice shaking. 'Tell me how that *feels*!'

I bowed my head, but didn't resent the question. It was one I'd often asked myself.

'It makes no more sense to me than it does to you,' I said quietly. 'And I don't suppose it ever will.'

Looking up, I saw that Reggie's anger had gone as quickly as it had come. He seemed to be laughing.

'My God, Tom. It's priceless. You picked the prize ticket, the one we all dreamed about, and now you haven't a clue what to do with it.'

Reggie laughed again, with genuine amusement, then pointed out over the lawn. The man on crutches had reappeared and was making his way clumsily back in the other direction.

'That's Dawkins,' he said. 'Cheshire Regiment. Lost a leg and a foot near Cambrai. Father's a country doctor. Fiancée died of the flu just before he got here. Poor sod. But look at him go. Every day. Backwards and forwards.'

He turned back and looked me in the eye.

'You know something, Tom. Out there, with the shells coming in, I don't think I ever felt happier.' He paused, as if to let me grapple with the idea. 'Oh, I was afraid just like everyone else. So frightened I used to keep my arms crossed so people wouldn't see my hands shake. But even when I was scared out of my wits, beneath the fear I felt oddly peaceful. All the anger that I used to feel at Hannesford just wasn't there any more. For days before a push I'd be in a funk, but afterwards, when I'd come through it and found I was in one piece, oh, the *elation*, Tom. I think I wanted it all to go on for ever.'

I'd never heard him say so much; Reggie had never been a talker. Back then, it had been me who used to know what to say.

I stayed at the sanatorium for nearly an hour, although after that burst of unexpected loquacity, Reggie showed no inclination to talk about his time at the front. Neither of us did. With so many years in France looming between us, it was easier not to begin. But somehow the silences that fell were not awkward ones, even though in that other world, before the war, we had never really been friends.

87

Before I left, I asked Reggie what he could remember about Professor Schmidt.

'Professor who?' he replied, his disfigured face betraying no emotion. 'Oh, yes. The pater's Hun. Don't remember much about him really. Apart from his dying, of course. Put a bit of a damper on festivities, didn't it? Why do you ask?'

'Just something Freddie Masters said. I seem to remember you falling out with him. Just before the Rose Ball, wasn't it?'

'Was it?' He shrugged. 'You're probably right. Damnably rude of me if I did. He was a guest, after all. But I really don't remember. I probably didn't care for his politics.' From somewhere behind me a clock chimed. 'Unlatch the French doors for me before you go, Tom, in case I want to go out. And tell my mother I want to be left alone for a bit. As for the ball, you can say I'll think about it.'

I left him sitting in the window, watching the endeavours of the man called Dawkins, backwards and forwards across the lawn.

The road out of Cullingford climbs steeply between thick hedges until it stumbles, as if by accident, out on to the open moor. The view from that point is always striking, and that day it was shot through with shards of bleak, wintry beauty. Looking out from the window of the Daimler, I tried to absorb some of its tranquillity. But my visit to Reggie Stansbury had left me feeling unsettled, and the prospect of going straight back to Hannesford did not appeal. To delay my return, and to answer a question that had occurred to me during my visit, I decided to go only as far as Hannesford village. I would seek out Anne Gregory again.

He came again the following day. Margot had insisted on it. There were plans for a tennis party and the numbers were uneven, and Margot was sure Tom must be good with a racquet. I don't remember who won, who lost, only the restful to-and-fro of the white figures against the green and the satisfying *plock* of the balls. The day after that there was an expedition to the Shepherds, and they begged him to join them there too. In no time, the pattern was set.

I suppose the timing of Tom's arrival was fortunate. His was a welcome injection of new blood into a group of people seeing slightly too much of each other. Harry liked his dry humour and his willingness to laugh at himself. Margot seemed intrigued. And for Lady Stansbury he was something of a find—affable, good-natured and perfectly capable of making up a four at tennis or holding his own at bridge. And he was presentable enough to please the young ladies while unassuming enough to put their mothers at ease. When Tom was present his hostess never needed to worry about finding someone to talk to the large, shy girl whose mother was growing anxious. Tom never demurred and never complained.

And of course, he was interested in photography. Lady Stansbury had gleaned this from his mother, though when I asked him about it he was oddly reticent. At Hannesford there was a darkroom at the top of the house that had been set up years before by Sir Robert's younger brother and which had lain neglected since his early death; Lady Stansbury had long thought to find someone willing to sort out all the jars and bottles and get it working again.

89

It was, she felt, just the sort of thing Hannesford Court *should* have. So Tom must come over one day to take a look. He must come whenever he liked. He should consider himself her guest. His week at Hannesford stretched to two, then into a third.

I was pleased that it did. However often he came and however long he stayed, he never seemed to surrender himself fully to Margot and Harry and their circle. At first I expected him to be engulfed by Hannesford's swirling gaiety in the usual way, to become another of the *coterie*, indistinguishable from the Julians and Olivers and Freddies. But somehow he never did. They were welcoming him in, I could see that, especially Margot, who was always the first to greet him. But I could see that he chose to remain a little to one side, away from the main current, observing its changing eddies and wary of its choppy waters.

Yet when he first asked me to dance I drew back. There were many among Harry and Margot's closest friends who barely noticed me, but Tom was never one of them—and at first I was suspicious of his kindness, afraid that he sensed my isolation and pitied me for it. So when he approached me at one of the many informal dances that studded the county season I refused him rather tartly, pointing out that Daisy Flinders had no partner while I was quite content to sit and watch.

He listened to that and nodded, and danced with Daisy Flinders. But before the next dance he returned and asked again, and this time I could find no obvious reason to refuse. At first we danced cautiously, two people feeling their way. But gradually I let myself relax. In my time at Hannesford, I'd almost forgotten how much I loved to dance.

After that I began to look forward to our encounters, and whenever a crowd assembled at Hannesford I'd find myself scanning the room to see if he was there. It happened gradually, but bit by bit my loneliness began to dissipate. I found my heart a little lighter when he was present. Often, on the way back from expeditions, he would fall into step beside me and we would chat comfortably until Hannesford came into view. Gradually, as the days passed, I ceased to dread the emptiness of crowded rooms.

5

By the time the car dropped me in Hannesford village, the clear skies of the morning had already passed and the day was turning colder. At the vicarage, I was told that Anne was out with Mr Uttley, hanging boughs of holly in the church. The spire of St Oswald's was still in sunlight, picked out in gold, but behind it the clouds were gathering in ominous battalions, threatening snow. Inside the church, it felt as though the cold of centuries lay undisturbed, and the two figures at work had not removed their coats. Even though it was still early afternoon, there was a lamp burning near the altar. When I stepped inside, the vicar gave me a friendly wave.

'Hello, Tom! Come in! Come in! You've caught us in the act, I'm afraid.' He beckoned me further inside, explaining that the tradition of decorating the church had been neglected for the duration of the hostilities. 'But this year Anne and I felt that a little holly from the hedgerow would not go amiss. No doubt there will be some who consider it *pagan*, but that can't be helped ...' He waved his hand again, this time to show off his work. 'And now, I think we've nearly finished here, so if you will excuse me ... I have work to do, and Mrs Uttley is expecting me.'

After a few more minutes of pottering, he departed, leaving me alone with Anne.

'So what's brought you to church this winter afternoon, Tom?' she asked me with a smile. 'Festive spirit?'

92

'Far from it,' I confessed, explaining that I was on my way back from seeing Reggie.

'Grim?' she asked.

'Yes, in a way. Though in some ways he's remarkably unchanged. I wanted to ask you about his face.' I watched her packing things into a basket. 'Perhaps I could help you back to the vicarage with that?'

But Anne wasn't going back to the vicarage. She had an errand to run for Mrs Uttley to one of Hannesford's outlying cottages.

'But you're welcome to come with me,' she added with a smile, 'if you feel like a walk.'

It was a little after two by the church clock when we stepped out of the church porch but it already felt as though another day were slipping away. Our path lay across bare fields and the air was full of rooks which cried out at the sight of intruders, wheeling in ragged patterns under the wide open skies.

'You were saying something about Reggie's face, Tom,' Anne reminded me after we had walked a little distance talking only of trivialities.

So I told her about my visit to Cullingford and about the extent of Reggie's injuries. 'I don't know much about these things but in London I saw men wearing masks to hide their injuries. Is that something Reggie might try?'

'I suppose he might.' Anne sounded dubious. 'It's not a medical procedure, of course, although I believe some doctors recommend them. But it seems horrible that soldiers feel they have to hide their faces away, doesn't it? Such a condemnation of the rest of us, really.'

I glanced across at her. After a morning

93

with Reggie, her vigour and her openness were refreshing. She walked quickly without losing her breath.

'Reggie does know about masks,' she went on. 'But Lady Stansbury says he just rages at her if she even mentions the subject. I'm afraid Mrs Uttley rather told her off about it. She said Reggie should be allowed to come to these things in his own time.'

I nodded. Mrs Uttley had always been reassuringly wise.

'Poor Reggie,' Anne went on. 'I'm not ashamed to say that I never really liked him very much. He was always so determined to be objectionable. And his temper used to frighten me. He only ever seemed happy when he was out with the guns, and I suppose even that's lost to him now.'

'He'll inherit Hannesford,' I pointed out. The thought was still strange. Hannesford had always been Harry's.

'And you think that's a consolation?' Anne sounded unconvinced.

'Not at the moment perhaps. At the moment he only wants to rage against the heavens. But at the same time I think he realises there are young men with similar injuries who are much worse off than he is.'

I paused to help her over a stile and for an instant her face was lit up by the declining sun. Our pace had never slackened and there was colour in her cheeks. My gaze lingered for a moment.

'Do you remember Professor Schmidt?' I asked as we continued, unsure how to broach the subject.

'Why, yes.' She looked surprised. 'I was there with him when he died, remember?'

'And do you have any recollection of Reggie

94

falling out with him at all? The vicar seemed to think he had.'

Anne looked thoughtful. 'Reggie and the professor ... Not that I remember. Why? Is it important?'

Behind her a flurry of rooks. Below, Hannesford village, already picked out by its early lamps. Beyond them all, the dark flank of the moor. 'No,' I said. 'I don't think so. Come on. It will be dark soon.'

*   *   *

When I made my very first appearance at Hannesford Court, Anne Gregory's had simply been one of many unfamiliar faces. It had been Harry who greeted me first and led me down to join the others, Margot who advanced to welcome me; and it had been those two who made the deepest impression. Anne had been part of the background, one of a crowd sitting neatly near the picnic things, a group of chattering young men and women. Everything had been new and vivid to me: the white dresses and the gaily coloured ribbons, the green of the meadow grasses; the fields and trees and strips of red poppy, all tumbling together on the rising land, then the lazy dreaming of the moor.

If anything struck me about Anne that day, it was her calm amid the hilarity of the other picnickers. When Margot and the others fluttered away and left me to introduce myself, I decided she must be shy or serious or both. It was only later that I began to understand the role she played at Hannesford Court, her quiet efficiency and her patience with Lady Stansbury's whims. But more often than not she was in the background, shrinking from attention. Hannesford was a busy canvas and certain figures dominated. Anne's wasn't one of them.

Oddly though, something happened that summer which made me think of her quite often. It was a foolish episode, a day of sunshine after two or three of rain and Daisy Flinders managed to slip in the woods, hurting her ankle. I was out with my camera that morning, hoping to capture some of the patterns of light and shade where the trees were at their thickest. I was wary of being seen. My interest in photography was still new to me then, and I felt an instinctive reluctance to allow the Stansburys to encroach upon it. I'd discovered it by accident, through an acquaintance who talked of little else. One day, out of politeness, I'd accompanied him to his darkroom, and had watched in the red half-light with unexpected fascination as the solemn rituals were performed and an image crept into being. Not a very good image, I thought—I felt strangely confident I could do better—but a miracle nonetheless. I suppose it was the first time I'd ever felt a sense of vocation.

But I was loath to share it, wary of becoming the sort of gentleman amateur who turns his hobby into a party piece for country weekends. My mother might have betrayed the secret to Lady Stansbury, but I myself took care to be discreet.

I stumbled upon the scene of Daisy Flinders's distress by chance. I was on the edge of a small, wooded escarpment and, below me, at a place where the groove of a footpath twisted downhill, Daisy was lying awkwardly while her sister wailed in distress and one of the Everson brothers flapped his arms and looked nonplussed. From my vantage point I watched Anne take control, insisting that the Everson boy should take Buttercup and return to the house for help. Having thus removed the principal cause of agitation, she set about her examination. I could hear her voice, low and soothing, as I pushed my way down through screens of bracken to join her.

Later, when I complimented her on her handling of the situation, she simply shook her head.

'People panic, you see. All I did was to keep things calm. Sometimes that's all any nurse can do.'

I didn't think much of it at the time. It seemed a casual remark and nothing more. But later those words returned to me in the company of young men who were ripped and bleeding and torn. I would remember those quiet, comforting tones—*keep things calm, keep things calm*—and do my best to emulate them. It was peculiar how often, having helped a man to die, I would think gratefully of Anne.

*   *   *

The first stars were already pressing through the blue surface of the evening when I made my way back to Hannesford Court. Behind me, west of the village, the clouds were still gathering, but ahead, above the house, the sky was clear, and the air felt very cold. I had dreaded the silence that awaited me on my walk home, but instead I found the village full of the sounds of a winter evening. At the rear of the Stansbury Arms, Turner the publican berated a boy over the state of the yard. From the church, the sound of organ practice reminded me of old Miss

97

Shaw, and I wondered if she was still alive and still robust enough to pull out all the stops.

Then, as I left the village behind me, a dog started to bark over at Winnard's Farm, and somewhere to my left, where by rights no dog should have been, another answered it: a timeless exchange, raw and plaintive and somehow infinitely reassuring. Closer to the house, before I could see it, there were strains of music. Someone in the Orangery was playing Harry's gramophone. When I stepped out of the trees and saw Hannesford waiting for me, its windows blazing under the deepening sky, I felt touched by an unfamiliar serenity. It was surprisingly easy at that moment to forget the many fine buildings I'd seen reduced to fragments: Hannesford, surely, would be there for ever.

I'd been right about the music. I found them all in the Orangery—Margot, Bill, Freddie Masters, Neil Maclean and, chatting somewhere in the palm frond undergrowth, Lucy Flinders and Laura Finch-Taylor. Even Denny Houghton and Violet Eccleston were there, the latter dressed in what looked like a purple turban. Although it was not yet five o'clock, there was champagne in a bucket and Bill had put on a recording of Caruso that I remembered from when Harry was alive.

'Tom!' Bill looked pleased to see me. 'Come in! Come in! Susan's just arrived so we thought a celebration was in order. She'll be down in two shakes, and then we'll all be here. Denny, you old ass, get him a glass. There's still plenty of time before we need to change.'

This unscheduled gathering rather surprised me, if only because Denny and Bill should still have been in their shooting gear, still stamping their feet in the gun room and draining the last dregs from their flasks.

'They had a rotten day,' Margot explained, taking me by the arm and drawing me into the room. 'Henson the gamekeeper is in disgrace, apparently. Hardly a bird to shoot at. Of course it isn't Henson's fault. He wasn't demobbed until the summer, poor man, and found things in a dreadful state. There was no one here to look after things while he was away.'

'Denny was the only one of us to hit a thing!' Bill chipped in from beneath a potted palm. 'The pater got in a frightful huff and we called it a day just after lunch.'

The sense of timelessness that had touched me only a few minutes before began to dissipate a little. The Hannesford shooting was famous; it was unheard of for the shooting party to be back so early.

'And your trip to Tenmouth?' I asked as Maclean came over to join us.

'Fascinating, wasn't it, Margot? These little lanes of yours are quite something, but Tenmouth is a nice little town—though cold enough down by the water.'

It seemed that Maclean had been largely left to his own devices there, while Margot and Lucy Flinders visited a milliner recently arrived from London. The three of them had lunched at the Angel, and they too had been back before it was quite dark. Maclean was telling me about the bookshop when the door opened and Susan Stansbury stepped into the room.

Except, of course, she was no longer Susan

Stansbury. She was Susan Eastwell, widow of Oliver. I'd met Oliver Eastwell on my very first visit to Hannesford and had seen him innumerable times since then, but had never really been able to take him seriously. It still seemed incredible that Susan Stansbury had ever been his wife.

'Hello, Susie!' Bill was greeting her fondly. 'Look, here's Tom. Isn't it splendid to have him back?'

Susan, perhaps alone of her family, looked very much as I remembered her. In many ways she was Margot's opposite, dark where Margot was fair and slender where Margot curved. She had always been the quiet, thoughtful one, a rarity among the Stansbury children, and strangers might not at first have guessed she was Margot's sister. Only when they looked more closely would they notice the same eyes, the same brow, the same fullness of the lips. No one had ever said the Stansbury children were plain.

'Tom. I'm so glad to see you. We're all so pleased to have you back.'

She took my hands in hers quite naturally, and leaned back to examine me. 'Freddie's been telling everyone you're about to be demobbed. Is it true?'

I laughed. 'Freddie seems to know more about it than I do but, yes, I'll be out officially any day now.'

She was no longer wearing mourning, I noticed. Was that significant? After all, I wasn't wearing uniform. And it was over two years since Oliver had died.

And yet there was an air of sadness about her that night, even though she chatted freely. When the impromptu gathering broke up and I found myself walking with her towards the Great Hall, I could see the sorrow in her eyes.

'I'm sorry, Tom. It's stupid of me. But being back here reminds me . . .' She tried to smile. 'There's so few of the old group left now, aren't there? Of the boys, there's really only you and Freddie.'

I bowed my head slightly. 'Susan. About Oliver. I was so terribly sorry when I heard . . .'

She looked up, and her eyes met mine. 'I know.' She smiled. 'And thank you again for your letter. You were always the best person at not saying too much.'

But it had not been an easy letter to write. It had been common knowledge for as long as I could remember that Oliver Eastwell was infatuated with Margot. Oliver had made no secret of his admiration, and Susan must have known all about it. After all there was nothing cunning about Oliver; life with him would have contained few surprises. And yet when he proposed to Susan out of the blue at that fateful Rose Ball, she had agreed to marry him. *Had* married him. I'd never really understood why. Because Oliver was rich and genial? Because in some way he represented an escape from Hannesford? With Susan it was hard to tell.

We paused at the entrance to the Great Hall. The others had gone ahead to dress, and the room was empty, already laid out for the evening to come. The fire had been built up in the hearth but away from it the room flickered in shadow. Susan regarded it for a few seconds. It might have been any year, any Christmas.

'Mama said you'd been to see Reggie, Tom. How is he? Will he come home?'

'I don't think he will. Not just yet.'

'Poor Reggie! He always did hate these big

101

events. When they brought him back from France, I planned to shut up the house in London and come back here, you know. I had some idea of nursing him, I think. But he practically ordered me away. Told me to go back to town and stay there. He was quite foul, actually. But I think in his own way he was trying to be kind.'

For all Reggie's misanthropy, I thought she might be right. Susan had always been his favourite. 'I'll drive you down there one day if you like,' I offered. 'If you think Reggie will see you.' I didn't particularly relish the idea of a second visit to the sanatorium, but it was hard to keep the thought of Reggie out of my head. The scars. The grey hair. Reggie sitting alone in the window.

I was still thinking of it when I went upstairs to dress.

*   *   *

By the time I'd cleaned up and was once more ready for company, it was snowing. I could tell that by the smell of brandy punch that filtered up to the gallery, and when I stepped close to one of the lofted windows and peered out, I saw it was true. Slow, heavy flakes were drifting across the park, picked out by the lights from the house, making careful landings on the lawns and on the dark surface of the lake. And in the Great Hall, it struck me that the aroma of hot brandy had lifted the mood of the place, as though snow on Christmas Eve was in itself enough to make the party festive. The Great Hall felt welcoming, cheery even; there was laughter, and that convivial, excited sound of many people grouped together for pleasure.

Most of what I remember about that evening concerned Margot in some way. She was the first to greet me as I came down, slipping away from the Finch-Taylors to take my arm and lead me towards the punchbowl, chatting away about her day in Tenmouth with all her familiar lightness and good humour.

'Such a shame you couldn't join us, Tom. But tell me, how did you find Reggie? He refuses to see the rest of us, you know...'

We talked affably for a time until we were joined by Lucy Flinders, shiny-eyed and full of laughter, clutching a glass of punch.

'Isn't it priceless?' she asked, the words tumbling out. 'Sir Robert has just been telling me all about *that*!' She pointed upwards, towards a point above our heads. 'I can't imagine how I didn't notice it before! Is it true, Margot? Did your brother really climb up there?'

The object she was pointing at was high on the wall of the Great Hall, forty feet or more above the floor. It was the head of a bear, stuffed and mounted in some forgotten era, its jaws set in a perpetual snarl. It was so much a part of the baronial bric-à-brac that it tended to escape notice, blending in among the stags' heads and antlers and the displays of antique weaponry. It would not have been a subject for remark had it not been for the large upturned chamberpot that crowned it like a helmet. The effect was somewhere between the comic and the grotesque. Judging by Lucy Flinders's expression, she considered it the former.

'Yes, it's true,' Margot confirmed. 'That's Harry's doing. It was quite a climb. And he had to do the whole thing with the chamberpot hooked over his

103

own head, didn't he, Tom?'

I nodded. It had been the Christmas after I'd first met the Stansburys, a time when anti-German feeling was already on the rise. Julian Trevelyan had started it, teasing Harry that the Stansburys allowed the Prussian bear such pride of place in their home. Harry had taken up the challenge, declaring that the bear needed a proper crown, to make clear the respect in which it was held.

The idea was embraced enthusiastically—Harry and his friends were young and the claret had been flowing—but the task was far from straightforward. From the floor of the hall the bear was clearly out of reach. But from the gallery above, a narrow ledge ran around the walls, no more than six inches wide. It seemed just possible that someone with sufficient daring and balance might find a way to edge around it, using the heads of mounted animals for hand-holds, but it was a perilous undertaking. Freddie Masters and Oliver Eastwell both made the attempt, each of them returning after only a few feet, declaring the task impossible. But Harry had done it. On such occasions Harry always did.

I'd not been part of the drunken group cheering him on, but I'd heard the ringing cheers when he finally slipped the pot into place. I arrived just in time to see him being heaved back to the safety of the gallery. The atmosphere had been raucous, wild even: young men egging each other on to acts of pointless bravado. A few years later when the recruiting banners came out, I was to see the same thing all over again.

Everyone had imagined Sir Robert would be incensed by the escapade of the chamberpot, and the party had retired to bed that night fully expecting that servants with ladders would have removed the offending item by the morning. But Sir Robert's feelings for his eldest son had always run towards indulgence, and instead of outrage he seemed to take a good deal of pride in the feat. No order was given to remove it and slowly the bear and chamberpot became one of the sights of Hannesford. Sir Robert would point it out to guests. *'Really must have it taken down soon. But quite a climb, there's no denying that. Young Harry's certainly not short of nerve . . .'*

And then, of course, when Harry's death was confirmed, no one spoke again of taking down the chamberpot. It had ceased to be a drunken jape in dubious taste and had become a permanent monument to Harry Stansbury's daring, a prefigurement of his selfless determination to defy the Teutonic invader.

'It's such a wonderful story!' Lucy Flinders exclaimed, her eyes still dancing. 'How I wish I could have been here in those days!'

Margot's eyes met mine for an instant but she simply smiled and said something flattering about Lucy Flinders's dress. When eventually the younger woman drifted away, Margot took my arm.

'Come on, Tom,' she whispered, 'there's a fire in the study. Let's leave this lot to it for a bit.'

After the noise of the Great Hall, the study seemed very quiet. The curtains had been drawn and it felt warm and inviting.

'Honestly!' Margot spluttered, as soon as the door had closed behind us. 'I'm sorry to drag you off, Tom, but really I had to get away. That stupid girl! *How I wish I could have been here in those days!* You'd think Harry and Julian had died a hundred years ago. It's as if they're no different from all those dead barons in the vaults. She sounded like one of the penny-trippers on May Day.'

She tossed her head and I noticed her eyes. Anger had always suited Margot.

'Really, though, Tom. This *is* murder, isn't it?' She found cigarettes and offered me the box. 'I mean all of us being here like this, pretending nothing's changed. How can you stand it?'

She dropped into one of the sofas and gestured at the space beside her. It was not a large sofa. Once such an invitation would have filled me with elation.

'I've known worse things,' I muttered, seating myself instead on the arm of the chair opposite her. I realised as I said them that the words sounded like a reproach.

'Of course you have. I'm sorry.' She turned her face to the fire. 'I know it's silly of me to complain. You must think me a spoiled little girl.'

Was that true? I'd certainly thought so once. But somehow it had never been enough to break the spell.

'Not at all,' I assured her. 'After all, everyone knows you lost Julian.'

'Yes, of course.' She said it flatly, then rose to poke the fire. 'Let's not talk about all that again, Tom. I'm not a very good saint, and if you try to tell me otherwise you'll only make me cross.'

She carried on teasing the fire until it grew fierce. Unsure how to reply, I nodded, aware of the way the heat from the fireplace was bringing a delicate flush to her cheeks.

'Do you have to be so formal with me, Tom? People tend not to be nowadays, you know.

And you've known me for so long now. If I can't be comfortable with you, then who can I be comfortable with?'

It was, I knew, an olive branch—Margot offering to forget the past.

'Forgive me. I suppose I've fallen out of the habit of being comfortable with people.' It sounded rather priggish.

'So tell me properly about Reggie,' she said, returning to her seat. 'When's he going to come home?'

We stayed in the study for ten minutes or so, talking about her brother and then, more comfortably, about life at Hannesford. Occasionally I let my eyes drift from the fire to where Margot was sitting. She was, undeniably, beautiful. Remarkably so. What a fool I'd been ever to linger at Hannesford. I'd known the danger from the very first, but had chosen to keep coming back. I should have left Hannesford that first summer and never returned. Instead all those years had trickled by in the Hannesford sunshine. I could have been achieving something, taking proper photographs perhaps, learning something. Now I was thirty and had nothing to show for anything. Not because of Margot. Because I was a fool.

When we returned to the Great Hall, the noise and bustle were undiminished but I felt impatient with it all. When the festivities at Hannesford were over, I would get back to London as quickly as I could.

*   *   *

Dinner that Christmas Eve was a strange and slightly

strained affair. Sir Robert, whose politics consisted chiefly of loathing Lloyd George, was nevertheless in agreement with the Welshman's policy of *making Germany pay*, a subject he elaborated on at great length over dinner. It was a position that seemed to command widespread approbation around the table at Hannesford that night, with Mapperley the banker bemoaning the fact that the war hadn't been taken on to German soil *so they know how it feels*, and young Bill Stansbury piping up to say that he'd have been happy to fight all the way to Berlin.

I noticed that Freddie Masters did not join in. The thirst for retribution so apparent among the British public had certainly not come from the troops; we'd looked into the eyes of our enemies and seen only reflections of ourselves. In Cologne, I'd seen my men share their rations with German children. But back home, there was hatred everywhere, ugly and undignified and demeaning. It made me feel again the invisible distance between those who had gone and those who had stayed.

Only Violet Eccleston spoke out against the prevailing mood, maintaining that revenge was a short-sighted luxury, that a peaceful, contented Germany had benefits for the British Empire. I admired her spirit but could see that she would not win any arguments that night. I felt I was intruding upon a scene that had been rehearsed many times before, one in which all the others around the table had long been assigned their roles. All in all, it was not a particularly festive meal.

But after dinner, with the fires blazing and the candles on the Christmas tree casting a fairy magic over the Great Hall, the mood improved. Sir Robert retired early, and after his withdrawal a weight seemed to lift from those who remained. High spirits were not easy in his presence. His persistent, barely disguised grief had come to feel like a reproach.

Lady Stansbury, on the other hand, was adamant that her guests should enjoy themselves, and there was something rather admirable in her dogged insistence that Christmas should be celebrated at Hannesford as it had always been. A son lost, another maimed, both her daughters robbed of advantageous marriages—it seemed inconceivable that the delicate, unworldly hostess I remembered could have survived such an accumulation of sorrows. But if any of those things were preying on her mind that Christmas Eve, she showed no sign of it. *The past is past*, she seemed to be insisting, as her guests arranged themselves at card tables in the drawing room or were persuaded to the piano for duets. Grief, it seemed, was a foe she was determined to resist.

But perhaps the individual who did most to infuse the evening with gaiety was Freddie Masters. I watched with considerable curiosity as he played the piano at his hostess's request, performing with lightness and some panache. When he sang—a sentimental song about lovers kissing in a cornfield—his voice was good, and, although I looked for it, there was nothing to suggest any irony in his delivery. Yet Masters had seen his share of horrors. Had he put them all behind him in some way I couldn't fathom? Or did he hope to forget them all in music?

But perhaps he simply played because he liked to. When Susan went over to him and whispered something, he moved without apparent effort into a

Bach cantata.

I sat up till eleven or so, watching Margot move from group to group, enjoying the warmth and the chatter all around me. And when eventually I did retire, my feet took me instinctively to the door of the room that had always previously been mine. I didn't realise my mistake until I'd stepped inside and found it stripped to its bones—the bed naked, the windows bare, its surfaces devoid of any bits and pieces to give the room identity. Strangely, for all its emptiness, it somehow seemed much, much smaller than I remembered.

Then, before returning to my new bedroom, I found myself moved to try the next door along— the door to Harry's room. Perhaps I'd expected to see something similar. Perhaps it was a way of reminding myself that Harry really had gone. But Harry's room had not been stripped. The light from the corridor revealed everything as it had always been, from the photographs on the mantelpiece to the old cricket pads shoved carelessly behind a chest. It was as if Harry had stepped out to wash his face and would be returning at any moment.

At least, it looked that way. But that wasn't how it felt. The air seemed too still. It had the feeling of a shrine. And it was as cold as the sepulchre.

That night I slept well at first, lulled by the warmth and the brandy and the good food, sinking into the eider-soft haven of my bed and knowing nothing more till I awoke in the darkness, juddering into consciousness, instantly aware of the silence wrapped around me. I could feel the panic rising as I braced myself for the sound of the whistle. But instead came the chiming of the church clock, low, made distant by the snow. Three o'clock. Reality reasserted itself and gradually my body went limp. Pulling the blankets more tightly around me, I waited for my heartbeat to slow. Somewhere, much nearer than the church, an owl was calling. I imagined it, brown-flecked and vigilant, somewhere in the Hannesford woods. For many years I was to take great comfort from owls and nightjars and the unearthly screeching of foxes.

I did not sleep again after that. Instead I lay there thinking, not of Margot, nor of Susan, nor of cold, dead Harry, stretched out somewhere beneath the frost-pinched fields of France. Instead I thought of the professor, dying with the stars above him and the scent of roses in the air and his cheek still stinging from that horrible, cowardly blow. He had died in Anne Gregory's arms. There had been tears in her eyes as she leaned over him.

Until that night, I'd never really thought about those tears. A man was dying. Of course there were tears. But Anne Gregory was a nurse, and she had not been crying as she tended the professor. Those tears, I thought, had been there already, before she saw him fall.

Dimly, I wondered what had made Anne Gregory cry that night.

From there, by steps I couldn't explain, I found myself thinking of Reggie again, somewhere in a ground-floor room in Cullingford, the story of his war written all over his body. Reggie, who would never again walk out with the guns on a winter morning.

I lay like that, barely moving, until the house began to stir and the sky brighten, until a madly joyous peal of bells announced that it was Christmas morning.

111

The year after Tom arrived was my happiest at Hannesford. I remember it as a time of comforting certainties, when all the strangeness of my new life began to simplify into routine. My confidence grew, and I started to see how vital I was to the smooth running of Hannesford Court. Lady Stansbury relied on me and trusted me. Harry and Margot were kind and accepted me as a useful and valuable part of their lives. I came to understand that when guests failed to notice me, the fault was theirs, not mine—a blindness in the eye of the beholder. I suppose it was the year Hannesford became my home.

And I came to believe that Tom would always be there, putting me at ease, making me feel a person rather than a shadow. His standing remained high with the Stansburys. He was a reassuring presence, and Lady Stansbury was a clever enough hostess to know that a successful house party depended on more than just its leading players. Tom was straightforward and dependable and always knew the right thing to say.

And I relied on him no less than she did. I knew it was absurd, but when he was present I felt I had an ally. And, stupid though it may sound, whenever I felt myself ignored or slighted, his smile across the room made good all sorts of hurt.

Of course I could see the effect Margot had on him. It wasn't a surprise. Every newcomer to Hannesford was struck by Margot, and every young man more or less smitten. From his very first visit, I'd seen the way Tom's eye would sometimes linger on her. That wasn't unusual, it was just what happened. Some young men saw enough in those first few glances to understand that Margot Stansbury was someone to whom they could never aspire, and, finding her unobtainable, discovered their passion hastily extinguished. Perhaps those were the lucky ones. Others allowed the fascination to take hold; some hopelessly, like Oliver Eastwell, with no expectation of success; others, like Julian Trevelyan, more confident of their own eligibility.

But Tom wasn't like any of them. He seemed indifferent to Margot's flirting, even pained by it. Once, when an expedition on the lake had been planned, I watched him sidestep with great dexterity Margot's suggestion that he should join her boat. And I knew, from his amused expression and his dry observations, that his opinion of Margot was not uncritical. He seemed determined to keep himself slightly apart from her, as if to be better placed to study her foibles.

Yet I knew he wasn't immune. Although he attempted nothing to further his cause, there was rarely an invitation to Hannesford that he did not, after deliberating, accept. Every Christmas, every summer, whenever Hannesford Court opened its doors. Often he was one of the last to reply, sometimes the last to arrive. But he came. If others were moths to the flame, Tom flew cautiously above it. But he was still undoubtedly attracted by its light.

He seemed to take little notice of Julian Trevelyan— languid, confident Julian, who was biding his time, waiting for Margot to make up her mind. Rich, impeccably connected, the most eligible of all Harry's friends; one of the greatest marriage prizes in the whole country. Everyone could see that Julian wanted Margot, and that Margot knew it, and was delighted. Tom, by contrast, was some distance removed from the circles in which Margot Stansbury would choose a husband. To the Stansburys, old money still had a value.

That first year, I didn't really care what Tom thought about Margot. I no longer felt myself alone, on the periphery of things, and that was all that mattered. My spirits rose, and in my room I thought of Tom. But another year followed, another season, another Rose Ball. Margot's preference for Julian Trevelyan became more marked. I don't think she loved him, but his attention flattered her. Julian could marry anyone he chose, but he attended Hannesford religiously and everyone knew why he came. Margot still smiled upon her other admirers, but more and more often Julian was her companion.

And Tom didn't protest. He didn't fawn or put himself forward. He was still a congenial companion, and we walked and talked together as we always had. His conversation was the same: light and funny, interested in things. But increasingly I felt the conflict in him, like someone pained by a wound he refused to acknowledge.

Perhaps that was why, by that last summer, despite the roses and the meadowsweet and the heady scent of wisteria, I felt so out of patience with him. After all, not every young man at Hannesford was infatuated with Margot Stansbury. Others also had their admirers. It was a fact in which I took a secret, almost primitive pleasure.

6

Waking very early, long before dawn, I was instantly aware that Christmas morning sounded different from other days. There were no shooting parties to feed and dress, for one thing, no early tradesmen at the back of the house, none of the common week-day commotion that gave the first hours of the day such a strong sense of purpose. But it was not quite a Sunday, either. There was too much activity for that, and an air almost of expectancy in routine tasks that marked them out as different. Enjoying the change, and comforted by the noises of the household waking, I stretched myself beneath my blankets and listened. Not until the other guests began to stir did I make any effort to rise.

There was a very strict code for the giving of gifts at Hannesford at Christmas, one that over the years I'd become familiar with. Guests were not expected to exchange them with each other, nor to present them to their hosts. On Christmas morning, however, every guest would find on their tea-tray a small token, exquisitely wrapped, from Sir Robert and Lady Stansbury. In my experience, it was nearly always handkerchiefs for the gentlemen, each one embroidered with a tiny representation of Hannesford Court. It was not considered necessary to thank the Stansburys for this kindness until the day of departure, but it was understood that guests would, in turn, present to the housekeeper or butler a suitable Christmas box for the servants' hall.

This thorny question of etiquette having been dealt with at a stroke, the party was free to enjoy the day, although it was largely an unstructured one, there being no shooting to entertain Sir Robert and, between lunch and dinner, no fixed plan for how the day should be spent. Much depended on the weather. If fine, there might be walks; if not, Sir Robert and the older gentlemen would retire to the library to play cards until it was time to dress. When I rose that morning, I saw a low, golden sun creeping above the trees and felt relieved. The snow of the night before had not been heavy. It would be a good day for walking.

The morning, of course, was spent in church. Tradition dictated that guests should gather in the Great Hall shortly after breakfast and proceed to Hannesford village in a stately column. Afterwards they returned in similar fashion, the party augmented by dignitaries from the village, all invited for hock-cup in the Great Hall. It was a tradition that had continued uninterrupted for as long as anyone could remember, until it, like so much else, had fallen victim to events at the front.

That morning I walked most of the way with Margot. Around us the trees were still laced with a perfect powdering of snow, although as we walked the path beneath our feet turned quickly to slush.

'So, Tom,' Margot asked brightly as the procession twisted through the woods, 'have you decided where you stand on the great memorial debate? Are you with Father? You'll get into terrible trouble if you side with the vicar, you know. Mama's terribly worried he's going to say something about it in his sermon today. If he does, Father will be furious.'

'I'm sure Mr Uttley is far too sensible for that,' I assured her.

116

'Perhaps. And he has been wonderful about arranging the service for Harry. Have you thought yet what you're going to say?'

I hadn't. The thought of it filled me with dread. Ahead of us, Lady Stansbury was saying something to Neil Maclean and the American was smiling broadly. Everything different, nothing as it was. What *was* I going to say at Harry's service?

In the event, the vicar chose to confine himself to a general message of hope and goodwill, and the village children, singing the Christmas hymns with full-hearted enthusiasm, created notes of genuine joy in a place that for some years had not known much of it. I'd sung carols in some strange places since I was last at Hannesford and had always marvelled at their power, even in the darkest times, to lift the mood of those who sang them. There was no logic to it. Peace on earth. Goodwill to men. And watch out for gas.

'Such a hard message at times like this,' the vicar agreed as he shook my hand after the service, 'when so many people are still in so much pain. But I believe deep down there is a place in all of us where the Christmas message is never wholly extinguished, wouldn't you say, Tom?'

His voice was full of kindness but I could see the weariness in his face. The vicar too, I sensed, had had a difficult war.

'I've told Sir Robert that I won't be coming back to Hannesford Court this morning,' Mr Uttley went on. 'Mrs Uttley, you know. I'm afraid she simply isn't well enough to attend, even though Lady Stansbury has offered to send the car for her. I do hope Sir Robert will understand. However, I'm adamant that Anne should go with you. Lady

117

Stansbury was most insistent, and my wife would be mortified if Anne stayed behind on her behalf. Would you be good enough to walk her home afterwards, Tom? If she will allow you, that is. She has become a very independent young lady.'

I promised that I would, and then Bill Stansbury began to round up people and shepherd them back to Hannesford Court. It was a matter of some importance on Christmas Day that the drinks should be served promptly after church so that there could be no danger of guests lingering into lunchtime.

An observer viewing the scene in Hannesford's Great Hall that Christmas morning might not have noticed any difference from previous years. The winter light cut in through the high windows as it had always done, touching the ancient tracery of beams and carvings with the same soft glow. Below, the lamps were lit and the fire played around a Yule log of immense proportions that would burn slowly and intensely for the rest of the day. In front of it, people eddied and turned, exchanging the same festive greetings, the same good-humoured salutations. The spirit of Christmas appeared in the ascendant.

Only if they had counted the young men present would observers have noticed any change. Ours was a party of old men and boys. Of men my own age there were pitifully few to be seen.

Yet all around the hall were unchanged numbers of young women, talking and smiling as if the young men of the party had simply stepped outside for a breath of air. I was reminded of Lady Stansbury's anxieties for the New Year Ball, her difficulties balancing the numbers. And for the first time it

118

dawned on me that this was not merely a passing social awkwardness. Those missing partners would never step back into the room, and nor would they be replaced from elsewhere, for everywhere it was the same. In every such gathering, that year and every year, there would be young women who did not dance because their partners lay dead in the fields of France. They would be sitting out those dances for the rest of their lives.

The thought made me shiver. There could be no going back to how things had been. I had imagined peace would be a resumption of the world I knew; I had been wrong.

On the other side of the room Bill Stansbury was talking to Laura Finch-Taylor, whose husband was nowhere to be seen. Her eyes were raised and meeting his with that knowing, slightly challenging gaze of hers, and he was blushing ever so slightly. How old was he? Nineteen? And untouched by the carnage. Once he would have been an unexceptional young man among many others. In that room that day he stood out as a rare, precious object. Perhaps Reggie Stansbury had been right. Even with half a face, the heir to Hannesford would not necessarily lack for a wife.

Oddly, while the gathering was still at its height, somebody said something that reminded me of Professor Schmidt.

I'd been making small talk with Sir Robert's new steward, a Borders Scot called Parker who had seen service in Mesopotamia and Greece as well as Flanders. Parker had been describing some of the most pressing works in which he was engaged.

'I don't mind telling you, sir, things had fallen into a pretty poor state. I'm surprised Sir Robert stood for it. But I believe my predecessor had been in ill-health for a year or two. And, of course, he had very little help.'

'Old Woodward?' I remembered him vaguely, a touchy, rather difficult man. 'What happened to him?'

'It was the influenza, I believe, sir. It wasn't so bad here as in the cities, they say, but he'd been a sick man already. Did you know him, sir?'

'A little. He had a daughter who was going to be a governess.' I recalled a nervous, quietly pretty, very serious young girl. Her father had sent her away to school, and she had returned to Hannesford the summer war broke out. Harry and Margot had made a point of inviting her to some of their picnics.

'I don't know about a daughter, sir, but his widow is still living in one of the cottages over on the other side of the lake. By rights some of those cottages should have a lot of work done to them. They're in a poor state. But there's still no labour to be had just now, and Sir Robert wants me to start on the old boathouse. For young Mr Bill, he says. I gather it's used as some sort of clubhouse, sir?'

I nodded. The boathouse was in reality a rather splendid summerhouse on the edge of the lake, gaily painted in blue and white and hidden away in the trees. Sir Robert had converted it into a retreat for his elder sons, somewhere they could hide away with their friends, a sort of shooting lodge without the guns. As they grew older, the place became a focus for Harry and his crowd, a place where the young men invited to Hannesford would retreat to smoke and drink whisky and make a great deal of noise. I had not been a frequent visitor.

But as I was explaining some of that to Parker, I was reminded of an incident I'd not thought of for many years. A hot, oppressive day, the summer before the war ... While Parker continued to describe the challenges that lay ahead of him, my mind wandered.

I'd been skulking in the rose garden when the professor found me. The old man had been out of breath, flushed and sticky in the heat. And he had been carrying a butterfly net. For some absurd reason, I could remember the butterfly net more clearly than anything else.

And I'd been cross with him for asking questions when I wanted to be left alone. *Had I been down at the lake?* That was the question. My reply had been quite curt, and when the professor asked if I'd seen anyone by the boathouse, I'd barely replied at all. Because that was the day I'd come across Margot and Julian Trevelyan walking hand in hand by the water. I'd watched them through the trees, like a common spy. And then I'd come away, desperate to be on my own. Of course, it wasn't seeing Margot's hand in Julian's that surprised me. Everyone knew how the land lay. What surprised me was the pain. I'd never for a moment expected to feel such pain.

So for a couple of hours or more I'd avoided everyone, hiding myself away in Hannesford's gardens, seeking out the quiet corners where I wouldn't be disturbed. When the professor found me, my craving for solitude was in no way diminished.

But the professor had asked again. He had been so persistent. And I couldn't bring myself to repeat what I'd seen earlier, so I only told him that I'd seen Reggie near the boathouse at some point, which was true. Reggie had been stalking away from the water scowling, and hadn't noticed me hidden in the shadows. I'd been glad to avoid him.

As Parker talked, it occurred to me for the first time to wonder why the professor had been asking those questions. He'd seemed in earnest, as if the matter was urgent, but I'd been too absorbed in my own affairs to ask him why. I just wanted him to go.

And then I remembered something that made me flush with embarrassment. So intense was my suffering that day, so great my self-absorption, that on coming from the lake I had dashed my fist against the rose garden wall. When the professor approached me that afternoon, I had been trying to hide the dried blood on my knuckles.

*   *   *

I didn't speak to Anne again until the gathering in the Great Hall began to break up. I found her near the door talking to the banker, Mapperley.

'There's really no need to walk me home, Tom,' she insisted, then hesitated. 'But if you're in the mood for some exercise, and if you don't mind the snow, you could help me with Mrs Uttley's Christmas deliveries this afternoon. The vicar was supposed to be coming with me to carry one of the baskets, but he really doesn't have time, poor dear.'

And I agreed readily to take the vicar's place, partly because the prospect of a walk with Anne was not unpleasant, and partly because the expression on Mapperley's face suggested that, had I declined, the banker would have felt obliged to volunteer his own services—something I felt sure would not have added to the festive spirits of either party. Besides, Christmas Day at Hannesford Court was going to feel strange. I wasn't sure I wanted too much of it.

Lady Stansbury must have seen me talking to Anne because when her guests from the village had departed she sought me out.

'Really, Tom, Anne is proving very stubborn. Having her here when Reggie comes home would be the perfect arrangement. But she simply won't be moved. If you get the chance, you will put in a word for Reggie, won't you?'

There was genuine hurt in her voice. First Reggie, now Anne. Lady Stansbury was not used to people turning away from Hannesford. I muttered something about us all having been through a great deal, about sometimes people needing to make changes, and to my surprise she placed her hand on my arm before she turned away. It was an unfamiliar intimacy, but a kindly one. And from a woman not always noted for sympathy towards others.

As I'd anticipated, I was pleased to get away from Hannesford that afternoon. The midday meal was a convivial enough affair, but it soon became clear that there was no great appetite for an afternoon in the fresh air. Bill and Margot were cooking up some scheme for an indoor treasure hunt, urged on by Denny Houghton and Lucy Flinders, and Sir Robert stated plainly that he intended to spend the afternoon going over his plans for the memorial. Margot, when she heard I was bound for the village, met my eye and raised an eyebrow, but made no attempt to dissuade me. Neil Maclean looked as though he would have enjoyed some time outdoors, but the current was against him. As I made my escape, Freddie Masters was patting the American on the arm and declaring cheerily, 'Don't worry, old man, only five hours till dinner time.'

At the vicarage, Anne was already pulling on her shawl when I arrived. The early promise of the day had faded and the sky was overcast, threatening an early dusk. But the air was fresh and I found myself suddenly possessed of an unaccountable sense of optimism. The tradition of these Christmas visits had its roots deep in the past, and the sense of continuity appealed to me. Anne smiled when she saw me hurrying up the icy path.

'No time to come in,' she ruled. 'If we're to get as far as Winnard's Farm and back before dark, there's no time to lose.'

It was a genuinely enjoyable afternoon. The skies were dark but there was no further snow, and the bleak profile of the moor, softened by skeins of trailing cloud, looked unworldly and mysterious. At every cottage we were welcomed warmly, Mrs Uttley having made that round for so many years that in many households the visit from the vicarage was considered an essential part of the festivities. We were frequently urged to step inside for cups of tea or glasses of eye-watering parsnip wine.

And yet amid all the warmth and friendliness, there was nearly always sadness. Between cottages Anne would tell me what I needed to know: a grandson lost near Arras; a son killed at Gallipoli; a brother who died a prisoner; a household where, at night, the door was left unlocked and a candle burning, so that a missing husband would be sure to find his way home.

But despite these sorrows I was made welcome

by families surprisingly eager to talk of their loss. I heard myself delivering the necessary platitudes in reply—*everyone always spoke so highly of his regiment; we all admired the Devons; men like that were an example to us all*—and I was struck by the genuine consolation the well-worn phrases seemed to bring. At every dwelling, so much need to talk, so much hunger for comfort. *Thank you, sir. It's made his mother so happy to hear you say that . . .*

And in almost every house, a photograph, prominently displayed. I hadn't realised that ours had become a nation of shrines. More than once, between cottages, I had to stare very hard at the horizon before saying anything to Anne.

By the time we came to the last house, the light was turning murky and the air smelled of damp leaves.

'Next is Mrs Woodward at White Cottage,' she explained. 'Widow of Sir Robert's old steward. He died of the flu last year.'

I nodded. 'Yes, I met his replacement earlier. I was wondering what became of his daughter. Julia, wasn't it?'

She stopped walking and turned to me in surprise.

'Did no one tell you?' she asked. 'Julia Woodward's dead.'

I blinked, taken aback. Only that morning I'd been imagining her giving lessons in some smart London house. 'The same illness?' I asked. 'The flu?'

'She drowned,' Anne replied shortly. 'In that deep pool below the donkey bridge. It was a few years ago now.'

'I'd no idea.' It seemed death still had the power

125

to surprise me, after all. 'How did it happen?'

Anne gave a little shake of her head and looked down.

'No one knows. The parapet on that bridge is very low, and the stones can be slippery. She probably slipped and fell. Though there's talk . . .' She tailed off, looking doubtful.

'Go on,' I prompted.

'There's talk she took her own life. She was found by old Robert Knowles. Remember him? Famous for his poaching. They say he took the stones out of her pockets before he raised the alarm.'

I shivered slightly. The warmth of the day was slipping away.

'That's horrible. When did all this happen?'

'A year or two into the war. She had a cousin in the BEF who died fairly early on. They say that upset her. She was always, well, a little *precarious*, if you know what I mean.'

In the cottage ahead of us I saw a figure moving across the window. 'I suppose we'd better be going in,' I murmured.

Anne put her arm through mine. 'Yes. But I'm afraid this visit may not be particularly merry.'

*   *   *

Mrs Woodward was a small, rather tight-lipped woman who ushered us into her parlour with the air of one fulfilling an inevitable but slightly unsavoury duty.

'Do take a seat, Miss Gregory, Mr Allen. You'll be wanting tea, I expect.'

It would be easy to say that the small, neat parlour smelled of sorrow. In fact it smelled only

126

of furniture polish, rather strongly, as though somehow the spirit of the place had been polished out of it. There was no photograph here, I noticed, no portraits, not even a collection of fussy ornaments on the mantelpiece. Nothing to give the room any character of its own, or to reflect any of its owner's. The only exception was a small shelf of books in one corner that seemed somehow out of place in its surroundings: volumes of poetry and some cheap editions of novels with one or two more expensively bound volumes scattered among them. Not, I suspected, Mrs Woodward's personal collection.

'A lot's changed since you were last here, sir,' my hostess observed, returning from the kitchen with a tea-tray. 'How long has it been?'

'Over five years now since I was last at Hannesford, I'm ashamed to say.'

'There's no shame in it as far as I can see, sir. You were away doing your duty, I've no doubt. And I wouldn't blame anyone for leaving Hannesford behind them, and that's a fact.'

It was said with such an air of bitterness that both Anne and I were a little at a loss for a reply.

'I understand from Miss Gregory that Hannesford must contain many unhappy memories for you,' I ventured. 'I'm sorry that I've not been able to offer my condolences before this.'

'Thank you, sir.' If anything, the widow seemed a little cheered by mention of her sufferings. 'But Mr Woodward had been unwell for some time before he died. And with the young men gone, and no one to help him, well, I said to him any number of times that it was all going to prove too much.'

Anne and I sipped our tea and allowed her to

127

expand for a few minutes on the subject of her husband's hardships.

'And my condolences too for the loss of your daughter,' I added when she eventually drew to a halt. 'I was so very sorry to hear of Miss Woodward's death.'

Mrs Woodward looked bleak. 'That old bridge there, it was never safe. I've often said it needed a proper railing. It's a miracle that no one else has gone the same way. But what with the war and everything, of course there was never any chance of anything being done.'

I nodded, wondering at the infinite ways grief could express itself. In Mrs Woodward it seemed to emerge as a sort of irritable pettiness.

'Captain Allen shares my fond memories of Miss Woodward,' Anne put in. 'We always enjoyed her company down at the Court.'

But Mrs Woodward only pursed her lips more tightly than ever.

'I'm afraid my daughter was a good deal too much at Hannesford Court, Miss Gregory. I know it was very condescending of Miss Margot to invite her, but if I'd had my way she would have stayed here and remembered her place. Those visits unsettled her, they did. Gave her ideas.'

Mrs Woodward seemed to be moving on to well-trodden territory.

'I don't like to speak ill of the Stansbury family, Captain,' she went on, with the air of someone who probably liked it very much, 'but the way that young man used to come round here after my Julia . . . He should have been ashamed of himself, pressing his attentions on a young lady like that. A true gentleman would never have behaved in

128

such a way.'

Up to that point, I hadn't been listening particularly closely, but this caught my attention.

'A young man? Do you mean Harry, ma'am? Harry Stansbury?'

'Not Harry, sir. No, it was Reginald Stansbury who was always pestering my Julia. Not that she was ever pleased to see him. She never gave him any encouragement, I'll give her that. Used to snub him properly, she did. But even so, that sort of attention, it wouldn't be good for a girl, now would it, sir?'

It wasn't a question I felt qualified to answer. Mrs Woodward took my hesitation for assent.

'Of course, I hear that he's in a poor way himself now. Lost his legs, they say. But he's better off than my Julia for all that, isn't he, sir?'

And I had no answer to that either. He probably was. I couldn't be sure.

*   *   *

It was getting dark when Anne and I made our way down the steep wooded slope that led from White Cottage to the park. Anne had her arm through mine because the melting snow had made the path a little treacherous, but neither of us stumbled. Our old familiarity with Hannesford and its paths had not deserted us despite our years away.

'I'm sorry about that, Tom,' she said. 'I should have warned you that Mrs Woodward can be that way. She feels the blows that have befallen her very keenly.'

'I'm sure she has every right to. It was a bit of a surprise about Reggie, though. Did you know about that?'

She shook her head. 'No. I've heard her complain before about the Stansbury family turning her daughter's head. But never that much detail.'

'Do you think it's true? Could Reggie really have been trying to court Julia Woodward? I've never thought of Reggie as one for the ladies.'

Anne seemed to share my doubts. Even on social occasions Reggie had never paid much attention to the opposite sex.

'I suppose Mrs Woodward might have imagined it,' I pondered. 'Reggie was always out with his gun. She must have seen him around White Cottage quite often.'

'Mrs Uttley would be the person to ask. She knows *everything* about the village. Or at least she used to, when she could still get out and about.' Anne thought for a moment. 'From what I remember, Mrs Woodward rather resented Julia being sent off to school. She thought it would give her airs.'

The path from White Cottage led down to the donkey bridge and the pool in which Julia Woodward had drowned. Stepping out of the trees and seeing it in front of us, we both paused. I saw Anne shudder.

'Come on,' she said. 'It's almost dark now. We should keep going.'

I nodded, but it was not of Miss Woodward I was thinking as we reached the far side of the crossing. I was imagining the scene Freddie Masters had described: the professor in evening dress on that same bridge, arguing with an unknown man. Then a blow, and the professor left fumbling on the ground. As we climbed away from the river, I told

130

Anne the story.

'What a very unpleasant thing,' she said quietly, as we stepped out of the trees. Before us Hannesford Court stood twinkling in the dusk. 'Come with me as far as the vicarage, Tom?'

'Of course,' I replied, indignant that she might think I'd abandon her in the dark.

'Well, hurry then. They'll be expecting you back soon.'

'Don't you miss it, Anne?' I asked her as we skirted the wood in the direction of the village. 'Hannesford Court, I mean. It was once part of your life too, you know.'

'Of course it was. But no, I don't miss it. I was there too long.'

Again I admired her certainty. We were silent for a spell after that and my thoughts drifted back to Julia Woodward.

'It's strange, isn't it? To hear a thing like that about Reggie after all these years. And Freddie's story about the professor too. It's as if we really only knew a fraction of what was going on around us. Could that be true?'

Anne tilted her head, as if searching for the right words. We had reached the village street, and ahead of us, beyond the inn and the church, the lights of the vicarage were just visible.

'It seemed a very small world,' she said at last. 'But I suppose in a small world people become very good at keeping secrets.'

We said goodbye at the vicarage gate. I thought of holding out my hand to her but hesitated, unsure of our etiquette for parting.

'Good night, Tom,' she said with a smile. 'And merry Christmas.'

That last summer grew hotter by the day. Beyond the Hannesford gardens, the square fields trapped the heat and a heat haze blurred the hedgerows. Tom was one of the last to arrive, appearing unannounced as he sometimes did, hot after a walk across the fields. Margot found him in the Great Hall and dragged him out on to the terrace. There he met my eye and took my hand in that way he always did, but I could sense he wasn't at ease. He was quieter than usual. He seemed preoccupied.

But it wasn't only Tom. Everything felt different that summer. The careless frivolity of previous years had been replaced by something more intense, and the little dramas and flirtations of the past had lost their gaiety. Suddenly they all seemed brooding and a little oppressive. I had a sense of too many desires threatening to collide.

It was a summer of secrets. Some I knew for myself, some I stumbled upon, others I suppose I never even guessed at. Looking back, it was hard to believe how brief it had all been, curtailed as it was by death and the threat of war: only a matter of weeks between the arrival of the professor and the night of the Rose Ball.

The professor was the first to appear at Hannesford because Sir Robert had urged him to come early to continue his work on the butterfly collection. I was pleased to welcome him back. I liked his old-fashioned courtesy and his comfortable, comforting manner, and often in those early days of summer, before the other guests began to trickle in, I would visit him in the library late in the evening and hear his thoughts on butterflies and moths. It was restful just to listen. He could be an astute observer too, I knew, but I gave that aspect of his character less thought. We tend to trust ourselves to keep our own secrets.

Next to return to Hannesford was Harry, smarter than ever, perhaps more handsome, flushed as he was by the triumphs of the Season. It had been four months since I'd seen him and I found him changed. Before then Harry had been only one element in the Hannesford landscape—a hugely significant one, of course, but still somehow in proportion to his surroundings. That summer he seemed to have *grown*, so that having him at Hannesford felt almost uncomfortable. Wherever I went, whatever my tasks, there was no escaping his presence. Everyone was talking about Harry; he filled the house. When he joined the ladies on the terrace after dinner, the simple fact of his being there dominated everything that passed; and when he stepped away to smoke a cigar, the terrace seemed suddenly empty.

Reggie followed him down to Hannesford, as closed and taciturn as ever, and it struck me that the greater Harry's presence, the less substantial Reggie's. Sometimes he seemed little more than a shadow, rising early and spending his days on outlying farms, shooting crows or trying for rabbits. Then came Margot with the Flinders sisters, then Freddie Masters, and not long after came Julian Trevelyan.

From the very first the difference in Julian's attitude towards Margot was quite marked. It had always been understood that he was Margot's most significant suitor, and gradually he'd emerged as the most favoured, confident of his position, lazily tolerating the antics of the others. That summer, however, there had been a change. Margot was to be his, and in subtle ways Julian made sure the others were aware of it. It was the summer when he began to assert his power. There was something icy and rather ruthless about it.

Then Tom arrived and I wondered how the change would affect him. But instead of seeing more of him, I saw less. He was as affable as ever, but less often present among the crowd. He chose to spend much more of his time alone.

And seeing him so much less engaged with things, instead of feeling sympathy, I simply felt impatient. I was growing restless. Being noticed, standing out just a little from the background, wasn't enough. I needed more than that to sustain me. And so when Tom greeted me with a smile, instead of feeling lighter or stronger or brighter than before, I simply felt the sands of my life running more swiftly between my fingers.

Already by then I'd started to make enquiries. I still knew people who could help, people with good contacts at home and abroad. But before I'd gone very far, the summer had caught up with me and the roses were in bloom, and Hannesford was seized by a heady breathlessness. That summer everything I thought I knew about myself began to change.

At five o'clock on Christmas Day the carol singers came to Hannesford Court. It was probably the oldest of all the Hannesford Christmas traditions and one I liked; it marked the point where the disparate activities of the afternoon were brought to a close and the evening began.

It also gave the day a peculiar symmetry. The carollers were welcomed into the Great Hall, just as the guests from the village had been welcomed earlier, but the singers were received in a very different way. The sherry and the hock-cup of the morning were swept aside and a barrel of Hannesford's own beer was rolled up from the cellars and placed on trestles near the fire, to be enjoyed by both the carollers and their audience.

The Lord of the Wassailers was usually Turner, the publican from the Stansbury Arms, with a choir assembled from the farms and cottages of Hannesford. The higher parts were taken by the village boys, and the ensemble invariably made up in gusto anything it lacked in finesse. Even so, I couldn't help but notice that this year the choir was a little smaller than it had been, and that the proportion of young boys to men rather higher; but the audience seemed inclined to overlook the change, and was warm in its applause.

Afterwards we dressed for dinner, and then I followed the sound of the gramophone to the Orangery where Bill Stansbury was once again convening his own pre-prandial gathering. Freddie Masters and Susan were there already, talking beneath a date palm, and Lucy Flinders appeared to be flirting with Denny Houghton by the ice bucket. Of Margot and Maclean there was no sign.

Bill greeted me cheerfully. 'Champagne, Tom? To wash down the beer. Did you have a good walk? This place has been like a morgue all day. The pater's guests spent all afternoon sleeping off lunch, I think.'

He chatted away merrily.

'No Laura tonight, Bill?' I asked without thinking, then realised from Bill's blushes the question might have been an indelicate one.

'She and Finch-Taylor are playing with the grown-ups today, Tom. She's a fantastic sport, of course, but I don't think Horatio approves of the gramophone. He can be a bit of a dry old stick at times, don't you think?'

I was agreeing that sticks didn't come much drier when the expression on Bill's face changed.

'Oh, lor!' he mumbled. 'I've had her for most of the afternoon. Your turn now, Tom, there's a good fellow.'

Looking past him I saw Violet Eccleston approaching at a jaunty trot. By the time she reached me, Bill had fled into the Orangery's undergrowth.

'Hello, Violet.' I grinned. 'Champagne?'

She accepted the proffered glass without a flicker of disapproval and peered around her.

'Do you think Neil Maclean will be joining us?' she asked without preamble.

'Apparently not.'

'That's rather a shame. There was something I wanted to ask him, Captain Allen.'

'Tom, please.'

'Tom, then.' She looked at me with sudden interest. 'Where do *you* stand on heavy industry,

136

Tom?'

Violet Eccleston had a remarkable talent for asking questions that simply made no sense to me.

'The current boom, for instance. Do you trust it? It can't possibly last, you know. But Sir Robert won't believe me. He's in danger of making some very bad mistakes.'

I looked around for help, but none came. Freddie Masters appeared to be telling Susan a story that involved a great deal of gesticulation.

'Neil shares my views, I think,' she went on. 'And he's terribly influential, you know. I wanted to ask him a question about foreign debt.' And then, looking around and noticing Susan, she surprised me with something that seemed to come from nowhere. 'Susan loved her husband a great deal, didn't she?'

Did she? It was hard to believe. I recalled other Christmases, and Oliver Eastwell, flushed with drink, roaring drunkenly as Harry and Julian tried to take off his trousers.

'I don't think I could say,' I told her, aware as I said it that I sounded stiff and a little ridiculous.

'Of course she did.' Violet Eccleston slapped aside the objection with disdain. 'It's obvious. Do *you* intend to marry, Captain Allen? I rather think it's your duty, you know.'

'Tom,' I corrected her, still hoping for rescue. 'Please call me Tom.'

And then, like an angel from heaven, Margot appeared with Neil Maclean behind her. I'd seldom been more pleased to see her.

'Hello, Tom! We'd been wondering what had become of you, hadn't we, Neil?'

She was wearing something dark, a shade of very

137

deep green, perhaps. I was struck by how *alive* she looked.

'No, Tom, no time for champagne. We've come to round you all up. You should be joining the others.' And she slipped her arm through mine. 'Shall we go?' she asked.

So I went. I told myself I was simply evading Violet Eccleston.

*   *   *

To my surprise, before we went in to dinner, Neil Maclean asked to talk to me in the library.

'Forgive me for taking you away from the others, Captain Allen, but I was hoping to have a word with you on a matter of some delicacy.'

My heart sank. 'In that case perhaps we'd better sit down.' I perched myself on the arm of a sofa. Maclean, it seemed, preferred to stay standing.

'You're probably aware, Captain, that over the last eight months I've been seeing a great deal of Margot. You don't need me to tell you that she's a very remarkable young lady. You and she are old friends. I know her happiness is very important to you.'

'Of course,' I replied, still horribly anxious about the direction the conversation was taking. Rather than meet the American's gaze, I allowed my eye to run along the shelves of books behind him. I had a ghastly presentiment that he was going to ask for my blessing.

'In that case I hope you can forgive me for taking this liberty. You see, Captain, when I first met Margot she was already . . . unattached. Her fiancé had died the year before. I understand he had been

138

unwell for some time.'

Julian. So that's what it was about. I felt my shoulders relax a little.

'That's right,' I confirmed. 'He'd been wounded quite badly. They had him in hospital in London at first, but thought he was well enough to be moved home. But then he suffered some sort of seizure, and I believe he was in a pretty bad state after that.'

'Did you see him, Captain?'

I shook my head. 'It all happened when I was at the front. In the last year or two of the fighting I didn't get home much.'

Maclean had begun to pace up and down.

'And what sort of man was he? He seems to have been held in very high regard.'

I began to understand then. Neil Maclean was a confident man, not one afraid of squaring up to the competition. But a dead rival was different. That battle was harder to fight. Maclean found himself on uncertain ground.

'Julian Trevelyan was always spoken of as the most eligible bachelor of his generation,' I told him, a little brutally. 'It was something both mothers and daughters seemed to agree on.'

'That good, huh?' Maclean pulled a face, and I smiled. It was one of those moments when I found the American very hard to dislike.

'Does she talk about him much to you, Captain?' he asked.

My eye had wandered back to the bookshelves and a thought was occurring to me that had nothing to do with Margot. 'Not really,' I replied.

Maclean sighed and mumbled something about a very difficult situation for everyone.

'From everything I've heard about the man,' he

said pensively as we left the library, 'he must have left a pretty big hole in Margot's life. Not an easy thing for a girl to recover from.'

He said it with feeling, and yet there was something in his face, a slight shadow of impatience, perhaps, that made me realise I'd found in Maclean someone else for whom the veneration of the dead was already beginning to pall.

*   *   *

Oddly, although I'd known full well that Julian Trevelyan was well placed to secure Margot's hand, for a long time I didn't think of it. I found him an unprepossessing rival. Rather cold, dismissive of others, a bit of a snob—there was too little to like about Julian for me to feel jealous of him, and I wasn't impressed by his money. I assumed if Margot married him it would be with regret, a sort of bowing to the inevitable. Of course I understood that he was a remarkable catch, but until the day I travelled down to Hannesford that final summer I hadn't understood Margot's love of the chase, her relish at capturing the biggest prize of them all.

I suppose it's one of those memories I'd like to be rid of, but it persists in vivid colours: the greens of the hedges, the sandy browns of the lane, the gold of the early barley fields stretching into an English haze. It was the middle of the afternoon and the station platform smelled of hot tar. The sky was a peerless, unforgiving blue. And everywhere there was that heavy, drowsy silence of the sort that presses itself upon country stations at the hottest part of the day, the sort that makes the clocks tick

140

louder. A lull between two heartbeats.

The path from the station ran through fields where tall grasses gathered the heat. More than once I had to stop to mop my brow. Then I came to a stile and there ahead of me was Hannesford Court, arms open, its old stone touched with amber. In that light, at that hour, it seemed as timeless as the land around it, ancient and slumbering, at peace in the sun.

I'd deliberately caught an early train, moved by some urge to avoid attention. So my arrival was unheralded, and there was no party of welcome to greet me on the wide stone steps. The white gravel sweep stood empty, its raked curves unblemished by recent wheels. I had to squint to look around me. Across the whole of Hannesford's tranquil face, nothing stirred. Facing me, the shutters were closed against the heat. But the great front door was pinned open, and without ringing I stepped inside.

And then, as I stood blinking on the threshold, there was Margot. Later, in France, when it seemed impossible to believe that such a world had ever existed, I could still recall the drowsy scent of roses. Margot in blue, a shade the colour of summer sea, her fair hair loosely pinned.

She hadn't noticed me. She was emerging from a door at the back of the house and the whole of the Great Hall lay in shadow between us; but where she stood she was caught in a brilliant square of sunlight like a figure in an old Dutch painting, her face angled away from me, exchanging a final word with someone unseen. I heard her laugh and then she turned, the laughter still on her lips, and the vitality of that smile, the lightness of her figure as she moved, filled me with a longing as intense as any I had ever known. If she hadn't noticed me then, I would have stepped away, afraid of myself, and let the moment pass.

But she did see me. She looked up and I saw her face brighten with a blend of excitement and pleasure and mischief. And triumph too. Definitely, triumph. To her, of course, I was no more than a silhouette against the light, a figure hesitating on the threshold.

'So *there* you are!' she exclaimed, and her voice was light with happiness. 'We wondered where you'd got to!' And she ran forward to greet, not me, I realised as I watched her, but the person she'd mistaken me for.

*   *   *

The rest of Christmas Day passed rather quietly. Sir Robert cornered me before dinner and thanked me again for agreeing to say some words about Harry. Susan told me that she'd telephoned the sanatorium and spoken to Reggie, and wanted to know if I was happy to drive her to Cullingford the following day. Violet Eccleston explained why reparations would destroy British shipyards. I drank some very fine burgundy. And after dinner Freddie Masters teased Wilfred Mapperley on the subject of chivalry.

Yes, that was the thing that, afterwards, I remembered most clearly.

By that stage of the evening, the party in the drawing room had broken up into little groups and somehow Freddie and Bill Stansbury and old Mapperley had found themselves together. The banker had been holding court on one of his favourite subjects, comparing modern manners unfavourably with those of some distant golden age, the dates of which were not made clear. Freddie Masters, with a gleam in his eye, had taken up the gauntlet. When I joined them, Mapperley was on the offensive.

'Nowadays young women think nothing of hanging upon the arms of men they barely know. You see it every day. In my day, a young lady would never have dreamed of such a thing.'

'Oh, come, sir . . .' Freddie's tone was reproving. 'How can you be so sure? I grant you they may not have acted in such a way, but who is to say for certain what young ladies dream about?'

The banker looked a little flustered.

'Nonsense, sir. These are degenerate times. In days of yore a maiden used to bestow a chaste token, a glove, say, upon the knight who won her favour. Nowadays girls simply throw themselves into the paths of young men without any dignity or decency at all. It is quite appalling.'

'A glove, sir? A glove?' Freddie managed to sound utterly outraged. 'I can see nothing chaste in the gift of a glove! On the contrary, I think you make my point for me. Think of it . . .' And Freddie began to illustrate his point with gestures. 'A glove has brushed across a lady's palm. It has caressed her fingertips. It has nestled in that sweet valley between her fingers . . .'

He paused and shook himself, as if waking from a dream.

'No, sir,' he concluded, 'there is surely nothing chaste about the gift of a glove.'

In reply Mapperley snorted with disdain and shortly afterwards stomped off altogether. As soon

143

as he had gone, Margot joined us.

'Have you been misbehaving, Freddie?' she asked, her voice full of laughter.

'Margot, my sweet, I'm rather afraid I have. You must forgive me. I simply couldn't help myself. Perhaps more brandy is called for.'

It was no more than a piece of impudence really, although I enjoyed seeing the banker's pomposity punctured. Even so, I almost certainly wouldn't have thought of it again but for the fact that when I retired to bed that night, I found spread out across my pillow, pale and lovely, a single glove of exquisite white lace.

One by one I watched them arrive that summer as they had always done, the established *coterie* of Harry and Margot's friends. I suppose I thought it a ritual that would go on for ever, so that in middle age Freddie Masters and Tippy Hibbert and the rest would still make their summer pilgrimage to Hannesford, perhaps bringing with them wives or even children, but coming nonetheless. I never imagined rifts or divisions or deceit. Not until that summer.

I tend to think of the weeks before the Rose Ball as a time of unrelenting sunshine, but May and early June had been damp and sometimes cold. Frustrated by the weather and still waiting for his friends to join him, Harry was more indoors than usual, and therefore more in my company. For all his breezy friendliness, I didn't find it easy. There was something unsettling about his presence as he paced around. It was like watching an animal that has outgrown its cage.

In the world I grew up in, references to the physical passions were unknown. It was a subject as veiled and opaque as the mysteries of the universe. But at Hannesford, I'd been a little shocked to discover, things were rather different. For an unmarried woman, of course, reputation was still everything. But discreet affairs, especially when the lady was safely married, were neither unknown nor, it seemed, particularly condemned. They were simply not spoken of. To make any reference to such a thing would be indelicate; to be shocked by it, unsophisticated. In the circles in which the Stansburys moved, indiscretion was a far more grievous sin than adultery.

Even so, I was not at all prepared for my conversation with Harry.

He'd come to find me because the rain had stopped and he was looking for someone to go walking with him. But I was busy, of course, preparing for the arrival of the other guests, preparing the list of rooms. It was a task that seemed to capture Harry's interest.

'The room list, eh? A diplomatic tightrope, I should think. So who goes where?' His tone was gay and flippant as he peered over my shoulder. I explained that mostly it was the same as the previous year, but he was already running his eye down the column.

'Let's see, *Rolleston, Rolleston, Fredericks, Smythe, Smythe, Adams, Adams ...*' His finger stopped. 'I say, Anne, would there be any chance that Adams and his wife might be moved to a couple of rooms over on the other side? Might be better if you could.'

At first I was simply surprised he had a view. He was still standing behind me, leaning over me a little, so I had to twist to talk to him. I explained the Adams generally had the same rooms every year and asked why they might wish to change.

'Ah, now you're embarrassing me, Anne,' he replied, moving away from the bureau and flopping into a seat beside me. He was smiling. He certainly wasn't afraid to meet my eye. 'You know how it is. I saw quite a lot of Tilly Adams at the Derwents' just before Christmas. We rather hit it off.'

He paused and waited, but I still didn't understand.

'But of course that was last year,' he went on, 'and these things change.' Finally he gave a little sigh, as if pained by my obtuseness. 'Really, Anne! Let's just say that this year it might spare me a little awkwardness if Mrs Adams and I were in bedrooms in very different parts of the house. Do you see?'

146

Only then did I blush, and Harry saw it and was amused. Lost for words, I tried to avoid his eye. But he reached out and touched my hand.

'I'm sorry, Anne. Now I've embarrassed you. My apologies. We shall say no more about it.'

I don't remember him taking his leave, only that I stayed at my desk for a good while longer, until I could no longer feel the colour in my cheeks. And that night at dinner, the more I avoided looking in Harry's direction the more impossible it seemed not to meet his eye.

7

Susan Stansbury had arranged to visit her brother quite early the following morning. Boxing Day was the day the hunt met at Hannesford Court, and, one way or another, despite a shortage of good mounts, it would occupy most of the Stansburys' guests for most of the day.

Both Susan and I were glad to escape it. As the Daimler was required to follow the progress of the hounds, we commandeered the two-seater and made good time over the moor, where the snow of Christmas Eve remained only in frozen, irregular patches. At the sanatorium the stray crutch had been removed from the front door and a Christmas tree had appeared in the hallway, but otherwise I found the place much as I'd left it: still a little stark, and with a very faint smell of boiled vegetables.

Reggie received us in the room I'd seen before, the large drawing room with French windows that overlooked the lawn. I thought he looked tired, as though he had slept badly. His greeting, however, was as pugnacious as ever.

'Come for another peek, eh, Tom?' he asked, raising his eyebrow. 'Well, don't go anywhere, old man. Susan won't be staying long. How's widowhood going, Susie? Still mourning that fat husband of yours?'

Had she turned on her heel there and then, I wouldn't have blamed her. But Susan simply turned to me, her face impassive.

'Light me a cigarette, will you, Tom? I expect Reggie's still smoking those foul American things of his.'

This made her brother laugh out loud.

'As a matter of fact I am. Our loving mother sends me a new box every week. Assuages the guilt, I suppose. Don't tell me she lets you smoke like that at Hannesford?'

Susan took a breath and exhaled languorously, then shook her head. 'It's one of the reasons I choose to live in London.'

Reggie laughed again, and this time sounded genuinely amused. He had always approved of Susan.

After a few minutes I left them together and took a stroll around the grounds. Beneath the moors it was a damp, grey morning and I saw no sign of the sanatorium's other patients. The gardens had a lank, unhappy feel to them and the lawn squelched slightly underfoot. It was a long half-hour. When I returned, I found the two siblings sitting quietly together, Susan's hand resting on her brother's.

'Reggie's going to come home for the ball, Tom.' Susan rose to her feet. 'We should go home and tell Mother.'

'I never said that,' her brother growled, looking up sharply. 'I said I'd think about it.'

'But he will, I know.' Susan addressed the remark to me. 'If only to make sure Mother doesn't have it all her own way, eh, Reggie?'

He snorted. 'If I come, it will be because this place is getting on my nerves. The sight of men on crutches is beginning to drive me insane.'

He did not seem entirely displeased by this outcome, however, and when Susan excused herself for a few moments, his voice, for all its mocking tone, was almost cheerful.

149

'So, Tom, how's Hannesford? Did you spend Christmas Day telling Lucy Flinders your war stories? Susan says that one's got an eye for a soldier. You might be the man to show her a few military manoeuvres.'

I shouldn't have been provoked, but I was.

'Actually, I walked out to see Mrs Woodward yesterday,' I replied, although I hadn't intended to mention my visit to the old steward's widow. 'Remember her, Reggie?'

I paused, watching for a reaction, but Reggie's face was too scarred to give much away. Only his eyes displayed any flicker of emotion.

'Yes, of course.' He began patting his pockets, looking for his cigarette lighter. 'I didn't know you and she were friends.'

'Oh, we aren't really. In fact she said, of all of us at Hannesford Court, you used to be her only regular visitor.'

That eyebrow lifted again. 'Me?' He shrugged. 'I used to go out that way with a gun fairly frequently, I suppose. She must have meant that.'

If he'd left it there I would have gone home feeling a little ashamed of myself. Attempting to needle a wounded man was not something to be proud of. But perhaps I was not the only one who could be provoked. Reggie's next comment was clearly intended to unsettle me, and I think he regretted the indiscretion almost as soon as he'd uttered it.

'If anyone used to sniff around that cottage, Tom,' he said, 'it was your friend the professor. Didn't you know?'

*   *   *

150

I suppose I was uncharacteristically quiet as we drove back to Hannesford. The image of Margot's glove on my pillow kept returning to me, playing on my thoughts. She had meant it as a joke, of course, I was sure of that, her way of joining in the fun at Mapperley's expense. And yet it was a sly and slightly unsettling joke too, one that seemed to be teasing me as well. For what? For the way I'd been before? Or for the way I was now—stiff with her, and always a little bit awkward? I couldn't tell. I'd lain awake for a long time, not sure what to make of it, stirred and embarrassed by turns. I wasn't at all sure it was one of Margot's better bits of humour.

And then there was Reggie's remark about the professor and Miss Woodward. What had that been? A jibe? A taunt? What was he hinting at? Had the professor really been a regular visitor to White Cottage? It seemed unlikely. It hadn't particularly occurred to me that the professor even knew the Woodwards. Yet as the two-seater edged back up the shoulder of the moor, I could recall at least one occasion when the professor and Miss Woodward had both been present, an expedition organised by Margot, down to the water meadows beyond the park. There had been a shower of rain the evening before and the fields had filled with buttercups overnight. We had set off early to avoid the heat, and there had been champagne waiting for us in the shade, then lunch in hampers and a huge basket of peaches, ripened to perfection.

Later, as the day grew hotter, Harry Stansbury had gone to find a place to swim. Sitting beneath a tree, I'd watched Margot applauding one of the Everson boys as he threw grapes into the air and

151

caught them in his mouth while Daisy Flinders chirruped with amusement like a budgerigar. Reggie had been there too, I think, which was unusual as he generally avoided such events. I could remember how pained he looked. He certainly didn't applaud as the grapes went in. On the edge of the group, Julian Trevelyan said little and smiled to himself. Margot's gloves had been resting in his lap . . .

There were others there that day, too. Laura Finch-Taylor for one: there'd been some discussion with her husband about whether it was too hot for such an outing. Eventually he had urged her to go without him, and she had thought about it and agreed that perhaps she would, and had smiled that familiar little smile. Where had she been when Jimmy Everson was catching grapes? I couldn't remember. I had a vague sense she had drifted off in the direction of the river.

And Anne Gregory must have been there somewhere because that morning she and Harry had gone ahead of the rest of the party to make sure the champagne was properly iced. But searching the picture in my head—that tableau of young people surrounded by buttercups—I couldn't find her. She'd had a talent for hiding herself.

The professor, though, I could recall. He had been walking with Julia Woodward around the edge of the meadow, talking to her of plants and flowers. I remember his earnestness and her pallor. At one point, their path brought them very close to where I was sitting. The professor had quoted something—a line of poetry, I think—expecting Miss Woodward to recognise the reference. But she had looked strained and wasn't really listening.

It occurred to me that as far as she was concerned, Harry and Margot were proving poor hosts.

Perhaps Professor Schmidt sensed that too, because as he and I walked back together at the end of the day he made a remark I still partly recall. *A very unhappy woman*, or something like that. But I hadn't paid too much attention to him. I'd been too preoccupied with my own concerns to pay much attention to Julia Woodward's.

*　　*　　*

When I called on Mrs Woodward that Boxing Day afternoon, I don't know which of us was the more surprised. I'd expected to spend the afternoon wallowing in the comforts of Hannesford Court, warming up after the drive across the moor, perhaps surrendering to a good book by the fire. It seemed a lifetime since I'd last had the opportunity for that. But instead, on impulse, I set out again shortly after my return from Cullingford, while the sun was still streaking the landscape with pale, golden light. Mrs Woodward would not have anticipated a second visit from me so soon, and when I presented myself on her doorstep she regarded me with some suspicion; but she ushered me into her parlour nonetheless.

The room was as fastidiously neat as before, but this time my inspection was less general. Instead I directed my attention to the row of books I'd noticed the day before. One, in a rich green binding, had caught my eye, but it wasn't until my interview with Neil Maclean in the library at Hannesford that I realised why it was familiar. This time, while Mrs Woodward was boiling the kettle,

I studied it more closely and saw that its binding was indeed identical to others in the Hannesford collection. On flipping it open I saw it was a volume of Keats's verse, marked with the Stansbury family stamp on the fly leaf. The volumes flanking it suggested that Julia Woodward had a taste for Romantic poetry. Had she borrowed the book? Or had she been in the habit of surreptitiously raiding the Stansburys' library to nurture her passion?

I was idly wondering which was true and whether it mattered when Mrs Woodward brought in the tea things.

'My daughter's,' she said shortly, gesturing at the object in my hands. 'She loved her books.'

'It's a fine volume,' I replied. 'Would you mind if I borrowed it for a day or two?'

In reply, she simply shrugged her shoulders, as if indifferent to both the request and the requester.

'As you like, Captain. You haven't come all this way just for that, I'll be bound.'

She passed me a cup of strong, dark tea. The china was old and rather fine.

'No, Mrs Woodward, I confess I haven't. After I left you yesterday, it occurred to me that I should have asked you about Professor Schmidt.'

'The German?' She looked at me sharply, surprise laced with suspicion. 'What about him?'

I did my best to look light-hearted and unconcerned.

'Only that I was rather a friend of his, you know, and I've always felt I neglected him in the days before he died. It's bothered me that I left him alone so much. But someone told me he was a frequent visitor here, and if so I'm pleased to hear he was in good company.'

154

'A friend of yours, was he?' Mrs Woodward managed to convey scorn and distaste at the same time. 'He wasn't a great favourite around here, sir, I'm afraid. Really, a man of his age, pestering a young girl! But then it wasn't long before we all found out what Germans were really like, was it?'

'Pestering, you say?' It wasn't a word I could reconcile with my memories of the professor. 'Surely not, Mrs Woodward.'

'I know what I know,' she replied tartly. 'And I've known older men than him make fools of themselves over a pretty face.'

'Very well.' I tried to keep my voice neutral. 'He was your daughter's admirer then?'

Again she shrugged her shoulders.

'I couldn't rightly say what he was, sir. But his attentions weren't welcome here. And for all his airs, he was no gentleman, bothering her like that. If I'd told my husband about it, he'd have bloodied his nose for him, gentleman or not.'

It took a little time to tease out the substance of Mrs Woodward's grievance. She was not reluctant to speak—in fact, if anything, she seemed glad of the opportunity to air her complaints. But she was so eager to condemn, to offer judgements and apportion blame, that the bare bones of her narrative were not easy to extract. I had to keep reminding myself that she had lost a husband and a daughter in the most unhappy circumstances. If her outlook on the world was sour, I could hardly begrudge her that.

The professor, it seemed, had not in fact been a regular visitor to White Cottage until the last few days of his life.

'I don't know what *happened*, sir,' the widow

155

admitted. 'My daughter refused to speak of it. But one day she came back here from one of her walks in a terrible state. Took to her room without so much as a word, and locked herself in. And then, hot on her heels, *he* came calling.'

'The professor?'

'Yes, sir. Asked to see my Julia. Very insistent he was. Said he was concerned for her. As if she were any concern of his! And all the time I could hear her shouting down that she wouldn't see anyone. So I told him he wasn't welcome and sent him on his way.' She saw fit to accompany her remarks with an anti-German epithet that out in the trenches would have been considered in dubious taste.

But it seemed the professor, whatever the reason for his visit, had not been deterred. From what I could make out, he had made further attempts to see Julia Woodward in the days that followed— according to Mrs Woodward, the days immediately prior to the Rose Ball.

'She wouldn't see him, though. Wouldn't see anyone, not that German, nor Reginald Stansbury either. Those were the two she mentioned by name.'

'So you turned away Reggie, too?' I asked.

But she shook her head. 'Didn't need to. He'd been a regular enough caller before that. Always knocking at our door he was, asking if Julia was at home, asking if I knew where she was. But he never came while she was hiding herself away like that. And of course he left Hannesford altogether a few days later. The war may have been a terrible thing, but I'll say one thing, we got some peace round here when it started.'

I recalled that Reggie had also quit Hannesford

shortly after the Rose Ball. Like me, like others that summer, he had made his way to London to set about finding himself a commission.

'And your daughter, ma'am? Did she ever explain what had upset her so?'

Mrs Woodward shook her head and shrugged, and there was something in that shrug that told me a great deal. It seemed to say there had been other occasions when her daughter had fled to her room, that it was not altogether unusual; and that on such occasions maternal sympathy had not been in ready supply. It was clear enough that mother and daughter had been cut from very different materials. Mrs Woodward was dour and implacable, and Julia Woodward ... How had Anne phrased it? Julia Woodward always seemed a little precarious.

'To tell you the truth, Captain, I didn't really want to hear about my daughter's doings down at the Court. I warned her she was better off sticking to her own. She stayed in her room two or three days that time. And when she came out, she took great care to avoid me, I'll tell you that.'

And it was spoken with a certain pride, as if proof of her daughter's degeneracy and her own rectitude. If Julia Woodward had a confidante that summer, it had clearly not been her mother.

*   *   *

On leaving White Cottage, my feet took me to the vicarage. I hadn't planned to go, but the path from Mrs Woodward's front door led down, through the steep woods, to the donkey bridge, and from there I took the route Anne and I had followed the day before. It was quiet in the woods that day, especially higher up, where the rumble of the water was muffled by the trees. But for once the silence didn't disturb me. I was too deep in thought.

What did I make of Mrs Woodward's story? Perhaps surprisingly, it never occurred to me to doubt its factual accuracy. She had described the events themselves with conviction: her daughter returning home upset; the professor calling; Reggie Stansbury calling no longer. But Mrs Woodward's interpretation of those events seemed highly questionable. I didn't believe for an instant that the professor had been pursuing Julia Woodward like some satyr through the woods. But he'd clearly wished to speak to her. Why had she been so anxious to avoid him? Perhaps, with a mother like hers, she had developed an instinct for hiding things away.

And Reggie ... At the sanatorium that morning he'd seemed to deny being a regular visitor to White Cottage. A lie? Or had I simply misunderstood?

Then, approaching the gate of the vicarage, I was seized by a sudden sense of distaste. The professor and the girl were both dead; Reggie was maimed and disfigured. What did their secrets matter now? I could understand why Freddie Masters had taken an interest in the story told by the professor's son: Freddie had seen the old man struck in the face and still felt uncomfortable about it, still regretted his failure to intervene. But I'd been oblivious to all of it. If Reggie had frightened a girl in the woods, if the professor had seen him do it, what business was it of mine? I had other things to worry about. In a few days' time I would set off back to London and make a clean break. I had the future to think about.

The vicar and his wife were at home, and Anne with them, and I passed a pleasant half-hour in their company. The vicar, it seemed, had accepted defeat in the matter of the war memorial. Popular opinion, in the village and in the country, was against him, and although he still fervently believed that the dead would be better honoured by the education of their children, he accepted that the argument was lost.

'Yet I feel we should be striving to keep those young men alive in our *hearts*, not on memorials,' he insisted. 'By carving their names in stone, I feel we begin to let them go. It is so easy to let stone monuments do our work for us, you see.'

Mrs Uttley, although still frail, seemed in good spirits and asked a number of questions about the Stansburys and their guests, most of which I was quite unable to answer. Anne sat quietly by her side, but when I rose to go she came with me to the front door. A few minutes in the sane and reassuring company of the Uttleys had contrived to make my visit to Mrs Woodward seem absurd and pointless, and I hadn't planned to mention it to Anne. But in the hallway, by the door, she stopped me.

'I've been thinking about what you told me last night, Tom,' she said quietly, holding my hat and coat, her face touched by soft light from the hall lamp. Outside, the afternoon was already in decline. 'About Freddie Masters and that argument he saw on the bridge. It made me think . . .'

She hesitated.

'Yes?' I asked, curious despite myself.

'You know how it is when you can't sleep? All

sorts of things run through your head. Well, I was thinking about who could possibly have treated the professor in such a way. Then I remembered something I hadn't thought about for ages. Not since it all happened, I suppose.'

I paused, one arm in my coat, and waited for her to continue.

'You see, after the professor's death I was in charge of packing up his things. It was ever such a sad thing to do. All his clothes and his papers. Such intimate things. And one thing I found was a green leather notebook.'

I knew the one she meant. The professor had been in the habit of carrying it with him everywhere.

'Remember, Tom? He used to make notes about butterflies and things. But the one I found was blank. It must have been a spare. And finding it made me realise that I hadn't yet packed the other notebook. We were supposed to be sending everything back to his son, you see, and the notebook struck me as quite important. I mean, if he was your father, you'd rather have that than his shirts and things, wouldn't you?'

Briefly and inappropriately I wondered what had happened to my own father's shirts. I rather thought my mother had given them to the gardener.

'Go on,' I said. 'Where did you find it?'

'But I didn't.' The omission clearly still troubled her. 'We never did find it. I assumed he must have left it lying around somewhere, because he often did that. So I asked the servants to look for it, but it never turned up. After a day or two we sent off what we had, and I told myself the notebook would reappear at some point. And then I suppose I

160

forgot about it.'

'So you never saw it?'

She shook her head. 'No. At the time I just thought someone must have tidied it away. Do you think it matters at all?'

I thought of the things Mrs Woodward had been telling me. The professor's notebook ... The professor wrote everything down. But even so, surely there was no point in stirring up quiet waters...

'Who knows? Remember, we were all quite easily shocked back then. A lot of things that seemed dreadful or scandalous before just seem petty now.'

She nodded and I went on my way, pleased at my own restraint. After all, the misdeeds of the past were in the past. Retribution belonged to Sir Robert and the politicians, and to all those who were going to *make Germany pay*. I wanted none of it.

But of course the past is not so easy to leave behind. It has the habit of seeping into the present like a bad drain. Why else did I wake at night, sweating in the silence? And why was I at Hannesford? Just because I'd been lonely in London? Because I'd needed company to see me through Christmas? I wasn't sure. But whatever motive had drawn me back, it certainly hadn't been a desire to forget.

By the time the last of Hannesford's summer guests had arrived the good weather was firmly set, and wherever you looked out the colours were bright and bold and uncompromising, the subtleties of spring long forgotten. But by then I was already too busy to enjoy them properly. A full house meant there was much to be done.

As for Harry, at first I was simply confused. I'd never been self-conscious in his company before. If anything I'd tended not think of him at all, or to think of him only as part of the problem of organising life at Hannesford. But now it seemed that wherever I looked my eyes would meet his. And I found I couldn't hold his gaze. I would look away, flustered, my cheeks inevitably betraying me.

But amid the confusion there was the taste of something sweet. The house filled with people, became loud with Harry's friends. Tippy Hibbert and the Everson boys, the Flinders girls, Julian Trevelyan—these were the people who in their own polite way barely noticed me. Yet even at the height of the revelry, Harry's eyes would sometimes seek out mine, and I would feel a little thrill of joy at knowing I was not forgotten.

Yet I was nervous too. That summer Hannesford surged with powerful currents. At times I felt reckless, more than happy to abandon myself to their flow; but there were other times, as the sun rose and touched the lawns beneath my window with tentative daylight, when the freshness of the morning made the Stansburys' world seem shadowy and dangerous and turbulent. On one such day, I found myself alone with Tom down by the lake.

162

It was a clear, sweetly scented morning, and I felt the peace of the place touching my soul. But Harry and Margot came looking for me there, in need of someone to make up a boating party. Their spirits were high and they were full of laughter. I hesitated, but I went with them.

As the summer took hold and the temperatures began to rise, some things became clearer. It was incredible, bewildering, almost impossible to believe, but the frequency of Harry's glances could not have been a coincidence. I couldn't pretend otherwise. I had inspired pity before, had inspired trust in some, but I had never before been desired. And in Harry's eyes, frank and challenging as they met mine, I was sure the spark I could see was one of desire.

Hannesford Court was in a state of confusion when I returned from the vicarage. Bill Stansbury had taken a fall out hunting and had broken his arm, or his elbow, or his wrist—opinion was divided. It was unanimously agreed, though, that he was lucky to be alive, and the incident had caused a good deal of excitement. Mrs Rolleston talked about the likelihood of complications. Colonel Rolleston fulminated on the importance of proper cavalry training for young gentlemen. Horatio Finch-Taylor, who rode to hounds with the caution of a fretful bishop, lamented the impetuousness of youth. Even young Denny Houghton seemed rather elated by it all.

'I tell you,' he kept repeating, 'I thought the game was up for Bill. Landed on his head, he did, the damned fool. Still, no danger of an injury *there*, eh?'

'It's all nonsense,' Margot declared when I came across her and Susan and Freddie Masters in a quiet corner of the library, not far from the cases where the butterfly collection remained, still only partially labelled. 'The doctor says his arm's bruised, not broken. He's just a bit shaken up, that's all. Neil's with him now, and Laura Finch-Taylor, who seems to imagine herself a nurse.'

Susan confirmed this version of events, although her face seemed a little paler, as though the incident had upset her.

'Come on, old girl.' Freddie held out his hand to her. 'Let's go and relieve the watchers, shall we? Better to be doing something than sitting around here prattling, wouldn't you say?'

164

Margot watched them go.

'Freddie's rather a *good* man, isn't he, Tom? I'd never really noticed before.'

The corner where we were sitting was shielded from the rest of the room by jutting bookshelves. Outside, the last throes of the afternoon were splashing the clouds with colour. In the library the lamps were lit. It felt much later than it was. I agreed that I too was seeing Freddie in a somewhat different light.

Margot smiled. 'I suppose before, with Harry and Julian attracting so much attention, it was always easiest for him to play the fool. And of course he's always been good fun, and quite unshockable.' She looked at me. 'And you, Tom? Have I shocked you?'

I thought of the glove on my pillow.

'I think my sense of humour just about survived the front intact.'

'Good!' she said. 'In that case you can dance with me tonight. It's Boxing Day, remember? Bill's going to set up the gramophone in the drawing room. If the poor lamb's up to it, of course.'

The poor lamb was. Bill Stansbury defied the doom-sayers by appearing, immaculately attired, in time for dinner, his left arm cloaked in a sling. He seemed rather proud of this souvenir of his adventure, and took great pains to assure everyone that a fall from a horse was nothing, that he had endured much worse hardships during his time in uniform.

His recovery proved a blessing, as that night's entertainment rather relied on his enthusiasm to make it a success. On Boxing Day, as Sir Robert used to announce with pride, the servants at

Hannesford got a proper day off. Although the truth of this assertion depended upon a rather elastic definition of what constituted a proper day, the myth was a well-established one. For months beforehand Sir Robert would shake his head and tell his neighbours: *'Cold cuts in the evening. It's every man for himself. But we get by, you know. We get by.'*

Sir Robert himself had evolved a very good method of getting by, namely to make sure that he and his guests were invited to dine elsewhere. For many years, this had meant dinner at Colonel Kirkpatrick's in Hanbury. The tradition had grown up when the Stansbury children were still small, so they had been left behind; and by the time they had grown into adults, the precedent was established, and it was universally understood that on Boxing Day Hannesford was theirs for the evening. Informal after-dinner invitations were extended to their friends in the county, and an evening of merrymaking was planned.

One result of Bill Stansbury's hunting accident, however, was that Lady Stansbury was not at all eager to leave Hannesford. I came across her at her writing desk in the small parlour, and saw at once that the incident had shaken her.

'I have never been the sort of mother that fussed over her children,' she declared with undeniable veracity, 'but when I saw how pale he was, Tom . . . Well, you can imagine, after what's happened to Harry, and to Reggie . . . Harry *never* fell, you know. And Reggie, well, he knew how to take care of himself. But Bill's so *young* . . .'

I assured her that youth was a great advantage when falling from a horse and that Bill seemed

166

well on the road to recovery. She nodded, a little distracted, then gestured towards the piece of notepaper on the desk before her.

'I've been thinking about Reggie, too. It's wonderful news that he'll be coming home. But it does mean we have a lot of arrangements to make. I was thinking that this room would do very well for him. It's a good size, and quiet, and there's plenty of space for a bed. I am writing to Anne Gregory to ask if she would come here tomorrow to help us prepare. She will know exactly what to do. Anne always does.'

But when I asked if she still hoped to persuade Anne to return to Hannesford Court, she shook her head.

'I'm afraid not.' She added a few final words to her letter, and then rose. 'Is there anything we can do about Anne, do you think, Tom? Mrs Uttley says she is quite determined. I wish we could dissuade her. It is such a long way to go.'

'Dissuade her? Is she planning a journey?'

Lady Stansbury looked at me in surprise. 'Why, to South Africa, of course. Didn't she say? Anne has decided to take up a post in the Cape.'

*   *   *

That night I was not greatly in the mood for dancing. I felt restless and out of sorts, and over dinner I managed to argue with Denny Houghton, a feat which beforehand I would have considered almost impossible.

As Sir Robert so enjoyed pointing out, there was no formal dining at Hannesford on Boxing Day. Instead a fine feast of cold meats was laid out in the breakfast room, and 'the young people' helped themselves. I was considered one of them, but the prospect didn't thrill me. In the company of Bill and Denny I felt old and tired, and slightly resentful of their frivolity. It was a gulf that consisted of far more than a few years in age.

Certainly my altercation with Denny was both foolish and pointless. Violet Eccleston started it all off. She'd heard Denny complaining about the Scapa Flow fiasco and had begun to argue fiercely that, from an economic point of view, the scuttling of the German fleet was actually an excellent thing for British interests.

'You must see,' she insisted, rather optimistically, 'that if those ships had simply been handed over to the Royal Navy, it would have meant even less work for our shipyards. We should have been punishing ourselves purely to spite the German people. And their plight is already pitiful enough as it is. I'm sure you wouldn't like to see it get any worse.'

But for once Denny Houghton did not simply let this go.

'What I don't like,' he replied rather haughtily, making a point of catching Lucy Flinders's eye, 'is people telling me that I should love the Hun. None of us should. Nothing's too bad for them, that's what I say.'

He sat back contentedly with the air of one who had taken a stand for common sense and decency.

'What I don't like,' I said quietly, 'is people telling me I'm supposed to hate the men I've killed.'

I hadn't intended it to be heard; I hadn't really intended to speak at all. The words came from a place inside me that rarely saw the light. But suddenly the room went very silent.

168

'What's that, Allen? Don't be shy. Speak up!' With hindsight, I realised that Denny, possibly alone in the room, simply hadn't heard what I'd muttered, but at the time it sounded like a challenge. So I raised my voice in reply.

'I mean to say, we killed them, didn't we? Did our bit and shot them down.' I could feel the rage rising in my chest, but my voice stayed even. There was something pale and cold about my anger that made my hands shake. 'Men from places like this, doing the same things we were doing. They just wanted to go home too. But we killed them anyway.'

'Steady, Tom.' Freddie Masters put a hand on my arm, but I wasn't to be stopped.

'I mean, for God's sake! *King and Country. For the Glory of God.* You think they weren't told the same? You think they *wanted* to be out there? You think they were out there in the mud and the gas because they wanted to be killing Englishmen?'

I knew I was making a scene but I couldn't stop.

'There were telegrams in Germany too, you know. They've got the same empty places at their tables. Empty beds. But they can't stand in church like we can and thank God for victory and try to persuade themselves it was all worthwhile. And now you want to starve their widows, too. Why can't you just let them be? Why can't we all just let them be?'

The depth of the silence that followed is hard to describe. Certainly it was enough to dampen my fury. I felt foolish: rude and ridiculous. I could feel Margot looking at me.

'It's all right, Tom,' she said softly. Next to her, Bill Stansbury looked embarrassed. Lucy Flinders

169

just looked scared. But it was Denny Houghton who spoke first.

'I say, old man, I'm terribly sorry. Of course, I didn't mean ... Just a turn of phrase, don't you know? We all know that not *all* Germans...'

And then Violet Eccleston broke the tension.

'Well, for my part,' she declared in a ringing voice, as if completely unaware of any awkwardness, 'I see the desire for revenge on the German nation as an entirely natural emotion though a damaging one, and economically, of course, quite disastrous...'

And somehow the sound of Violet launching into one of her familiar lectures eased the atmosphere and allowed people to breathe freely again. When I mouthed an apology to Denny Houghton, instead of looking resentful, he simply looked relieved.

'Very good, Tom,' Freddie Masters whispered as the conversation became more general. 'Full marks for *politesse*. If that's what you intend to give them at Harry's memorial service, I shall make sure I get a front row seat.'

After dinner, other guests began to arrive. Very young men, rather more young women, scarcely a face I recognised. It was a gathering that always had a slightly impromptu feel to it, but the mood seemed a little more reckless than usual. At first I felt too ashamed to join in, but Denny Houghton came to find me to apologise again and I realised that only by joining the rest of them could I show I bore no grudge.

But I was too shaken by my own anger to enjoy myself. Violet Eccleston made a point of coming up and commending me on my outspokenness, then Bill Stansbury sauntered over and made a show of

170

chatting at great length on inconsequential subjects. Eventually I decided it was easier to dance.

The gramophone did good service, and the evening passed surprisingly swiftly. I danced with Susan Stansbury and with the doctor's daughter from Hannesford, and with a number of enthusiastic young ladies from surrounding parishes who I found difficult to tell apart. I danced with Margot early in the evening, and again later when, flushed and radiant, she came and sought me out. On both occasions I was struck by the difference in her, that difference I'd noticed on my first evening back at Hannesford. I'd danced with Margot many times before, but had never previously felt her move so freely, as if she cared for nothing but her own enjoyment.

'You know, Tom,' she murmured as we swirled around the hastily cleared drawing room, avoiding furniture and other couples. 'I've never really known you angry. Even that other time, at the Rose Ball, when I told you I was going to marry Julian. I thought you were angry then. You told me what a silly fool I was, remember? But it wasn't like tonight.' She looked into my face, slightly puzzled. 'What a man of surprises you are, Tom Allen.'

I didn't reply. I didn't want to talk. I didn't want to think.

Margot said nothing more until the gramophone stopped itself abruptly in the middle of the piece and left all the dancers looking awkwardly at one another.

'One moment!' Bill cried, and with a deft, one-armed manoeuvre succeeded in restarting the machine; but when the music began again Margot was claimed by a lanky youth who bowed

171

in an exaggerated manner and addressed her as *Marguerite*.

As I withdrew to the fringes, I saw that Lucy Flinders was dancing with Denny Houghton, her eyes bright with excitement, and I wondered at the strange alchemy that could transform such a very ordinary young man into a young girl's handsome prince. From whatever angle I viewed him, I could only see a rather callow youth with an oddly shaped chin.

Near them Susan was dancing with Freddie Masters. In contrast to the younger couple, there was no breathlessness in the way they danced, indeed they barely moved around the floor. If anything, even though dancing, they gave off a sense of *stillness*. Neither seemed particularly inclined to talk.

And then I found myself thinking of Anne. Why had she said nothing to me about her plan for South Africa? It seemed strange she hadn't mentioned it. The *fait accompli* unsettled me. Unreasonably and irrationally, it felt as if I were being left behind. Since meeting Anne again I'd noticed the parallels between her position and my own. For both of us Hannesford had perhaps been a trap as well as a refuge. But Anne had laid her plans and I had not. She was waving Hannesford goodbye.

And taking another look around the room at the bright, handsome people dancing there, I was gripped by an intense, disturbing sense that, unlike Anne, I had no idea who I was or where I was going.

* * *

172

Bill Stansbury's guests stayed until midnight. Long before then I had slipped away to my room. I didn't say goodnight to Margot, although I knew I should have done. Only Freddie Masters noticed me leave. From the other side of the room he raised an eyebrow by way of farewell.

Upstairs, I lay down with the lamp still burning and let my thoughts wander. The fire in the grate crackled in a sporadic, comforting fashion and the drift of music from below was soothing. For a time I allowed myself to imagine Margot dancing, surrendering herself to the music in that way I'd never felt before. And I thought of Anne, escaping Hannesford, making a life for herself that did not revolve around the Stansburys' seasons.

And then, when it all became too difficult, I thought of the professor again.

Perhaps Freddie Masters's little mystery only occupied my thoughts because it was a diversion from more difficult questions. But the professor's letter and Freddie's description of the scene at the donkey bridge sat awkwardly with my picture of the past. I'd always seen my time at Hannesford as my own story; the story of my own foolishness. Now I looked again and saw that I was only a small part of it. There was the professor on the donkey bridge. There was Anne Gregory with tears in her eyes I'd never thought to explain. There was Freddie Masters, stalking off into the woods at the height of the party. And somewhere there was Reggie, out of sight, sullen while the band played. Thinking of what? Of his grievances? Of Julia Woodward? I'd noticed none of it. Not a thing.

173

The day of Margot's expedition to the water meadows dawned clear and cloudless, the pale blush of the morning sun promising heat. I'd already volunteered to go on ahead of the others, although I knew that everything would be as it should be, that the hampers would be in the proper place, the rugs laid out in readiness, the champagne on ice. But the thought of being alone appealed. Everything that summer was happening too quickly. Hannesford was crowded with guests, and the Rose Ball was approaching apace. Event was piling upon event and there was constant activity. Tongues were wagging about Julian and Margot, about the date of an announcement. Tilly Adams had argued with her husband and was publicly tearful, fuelling all sorts of speculation. The Everson boys were in naked competition for the affections of Buttercup Flinders, who seemed to be showing a preference for a man called Cartwright. And Harry . . . It was easier not to think too much about Harry.

But I wasn't to have things my own way. That morning he was waiting for me by the steps to the terrace, already dressed for the walk.

'Did you really think I'd let you go alone? Come on, Anne, I know the spot we're heading for. It will be far more lovely without the rest of them there.'

There was no escape. Harry was not easy to rebuff. So we walked out through the woods and fields together, while the morning was still cool and the countryside quiet.

It was an hour or more before the others joined us, bringing with them all the noise and foolish drama I'd been dreading. There had been peaches

174

and champagne waiting for them, and very perfect sandwiches, and then there had been games and running around until the heat of the day sapped everyone's energy and people sought the shade. Harry went off to swim. Margot held court among a small circle of admirers. I slipped away into deep shadow further down the river. As I went I noticed Tom sitting alone under a tree, and I was seized by an acute desire to join him there as I might have done the previous summer—to sit quietly with him again and talk about ordinary things, to feel at ease and at peace and happy.

But even as I changed course to go to him I saw he was about to be joined by Julia Woodward and the professor. I hesitated for a second or two, a little unbalanced by the strength of the urge I felt for his company. I'd thought that was all over. I was no longer that girl. I'd let Tom go.

But that day, by the river, I was sorry to walk away.

8

The guns were out again the day after Boxing Day. This time rather more of Sir Robert's guests were in attendance: for those who did not shoot, the days between Christmas and New Year could hang a little heavily, and no doubt many had come to feel that a certain amount of sporting enthusiasm was expected of them. Neil Maclean was one of the ones who joined the party, and Margot, who did not often follow the guns, went with him. I was happy to leave them to it.

In the breakfast room I found Violet Eccleston and Freddie Masters seated next to each other. Freddie, it turned out, had defected from the shooting party because he and Susan planned to motor over to Tenmouth to call on some mutual friends. Delighted to have an audience, Violet's chosen subject that morning was aviation, about which she seemed extremely passionate.

'Of course, Alcock and Brown garnered all the publicity,' she was saying as I joined them, 'but it's the achievement of the Smith brothers that has the greatest implications for the Empire.'

'Australians,' Freddie explained when I looked blank. 'They've just made it from Hounslow to Australia.'

'In twenty-seven days!' Violet added triumphantly. 'Their achievement answers a great many questions.'

'Except *why*?' Freddie muttered drily. 'Much comfier by boat.'

'Think of what that means!' Violet went on,

with evangelical enthusiasm. 'India in ten days. The Cape in under a week.' She lowered her voice. 'I assure you, gentlemen, that if you wish to find a safe home for your investments, aviation is the place. Traditional industries are in for a rough ride. It is one of only two strategies I could honestly endorse.'

'And the other?' I thought the interest in Freddie's voice did actually sound quite genuine.

'Why, gold, of course. Gold mines are always a safe refuge in troubled times. Assuming you choose ones that have gold in them.'

'But aren't the troubled times coming to an end now, Violet?' I asked. 'I know the war years were difficult, but now things can get back to normal, can't they?'

She looked at me with a mixture of scorn and exasperation. 'Really, Captain Allen! Normal? What's normal now? Everything is different. You sound just like Sir Robert!'

Freddie cleared his throat. 'Perhaps not over breakfast, Violet. I think Tom's introduction to the economics of the peace should wait until you're both sitting more comfortably. Perhaps with a stiff drink...'

With that, he made his escape. Violet, unabashed, moved on to the subject of Neil Maclean, for whom, like aviators, she seemed to have a great deal of admiration.

'It's such an honour to be here with him,' she confided. 'When I heard he was going to be joining the party at Hannesford for Christmas, I confess my excitement knew no bounds. He really is a very important man indeed.'

I waited while she swallowed a large mouthful of

scrambled eggs.

'He has consistently anticipated events,' she explained. 'In a business sense, I mean. That is how he has become such a pre-eminent figure over there. Everyone is always watching to see what he will do next. And I rather think he shares my concerns about the state of Europe...'

I confessed that I hadn't realised Maclean was such an influential figure.

'Oh, enormously. The financiers over here simply fawn on him. It's not at all surprising that Lady Stansbury thinks he would make such a good match for Margot. Unlike Sir Robert, Lady S seems to have a good idea of which way the wind is blowing.' She paused. 'You do know that's what Lady Stansbury intends, don't you, Tom?'

I told her that Bill had mentioned it.

'Oh, good. I'm glad that's clear. Of course I completely understand why you men find Margot so attractive. She's one of the lucky ones, isn't she? Neil will suit her very well.'

I ventured to ask if Margot had shown any sign of sharing that opinion.

'Any display of partiality, you mean?' She frowned. 'Well, they do spend a lot of time together. And she seems very comfortable in his company. But of course that isn't really the point, is it, Tom? I think we both know that Margot is a sensible girl in these matters. Why else would she have become engaged to a frightful man like Julian Trevelyan? Of course she'll marry Neil. Any girl would.'

Violet Eccleston could be a bit much, first thing in the morning.

When I finally escaped the breakfast room, I

178

found Freddie Masters in the library, smoking and waiting for Susan to appear.

'The funny thing about Violet,' he remarked, 'is that the more appalling she is, the more I like her.' He raised his eyebrows and peered at me theatrically. 'If it's not a rude question, old man, what are you doing with your father's money? Land, government bonds, that sort of thing?'

I shrugged, embarrassed. 'I confess I leave it to the lawyers.'

'Well, if I were you, my friend, I'd think about dropping them a line to mention you're keen on gold. It's just an inkling I have.' Freddie smiled and stubbed out his cigarette. 'Confound the girl. Now she's got me wondering how on earth one invests in aeroplanes.'

*   *   *

When Freddie and Susan set off for Tenmouth the house felt very empty. Bill Stansbury had taken his bruised arm off to follow the guns, Lucy Flinders had gone with him, and most of the other ladies had followed them. Horatio Finch-Taylor, Mapperley the banker and the other male guests were all part of the shooting party, so I had the rare pleasure of being left at Hannesford to my own devices. I'd been looking forward to it.

My plan for the day, hatched in the sleepless early morning, was simple. Rather than resist the itch, I would allow myself to scratch it for a few hours. Since the professor was on my mind, I would take a little time to think about him. Somewhere in the library there was a lot of paperwork that accompanied the butterfly collection, and I was

179

pretty sure the professor's own notes would still be there too, all the jottings he'd made in the days before he died. I didn't expect to find anything momentous among them, but in the absence of his notebook it seemed worth a try. If nothing else, I'd be able to tell Freddie Masters that I'd done what I could to throw some light upon his mystery.

So, very systematically, I set to work. It didn't take me long to find the papers. They were exactly where I'd expected them to be, still arranged as they had been when the professor was alive. Mostly they were the notes of the original collector, Sir Robert's great-uncle, who had neglected to label the remarkable collection he amassed. Interleaved with the original papers were notes the professor had added. I recognised his spidery, slightly old-fashioned handwriting. He had worked in English, as he always did, even when writing in his little notebook. *I think in English now*, he'd once explained to me. *I have been living here nearly thirty years. If I ever go back to Germany, I shall have to learn to think in German again.* And of course, had he lived longer, he almost certainly *would* have gone back. He would have had no choice. Staying on would have been too difficult. In a way, I was glad he'd never been forced to make the decision.

My morning was not, in the end, particularly profitable: partly because the notes were no more and no less than they should have been— observations about details of various Lepidoptera; partly because I'd reckoned without the lingering presence of Violet Eccleston. She found me in the library shortly after I'd started work, and the sight of something resembling scholarly activity delighted her. I told her that Professor Schmidt had been a friend of mine, and that I wanted to make sure his notes were left in good order. After that she settled down nearby, apparently content to talk uninterrupted while I worked.

Her thoughts, it seemed, were still on Margot's prospects of marriage.

'Of course, Lady Stansbury's daughters are the exception nowadays,' she explained. 'My generation of young women find themselves in peculiar circumstances. A very large number of us will never marry. We may as well be frank about the situation. It is a simple question of mathematics.'

I let her run on, only half listening, my mind on butterflies.

'For Margot, of course, who has both looks and fortune, the situation is rather different. She will not be greatly inconvenienced by the changes. Indeed, for women who have one of those attributes—either exceptional looks or exceptional wealth—there is every chance that their lives will develop as they have always imagined. But for those who have neither . . .'

I heard her give a little cough, as if to clear her throat.

'For the rest of us . . . Well, I for one must accept that all the things that were, for my mother, the very point of her existence—I mean marriage, motherhood, the joy of children—these are things I shall never experience. Of course, I shall . . . These things are not . . .'

And to my amazement her voice began to break. It had never even occurred to me to wonder what feelings lay behind those stoutly defended barricades. I'd supposed her façade of breezy practicality utterly unbreachable.

181

'Violet . . .' I began, half rising to my feet, but she waved me away with a little stab of her hand.

'No, please, Captain Allen. Tom. No flattery. It is quite pointless. The truth is better. I shall never marry, and I am quite resigned to the situation. And so must many other women be.' She took a deep breath. 'Of course, it goes without saying that there have always been a certain number of women who, because of their precarious position in society, are less likely to marry—governesses, ladies' companions, the genteel, impoverished women forced into those sorts of roles. But the truth is that now their numbers are vastly multiplied, and society really has no idea at all what to do about it.' She took another breath and her voice was steadier. 'Of course, in primitive societies the solution would be polygamy, but I cannot see that option being readily embraced.'

She had regained her equilibrium, and I ventured to suggest that perhaps Mr Lloyd George might be more amenable to such a policy that she supposed. But the sally was lost on her. Violet Eccleston did not engage in scurrilous rumour.

'Our only option is nothing less than the re-shaping of society's whole concept of womanhood. And although the circumstances are deeply unfortunate, the opportunities for my sex are boundless. I see no reason why in the future there may not be very great numbers of female scientists, female surgeons, even female judges.'

I listened, admiring her fortitude, the courage behind her words. Only when she finally paused did I change the subject.

'Tell me, Violet. I wanted to ask about something you said at breakfast. Why didn't you like Julian

Trevelyan?'

'He was the sort of man who is disliked by his servants,' she replied without a moment's hesitation. I waited for her to elaborate but instead she seemed to be gathering herself for further comments about female advancement.

'You think he would have made a poor husband?'

'Well, really, Captain Allen, that all depends on what one feels a husband should be. He was very wealthy, but I cannot imagine that he would have given Margot a lifetime of pleasant and diverting company.'

'What about Harry Stansbury?' I asked. 'What did you think of him?'

'Barely knew him. Not a great thinker, I should say. He and I were not the closest of friends, obviously. Why do you ask?'

But I didn't give a reason. I was going to be speaking at Harry's memorial service in four days' time and still hadn't the slightest clue what to say.

Violet stayed with me until the clock struck eleven and reminded her that she had promised to sit with Mrs Rolleston. I was left alone with the professor's notes and continued to study them slightly absently until disturbed by the throaty rumble of a motor car approaching the house. When I went to the window I saw Anne Gregory alighting from the Daimler. Lady Stansbury, it seemed, had sent the car as her ambassador, to make sure Anne really did come back to help for the day.

As I watched her small figure approach the house I wondered if it were true, that comment Violet had made about governesses and ladies' companions. Had Anne's position at Hannesford robbed her of the chance of marriage? I'd never really considered the matter before. It was certainly true that at Hannesford Court Anne mixed in circles where she often went unseen; the Julian Trevelyans of this world did not pay much attention to their hostesses' companions. And with Margot always there, always nearby, what chance for anyone else to shine? Yet as she crossed the gravel sweep, I knew I was pleased to see her. She had always been good company, an easy person to talk to. And whereas I'd once found it easy to talk to everyone, now there only seemed to be Anne. I wasn't surprised by Lady Stansbury's reluctance to let her go.

Returning to the professor's papers, I found my concentration wandering. The notes were mostly the professor's thoughts on provenance—where in the county or in the country particular specimens might have been collected. When he believed a specimen had been local to Hannesford, he'd sought to test this theory by his own observations, and these notes were the only ones that made reference to anything I found familiar:

Polyommatus alexis—Common Blue. Hannesford. Meadow south side of lake, 26th June 1914.

On one such entry I even found a reference to myself:

Euchloë cardamines—Orange-tip. SW of Hannesford. Below apple trees, above gorge of River Hanna, 23rd June 1914, walking with TA.

I could remember that expedition. I'd shown the professor the walk to the ruined chapel that stood a couple of miles beyond Hannesford village. It had been an enjoyable afternoon, at a time when there seemed nothing remarkable in an Englishman and a German strolling through the countryside talking of harebells and architraves. The only person I remember passing was Harry Stansbury, out walking a young dog of his brother's. We'd come across him in the woods below the chapel, where the path follows the river. Harry was coming towards us, heading back to Hannesford. It was unusual to see him so far from his friends—he was not generally one for his own company— but I remember how relaxed he seemed at that moment, how content to be in that beautiful place on that beautiful day. After learning of his death, I often thought of that meeting in the woods. It was perhaps the best image I could find to remember Harry by.

The ruined chapel was a private spot on the flank of a hill, a secluded place that trapped the sun and the silence. Red clover grew in the grass between the low walls, and the turf was closely cropped and good to sit on. From there you could look out over the trees towards the moor, and once or twice I'd passed the better part of a day there, reading and smoking, without ever seeing another soul.

But that day, the chapel was not deserted. We had found Julia Woodward there, seated on one of the low walls, looking out at the panorama below. I remember being struck by how serene she looked. She told us she often walked that way and she said it with a smile, as if treasuring a secret all of her own.

Anyway, it was a good walk. The professor must have enjoyed it too, I thought, because his notes showed that a couple of days later he'd walked that way again.

Agapetes galathea—Marbled White. Old chapel above river gorge, SW of Hannesford, 25th June 1914. HS, Miss AG. Peinlich.

The initials indicated Harry Stansbury and Anne Gregory, who were both people the professor might have come across on one of his expeditions. But the German word meant nothing to me. I made a mental note to ask Freddie Masters about it.

Meanwhile, it was almost lunchtime. I would go downstairs and see what plans Anne had for the afternoon.

It was never easy to be alone at Hannesford. The day after the expedition to the water meadows I sought refuge in the library. I found the professor there as I knew I would, the great trays of butterflies and moths spread out around him like exotically embroidered panels. He had been out walking with Tom earlier that day—I'd seen them set off together, chatting and relaxed. But that evening the professor seemed a little reflective, as if preoccupied with something other than butterflies.

However he smiled as if pleased to see me, and when I was settled began to tell me about the specimens in front of him. It was not unusual for him to talk freely in that way when we were alone in the library, as if merely speaking his private thoughts aloud. The professor had a way of putting people at ease.

But that evening he surprised me with a question.

'Ah, Miss Gregory, tell me. This creature here . . .' He pointed to a bright yellow specimen with small spots on its wings. 'Butterfly or moth?'

I peered at it. A butterfly, a very beautiful one.

'And this one?' He indicated a specimen of similar size in pale, muted colours, mostly grey.

A moth, I thought.

'And what then, would you say, is the difference between butterflies and moths?'

Suspecting a trap, I simply mumbled something about moths coming out at night. The professor greeted my reply with a little shrug.

'Some do, some don't. And butterflies sometimes fly by night. But surely, when you answered just now, you couldn't tell the nocturnal habits of this little fellow just by looking? It must have been something else that made you decide.'

'Yes, of course. It was the colours.' I considered the two specimens again. 'Butterflies are bright and moths are dull.'

The professor smiled. 'Yet look here. And here, and here.' His finger moved to various brown-winged examples. 'All these are considered butterflies, but their colours are very plain.'

So I asked him what point he was making, what the difference really was between the two. The question seemed to please him.

'Scientifically speaking, we *can* identify differences. Of course in some countries, the language does not even attempt to differentiate between the two. But here in England people do not rely on science. They answer my question quite instinctively, as you did. They decide just by looking.'

The professor removed his spectacles and gave them a little rub against his waistcoat.

'Which is a little like English society, is it not, Miss Gregory? Take our recent picnic, for example. I was introduced there to your Miss Woodward. To the humble foreigner she looked very like the other ladies present. She is pretty, she holds herself well, she has just enough education, but not too much, because of course in this country too much education is a terrible blunder. She is invited by Miss Stansbury and her brother, just as the other young ladies are invited. And yet she is not the same, is she? She is not quite a butterfly. And although nothing is said, this is something everyone present is aware of. These subtleties are fascinating to me.'

'I suppose that's true ...' I watched him rub the bridge of his nose. 'People *are* aware of these distinctions, yes. And although it was kind of Harry and Margot to invite her, I don't think they realise that generosity of that sort is not always a kindness. Miss Woodward didn't seem in very good spirits.'

'Tom Allen and I came across her on our walk today,' the professor mused, 'in a rather lovely place. She seemed a good deal happier.'

He returned his glasses to his nose, but did not seem greatly happier himself. I had the impression he was still turning over in his mind something that troubled him. So instead of replying, I allowed my eye to wander to the specimen tray, to the brightest, most colourful specimen I could see, still iridescent and exquisite despite its age.

In the professor's analogy, what was I? A very small, brown butterfly, perhaps. Like one of those in the Hannesford collection. If so, I was one quite easily taken for a moth.

I found Anne in the small parlour where she was in conference with the housekeeper, Mrs Hodge, discussing the changes needed to make the room suitable for Reggie. Already it had been stripped of its usual furniture and bore no resemblance to Lady Stansbury's elegant little writing room. When I put my head around the door, Anne greeted me with a cheerful smile and I felt the slight sense of resentment I'd been carrying around all day begin to melt a little.

'Are you going to be here this afternoon?' she asked. 'I've something to tell you.'

And so I abandoned the plans I'd been making for a brisk walk and waited indoors, enduring Mrs Rolleston over lunch and Violet Eccleston over coffee, until Anne took a break from her labours and found me in the library, still surrounded by the quiet ranks of the professor's butterflies.

'Come on,' she said. 'The sun's still shining. Let's get some fresh air.'

We walked down to the small rotunda on the far side of the lake. The air was sharp, and beneath our feet the ground was frozen in places and a little treacherous, but the sun sparkled on the water and the world was bright. When we reached the place where the path skirted the water's edge, I had to screw up my eyes to look at her. Even then I could make out little more than her profile against the light. From somewhere in the distance we could hear the occasional pattering volleys of the shooting party.

I felt awkward asking her about South Africa but Anne seemed neither surprised nor uncomfortable.

She simply explained that an opportunity had arisen, that it had come to her through someone she'd worked with closely in the past, and that she was at liberty to defer the post until she was no longer required by the Uttleys.

'That made it difficult for me to decline,' she concluded. 'And besides, apart from the Uttleys there's really nothing to keep me here. I've already stayed much longer than I should have done. It will do me good to travel.' She turned to me. 'What do you think, Tom? A good plan?'

With the water so bright behind her I couldn't make out her expression, but there was something in her voice, a seriousness beneath the lightness, that made me hesitate.

'It seems a shame,' I said, 'to go so far.'

'I once thought of going further. To Australia, perhaps.'

I looked past her, at the shining water, and wondered when that had been, what urge had prompted it. It was strange how little I really knew about Anne.

'I should be sorry to see you go.' I gave the words a twist of lightness that contrived to turn them into a commonplace. But even the most trivial pieces of politeness can also be true.

Anne simply laughed, however, and said, 'Thank you, Tom,' and we continued to walk.

In the end, I discovered that the thing she'd wanted to tell me was nothing to do with South Africa anyway.

'It's a terrible piece of tittle-tattle, really,' she explained. 'I don't know that I should be repeating it. It was something Miss Thomson, the doctor's daughter, told me when I called on her this morning. I mentioned that we'd visited Mrs Woodward, and said how sorry you'd been to hear about Julia, and she pulled that face that people pull when they want to tell you something but don't want you to consider them indiscreet.'

'And what was it?' I was always a little wary of village gossip.

'Something that happened before the fighting started. Miss Thomson was only a girl, but she remembers a time when Julia Woodward came to see her father very late one evening, without an appointment. In a state, she said. She remembers walking past the door of her father's room and hearing Miss Woodward's sobs.'

I said nothing. Perhaps I had an inkling of what was coming.

'Well, obviously the doctor never said anything to anyone, but Miss Thomson was hiding at the top of the stairs when he showed Miss Woodward out. She remembers him saying that the worst was over and that she should rest and try to recover her strength. And he said, given her situation, she would perhaps come to see that it was all for the best.'

'And when was this? Could Miss Thomson remember?'

'She wasn't sure. Not long before the start of the war. Honestly, Tom, you'd think a doctor's daughter would know better, wouldn't you? But she didn't seem at all ashamed of her eavesdropping. And, of course . . .' Anne didn't blush. 'Of course it was pretty clear what she was suggesting.'

I simply nodded. There didn't seem to be anything to add.

Our walk soon brought us back to the house,

192

where Mrs Hodge was looking out for Anne, awaiting further instructions. We parted with a smile and a nod, and I was sorry we couldn't have stayed out longer.

*   *   *

After that I was alone till mid-afternoon when Margot and Lucy Flinders abandoned the shooting party and sought refuge from the cold. They found me in the library, still seated in front of the neat lines of butterflies and moths.

I rose politely when they came in, but I didn't really want to be disturbed. I'd been thinking about Reggie; or rather, of the two Reggies—the crumpled, broken invalid at the sanatorium in Cullingford, and the brooding young man who had once haunted the Hannesford woods with a gun under his arm. I'd never imagined the latter as a seducer of young girls, but such things did happen; it was an old story. Even so, I'd no desire to confront the other Reggie about it. It was, after all, no business of mine.

'It's positively frigid out there,' Margot declared, falling into the chair opposite mine, 'and everyone says it's going to snow. So Lucy and I thought we'd come in and have some tea. Will you find it an awful bore to entertain us, Tom?'

'I'm afraid you may not find me very entertaining,' I replied, sounding rather stuffy.

Margot's cheeks were glowing from the fresh air. Next to her, Lucy Flinders's youthful prettiness seemed little better than insipid. But somehow, at that particular moment, her radiance felt like a reproach. It reminded me of that time when her

193

perfection had been all I could see, when Reggie's passions and Julia Woodward's unhappiness had both somehow slipped beneath my notice.

I'd never paid enough attention to Anne, either. And soon she would be in Cape Town.

'Then we shall entertain you, shan't we, Lucy?' Margot was never one to be deterred by a lukewarm welcome. 'We've already rung for tea, and we're hoping for scones. Mrs Adkins loves Tom, you see, Lucy. There are always scones for Tom.' She turned back to me. 'We were talking about you as we walked home. Lucy didn't believe me when I told her about your photographs.'

Lucy Flinders flushed. 'I didn't exactly say that, Captain Allen. I only said I was surprised to hear that you were a photographer.'

'I'm not,' I replied shortly. 'I never was. I used to dabble a bit, that's all. A long time ago.'

'But Margot says you were very good.'

'I'm not sure Margot is a reliable judge. She's far too polite to say what she really thinks.'

But Margot denied the charge hotly, horrified at being labelled polite.

'Nowadays everyone says I'm far too frank,' she concluded. 'Anyway, Tom, you really ought to photograph Lucy. Don't you think she'd make a wonderful subject?'

Happily, she didn't wait for an answer, rattling on to a different subject before I could reply. I was relieved when they finally left me alone.

But the conversation had set me thinking, and when the tea things were cleared away, I made my way to the narrow flight of stairs at the top of the house, stairs that led to a corridor where guests generally never ventured. This was where the old

194

schoolroom could be found, and a room called the music room where no one ever played music, and the rooms used as quarters by a succession of governesses; it was where Anne's room had been, before her departure from Hannesford. From these rooms you could look out through Hannesford's small upper windows, over the avenue and lawns, across to the lake and the wooded slopes beyond.

I poked my nose into the old schoolroom first. It was not a room I knew well, but I found it neat, the little desks and chairs covered with dustsheets in the way they had always been. It felt very cold. And as soon as I stepped inside, I thought of Harry.

I'd almost forgotten that the schoolroom was a place Harry used to visit as an adult. He would escape there to smoke a particular brand of Indian cigar that his father found objectionable— something rather nasty that gave off an evil smell. I'd always suspected that his partiality towards them was more an affectation than anything else— or perhaps a convenient excuse to retire from his father's company. But as I stood in the doorway of the schoolroom that day, the stale smoke of those cigars seemed to linger in the air, as though Harry had smoked his last one only a month or two before. It was peculiar: Harry's bedroom, so carefully preserved in the state he'd left it, had not spoken to me of him at all. It had felt like a museum. Harry seemed more real to me here, in an empty room he visited only occasionally, a room still vaguely redolent of bad tobacco.

But it was not the schoolroom I'd come to see. The room I sought lay at the other end of the corridor and when I tried the door I found it locked. It was the room where, in the early days of photography, Sir Robert's errant younger brother had chosen to construct his darkroom.

My search for the key led me back to warmer regions and eventually to Lady Stansbury who, according to the housekeeper, kept that particular key on her own ring. I found my hostess in the room that was to become Reggie's new bedroom, apparently examining the bell pull.

'We need to replace it with a longer one,' she explained. 'Anne thought of it. Reggie, you know, in his chair . . .'

She looked surprised when I asked her for the key I was seeking.

'The old darkroom? Yes, of course. I'd forgotten. I should have thought of it before. I've always kept it locked, you know, between your visits. I think of it very much as your private place.'

I hadn't known that, and found it strangely touching. Of course Lady Stansbury wasn't to know I took great pains at the end of every visit to hide all traces of my work.

She led me to her writing desk, now relocated to a small, high-ceilinged room at the back of the house. As she took the key from her ring, my eye fell upon a letter open in front of her. The handwriting was vaguely familiar.

'From Oliver,' she said quietly. 'Susan's Oliver. He wrote it the year before he died . . .' She pushed it closer. 'I read it often, to tell the truth. I don't know why. I should probably put it well away, somewhere out of reach.'

I took it gently. It was a letter of condolence written shortly after Harry's death. It had always struck me that Oliver Eastwell's handwriting was somehow suggestive of his character: he wrote in large, looping letters, unsophisticated and slightly exaggerated. If Harry's fine handwriting had been the calligraphy of sonnets, Oliver's was the scrawl of comic verse. I couldn't help thinking how incongruous such a letter was. For his first twenty-five years, Oliver had chortled his way through life flushed by claret. Then suddenly he'd been required to turn his hand to letters such as this one.

And he had written it well. Better than that. He had written it beautifully. In every line there was honesty and depth of feeling. It was as if, amid the roar of the guns, the fat, foolish Oliver I thought I'd known had somehow found a different identity.

. . . I had always hoped that at the end of this we might come back to Hannesford—Harry and I and Julian Trevelyan, Tippy Hibbert, the Eversons, all the old fellows—and work out how to make the world a better place. But Harry was always the heart of our group. Our brains and our spirit. Without him, I cannot think the rest of us will know how to function. My only hope is that we might yet contrive to make something of our lives that might be considered a monument to Harry . . .

When I looked up from the letter Lady Stansbury was watching my face.

'All of them, Tom. All those foolish, beautiful boys. I never dreamed that not even one of them would come home.'

There was nothing to say to that.

I left her at her desk, rearranging her papers.

197

Our summer came to an end on the night of the Rose Ball. Elsewhere, I suppose, it continued, at least in name. The Season staggered on, eyes glancing nervously abroad. The horses ran at Goodwood. At the seaside, children still swam. The hot weather lasted well into autumn.

But at Hannesford it finished that night, with the professor lying dead on the terrace. There was no more dancing after that. By the time the doctor had been found and Sir Robert informed and a decision made about where to move the professor's body, carriages were already beginning to arrive. For the most part people crept away rather quietly. Next morning the house party at Hannesford began to break up.

I spent the last hours of that last night with Tom. When the guests had all gone, I found him on the terrace, alone and looking out into the night. Neither of us seemed to feel like sleeping—I suppose we both had too much on our minds—so we began to walk, drifting without purpose through the quiet gardens where a few hours earlier there had been music and lights and flirtation.

We didn't even speak very much. A few words about the professor, about what a good man he had been, about how much we had both liked him. And of course a little about the other event of the evening, the news that had set every tongue wagging. Oliver and Susan. Quite out of the blue. Hannesford had been abuzz.

I didn't mention Margot, although I knew that she too had made up her mind that night. Lady Stansbury had been told, and it was to be formally announced in three weeks' time, after a visit to the Trevelyans, when everyone would be back in town. Tom knew about it too. I'd seen him talking to Margot.

For a lot of the time we simply strolled in silence, happy not to be alone. Whatever Tom was thinking, our measured tread over the lawns seemed to help. When he told me he intended to leave the following day, I simply nodded. By then the sky in the east was already beginning to pale. I was too tired to be miserable, too tired to think very hard about all the folly and weakness that had brought me to that empty dawn. I would miss him, I knew. I was more wretched than I'd ever been.

News of Harry's commission had come through just before the ball. It was unexpected and he was jubilant. I barely saw him in the three days that followed. There was no time for anything but formalities and brief farewells, hasty visits to neighbouring families to impart the news and take his leave. Strings had been pulled on his behalf and he must get to London to seize the day.

During the ball itself, he'd been able to talk of nothing else. There was going to be a war and he was going to be in the thick of it. He wanted everyone to know. But I hadn't wanted to listen to him. When Oliver Eastwell asked me if I didn't think Harry would make a damned fine soldier, I think he was shocked to find me so unsmiling.

And then there was Reggie. In the days that followed the ball he too had been desperate to get away. In the midst of the excitement about Harry's commission his packing had gone almost unnoticed, and in the end he scarcely even said goodbye to his family. Quite by chance I'd been crossing the Great Hall when he was waiting for the car to take him to the station. We exchanged a few rather stilted words, neither unfriendly nor particularly meaningful. Reggie had been eager to be gone. I'd been struck by how rigid he seemed, as if every muscle in his body was tense beneath his topcoat.

A few months later, in early 1915, I followed him to London. I went as soon as I decently could, when the demand for nurses gave me every excuse for going. Leaving Hannesford felt like a release; had it not been for Mrs Uttley I would never have gone back. And I would certainly not have returned to my role as Lady Stansbury's companion, not even for one last day to help with Reggie's things, had I not been sure that permanent escape lay within my grasp. But by then my path was clear. An offer of work in South Africa had been confirmed by interview in London; and with my course set and my future planned, the thought of returning to help at Hannesford Court for just a few more hours didn't seem too great a concession.

Even so, when the Stansburys' car deposited me on the gravel sweep that winter morning, I felt a reluctant helper. Stepping back into my old role was uncomfortable, and when I settled down with Mrs Hodge to work out the arrangements for Reggie's return, it was almost possible to forget how things had changed, to expect any minute to be interrupted by Harry bursting through the door or by the hilarity of Oliver Eastwell and the Everson boys embarking on one of their escapades.

But when I paused and listened, I noticed the silence. No Harry, no Oliver. Hannesford had never been this quiet. When Tom put his head round the door quite late in the morning, my heart quickened at the sound of his voice. But I resisted temptation and stayed at my post until a little after lunch. When I finally went to find him, the sun was shining and he seemed pleased to join me for a walk.

I spent the last part of that afternoon in Reggie's bedroom, supervising the removal of relevant items to his new room on the ground floor. It was a melancholy task, surveying the bits and pieces Reggie had walked away from, trying to anticipate which of them might smooth the awkwardness of his return. And it felt wrong to be doing it. It should have been someone who knew him better than I did, who would have known what little things might give him pleasure. But there was only me. I left the clothes to Evans and concentrated on Reggie's other belongings.

On the wall above his bed was a painting of gundogs on the marshes at dawn: that could be moved, and so could the photographs on his dressing table: one of his sister Susan and, more surprising perhaps, one of his mother as a young woman, still beautiful, her eyes slightly dreamy as if seeing a world far beyond the camera.

Other things were harder. Was the old leather dog-collar by his bed a treasured memento of a favourite animal, or had Reggie simply dropped it there unthinkingly on the morning of his last departure? I would have to ask Evans about it. There were no books in evidence, but a box beneath his bed was stuffed with papers and magazines—the faded racecards of forgotten point-to-point meetings, clippings from sporting periodicals, old bills from Lamingtons of London. Scattered among them were other things: a cigarette case, matchbox holders, collar studs, an old snuff box, a woman's button with a fragment of fabric attached to it. Together they conveyed the sense of items carelessly discarded. Even so, there was an intimacy to the collection that made me feel I shouldn't be prying, and I was on the point of returning all the contents to the box when a broken cufflink caught my eye and surprised me with a sudden shock of memories.

It was one of Oliver Eastwell's, a distinctive design in white and yellow gold the shape of a beehive. I could even remember the evening when he first wore it. He'd had the pair made specially, to commemorate the victory of a horse called Beehive in a race at Newmarket, a horse Oliver had backed at long odds to the derision of his friends. He had revealed the new cufflinks with enormous pride, to the groans of Harry and the rest of them, and had threatened to wear them every night of his stay. I smiled to think of it; it had been typical Oliver— extravagant, slightly foolish, deliberately playing up to the expectations of his companions.

I'd heard the news of Oliver's death when I was in France and too busy to dwell on it. It had been little more than another death to add to the list, another name among many. Sometimes it was hard to remember who was alive and who was dead. But the sight of that flamboyant, slightly tasteless cufflink brought with it a strong sense of the person I remembered, and I paused, stricken, for the first time really feeling his loss. For some reason, on returning it to the box, I decided to bury it deeply. I'd no idea how it came to be among Reggie's things.

It was as I slipped my hand to the bottom of the box that my fingers touched something firm, a book of some sort, bound in very soft leather.

In the end I didn't return to the darkroom straight away. On leaving Lady Stansbury, my company was claimed by Violet Eccleston who required me to play whist with her and Mrs Rolleston. The game came to an end with the return of the shooting party, which gathered for beer and refreshments in the Great Hall. There I saw that Anne had not yet returned to the vicarage. She was standing by the fire, talking to Lady Stansbury, whose face betrayed no trace of the emotion I'd seen there earlier. She was the perfect hostess once more.

'Please, Tom,' she implored when I approached them, 'tell Anne that she must join us for dinner. She has done so much today. The Daimler is at your disposal, Anne, dear, to run you back to the vicarage to dress. And it would be wonderful to have you here. It would be quite like the old days, wouldn't it, Tom?'

'It would certainly be lovely if you could join us,' I agreed, meaning it. 'Might Mrs Uttley be able to spare you for one night?'

'Not tonight, I'm afraid.'

Her regret seemed genuine. Lady Stansbury must have thought so too, for she renewed her efforts.

'Tomorrow, then? I shall write to Mrs Uttley first thing. I'm sure it can be arranged, Anne. I know Mrs Uttley too well to think that she will grudge us your company for just one evening...'

That night the assembled company seemed a good deal more relaxed than it had been, as if finally settling into the new way of things. Denny Houghton looked red-cheeked and merry, and in his company Lucy Flinders was transformed from the pallid girl of the afternoon into a vivacious, rather comely young woman. They were talking to Colonel Rolleston and making him laugh in a series of low, booming grunts, like the rumbling of a waking bear.

Margot was talking gaily to Neil Maclean, and Freddie Masters seemed to be entertaining a group of Sir Robert's friends with a tale of Whitehall. Not far from him, Susan was chatting to Violet Eccleston. I wondered idly whether Susan had ever seen the letter I'd been shown that afternoon. Was it she who had inspired such surprising eloquence in her husband? Or had it been there all along, lurking inside him?

Soon people drifted off to dress for dinner and the gathering began to break up. As the numbers thinned, I saw Anne making preparations to depart. She exchanged some last words with Lady Stansbury then paused and glanced around the room. When her eyes reached mine she smiled and I crossed the hall to join her.

'See me to the car, Tom?' she asked softly. 'I've got something for you.'

Outside, all those who had predicted snow were being proved correct. Occasional flakes were already falling as we made our way out on to the front steps, and the clouds above were leaden, threatening worse. The chauffeur, waiting patiently by the door of the Daimler, looked cold beneath his uniform.

'I should be going, Tom,' she said, pausing at the top of the steps. 'It's just that I wanted to show you something.'

She reached into her bag, then paused.

'I've never really thought that badly of Reggie before,' she said. 'I knew he could be objectionable and lose his temper, but I thought it was all bluster. I'd never have believed he might have done something as low as hitting the professor.'

I felt my eyebrow lift in surprise. 'But you believe it now?'

She bit her lip. 'You see, I never thought him underhand. I never thought him a sneak or a thief. But now there's this.'

She pulled from her bag a small notebook bound in green leather. The professor's notebook.

'I found it this afternoon. It was among Reggie's things. It wasn't even very well hidden. At the bottom of an old box, underneath some magazines. No, don't read it now. There isn't really anything to look at. The pages have been torn out, you see. All the ones for the time that mattered.'

I raised my eyebrow again and took the little book from her.

'I should really put it back soon,' she added.

I nodded and slid it into my pocket without speaking, then gave Anne my arm and accompanied her to the waiting car.

When the Daimler pulled away I watched it go until it was out of sight down Hannesford's long, tree-lined drive. It was too dark to tell whether or not the figure inside was looking back at me.

*   *   *

The only other thing I remembered about dinner that night was the story Freddie Masters told over the port. It was the first time since I returned to Hannesford that anyone had referred directly to the fighting, and at first I felt uneasy with the subject, unsure how Sir Robert and the others would react. But Freddie was more than equal to the situation, and when Mapperley, the banker, asked him a question he answered without hesitation.

'To be honest, my friend,' he declared, 'it was all thanks to one man's brilliance. He probably saved my life.'

'What's that, my boy?' Sir Robert had overheard, and the attention of the whole table turned to the speaker.

'My recollections of the action near Mons, sir,' Freddie explained. 'Mapperley here was asking how on earth we'd managed it. Of course, everyone must promise not to tell. It's all absolutely hush-hush.'

Sir Robert looked round the table. 'Go on, my boy. Let's hear it.'

'You see, sir, it was the autumn of last year and Jerry was falling back on all fronts. We were going forward with every attack, so there was no digging in. We just sheltered where we could.' He paused to help himself to more port, then looked across at me.

'Disturbing, wasn't it, Tom? We'd all got so used to not going anywhere, some of us had no idea what to do if we weren't in a trench. Well, anyway,' he went on, 'I found myself in something of a ditch alongside a fellow called Wiggins. A Harrovian, I believe, God bless him. My men were done in, and so were his, and no more than fifty yards away there was a band of Germans in a similar state but in a rather better ditch. Now, all of us knew that the next day we'd attack and go forward, and that they would counter attack and be beaten off. It had been

206

the pattern for weeks. By the end of the day rather fewer men on both sides would be sitting in similar ditches, waiting to start again.'

He paused to sip his port, his face a mask. I had no idea if I was listening to tragedy or comedy or both.

'Now, the approach to their trench was up a nasty little slope with a lot of wire and what-not, and I confess I didn't fancy it that much, and I was just thinking I'd better write a letter home when this fellow Wiggins comes up and asks me if I spoke German. I told him I did speak a bit and he said to me, "Good-o, in that case I'm going to sort this out." And he did.'

Sir Robert peered at him. 'I'm sorry, I don't understand.'

'Perfectly simple, sir. Wiggins was a practical man and he decided the simplest way to get hold of the next trench was to *buy* it. I have to say, his logic was quite impeccable, and the German officer facing us found the whole thing most amusing. "You're sure, Tommy?" he kept asking. All this was conducted by shouting across the darkness, of course. "I should warn you, Tommy, it's a terrible trench."

'"But we want it all the same," Wiggins told him. "It isn't as if you haven't got plenty of others."

'You see, we knew the enemy supply line had broken down, and we guessed that his men were hungrier than ours. And this man Wiggins had a canny little Welsh sergeant who the previous day had unearthed a veritable treasure trove of charcuterie—sausages, hams, all sorts. No idea where he found it. So Wiggins waited till the wind was in the right direction, then ordered his men to start frying up some bacon, then some sausages. He was relentless. By the time they'd got the bacon really crisp and black at the edges, we'd agreed four pounds of sausages, a pound of ham, a fruitcake and a box of cigars, and lobbed them over, all against their officer's solemn word. Next day we went forward and took forty-five prisoners without firing a shot.'

'Prisoners?' asked Maclean, amused. 'Were they part of the deal?'

Freddie shook his head solemnly. 'Not at all. But after tasting the sausages most of them decided to stay put and hope for seconds.'

The story had been a great success and Sir Robert had roared with laughter, calling the teller a capital joker and rewarding him with a slap on the back as they left the table. But when I came across Freddie Masters in the library that night, the fire low and the room in shadow, I found him in reflective mood.

'Really, Freddie, why on earth do you tell such tales?' I asked. 'I've never heard such nonsense.'

'Ah!' He leaned back in his seat completely unabashed. 'But a good story, nonetheless. You must admit that. There were rumours of some such thing, you know. And it's true that Wiggins was a bright fellow.'

'So how did you really bring in all those prisoners without taking any casualties?'

Freddie Masters grimaced at the question. 'The truth? You want the *truth*? I'm afraid the truth is much less pretty. We were just going forward when what was left of the Boche artillery opened up and hit their own line. Hammered away at it like no one's business for what seemed like an age. By the time we strolled across, the ones who weren't dead were too dazed even to put up their hands, poor bastards.'

He paused, rocking his brandy glass gently in his palm. 'Do you know what 1919 has taught me, old man?'

I shook my head.

'It's taught me that the likes of Mapperley might ask damned-fool questions, but they don't thank you if you give them answers. Not true ones, at any rate.'

'But isn't it up to us to tell them the truth? However unpleasant?'

Freddie Masters looked back at me through the smoke of his cigarette and shrugged. '*You* know the truth, Tom. *I* know the truth. Or we know our own bits of the truth, at any rate. But the likes of Mapperley and Sir Robert? I'm not sure they'll ever know it.'

Sitting there in immaculate dinner dress, slim and rather elegant, Freddie Masters didn't look like a man who'd ever been within twenty miles of a trench.

'And do you know why?' he went on. 'Because they don't want to know. They sent their precious sons out there to do their duty and win their spurs and defend the flag, and God Save the King. So if you point out that they died in rows, in holes smelling of shit, they simply don't hear you. *He's* come back bitter, they think. Or they tell you you're not yourself and suggest a good tonic. Or they begin to sneer and decide there's a bit of the conchie about you.' I watched him shake his head. 'There are thousands and thousands of people in this country who have lost loved ones, and they need to

209

make the best sense they can of it. Believe me, old man, the last thing those people want to hear is the truth.'

He eased himself out of his chair and refilled our glasses.

'I'm sorry, Tom. I didn't mean to give you a lecture. Besides, what do we mean by truth anyway?' He flopped back into his chair. 'Sir Robert and the rest of them are the guardians of the Glorious Dead and theirs is the truth now. They're not going to listen to us.'

'You have a pretty bleak vision of things,' I observed.

'My apologies, old man. I keep forgetting that you've come back a veritable bouquet of sunshine and roses. Tell me, how do you sleep?'

The question startled me.

'I mean is it coincidence that you and I are usually two of the last to bed? I don't know about you, Allen, old chap, but I'm a dreadful coward about bedtime. For two or three months after it was over I just tried to stay awake. What about you? Sweet dreams?'

'Not very often,' I confessed. I didn't add that I found the moment of waking far worse.

'We're not alone in that, you know, Tom. But fellows don't talk about it. And even now I still hope that one more brandy will see me through the night. It never does though.'

I didn't reply. It hadn't really occurred to me that every night, in a million dreams, the shells were still falling.

'The funny thing is,' Freddie went on, 'that when I was actually out there, I don't remember any nightmares at all. Why is that, do you think?'

'Too tired to dream, I suppose.'

'That's probably it.' He drained his glass and grinned. 'And of course if you're actually *in* a nightmare, what is there left to dream about? Still, under the circumstances, one could do without fools like Mapperley bringing the whole thing up again just before bedtime . . .'

*   *   *

Instead of following Freddie to bed that night, I took the key to the darkroom and made my way by candlelight past rows of silent bedrooms to the narrow upper staircase. I'd often walked that way late at night, excited by a picture I'd taken and unable to sleep until it was developed. Once I met Harry as I went. It had been one of those hot nights not long before the Rose Ball and I'd been unable to sleep for thinking about Margot and Julian Trevelyan. That summer had been full of ugly emotions.

It must have been very early in the morning when I bumped into Harry—probably only an hour or so before dawn. The house was hotter the higher you climbed, and I'd been going up the staircase as Harry was coming down. There'd been an unsmoked cigar protruding from his pocket and his dress shirt had been open at the neck. He'd given me a strange look.

'Taking up cigars in secret, old man?' he asked.

'Couldn't sleep,' I replied, embarrassed. 'There's something I'm working on . . .'

'Ah! The smoke and mirrors! Of course.'

Harry had tugged at the neck of his shirt as if to let in more air. In some lights his resemblance to

Margot was very marked. They had the same eyes, the same cheekbones, the same generous mouths. Harry was certainly good-looking, but there was more to him than that. It was his instinctive and boundless self-confidence that made him so attractive. It was that on which his charm was based.

'It certainly is infernally hot, isn't it, old man? Too hot to lie down. I haven't had a wink of sleep all night.'

And he had smiled at me in that way of his, as though he were really smiling about something else. Oddly, the whole incident didn't seem so very long ago.

When I reached the darkroom the key proved reluctant in the lock, as if not turned for some considerable time. The corridor at the top of the house was much colder than the floor below and silent with that sense of emptiness that gathers in neglected places. Inside the room, the air was very still and my candle burned with an unflickering flame. The place smelled musty. The candlelight was enough to show that the room had barely been touched in my absence, and very briefly I felt that sense of dizziness that came to me sometimes, as if the last five years hadn't happened. My old camera waited, shrouded in a leather cover, in one corner of the room, exactly where I'd left it. I had abandoned it deliberately. I'd come to associate it with Hannesford.

Placing my light on the floor, I knelt beside one of the fitted cupboards that lined the walls. The wooden skirting at its base was loose and lifted off as easily as I remembered. From the cavity behind it I retrieved a small leather case, secured with an

212

old belt strap. It struck me that I probably hadn't set eyes on it since that night I'd met Harry on the stairs. But it was too cold to examine it there and then. By the time I locked the darkroom door behind me, it felt as though the cold had crept deep into my bones, and my fingers were filthy with dark grey dust.

In the warmth of my room, I spread the contents of the case across my bed. There were more of them than I remembered, photographs I'd forgotten taking—portraits, landscapes, photographs of Hannesford from every angle. I worked through them without system, studying each as it caught my eye. A picture of the village, very early one morning, mist swathing it like smoke; a view of young boys swimming naked in the pool below the watermill; a party of Hannesford golfers next to the Daimler, all caps and tweeds and smiles. Then there were the preparations for the Rose Ball, the gardeners clipping hedges and girls scrubbing the steps of the terrace; slippered horses on the Hannesford lawns; men at work in the fields. Grinning faces peered back at me, absorbed by the moment, smiling as if the clear skies above them would never darken.

I felt the sadness spilling out from each of them. Harry Stansbury struck a pose, dashing in flannels. Oliver Eastwell smiled at an absurdly small puppy. Julian Trevelyan lolled in the sun by Margot's side, as if nothing could ever deprive him of all the good things that were rightfully his. But as I fumbled through the images the sense of loss went deeper. It wasn't just people. There was loss in the images of motor cars parked in rows at country point-to-points, of the village maypole decked with ribbon,

213

loss in the shire horses cutting furrows beneath the dark eye of the moor. They were all *the past*. Nothing was the same. They were fragments of the world I'd thought we were defending. Yet it was gone already, despite those endless ranks of wasted lives; gone without anyone really noticing its passing.

But the photographs themselves were far better than I remembered. Out at the front I'd come across professionals employed by the ministry, men who spoke in casual jargon of makes and shutter speeds, and explained what they were doing with a cheery assumption of superiority that left me feeling foolish and deflated. I had been an amateur, nothing more.

Yet now I looked at them again, I saw that the jumble of photographs around me amounted to something more than I'd realised. I'd been lucky. I'd captured something I thought was permanent, only to discover it more fleeting and more fragile than the most delicate strip of film. Already time had started to cloud our memories. The first shoots of oblivion were pushing through the soil. Soon the forest would be full-grown.

And what of the present? What things around me now would people look at later and say, *Yes, that's right, that's how it was after the fighting . . .*? For a moment my imagination began to stir, my mind began to reach for images. But I had left the camera behind me quite deliberately, and the thought of taking it up again filled me with doubt. Over time, it had come to be my excuse for wasting my life at Hannesford.

One of the last photographs to go back into the case was a portrait of Margot. On four or five

214

occasions she had insisted on sitting for me. They were, on the whole, respectable attempts—good likenesses, properly composed. But they seemed to me poorly done, too flat, too lifeless. I'd failed to capture that spark that made Margot so vital and so dangerous. They were photographs of a pretty young woman, nothing more. The last one I came to was signed across the back.

To Margot, with love,
Tom

I winced as I recalled it. I'd given it to her one Christmas, the year before the fighting started, when the house was packed with her admirers and her star was at its brightest. The next day I'd found it in the library, still in the place where I'd presented it to her. A few hours later, when it hadn't moved, I quietly returned it to the portfolio from where it had come. Margot had never missed it.

I hesitated with it between my fingers, then made up my mind. The fire was burning low but was warm enough. The photograph burned brightly for a moment and then was gone.

Sunday was one of Mrs Uttley's bad days. I knew it as soon as I went to rouse her and found the old lady already awake, her face drawn and her lips pinched, her attempt at a smile little more than a thin counterfeit. The winter was the worst time for her, and the days when she suffered very badly were becoming more frequent. On such days I knew there was little I could do to ease the pain. Dr Thomson visited regularly and was assiduous in his attentions, but both of us—and our patient too—understood that we could aim only at comfort, not at cure.

That morning, to distract her, I entertained her with tales of my visit to Hannesford Court, with the things I'd seen and done there. I even told her about Freddie Masters's encounter in Germany with Professor Schmidt's son, and the suggestion that the professor might have witnessed some sort of unpleasantness in the days before his death. The vicar's wife listened to it all with her eyes closed, and although she nodded I wasn't sure how closely she was following.

The only question she asked was about Tom. She wanted to know if I found him changed by the war. It was a question that made me hesitate.

'A little, perhaps. I suppose it will take him a while to get used to things. Do you remember how at ease he always was in company? Now he seems quieter, as if everything still feels foreign to him.'

'Well, I suppose he's witnessed some terrible scenes,' Mrs Uttley concurred, her breath coming haltingly. 'I'd like to see him again. If you see him at church, Anne, do please ask him to call.'

But I didn't go to church, at least not directly. The

216

morning was bright and the sky clear, too good a morning to waste. A footpath ran behind the vicarage to a knoll above the village where I could stand with the sun on my face. There had been only a thin drift of snow overnight, enough to whiten the fields and cover the roof of the church without making the paths too difficult. Standing there, surveying the scene and breathing in the freshness of the morning, I was close enough to the church to hear the singing of the hymns. Somewhere in there, Tom would be singing too.

Kind, reliable, ordinary Tom. It was almost impossible to believe he was really there. The maelstrom had carried so much away. But Tom had come through it. It was a miracle I'd never dared imagine.

I waited until the beginning of the last hymn before hurrying down to the church. When the service came to an end I was seated demurely at the back, as though I hadn't missed a moment.

9

On Sunday morning I did what was expected of me and went to church. Anne was there too and I was pleased to go with her afterwards to call on Mrs Uttley. Sunday mornings were slow, slightly formal times at Hannesford Court, and an excuse to be engaged elsewhere appealed. In addition, I suppose I hoped to talk to Anne about the professor's notebook. I'd examined it more closely that morning, but it was as she had said. The pages relating to the last week of the professor's life had been quite deliberately removed. Its significance was less in its contents than in where it had been found.

What was left proved that it had once been a diary of sorts, the dates written by hand and neatly underlined. The first part of each entry was scientific: the English names of butterflies appeared alongside their scientific names, and I guessed those entries were the raw material for the notes in the library. Beneath those sections were brief jottings about the professor's other activities and his observations about Hannesford life. It was easy to see where the missing pages had been torn from the binding.

Perhaps those lost pages were preying on my mind during my visit to the vicarage, for Mrs Uttley seemed unable to settle in my company. Only when I was about to take my leave did her manner change. That was when she decided there was a particular book she wished to show me, and Anne was asked to fetch it from the vicar's study. As soon as she was gone, Mrs Uttley turned to me with sudden vigour.

'Forgive me, Tom, but I did so much want a quick word with you alone. This is one of those days, I'm afraid, when I become a very cantankerous old lady, and very difficult to nurse.'

She raised herself a little on her day bed, waving away my offer of assistance.

'Anne has been telling me about your interest in Professor Schmidt. She says you're worried about some unpleasantness the professor witnessed here at Hannesford. Ever since she told me that, I've been thinking about it. It's been going round and round in my head all morning.'

'The unpleasantness?' I asked, and she nodded.

'You see, I think I know what the professor referred to. I've never spoken of it before, not even to the vicar, and it will be a relief to share it. It has often preyed upon my mind.'

'So something really did happen?' I felt oddly wary. Perhaps part of me still hoped that everything could be neatly explained away.

But Mrs Uttley nodded. 'I'd no idea the professor was aware of it too, but from what Anne was telling me I suppose he must have been. It was an ugly business.'

She paused and a grimace of pain passed across her face.

'You see, Tom, sometimes a vicar's wife is told things by parishioners that they would never dream of sharing with the vicar. A good many women here have confided in me over the years, and I have kept their secrets for them. In many ways my husband is not a very worldly man. I know it is vain of me to say so, but there were times when I thought it better a young girl should talk to me in confidence than to no one at all.'

I took her hand and squeezed it, and she smiled weakly.

'Anne told me you'd seen Mrs Woodward, Tom, so you know about that occasion when her daughter took to her room. Well, there was something else. Something I didn't want to tell Anne.'

Her eyes closed and she swallowed hard, but when she opened them again they were clear and certain.

'Julia Woodward was an unhappy girl, you know. Never very robust. Her father wanted her to be a governess, and her mother hated the idea of her having any education at all. I think she would rather have had her daughter a scullery maid than have ideas above her station. They both bullied Julia in different ways, her father with his shouting and her mother with her silences. In the end she went to school and came back a young lady, but I think she found herself lonelier than ever. She was a nervous young thing and she crumpled easily. She wasn't cut out to be a governess.'

Mrs Uttley paused. There was still no sound of Anne returning.

'Julia Woodward used to call here quite often the summer after she'd finished school. Lady Stansbury had invited her to the Rose Ball, you see, and she was terribly nervous about it. She was to go with her cousin, who was a second lieutenant in the regiment Harry was hoping to join. She used to sit here and tremble about the whole business—she really was all aflutter. So when I didn't see her for a couple of days I was a little surprised and a little worried, and I paid her a visit. In fact, I called two days in a row, and each time her mother said Julia was ill and not receiving visitors.'

'That's right.' I nodded. 'That's what Mrs Woodward told me.'

'But the second time I called, Tom, I caught a glimpse of Julia at her bedroom window. Just when I was leaving, it was. I was only a few yards away, so I could see her quite clearly. And her face was bruised, Tom. Badly bruised. As if someone had beaten her.'

The old lady's hand was still in mine and I felt her fingers tightening a little.

'What did you do?' I asked softly.

'Well, what *could* I do? Julia Woodward didn't go to the Rose Ball, obviously, and I was all set to make a fuss. I thought her father must have taken his fists to her. But the next day I had a note from Julia asking me to call when her mother was out. The swelling was down a little, but she still looked dreadful.'

'And did she tell you what happened?'

Mrs Uttley sighed. 'No, she just begged me not to say anything to anyone. I said that if it was her father who'd hit her like that, the vicar would certainly have a word with him. But she denied it and made me promise not to speak to him about it. She'd managed to hide it from her father, you see, by taking to her room. Anyway, I gave her a lecture about someone having behaved like a brute, and me intending to find out who. Then she broke down. She still wouldn't tell me exactly what had happened, but she said enough for me to understand it had been someone at Hannesford Court who was responsible. In a rage, she said. She said she had provoked it. She said it was her own

221

fault.'

'But that's outrageous!' I exclaimed. 'Are you sure? You could not have misunderstood?'

'I'm afraid not, Tom. She was very clear about it. And not for one moment did I disbelieve her. I remember how she trembled as she spoke of it.'

'But are you sure she meant someone staying at the Court? Not someone from the village?'

The old lady shook her head. 'A gentleman, she said. She was terribly upset.'

'But *who*? Did she give you no indication at all?'

'She wouldn't tell me anything, not even how it had come about. A misunderstanding, that was all she would say.'

Out there in France, before I'd lost myself in the fighting, I would sometimes think of Hannesford. Solid, unchanging Hannesford, a vision floating high above all the squalor and the chaos. But in the vicar's cold front parlour, things looked very different. *Ugly*. That's what Mrs Uttley had called it. *An ugly business*.

'There was nothing to be done,' Mrs Uttley went on. 'Julia was adamant. She said she'd rather die than have it talked about. She begged me over and over again to say nothing, and of course I gave her my word.'

I squeezed her hand again. 'But you've decided to say something now.'

She bit her lip, as if in pain. 'Well, it can't hurt Julia Woodward any more, can it, Tom? And I've always hated to think of some brute masquerading as a gentleman.'

She smiled, as if at her own folly.

'I don't make a very likely vengeful Fury, do I? And it seems such a small thing, given all that's

222

happened since. All those young lads dead. But what's wrong is still wrong, isn't it? It's our duty to remember that. *That's* what we owe to all the men who went out there and died and deserved better. To carry on telling right from wrong.'

She looked away from me, through the window, to her garden still laced with traces of snow. Beyond it, at the crossroads, work would soon begin on Sir Robert's stone memorial.

Only as I was leaving, when it was too late to ask, did I wonder why she'd been so reluctant to share her story with Anne.

*   *   *

That afternoon young Bill Stansbury decided to get up a party for cards. It was Sunday, the weather was grizzly and he'd recently learned a new game called July Cup that he was anxious to try out. 'Not for the grown-ups,' he declared, 'because it can get rather rowdy. But it's all the rage in town, it really is!'

The proposal was seized upon with enthusiasm. Denny Houghton and Lucy Flinders were eager for entertainment, and Margot laughed and said that Sundays were deathly, so why not? Neil Maclean warned everyone that he was a terrible card-player but intended to improve. Freddie Masters was easily roped in, and Laura Finch-Taylor indicated with a smile that she too was not averse to cards.

But I declined to join them, and Bill looked a little put out. I sensed that he was beginning to find me something of a disappointment—not perhaps the cavalier warrior he'd hoped for. Once perhaps I'd have stayed and done my bit. But Bill would survive without me. There were worse things than a dull, drawing-room afternoon. When the card party settled down to play, I slipped quietly out of the house.

I'd left my camera in the darkroom, exactly where I'd found it, but that afternoon it was in my thoughts. Although the brightness of the morning had faded, the light was still good, and I found myself looking about me. Somehow, somewhere, I'd lost my old way of seeing shapes and light. I'd been preoccupied with the business of survival, with the next set of orders, with the welfare of my men; with the cold, with snipers, with listening posts and gaps in the wire. After those, peace had seemed an oddly dreary landscape. But it was a landscape nonetheless, and I began to wonder, for all its disappointments, how it might be captured on a square of film.

First I headed towards the trees, but I was still not entirely comfortable with the silence of the woods. So instead I turned to the outbuildings and the stable blocks where, even on a Sunday, there was a comforting sense of human activity.

To the rear of the house there were signs of neglect I'd never noticed before. Had they always been there? Or had the weeds between the paving stones sprung up only when the men went away? Whatever the answer, the place suited my mood. The reproach of the rusted gutters and the empty stables rang true to me in a way that Hannesford's plush red dining room did not.

At one point I clambered into the loft of one of the stable buildings and peered down into the stable yard below. Unaware of my presence, a young groom was sweeping the yard, handling the broom with a slightly clumsy, high-elbowed action.

224

The man's cap hid his face and his back was turned, and I thought how well the corner of the stable block framed his figure. I liked the man's patient strokes, the curve of his back contrasting with that high elbow, the straight lines of the buildings.

His job complete, the groom straightened and I realised then that he had only one hand. The ungainly sweeping motion was the result of guiding the brush with the stump of his other arm. Still unaware of being watched, the man paused a moment, then disappeared into the stables. And I did not linger either. Despite my coat, I was beginning to feel the cold. As I walked away I was remembering another scene, one both different and the same—the gardens of the sanatorium in Cullingford, and a small figure on crutches moving backwards and forwards against the vast backdrop of the moor.

I set off towards the lake still deep in thought. Remnants of snow lay on the lawns, frozen now and crunching rather than squeaking beneath my feet. The afternoon was overcast and the clouds dark. Dusk would come with a rush. Ahead of me, a solitary figure stood looking out over the water: Susan Stansbury, a fellow refugee from the card table.

'Why doesn't it freeze?' she asked when I came up to her, gesturing at the surface of the lake. The water was still and gunmetal grey.

'It does,' I told her, 'but only on the other side. This side the current below the surface does peculiar things. All that river water rushing in.'

'Of course.' She turned and smiled. 'I wasn't thinking. That's why we were always told as children never to swim from this bank.'

We fell into step and began to make our way along the water's edge.

'Do you remember when Oliver got thrown in here, Tom? By Julian and Harry. He couldn't swim and Freddie Masters had to fish him out. That was years ago. I hardly knew him then.'

'Probably before my time,' I replied, but I didn't find it hard to imagine. It had been Oliver's role in life to be pushed, Harry's to do the pushing.

'You didn't really know Oliver very well, did you, Tom?'

The question embarrassed me. It was as though Susan had read my thoughts. 'I'm beginning to wonder if I ever knew anyone very well,' I told her.

'It isn't true, you know, what you think about Oliver and me.'

I paused then and met her gaze. 'What do I think?' I asked.

'That I didn't love him. That our marriage was all a bit of a charade.' She began to walk again, and after a moment or two I followed. 'I remember how shocked you were when I told you we were engaged. At the Rose Ball, remember?'

Yes, I remembered. Champagne corks. Congratulations. Wide grins. Endless toasts. Harry smirking as if the whole thing were a capital joke. I'd watched it all and had felt a little perplexed by it.

'Nothing made much sense to me that night,' I told her.

'Of course. Margot.'

I nodded. It was the night Margot told me she was going to accept Julian Trevelyan.

'You must have known she was going to marry Julian, Tom. Everyone did.'

226

And it was true. All those years had really just been part of an elaborate courting ritual, and I had been left with nothing but a sense of my own ridiculousness.

'It's funny, isn't it,' I reflected, 'how being aware of our own stupidity doesn't stop us making idiots of ourselves?'

We carried on walking, towards the trees that fringed one end of the lake.

'And you were right,' I went on. 'It never occurred to me that you might be in love with Oliver. Were you?'

'Not at first.' She spoke softly. 'And I never expected to be. I knew he was proposing to me because he had no chance of getting Margot.'

'So why on earth did you accept him?'

'It sounds foolish, but I think it was the way he asked me. He was so pathetically humble about it. And I remember thinking how those others were always so beastly to him. And I suppose I thought if we were married we could both of us get away from Hannesford, from Harry and Julian and their horrible friends. I suppose I thought it would rescue us both. And then of course the war came and everything changed.'

We had come to the edge of the trees. The path led onwards, into the wood, still skirting the water.

'You remember what it was like, Tom. Harry and Julian and the rest of them were so full of bravado, going on about what they'd do when they got to Berlin. And suddenly I saw Oliver was desperately afraid. He *let* me see, you understand. He never showed it to anyone else. Not his parents. Certainly not his friends. He chose me. And I felt ... touched. Honoured by his confidence.'

227

She shrugged. 'But of course he joined up anyway, because everyone else did. He felt he had no choice.'

I didn't say anything. Ahead I could glimpse the boathouse through the trees. Susan was looking at it too, but not really seeing.

'I remember the day he went. I saw the look on his face as the train pulled out, and I prayed, more than I'd ever prayed for anything in my life, that God would look after him and send him home.'

She attempted a weak smile, as though embarrassed at her own naivety.

'He used to write to me, Tom, and his letters were so brave. Not like the ones he sent his mother, which were bluff and hearty and full of how he was eating well and keeping warm. Much braver than those. He used to write about how horribly frightened he was. And I'd read those letters and feel certain my heart would break. It seemed incredible to me then that there'd ever been a time when I didn't care for him. I was terrified I'd never get the chance to tell him properly what I felt.'

We were silent for a little then, until we came up to the old pontoon where the rowing boats had once been moored.

'His leave was awful,' Susan went on. 'Never a moment to ourselves. Always his parents, his mother. It wasn't until his last leave, when we were married, that we were ever truly alone. It was just before the big push. Passchendaele. And at least that time, beyond any doubt, he knew I loved him. He'd never expected me to, you know. Never really expected anyone to love him for himself, the poor dear. Those last three days together . . . I think he thought some sort of miracle had happened to him.'

Her eyes filled with tears but she smiled.

'Do you know, Tom, it sounds wrong, but in a way I'm just so glad he knew. Perhaps if there hadn't been a war we'd have lived together politely for fifty years and neither of us would ever have known. Does that sound wrong?'

'I think perhaps he was a lucky man.' And I meant it. Better to die knowing you've something to lose, that you've made enough of your life to have something worth keeping.

We had come to the boathouse and on a whim I tried the door. After two or three firm pushes it swung open and we peered in.

Inside it seemed time had limped to a halt. The furniture, uncovered, stood where it had always done, as if expecting visitors, and on the sideboard the half-full decanters seemed to have been abandoned without formal leave-taking. But in the years since the Stansbury boys had left it, the place had been claimed by dust, and by the spiders which had spun dense grey webs across the windows. I saw Susan shiver. When we stepped inside, neither of us moved very far from the door.

'Oliver used to tell me a little of what they got up to down here,' Susan mused. 'He said it was a lawless place.'

'I think it was. Young men at play.'

Beneath one of the long sofas something caught my eye and I stooped to pick it up. Remarkably, it was something I recognised: a golden beehive, grey with dust.

'Oliver's,' I said, holding it out to her.

Susan took it and studied it with a sad smile. 'That's right,' she agreed. 'I'd forgotten all about these. Do you remember how proud he was of them? I think someone took them off him at cards in the end, only a day or two after he first wore them. Julian or Harry, perhaps. I can't remember who. I wonder how it ended up here.'

The room felt colder inside than out, and we turned to go. I was the first to break the silence.

'Susan, I know this may sound out of place, but there was something I wanted to ask you about Reggie. About his temper. Do you know if he ever went further than just raising his voice?'

She looked at me, puzzled. 'What on earth do you mean?'

'I mean did he ever lose control of himself? Did he ever raise his hand in anger, to use the old phrase?'

Out there in the cold winter air the question seemed bald and impertinent, and I was embarrassed by it. Susan looked slightly shocked.

'I shouldn't think so. Reggie was never violent. I think his temper blew up too quickly for that. He never bottled anything up for long. Why would you ask such a thing?'

'Oh, it's nothing. Just a conversation I was having with Freddie Masters. I was wondering why Reggie ran away from Hannesford so quickly after that last Rose Ball.'

We had reached the point where the trees gave way to parkland and ahead of us, across the snow-patched lawn, stood Hannesford Court. While we watched, the outside lamps were being lit. Susan seemed to be thinking.

'There *was* something,' she said at last. 'Before he left. He said he'd done something he regretted, that he needed to get away to think things through. I didn't pay much attention to it at the time. I thought it was just Reggie being Reggie.' She paused. 'If you want to know what it was, I suppose you'll have to ask him for yourself.'

*   *   *

At five o'clock, when the last of the light was gone, Bill Stansbury set up the gramophone in the Orangery again, defying the convention that nothing too frivolous or too noisy should be attempted at Hannesford on a Sunday. Hearing the music and the sounds of people enjoying themselves, I felt it was a good innovation. The lure of lively company was strong after my walk in the dwindling winter afternoon; a glass of champagne with Margot or Freddie would be a very acceptable tonic. But on my way downstairs I encountered old Colonel Rolleston, who insisted that I joined him for a whisky and soda in the drawing room. There he explained to me his theories about the future of warfare, mostly based on his own observations of the fight against the Boers. With so many Colonel Rollestons offering their advice through the letters page of *The Times*, I reflected, it was surprising that the war had lasted so long.

But despite the colonel's monologue, once settled in the drawing room I had no desire to move. It was warm and relaxing, and there was a faint scent of white lilies garnered from the hothouse. Most of all, once the colonel had disappeared to dress, it was quiet in a comfortable way: the crackle of the fire, a grandfather clock that chimed the quarters, the mutter of conversation from one corner, where Sir Robert and Horatio Finch-Taylor had their heads together. I didn't

231

much want to make conversation, but I didn't much want to be alone either. In that sense, it was the perfect spot.

Eventually my solitude was disturbed by Freddie Masters and Neil Maclean, both changed for dinner and looking very dapper.

'Cigarette, old man?' Freddie asked, holding out the box. 'Neil here was just telling me there are parts of North America where it is not absolutely obligatory to carry firearms in public. Did you know that?'

I waited for Maclean to respond, but the American just laughed and helped himself to a cigarette.

'Allow me.' Freddie produced his lighter, an elegant affair of green and gold, and lit my cigarette first, then Neil's. Before lighting his own, he let the flame die for a moment.

'Who won the July Cup?' I asked.

'Bill, of course.' Maclean grinned. 'He was the only one who understood the rules. Then he made us play a game called St Petersburg, which he claimed had been banned by the Bolsheviks in Russia. If true, they have my hearty support.'

'Oh, don't start on Russian politics, old man,' Freddie put in. 'You might cause a riot. Allen and I could have been sent to march on Moscow, you know, if some people had had their way.'

But before the conversation could turn to the Bolshevik menace, the sound of voices in the Great Hall told me that Anne had kept her promise and was arriving for dinner. When Lady Stansbury led her into the drawing room, our eyes met and she smiled.

That night the conversation taking place around

me at the dinner table was of the very dullest kind; possibly, I speculated, the dullest ever to take place there. I'd been hoping to speak to Anne, but she was at the far end of the table where Lady Stansbury could talk to her about Reggie. Instead I found myself trapped inside a triangle that had at its points Sir Robert, Horatio Finch-Taylor and the banker, Mapperley. With only Lucy Flinders and the hard-of-hearing Mrs Rolleston as allies, I could find no way of breaking out and had to endure at length Finch-Taylor's views on the stock market and Mapperley's complaints about the miners. I would have paid good money for Violet Eccleston to be seated a little closer. Violet, I was sure, would have given them a run for their money.

And then after dinner my hopes for a private word with Anne were dashed when Lady Stansbury pressed her into partnering Mrs Rolleston at bridge. Eventually I suggested to my hostess that I might save the chauffeur a much longer journey by walking Anne home across the park. She looked at me as if I were mad.

'Don't be absurd, Tom. I'm not having Anne walk to the vicarage at this time of night and in this weather. It's out of the question.'

But at the end of the evening, Anne herself suggested to Lady Stansbury that she should walk; she had a slight headache, she explained, and had often walked the path with a lantern. She would much prefer that to being shaken up in the Daimler.

So a distinctly bemused Lady Stansbury took up my offer, and a little before midnight we set off across the park. I walked with the collar of my topcoat turned up and my shoulders hunched,

233

a storm lantern in one hand. Anne was cloaked and cowled like a monk. After the warmth of Hannesford the first touch of the night air took my breath away.

As we went I told her about my conversation with Mrs Uttley. It occurred to me that I might be betraying a confidence, but it didn't feel like it, not with Anne. We'd both seen too much of mankind's barbarity to be coy with one another, and talking to her was very much easier than talking to anyone else at Hannesford. When we arrived at the vicarage the building stood in darkness, blind eyes reflecting back our lantern.

'I told them not to wait up,' Anne explained. 'I have a latch key.'

We hesitated under the porch, the lantern drawing a yellow circle around our feet.

'Will you come in, Tom?' she asked. 'If the vicar were up, he'd insist you had a tot of something to keep out the cold.'

I hesitated. Five years earlier, I knew, even the suggestion of such a thing would have been unthinkable. But the receding tide of war had left the shore less firm beneath us.

'Thank you,' I muttered, and I wondered if I were blushing. 'But of course I shouldn't. I can tell you all the rest another time.'

I was surprised to feel her hand on my elbow, firm and decisive.

'Come in,' she said. 'It's stupid not to. Besides, you might be able to breathe some life into the fire.'

I went in a little hesitantly, not at all sure I should be agreeing. But Anne's certainty had surprised me. It had always been me who was the confident one.

In the vicar's front parlour, while Anne lit the lamps, I roused a spark of life from the embers in the grate. Then we knelt together on the hearth rug, still in our coats, as close to the flame as possible. When we spoke, it was barely above a whisper.

'Go on,' she said. 'I want to hear the rest.'

So I finished relating the story Mrs Uttley had told me and moved on to what Susan had said about Reggie's sudden departure from Hannesford.

'*Something he regretted*. Those were the words Reggie used.'

'Surely not,' she breathed. 'Surely Reggie couldn't have done such a thing? Lose his temper with the professor, yes, but hit a woman?'

'If it was him who struck the professor, that would make sense of the stolen notebook. And according to Mrs Woodward, Julia was consistent in rejecting Reggie's advances.'

'What are you going to do? Will you ask him about it?' Anne looked up at me and I saw the fire reflected in her eyes.

'I suppose so.'

'I don't envy you.' She laughed but I knew she was being serious. We were silent for a few seconds after that, and Anne shivered, then drew a little closer to the fire. The movement brought her shoulder against mine. Instinctively we both moved slightly apart.

'This thing with Julia Woodward, it's so horrible, isn't it, Tom? Not like France. Horrible in a different way.'

She raised her hand to brush a tendril of hair away from her face, and I felt her weight press against me again. When her hand returned to the

235

ground, the pressure did not wholly dissipate.

'I suppose really it's none of our business,' I said softly.

'But isn't that what some people said about Belgium?' she asked. 'You can't let the bullies win, can you? In the end we had to fight. We had to do the right thing. However awful it proved.'

Her face was very close to mine, close enough for me to smell her scent. In the firelight her features seemed softer, almost serene. Beautiful, even.

'And in some ways the war was so *simple*, wasn't it, Tom? We didn't have to think very much. Remember what Reggie told you?' She lowered her eyes. 'About finding himself happier in France than he'd ever been before? A little part of me understands that.'

She said it very quietly, as if it were something shameful, something that she had harboured in her conscience for a very long time.

I waited and said nothing, and slowly, a bit hesitantly at first, Anne began to tell me about the time when she realised she was never going back to Hannesford Court. It was in a hospital in France, she said, in the spring of 1918, the first time she'd ever thought the war might be lost. So swift was the enemy thrust that in the space of a few days her hospital had gone from well to the rear of the fighting to being almost on the front line, almost in range of the guns.

'And the casualties, Tom . . . I'd never known anything like it. We were simply overwhelmed. We became little more than a clearing station, really, trying to get men on to the trains in a state where they might perhaps, if lucky, survive the journey. There was no nursing them. There was no time.

My job was to assess them as they came in. We couldn't treat everyone, you see. We had to decide who we would save. *I* had to decide. *This one for the train, this one for bandaging, this one through to the surgeons. This one, no point.'*

She paused, as if remembering, her eyes still focused on the fire. Seeing her so weary, so drained, I wanted to reach out and place a hand on her shoulder.

'But I never even hesitated,' she went on. 'There was no time for qualms or doubts. Everything had become simple. Life or death. No shades of grey. I seemed to have so much energy, I could go on for ever. I hadn't slept properly for days but I felt in total control. I was doing it well, too, I knew that. Making a difference.

'And that was when it hit me. There, in that slaughterhouse. I was fighting with my last ounces of strength a battle I knew I couldn't win—and do you know what, Tom? For the first time in my life I felt truly free. It was a terrible shock. It was as if, before that day, I'd never really been alive, I'd just been floating along with the current.'

She looked up at me and there was something in her eyes, like someone seeking absolution.

'Isn't that unspeakable, Tom? To discover myself content amid such terrible suffering?'

And looking at her then, her eyes slightly misty, searching mine, I felt a surge of tenderness unlike anything I'd ever felt before. I wanted to reach out and touch her cheek, to stroke away the memories.

'Not unspeakable,' I said. 'It was part of surviving.'

In reply I felt her place her hand over mine. I felt the pressure of her fingers. There was something in her eyes I couldn't read. But before I could speak, she turned her eyes to the fire again.

'You know, I cried that night, when I was finally by myself. I don't know why. I'd never cried before.'

'Exhaustion,' I told her, although I knew it was grief. Not for her patients. For herself. I didn't tell her there had been times out there, with the shells falling and casualties high, when I too had cried. Not straight away. Afterwards, in the rear, when I was finally alone. Grief for the young man I'd lost, the one who still flinched at the sight of death.

One of the coals in the grate tumbled away from the flame and we both jumped a little, then reached for the poker at the same time.

'After you,' I whispered. Our faces were only inches apart.

She leaned further forward and manoeuvred the coal back into place. The urge to draw her back so that she was close to me, resting against me, was almost more than I could bear.

But then I remembered where we were. I thought of the vicar asleep upstairs. Anne must have felt me draw back.

'What is it?' she asked, studying my face.

'I should be on my way, Anne.'

She straightened a little, moved away. 'Yes, of course.'

Suddenly we were both getting to our feet, both of us awkward.

'Thank you for walking me home, Tom.'

'It was my pleasure.'

Our eyes met and we smiled again, more comfortably this time.

'You're a good man, Tom Allen,' she said. 'Now go. We can talk again tomorrow.'

Out in the sleeping village, and in the woods beyond, I found the silence didn't trouble me. I could hear my feet crisp against the frost and hear my own breath as I walked; I could feel the blood running warm in my body. A beautiful night. The fear could wait until I slept.

* * *

Freddie Masters was still up, alone by the brandy decanter, when I got back. I was pleased to join him for a little; I felt too alert and energetic to draw the evening to a close. But that evening Freddie was a little quieter than usual and for once I was the more talkative. When I finally said good night and left him, he watched me go with an expression that was distinctly quizzical.

But even after that, I couldn't sleep; my brain was too active and I had a fancy to look again at the photographs from the night before. But that morning I'd returned them to the darkroom, and it was a long way to go to fetch them back. So instead I lay and looked at the ceiling and thought of how cold the vicarage had become, how small the fire . . .

Eventually I took a book from my bedside and tried to read. It was the volume of Keats I'd brought back from Mrs Woodward's cottage, and as I leafed through it my thoughts returned to Julia Woodward. The gossips said she'd taken her own life. Was that really true? Because her cousin had died at the front? Or because of something that had happened to her at Hannesford while the rest of us were looking the other way? If Reggie was responsible for such despair then he deserved to answer for it, regardless of his injuries.

The volume between my fingers was an attractive one, generously laid out, but the most memorable things I found there that night were not poems. I'd begun to turn the leaves idly, not really concentrating on the verses, when I came across a flower pressed between its pages: a simple red clover, its colours only a little faded. The flower's juices had marked the paper slightly, and I felt saddened by the thought of Julia Woodward placing it there, the memento of a happy day somewhere in the meadows. Her happiness had been too fleeting. In the end Hannesford had betrayed her. Perhaps it had betrayed us all.

It was only when I was about to put the book aside that I noticed the handwriting on the title page. Neat, careful writing that seemed vaguely familiar. Handwriting that was very much on its best behaviour.

To my sweet apparition of the woods, in the hope that some day you might feel for me one tenth of the passion you feel for Mr Keats.
With all the unruly, unrepentant love of your very own

RJKS

Reginald John Kendall Stansbury. Reggie. I read the inscription a second time, even spoke it aloud in an attempt to understand its import. Despite the evidence before me, I could hardly believe Reggie had written such a thing. Sullen, silent Reggie.

But then again, why not? Just because there was real honesty and emotion in the words? Reggie in love. It was a strange thought.

240

When I finally set the book down I still wasn't sure what to make of the inscription. But I'd begun to conclude that I didn't know Reginald Stansbury half as well as I'd imagined.

*   *   *

Sleep, that night, proved determined to elude me. Some time before dawn I gave in to my wakefulness and rose to fetch the box of photographs. I went cursing the cold and my own folly, and when I reached the darkroom, overcome with impatience, I placed the old case on the workbench and began to rummage through its contents. There was one particular picture I wanted to see again. Had I imagined it? No, there it was, between two portraits of Margot. A photograph of Anne Gregory arranging flowers.

I placed it under the light and studied it closely. The previous night I'd flicked past it without paying any particular attention. As a composition it was good enough, and the lighting was satisfactory, but it had not stood out. This time I looked at it more closely, comparing past and present. This time, perhaps for the first time, I really studied Anne's face.

And to my surprise, the past confirmed the present. Those eyes ... How had I not noticed them before? All that feeling ... She had been someone with a talent for evading notice. But those eyes! How could I not have been struck by them? At the vicarage I'd thought I was seeing them for the first time. But there they were, in my own photograph: clear, striking, direct. Everything else in the picture—the flowers, her hands, her face—

gave way to them. They were the living, vivid centre of the scene. Beside them, the portraits of Margot seemed doubly superficial and devoid of emotion.

As I tidied the pictures back into the box, I shivered slightly. All those photographs bearing witness to how little I had seen.

Then, as I made my way downstairs with the box under my arm, I heard the squeal of a hinge and a door at the far end of the corridor opened. I paused instinctively and the figure of a woman emerged wrapped in some sort of dark peignoir. She carried a candle, but at first, as she closed the door softly behind her, her face was turned away from me. Then she looked up and saw me there, and I realised it was Laura Finch-Taylor. The room she was leaving was undoubtedly Bill Stansbury's.

I had no idea what reaction I expected from her under such circumstances, but she hesitated for only a fraction of a second before continuing calmly towards me down the corridor. Before we passed she met my eye and arched one eyebrow.

'How very like old times, Captain Allen,' she murmured.

She said it without a trace of embarrassment.

*   *   *

I'd spent the night before the Rose Ball lying awake too. I'd been thinking about Margot, trying to decide exactly what my feelings were. I could imagine no tranquil future happiness with Margot, no easy contentment, no meeting of minds. Such thoughts were absurd. I knew that. And yet I couldn't rest for wretchedness at the idea of Julian Trevelyan taking her in his arms. I tried to close my eyes, but sleep would not come.

It must have been about four in the morning when I heard a door shutting in the corridor outside, and then a patter of footsteps. It was, of course, not unknown at country house gatherings for the hours before dawn to witness a certain discreet realignment of sleeping arrangements, and I had learned not to be curious. But there had been something about the way that door was flung shut that disturbed me slightly. It was so very flagrant, so very far from discreet; and surely there was something a little wild about those vanishing footsteps. After a moment of hesitation I slipped from my bed and peered into the corridor in the direction from which the sounds had come.

Of course I was too late. Whoever it was whose footsteps I'd heard, they had already disappeared. My room was next door to Harry's, and it struck me that it might have been Harry's door that had slammed. I waited for a second or two and was about to retire when something made me look in the other direction. There, at the other end of the corridor and mostly in shadow, Harry was watching me, smiling.

'Good morning, Tom,' he whispered, perfectly relaxed. He was still in evening dress but his tie was undone, hanging loose around his neck. 'Up early?'

Before I could reply, from very close to where Harry was standing, came the sound of another door clicking shut.

I waited until the following day to check, but I already knew it had been Laura Finch-Taylor's room that Harry was leaving.

I didn't sleep well after Tom's late visit to the vicarage. Although I was tired enough, my thoughts wouldn't settle and at first I slept only in snatches. Yet somehow I awoke feeling refreshed, and on opening the shutters found the dark shoulder of the moor transformed and softened by snow. The weather seemed to suit my mood: crisp and clean and bright with promise. I had visits to pay on Mrs Uttley's account that morning, and even though the chill had crept into my bedroom so that my breath clouded the air as I dressed, I was looking forward to the exercise. I would wrap up warm and walk quickly. My path would take me quite close to Hannesford Court.

Outside, the sound of snow beneath my boots and the raw air against my cheeks helped to keep my thoughts practical. I didn't really want to think about the previous evening. In that clear, winter light, it had already begun to seem unreal, as if the firelight had created a world of confidences and closeness that existed only while the flames still flickered. By daylight it all seemed hard to believe, and I blushed at the thought of it. I had leaned against Tom's shoulder. For a moment I'd even thought . . .

Ahead a blackbird fluttered from the hedgerow, leaving a little cascade of snow behind it. I watched it go. No, I wouldn't think of my evening with Tom. I had a life to lead, one that I must make for myself. Surely I'd seen too much of the world to allow my plans to become muddled by a pair of smiling brown eyes.

Besides, my conversation with Tom had brought back all sorts of things I didn't want to remember.

244

Things about that summer, about the Rose Ball. My naivety, my foolishness. Even the joy I'd felt in those summer months was painful to look back on: perhaps more painful than the rest. And Tom had been unaware of it all. His thoughts had been elsewhere, and a part of me still blamed him for it.

It was strange, in the midst of that snowy landscape, to remember the Rose Ball. I'd been a different person that summer, a person I barely recognised. The week of the ball was always my busiest. It was the week when the Stansbury family turned their backs on London and returned to the joys of country life; a week when the nights were short and the evenings long and the scent of roses seemed to grow headier with every day that passed; a week when the sun always shone and the mercury rose and tradesmen rushed to and fro like bees made drunk with pollen. Hedges were trimmed and flowers staked, and the lawns were combed to velvet perfection by patient, leather-shod ponies. A week of excitement and energy and expectation. There was no other part of the year quite like it. Its magic was intoxicating.

And the professor? During the quiet days early in the summer I'd enjoyed his company, but that final week I'd been so breathless, so caught up in other things, I'd had no time to think about him. I couldn't even remember seeing him during the ball itself. The first guests had arrived while the sun was still high above the horizon, awkward and incongruous in their evening clothes with the day still so hot. But soon the carriages began to arrive with a rush, and the guests had spilled out over the terrace and on to the lawns. The professor must have been there in that crush, but I couldn't remember where. The band was playing as the night fell, and the lanterns

245

in the trees looked like strange moons. Everything had been perfect. It was almost impossible to believe that while the dancing was at its height something so contemptible had been happening down by the donkey bridge.

Who would have treated an old man in such a way? Surely no one I knew. Visitors to Hannesford did not strike other guests. Yet there had been a look on the professor's face as he tottered up those steps; I had seen at once his distress, the shock in his eyes, his shortness of breath . . .

Who could I vouch for? All evening I'd been watching the party move around me. Surely I must have noticed who was absent in the minutes before the professor died? Reggie Stansbury, for instance . . . He'd been present throughout, hadn't he? I remembered him dancing rather sullenly with a friend of Margot's not long before the professor's death. Could he have slipped away after that, down to the river? I couldn't be sure. Then there was Oliver Eastwell. Everyone had been toasting his engagement. Surely, of all people, he had been in the public gaze throughout. Freddie Masters? I'd seen him early on. He had brought me a glass of champagne on the terrace as the evening was turning golden. And later that night, towards the end of things, he'd bumped into me and said he was looking for Oliver. So perhaps Oliver hadn't been there all the time after all . . .

No, it was too difficult. I hadn't been taking notes. And that evening my eyes had been very much on one person. He at least, I knew, had not been absent from things around the time of the professor's death.

10

That morning I was oblivious to the snow, locked in the darkroom, frowning in the artificial gloom. Being there again was like stirring up the dust of an ancient tomb, revealing objects and artefacts carefully placed there by forgotten hands. Except those hands had been my own, and it was my own past I was uncovering. Everywhere else the world had changed, but that room had waited for me. Nothing had moved, nothing had altered. It was an eerie feeling.

To my amazement, the negatives had survived. It had been hard to imagine that they would. The uncertain alchemy of chemicals and light, the fragility of film ... Less robust, perhaps, even than human memory. But there they were, intact, complete in all their details—and ordered in a way memories can never be. I rolled up my sleeves and began to examine them.

I emerged only once, to visit Mrs Hodge, the housekeeper, in the servants' hall. Much to that lady's consternation, I had questions about housekeeping. I think she thought the fighting had turned my mind.

After that I remained out of sight for most of the morning. When I was finally finished, just after eleven, I went in search of Freddie Masters and found him in the billiard room, quietly practising cannons.

'Hello, old man!' Freddie greeted me cheerfully. 'Come to pot a few balls? A peculiarly soothing way to pass the time, you know. And nowadays I usually have the place to myself at this hour. Although obviously I'm delighted to see *you* here, old fellow.'

I took a cue from the rack and regarded it absently. 'I was hoping to talk to you about the professor,' I told him.

Masters nodded, apparently unsurprised. 'Still barking up that tree, eh? I rather thought it was still on your mind.'

My instinct was to be open with him, but for some reason I didn't want to tell him all about Julia Woodward. It seemed too intrusive, almost indecent. But I did have something I needed to ask.

'Look, Freddie, I know it's a long time ago, but can you remember what you were doing on the Saturday before the Rose Ball?'

He paused, stretched over the table. 'I shouldn't think so, old man. Can you?' He played a tricky cannon with perfect precision.

'I think I can. You see, I've been looking through all the photographs I took that week, working out what was going on here each day. The negatives are all in order, so they form a sequence. The Saturday was the day the professor wrote to his son, remember? And the day he witnessed . . . whatever it was he witnessed.'

'If you say so . . .' Masters chalked his cue, his head angled slightly, waiting for me to go on.

'The day I'm thinking of was a very hot one. The professor was out with his butterfly net, and Julian and Margot were around, and so was Reggie, because I saw all of them down by the lake at different times. I've been trying to remember who else was here. Tell me, what day did you and the Everson boys go off to that horse sale?'

Freddie's face lost its guarded expression. 'My

248

word! I'd forgotten all about that. It was certainly around that time, wasn't it? You think it was the same day?'

'I'm sure of it. Have a look at these.' I handed Freddie a small pile of photographs. 'Recognise this fellow?'

It was a picture of a young man in blazer and cravat, leaning against the bonnet of a motor car and smoking a cigarette, apparently unaware of being photographed. The picture was taken from slightly behind him in such a way that both car and figure were dwarfed by the massive backdrop of Hannesford Court. The next photograph in the sequence was taken from a different angle, and Freddie's face, unlined and serene, was clearly visible.

Freddie raised an eyebrow. 'Recognise him? Barely. I think he was lost in action. I miss him sometimes. How is it I've never seen these before?'

I shrugged. 'I don't suppose I developed them until a day or two later. Probably not till the night before the Rose Ball.'

'They're good. Very good.' Freddie was moving through the pile, giving each his full attention. The next half-dozen were taken from a distance and showed others gathering by the same vehicle. 'It was the break-up of that fellow's racing stable near Bearhampton, wasn't it? There was quite a crowd of us. We took two cars—the Daimler, and Tippy Hibbert's old Lanchester. But I couldn't tell you what day it was.'

'No need. Look at the next one.'

Freddie turned to an image of two young housemaids beating a carpet in the stable yard. One of them was just preparing to strike, and the other was smiling, apparently about to speak. The photograph captured the expressions on their faces, a fragment of laughter and light-heartedness captured for ever against the heavy darkness of the carpet and the lighter stones of the stables beyond. The effect was oddly moving, an insignificant moment turned by the camera into something meaningful and memorable. Yet I barely remembered taking it. Finding it again surprised me with a sudden wistfulness.

'You lot were taking ages to set off,' I explained, 'so I went for a wander and came across those two at work. It makes a good photograph, doesn't it?'

'It makes an excellent photograph.' Masters was still looking at it.

'Well, I showed it to Mrs Hodge and she's prepared to swear that picture was taken on a Saturday. At Hannesford there's a fixed time and place for everything, you know, including the beating of carpets.'

Freddie moved to the next photograph in the sequence. Two motor cars were lined up on the gravel, the occupants waving at the house. I'd been too far away to capture their faces, but somehow the picture brought back to me the smell of polish and motor oil and hot leather, the little whoops of excitement as they pulled away.

'So who went?' I asked him. 'There was you, the Everson boys and Tippy Hibbert. Can you remember who else?'

'That fellow Cartwright who was killed in the Dardanelles. That's him there, with his back turned. And Buttercup and Daisy Flinders, of course. Let me think. . . . I'm sure there was someone else. . .'

'Harry?'

250

He shook his head. 'No, he didn't want to come. I remember being surprised. He seemed oddly keen to stay behind.'

'What about Oliver Eastwell?'

'No, not Oliver either.' Again Freddie sounded very certain. 'I suppose he stayed to moon after Susan. Or possibly Margot. Who knows? And, as you say, Reggie didn't come with us. Said he had a prior engagement. I remember that clearly because he was in such a good mood. You tend to remember Reggie's good moods.' Suddenly he snapped his fingers. 'Of course! That's it!'

'Who else?'

'Young Bill Stansbury, of course. He was only a lad then. He went in the Lanchester with Tippy Hibbert and the girls. Every time Buttercup spoke to him, he used to blush up to his ears.'

It was strange, but once Freddie said it, I began to remember. They had been gone all day, arriving back with tales of stopping at an inn and drinking cider on the river bank. And while they'd been away . . .

'So, Allen, old man . . .' Freddie began to line up a shot but seemed to think better of it. 'Are you going to tell me what you're thinking?'

But I wasn't. Not just then. There was still too much I didn't understand.

*　　　*　　　*

Shortly after that I drove over to the vicarage in the two-seater. I found Mrs Uttley sitting in one of the armchairs near the fire, and on my arrival she called excitedly for Anne.

'Look, dear,' the old lady exclaimed when she

251

appeared, 'Tom's here with a motor car and wants to know if you can be spared for lunch. Isn't that exciting? I've told him that Miss Thomson is due to sit with me, so there's really nothing at all to keep you here . . .'

'Of course, Miss Gregory may have other plans,' I pointed out.

But Miss Gregory did not. If I could allow her a few moments to change . . .

We drove to the George at Hanbury. I was reluctant to go further in case it snowed again and made the road over the moor impassable. Even as it was, the lane that led to Hanbury was a little treacherous and I took it slowly. Neither of us felt the need to refer to the previous evening, but the silence between us as I drove was comfortable and companionable. As we dropped down into Hanbury, I began to tell her about the inscription I'd found in Julia Woodward's book.

'It certainly took me aback,' I confessed when we'd been shown to a table in the old panelled dining room. 'I'd begun to see Reggie in such a bleak light, you see. But that note is so, well, *tender*, I suppose. I'm sure the whole thing is just some sort of misunderstanding.'

Looking up from the menu at just that moment, I thought I detected a trace of scepticism in Anne's eye.

'I was thinking like that too, Tom. But it doesn't work. Someone *did* hit the professor, and someone *did* hit Julia Woodward. We can't escape that.'

She looked around, making sure that we were not overheard. But the dining room was busy enough for our conversation to go unnoticed.

'I was just trying to make it all go away, you see.'

252

She met my eyes with perfect frankness. 'And do you know why? Because I didn't *want* to believe that something horrible happened to Julia.'

She swallowed hard.

'What does it say about us, Tom, about all of us, if it did? What does it say about Hannesford if someone could hit her like that and then just rejoin the rest of us, and no one notice anything at all?'

I let my eyes wander around the room. It was market day at Hanbury and the panelled dining room of the George was busy with well-to-do farmers and the like, busy getting on with their lives. Sturdy, honest folk. Yet I knew what Anne had said was true. I too would have found it much pleasanter to believe in an Eden free of serpents.

To change the subject, I told Anne about my morning in the darkroom and my conversation with Freddie Masters, about why I thought the Saturday before the Rose Ball was so significant.

'Whatever the professor saw, he saw it on that Saturday, and that was the day when most of the party were away at Bearhampton. What about you, Anne? Can you remember anything about that day?'

She seemed to hesitate before replying. 'I don't think so,' she said, frowning slightly. 'It's so long ago. But I do remember them going off to look at the horses.'

'Anything else? Can you recall what the others were up to that afternoon?'

She looked down, still a little furrow between her eyes.

'I don't think I can be much help. All those days seem to merge into one, don't they, Tom? What were *you* doing that day?'

So I told her what I could remember: about seeing Margot and Julian by the lake, and Reggie in the woods nearby; about sneaking off by myself for a time; about the professor finding me in the rose garden and asking questions about who I'd seen near the boathouse. And if I didn't tell her why I'd been lurking in the rose garden, or why I'd been in no mood to pay the professor much attention, it was because I'd decided that reminiscences about my romantic agonies could be of no interest to anyone but myself.

'And was that the day Julia Woodward went home so distressed?' Anne asked.

'I think it must have been, according to her mother. So let's imagine for a moment that the professor saw something that afternoon. A lot of people weren't at Hannesford that day. If Mrs Uttley's right and Julia Woodward had some sort of confrontation with someone who was staying at Hannesford Court, that narrows it right down. So, if we can work out what everyone was doing that afternoon, what Harry and Reggie were doing, for instance . . .'

'Tom! Please!' To my surprise, her tone was sharp. 'All this is too ghoulish. I really don't think it's possible for us to play detective after all this time. This isn't a game.'

'But, surely . . .' I felt rebuffed. 'Haven't you just told me we can't pretend nothing happened?'

'And I do think you should talk to Reggie about it all. It's just I think it's too late for us to start working out alibis.'

I didn't agree. I hadn't wanted to revisit the past, but somehow I'd found myself tangled in its threads. Around us the dining room of the George

254

was still busy, but I was aware our voices had risen slightly.

'But, Anne, if we rule out all the young men who went to Bearhampton that day, we're left with Harry and Reggie, Julian Trevelyan and Oliver Eastwell. Now I had a word with Susan before I came out and reminded her of the day of the bloodstock sale. She wasn't sure, but she thought she'd spent that afternoon with Oliver. She says they went for a walk. I haven't had a chance to speak to Margot, but I suppose it's likely she was with Julian most of that day too.'

'What about the older men? Sir Robert's friends? People like the Finch-Taylors?'

'But most of them wouldn't have come till the Monday—you remember how it used to work. It was only Harry and Margot's friends who made a week of it.'

'So that leaves Reggie,' Anne concluded.

'And Harry.' I said it lightly. Golden Harry. Even to think such a thought at Hannesford was sacrilege. Perhaps that was why I'd been so eager to drive out of the village.

'No, not Harry,' Anne replied, with a firmness that surprised me. I had assumed she was no more an adherent to the myth of Harry's greatness than I was.

'Why not? I mean, it could have been him.'

But Anne seemed certain. 'No. Harry had his faults, Tom. But not violence. Whatever you think of him, that couldn't be true.'

'Honestly,' I assured her, 'I'm not trying to cast aspersions on anyone's good name. Certainly not Harry's, who isn't here to defend himself. But I also found this . . .'

Our coffee had been cleared away and I was able to slide the volume of Keats across to her, open at the page where the pressed flower lay.

'First, read those lines I've marked.'

At these voluptuous accents, he arose
Ethereal, flush'd, and like a throbbing star
Seen mid the sapphire heaven's deep repose;
Into her dream he melted, as the rose
Blendeth its odour with the violet,—
Solution sweet:

Anne smiled. 'I remember that scene. Are you trying to embarrass me, Tom?'

'Now look in the margin. There. I noticed it this morning.'

The words had been written in pencil and had subsequently been erased. But their impression on the page was still visible. Next to those lines of verse, someone in the past had written the words:

Sweeter even than violets.

Anne pushed the book back to me.

'And what are we supposed to make of that?' Her tone wasn't particularly encouraging. But I went on anyway.

'I know it's hard to tell, but I don't think that's Reggie's handwriting. It could be Harry's though.'

'Yes, it probably could. But it could be anyone's really. It could be Julia's.'

I looked at it again. 'It's a man's hand, surely?'

Anne shrugged. She seemed a little listless, I thought, as though I were playing a rather silly game.

256

'It could have been any lecherous old colonel in the last fifty years, relaxing after dinner at Hannesford. I'm not sure what you're trying to say, Tom.'

I felt deflated. Suddenly I wasn't sure, either.

'I just thought . . . Well, it's the page where she put the flower. I suppose I imagined a lover might have written it, perhaps when they were out in the fields somewhere. A sort of playful compliment.'

But Anne had gone quiet and I felt that by playing the detective I'd overstepped some invisible mark. After all, we were talking about real people, real suffering. She was right to say it wasn't a game.

When we drove back to Hannesford our silence had a different quality to it, and when I dropped Anne at the vicarage she did not suggest that I came inside. As I left the village behind, I wished to blazes that Freddie Masters had never said a word to me about the professor and his letter.

My light, optimistic morning had turned into a bleak afternoon.

I watched Tom go and felt ashamed. Over lunch my good mood had evaporated, and I'd been short with him. But it hadn't been his fault. Up till then I'd found the story of the professor's altercation on the bridge as disturbing as he had. But that morning it wasn't what I wanted to talk about. Not with Tom. All that casting back, trying to pull secrets out of the shadows ... In the bright, bustling sanctuary of the George I'd felt cold and anxious. The past could be an uncomfortable place. There were things buried there it was better not to uncover.

And yet, perhaps Tom was right about that Saturday, that long hot afternoon after the others had driven away ... I remembered it more clearly than I'd admitted. The house had been so quiet, and the grounds of Hannesford very still in the sun. Could such a day really have cloaked something so sordid and despicable? Could the heat and the haze and the murmur of wood pigeons have blinded us all to such a thing? It was hard to imagine. In fact, it was hard to imagine anything very shabby or tawdry hiding itself beneath all that mid-summer perfection.

I could remember standing at my bedroom window that afternoon, looking out over the empty lawns from the very top of the house. The gardens were breathless, but up there I could feel the faintest of breezes brush against my skin. What had I seen as I looked out? A landscape bleached by sunlight, shadow made deep by the thickness of the trees. Nothing that would have helped Tom answer his questions. But I had not really been looking. My

258

thoughts had all been on the room behind me: its stifling heat, the stabbing white light where the shutters parted; the watching, questioning darkness that lay beyond. I'd been full of wild emotions that day, feelings that thrilled and frightened me. I'd called up a storm and I would ride out its tempests.

I'd stayed looking out of the window for only a few moments before reaching out and closing the shutters against the light.

When I returned the two-seater to the stable block after my trip to the George, I found Margot waiting for me, dressed for motoring.

'Mother's gone to the Kirkpatricks' in the Daimler,' she explained, 'and Neil and Freddie and Susan have gone off in Neil's car to investigate those diggings they were doing on the moor in the summer. Everyone else is out with the guns. And now I've had a message saying that Mrs Bramley is a bit poorly, so I wondered if you'd be a dear, Tom, and drive me over to Stonebridge so I can visit her? Of course, if you need to come in and get warm first . . .'

Mrs Bramley had been the housekeeper at Hannesford when the Stansbury children were small, and in retirement she had retained a place in their affections. She had always struck me as quite an acerbic old lady, but perhaps a spoonful of vinegar had been the right medicine for her employer's unruly brood. Harry and Margot in particular had always seemed unfailingly fond of her.

I liked to drive, and in former times the two-seater had not been so readily available: the young men of Harry's crowd had all been keen motorists. So it did not strike me as a great sacrifice to go out again in Margot's company. After all, I was well wrapped against the cold.

'So Susan has gone out to look at those diggings, has she?' I asked as we nosed out into the country lanes. 'I didn't know that was her cup of tea.'

'It isn't.' I was aware of Margot looking at me curiously. 'But I rather think Freddie Masters

260

might be.'

It took a moment for the implications of that to sink in.

'I'm sorry, are you saying you think Susan might be keen on Freddie?' The idea was entirely new to me.

'Well, I think she likes him very much. Haven't you noticed how often they are together? Since the others died, you know, Freddie has been something of a rock. Susan has seen a good deal of him in London. People don't realise it at first, but Freddie's terribly *competent*. I think Susan's come to rely on him quite a lot.'

'But what about Oliver? Susan was telling me only yesterday . . .'

'How much she misses him? Well, I think that's true too. But it's been more than two years now and, if you think about it, there aren't many men like Freddie around. He's rich, he's got a promising career, he had a very good war and he's ever so popular . . . Susan must realise he won't wait for her for ever.'

'Wait for her?' I blinked and took a corner slightly too fast.

'Oh, Freddie has been in love with Susan for years. Long before Oliver showed any interest. But Freddie never knew what to say. I think that's why he used to clown around so much, the poor fish. Showing off, I suppose. And then, before he even knew he had a rival, Oliver had blundered in and scooped the pool.'

I thought again of that night at the Rose Ball, the crowds arriving, drifting out into the gardens in the early evening sunlight. Susan had been at the door, next to her mother, welcoming guests. And

261

Freddie? Hadn't it been him who made a fuss of seizing champagne from a footman and carrying it out to someone on the terrace? It was a typical piece of Masters showmanship, carried out with deliberate, ostentatious gallantry.

After that I couldn't remember seeing Freddie again until much later. Surely he'd been present when news of Oliver and Susan's engagement broke? I tried to recall the scene but could only remember Oliver's face, flushed pink with triumph. So perhaps it was not surprising that Freddie had been walking alone in the woods that night; not surprising he had turned his back on the Rose Ball, and had been in no mood for company when he saw the professor below him on the bridge. Poor Freddie. He'd had to watch the crowds toast Susan's engagement to someone she didn't love. And then he'd had to watch her fall in love with her own husband . . . But he had waited. I felt humbled by such constancy. Compared to that, my own travails seemed poor stuff indeed.

I enjoyed that afternoon with Margot. Away from Hannesford society, in the fresh, open countryside, she seemed calmer and less flirtatious, and her little joke with the glove seemed forgotten. I felt again something of the bond that grows up between people who know each other well enough for certain things to remain unspoken. We talked about the first time I'd come to Hannesford, those early days of our acquaintance on which the shadows of later tragedies fell less sombrely. Then we discussed mutual friends in London, laughing at their quirks, enjoying a shared awareness of their eccentricities.

The visit to Mrs Bramley was entertaining too.

The old housekeeper denied being poorly with great vehemence, and described her niece, who had been responsible for the rumour, in language that was decidedly piquant.

'Just a little deaf today,' she said fiercely and rather loudly, then went on to rail against Lloyd George (whom she considered insufficiently English), the local blacksmith (insufficiently courteous) and the Kaiser (responsible for munitions girls who did not know their places). When she began to berate us both for not yet being married, our eyes met in embarrassment.

'I *was* nearly married...' Margot blushed slightly as she attempted to answer the charge. 'To Julian, remember, who died in the war. And Tom ...' She looked at me. 'Tom has spent too long being a soldier,' she concluded.

'I don't hold with all this mourning,' Mrs Bramley retorted crossly, looking at Margot. 'There's a good deal too much mourning nowadays. It's time we all got on with things.'

Delicacy and restraint were not Mrs Bramley's strengths, and back in the two-seater, out of sight of her cottage, we burst into laughter.

'Is she always like that?' I asked. 'Or was today exceptional?'

'No, that's exactly how she always is,' Margot assured me. 'Have you noticed the way everyone else lowers their voices when they talk about Julian in front of me? But not Mrs Bramley. She just dives straight in. *Don't indulge the children*, that's her motto. It was the same when I had the measles.'

The sunset was dramatic that day. As we drove home the western sky was already ablaze, touching the remnants of snow on the moor with an orange glow, angling dramatic shadows across the landscape. When the two-seater pulled up by the stables, Margot turned to me.

'Thank you for taking me, Tom. And thank you for coming down to see us. I hoped you would. You and Freddie are a sort of link to the old days, you see.' I saw her bite her lip. 'It must sound stupid to you, but it really helps. To know we didn't lose quite everything.'

I was surprised. It was unusual to find Margot in reflective mood. And when I held open the door and helped her out of the car, she reached up and kissed me lightly on the cheek.

*   *   *

That night Dr Thomson and his daughter joined the Hannesford party for dinner, and Violet Eccleston succeeded in arguing Sir Robert into a fury. The subject of debate was the League of Nations, but I knew it wasn't really the League that annoyed Sir Robert, it was Violet Eccleston herself: her confidence, her manner, the strength of her opinions. The argument flared dangerously for a few moments, and Lady Stansbury's attempts to smooth over the upset were less deft than usual; even Freddie Masters was only partially successful at cheering everyone up. All in all, it was not one of the brighter evenings I'd ever known.

After dinner, when I found myself alone with Sir Robert and mentioned Reggie Stansbury's imminent return to Hannesford, my host simply studied the floor and replied, 'Yes. Reginald. A bad business. Lucky to be alive.' When he then turned the conversation directly to the subject of the war memorial, I felt awkward and uncomfortable, and wished I hadn't spoken.

But even though the evening dragged, I found myself late to bed again, once more sitting up with Freddie Masters and the brandy.

'So tell me, old man . . .' Freddie came to the subject as if at random, leaning back in his armchair and stretching his legs. 'Have you worked out yet what you're going to say at this memorial service? It's all happening the day after tomorrow, you know.'

I shook my head. 'Not really. I'm not even sure why I was asked. You knew Harry much better than I did.'

Freddie studied the tip of his cigarette. 'I believe my name was mentioned, but Sir Robert didn't approve. Not enough gravitas, you see. I think he's afraid I'd tell improper stories.'

'And if it *were* you, what would you say?'

'Oh, if it were me . . .' He waved his hands airily. 'If it were me, I should stand up and say that Harry was the most capital fellow ever born, brave as a lion, wise as an owl, loyal as a hound. I'd give them the whole menagerie, then sit down. That should please everyone. But something tells me you may find that more difficult than it sounds.'

'Yes, I suppose I might.'

Masters considered me carefully, brandy glass cradled in one hand, cigarette in the other.

'You didn't like Harry very much, did you, old man?'

It was, of course, the question no one at Hannesford ever asked. For most, it was a question that would never even have occurred.

'No, not a great deal,' I conceded. 'Does that

265

surprise you?'

'Not much. Why should it? Harry was only really interested in himself.'

It was said so calmly that I blinked. No one *ever* spoke ill of Harry.

'But *you* liked him?'

Freddie Masters shrugged. 'He could be good company. And he tolerated having me around. But he was a terrible snob, and at times really rather ruthless. Of course most people never saw beyond all that charm.' He attempted a smoke ring. 'He really could be uncommonly charming, you know, when he wanted to be. Harry loved to be loved. I suppose that's where his true talent lay.'

'Yes, everyone always loved Harry, didn't they?' I think I grimaced.

'Perhaps you should take that as your text. Make things easy for yourself. Meanwhile, old man, on the subject of the Stansbury clan, here's another question for you. What's going to happen when Reggie Stansbury comes home?'

I wasn't sure I understood. '*Should* anything happen? Anything in particular, I mean?'

Masters put his head back and blew out another column of smoke.

'Well, these are strange times at Hannesford, aren't they, Tom? Here we all are, trying to make the best of things, trying to make sure our hostess's party doesn't fall off the tightrope, but it's a tricky business. Those of us who went out there want to forget all about the blasted war. Those who stayed here are determined not to let anyone ever forget it. Suddenly all the men who died are heroes, but the ones who came back are ungrateful fellows who get a bit moody and a bit awkward and rather let

266

the side down. That's if they're not out-and-out Bolsheviks or troublemakers.'

He contemplated the ceiling. 'Everyone here has some sort of scar, you know. Even the ones who made a great deal of money out of it. It's a volatile mixture. And now Reggie is being thrust into it like a battered grenade. The question is whether or not he's going to explode.'

And that was a question I couldn't answer. I simply told myself I'd be wise to stand well back.

*   *   *

That night, in the sanctuary of my room, I returned to the box of photographs. There were at least a dozen of Harry Stansbury: Harry in tennis whites, Harry on a polo pony, Harry sitting on a gate, smiling down at Margot who was smiling at the camera. I idled through them, studying each one, wondering what truths they might contain. But nothing struck me. The picture I'd shown Freddie of the housemaids and the carpet had breathed life, had spoken of something more than just two people hard at work. But the pictures I had of Harry seemed bland; simple likenesses, nothing more. In fact, photography at its very worst.

There was one of Harry with Julian Trevelyan, both of them holding tennis racquets, Harry resting his hand on the other man's shoulder. What truths did it contain, that image? That Harry and Julian were friends? That Harry, smiling broadly, valued the other's company? That Julian, standing slightly forward, had been more intent on the camera than on Harry? No, it told me none of those things. It told me only that one day, at a particular time, the two men had stood on the same terrace and had been photographed. Even their game of tennis could only be assumed. Rain might have cancelled play. Or the racquets might simply have been props, seized upon for the sake of the photograph. The camera told simple truths: it lied only in its implications.

Yet when I came to a picture of an expedition to the Three Shepherds, I studied it with interest. I had taken it, I knew, on the Friday before the Rose Ball, the day before I'd seen the professor in such distress. Ostensibly it was a group portrait. There were all the familiar faces—the Eversons, the Flinders girls, Freddie Masters, Tippy Hibbert. Harry Stansbury and Anne Gregory were kneeling together by a huge hamper, both smiling at the camera. Julia Woodward was there too, in the background, her smile a little guarded, her expression strained. She was partly obscured by Oliver Eastwell, who sported an elaborate cravat and was pulling a silly face. Next to him, Reggie Stansbury stood with hands in his pockets, his lips curved into a rare and rather attractive smile. He looked happier than I could remember seeing him.

But I knew it was not really a picture of any of those people. For me, it had been a portrait of Margot: Margot at the very centre of the picture, laughing at the camera, her eyes returning its gaze bold and unabashed; Margot's face, Margot's figure. Margot's hands lightly curled around a parasol. God, the agonies of hope and desire and yearning I'd felt that day. Yes, she had been self-centred and spoiled and vain, I had never doubted any of that. But even with the benefit of hindsight, I couldn't deny she was beautiful.

268

*   *   *

Sometimes you dream of something for so long that the dream becomes part of the furniture of your brain, to be turned to when required for comfort or support. The thing itself, the messy reality of it, ceases to be important. The dream is safer. It is the dream that matters.

The trenches had been a bonfire of dreams; they had burned with the smell of cordite and mustard gas. Most died still clutching them. Those who survived let them go and came back empty in ways they'd never imagined.

It was a long time after midnight when I heard my bedroom door open. I was in bed by then, stretching luxuriously beneath the blankets. I had kept the fire going and the room was still warm, but the flame was quietly dying. A single lamp burned by the bed.

Margot was wrapped in a gentleman's dressing gown that covered her from neck to toe and looked rough as wire. Above it her hair hung loose and golden around her shoulders. Her throat was bare. She looked tousled, as though fresh from her bed.

'Hello, Tom,' she said softly. 'I saw your light.' Her eyes fell on the photographs, lying muddled in their open case. 'Remembering old times?'

She moved silently across the room and perched on the edge of the bed.

'I suppose I was.' I felt disconcerted by her presence, by her closeness. 'Can't you sleep?'

She shook her head. 'I peeped out and saw your light. I thought you must still be awake too.'

269

I didn't know what to say. Her eyes were very intently on mine.

'Tom,' she said, 'you don't want to marry me, do you?'

I shook my head. I'd never wanted to, I knew that now. Not even when the thought of her marrying Julian Trevelyan seemed like hot steel twisting inside me.

'Good. I wanted to be sure.' She rose and let the dressing gown drop to the floor.

She slipped beneath the covers of my bed as though it were the most natural thing in the world.

*   *   *

I'd dreamed of Margot's body against mine. I'd dreamed of my fingertips against her skin. I'd imagined the bliss, the overwhelming joy of it. And not one caress, not one kiss, not one shiver of ecstasy was even a fraction less than I'd imagined. But even as the dream became real, I felt the world tilting, slipping out of control. I had never imagined my desire shot through with doubt or confusion or guilt. I'd never imagined complexity. We dream in simple colours.

'Why?' I asked her, when the fire had burned low and there was only the lamplight and her eyes. She lay close to me, her body against mine, her face on the same pillow. 'Why me? Why now?' I was bewildered.

Margot smiled and traced a fingertip down the line of my jaw.

'Questions, questions ...' Her eyes had been following her fingers. Now they moved back to meet mine. 'I could ask you the same. Why me,

270

Captain Allen?'

'Margot, you know. I've always wanted you. Always.'

'No.' There was tenderness in the way she contradicted me. 'You used to. It was different before. I used to see something in your eyes. A sort of yearning. It ran so deep it frightened me. But not any more. You've changed.'

'But tonight . . . Surely that shows . . .'

'It only shows I took you by surprise.' She rested her palm against my cheek. It felt cool, exquisite. 'And that you haven't quite forgotten all those things you used to feel. But you're different now. Now you look past me in a way you never did before.'

'So was this . . . was this to try to get that back?' A little spark of outrage.

'Ssssh . . .' She reached for me and kissed me. 'Quietly, Tom.' Her fingers stroked my cheek and I let myself be soothed.

'If you must know,' she whispered after a few moments, 'my motives in coming here tonight were entirely selfish.'

'I don't understand.'

She rolled away a little then, on to her back, and propped herself up on a different pillow, pulling the bed sheet chastely to her neck.

'Do you have cigarettes?' she asked, then to my surprise she giggled. 'Do you have any idea how shocked Mother would be if she knew I was smoking in bed?'

We both laughed, and I fetched cigarettes from the bureau. Standing naked in front of her felt strange but not uncomfortable. It occurred to me that Margot, too, seemed unembarrassed. She must

271

have seen the question in my face.

'As you've probably gathered, Tom, there have been others, you know. Lovers, I mean. Does that shock you?'

It did a little. I shook my head and slipped back beneath the blankets. Compared to the rest of the room, the bed was gloriously warm.

'I suppose it started when I was . . . When we were waiting for Julian to die. With one of his brother officers. Oh, don't look so appalled, Tom! Everything was different then. Everything had changed. People gave up waiting for things. There was no *time*, you see. People measured the future in weeks. And Julian was . . . Julian was damaged beyond repair. His friends were alive, and comforting, and the moment was everything because they might never come back.'

She turned slightly so that she faced me, and rested her hand on my chest.

'In fact none of them ever did. There were three of them in all, and all of them were dead within a few months. And then Julian died too, much sooner than we'd expected, and after that no one would come near me because I was practically a widow, and widows are sacred now, you know. I was terrified of being seen to smile because that would be taken as a crime against the dead. But now . . . Well, it's 1919 now. The war's over. Restaurants stay open after nine o'clock. I think I'm allowed to be alive again now, don't you?'

'And this . . . tonight . . . is being alive?'

She took a cigarette from the box but didn't light it. 'Well, what would *you* say?'

'It's better than being dead.'

She laughed out loud at that. 'So quick with a

272

compliment! You never were one to flatter me, were you, Tom?'

She put the cigarette down again and snuggled closer to me, rubbing my upper arm as if to warm it.

'It must be getting cold out there.'

'It is.' I didn't touch her in return. I was trying to work out what had happened, what it meant. 'So why tonight?' I asked.

'If you must know, I thought this was Horatio Finch-Taylor's room.' She said it with perfect seriousness, waiting until I smiled before she laughed. Then she reached down for my hand and linked her fingers with mine.

'I suppose I was curious, Tom. About you. About us. All those years I knew you wanted me, but I had other plans. I was so certain of everything in those days. Then, when I heard you were coming here this week, well, I couldn't help but wonder ... But you'd changed. You'd grown out of me. I like you much better for it, you know. And perhaps now you and I can go our separate ways without always wondering.'

I looked at her, her face bathed in soft light, framed by her tumbling hair, and thought I had never seen anything or anyone more beautiful. Yet I felt no despair at her words. Not even any regret.

'Is it so easy to go our separate ways?' I asked. 'After this?'

'Of course. I knew the answer to that as soon as you came back. You looked at me so differently. All that fire had gone, hadn't it?'

'I still find you incredibly beautiful.'

'Ah, but that's different. I can always tell. With men, I mean. Whether it's that or something deeper. I think sometimes I can tell better than

273

they can.'

She moved her hand from mine.

'There's another thing, Tom. Another reason why I came here tonight.' She hesitated, her eyes looking past me as though searching for the right words. 'It's because you remind me of how things used to be. Everything's so different now. All the others are gone. Everything's spoiled. But somehow the madness didn't seem to touch you. I look up sometimes and see you sitting where you used to sit, exactly as you used to be, and it's almost as if things are still as they were, and I'm still the person I used to be, back when everything was perfect and nothing, nothing, nothing really mattered.'

It was the first time I'd ever seen Margot so vulnerable. What was it Bill had said? *Still the same bright, beautiful Margot.* That was what people always said. Margot's flame was never seen to flicker.

'So what happens next?' I asked.

'I grow up and face this strange new world, and do what Mrs Bramley says. Get on with things.'

'And Neil Maclean?'

She looked at me questioningly, then shrugged. 'Neil confuses me. He seems to like me, Tom. I mean actually *like* me. I don't know why. God knows I've got enough faults. He doesn't need to marry, and even if he did, America must be full of brides. But he keeps coming back. Of course, he doesn't really know me. And when he does, I suppose he'll change his mind. What do you think? Do you like him?'

'Yes, I do.'

She laughed quietly. 'Better than Julian?'

I didn't need to reply. Margot pulled a face.

'I was a fool, wasn't I? About Julian, I mean. I was flattered, I suppose. He was the one every mother wanted for their daughter. I think I knew all along I didn't really care for him. And then, when he went off to fight ... This sounds terrible, Tom. When he went off to fight, I realised I didn't mind. Not at all. I tried to, but I didn't. It was like waving off a stranger. Does that sound hateful?'

'It sounds honest.'

'Thank you.' Margot looked pensive. 'I think if Neil were ever to ask me to marry him, I'd be honest with him too. I mean, about my past. About things like this.'

'Then Neil's a lucky man. I hope he realises.'

'Thank you,' she said again.

Our eyes met and we both smiled. Her face was still very close and I was aware of her throat, the hollows of her neck, the creamy perfection of her shoulder. I could feel the warmth of her body. It was a strange moment to look at her and know for certain that all those feelings I'd once had for her were gone, replaced by something quite different. I'd no more loved her than she had loved Julian Trevelyan. I hadn't even liked her very much. I had been consumed by desire and envy and wounded pride.

But now all that was gone. It was time to get on with my life, and Margot was not my life, I knew that. And for the very first time, perhaps, I could look at her and feel something that was untainted and honest and unselfish. Margot was Margot, and I was glad of it. I realised I wanted her to be happy.

'If Neil ever did propose ...' It was warm beneath the blankets and she was beginning to sound drowsy. 'I wouldn't say yes. Not yet. I'd make him wait. Wait until he knew me properly. Give him lots of time to change his mind. And you know what, Tom?' Her eyes were closing. 'If he still wanted me, after all that . . . You know, I really think I could make him happy.'

'In that case I'd be the first to congratulate you.' I meant it. I really did. And meaning it felt like freedom.

*   *   *

Long before first light I carried her sleeping to her bed, then returned to my own. It's in the nature of dreams that, come the dawn, you wake and find them gone.

11

The instructions Lady Stansbury had received were very precise.

'Reggie wants you to pick him up in the Daimler, Tom,' she explained. 'Just you, no chauffeur, no family. He was most insistent.'

Outside, the snow had retreated further beneath a bright winter sun, holding out only in patches on the upper slopes of the moor. The sky was cloudless. I could think of no good reason to refuse.

'Will eleven o'clock be all right? That's when he's expecting you. The people at the sanatorium are sending all his things ahead. And a Nurse Withers is coming with them. The matron says she gets on well with Reggie.' She paused a moment, then sighed. 'Oh, dear! I do hope Reggie isn't going to

276

be too difficult!'

I assured her that eleven o'clock would suit me very well. When Freddie Masters heard of the arrangements, he gave a low whistle.

'Roped in to fetch the prodigal son, eh? Or was Harry the prodigal, and Reggie the faithful one? Hard to say. Either way, old man, try to keep him calm. It would be nice if this thing didn't blow up in our faces...'

But Reggie Stansbury's return to Hannesford was not the problem uppermost in my mind. For the first time that I could remember, that morning I'd slept through the dawn. Instead of waking abruptly, alert and terrified, I had emerged from sleep in slow, muddled stages, uneasy and confused, troubled by a sense of transgression. And when eventually my mind cleared and my eyes had focused on the patterns of light clustered at the window, for once clarity did not bring consolation.

The photograph of Anne arranging flowers lay at the top of the pile by my bed. It's hard to say what I felt when it caught my eye. A shaft of brightness, I suppose, followed by a horror of shame. I felt myself freer in spirit than at any time since I'd first come to Hannesford. But that freedom had come at a price. When I took pen and paper and addressed a short note to Anne, asking if I might call that afternoon, I did it with a heavy heart. I seemed to be making an unholy mess of things.

I didn't see Margot until I was about to set off for Cullingford. Our paths crossed in the Great Hall where she and Susan were preparing to walk into the village. The three of us exchanged greetings, and when Margot met my eye she smiled. Not an arch smile, not a conspiratorial one, but honest and

277

unembarrassed. I hope I replied in kind, but it was hard to tell. The situation was going to take a little getting used to.

In contrast, my journey across the moor was uneventful and I welcomed the sense of being alone there on a clear day in winter. Cullingford, by comparison, seemed cramped and a little drab, the streets muddy and in places bedraggled with slush. I reached the sanatorium just before eleven and found Reggie waiting for me alone at the top of the front steps, wrapped up in topcoat and cap, smoking fretfully. He had positioned his chair so that he had a view of the drive, and when he saw the Daimler approaching he pulled out his watch to check the time.

'How like you to be punctual, Tom,' he called as I climbed out of the car. 'A tidy mind and all that.' The sneer was implied rather than audible and I didn't respond. It wasn't even true. Before my army days, my punctuality had only ever been so-so.

'Ready to go?' I asked, looking around. 'No one you need to say goodbye to?'

'For God's sake, Allen . . .' Reggie discarded his cigarette on to the gravel. 'Just get me out of here.'

There were three steps up to the front door and I paused on the first of them, looking up at the house, expecting assistance.

'No one's coming out.' Reggie's face was pale and his voice brittle. 'I told them not to. We had a row about it. I told them you'd carry me down. Think you can manage that? You'd better open the car door first.'

I knew better than to ask further questions, but readied the front passenger seat of the Daimler and returned to where Reggie was waiting. The

278

lifting wasn't easy. Even without legs, he was a considerable burden, but I managed to scoop him up and lift him down the steps; between us we succeeded in manoeuvring him into the car. The blanket covering his lap fell to the ground in the process and I had to retrieve it from the gravel.

'Humiliating, isn't it?' Reggie said it through clenched teeth.

'What about the chair?' I asked.

'You can leave that. They've sent one ahead. Little Nurse Withers will have it ready for me. Little Nurse Withers is a paragon of all virtues and as organised as you are, Tom. Her life must be completely joyless.'

I ignored him and clambered into the driver's seat.

'Where to?' I asked cheerfully.

'Don't be an ass, Tom. You know where we're going. Just drive.'

But I wasn't in a mood to be dictated to. 'Actually, I had another idea. I was in Stonebridge yesterday and I passed that pub you used to like. The Falcon, is it? They used to do a good lunch.'

Reggie looked at me, a muscle twitching near his jaw.

'And how exactly would I get inside the Falcon? Up a nice ramp perhaps? In the chair they keep for passing cripples?'

'Same way as you got down those steps, I suppose. I've carried men under worse circumstances, you know.' And it was true, though I didn't like to dwell on it.

'Oh, and a nice spectacle that would be, wouldn't it?' Reggie sneered. 'Look over there! There's nice Captain Allen taking his legless friend for an outing! Don't stare. For God's sake, don't stare. Used to be the best shot in the county, you know, but he was no match for a German howitzer. Quick, make way for the cripple!'

'All right.' I spoke so quietly that at first I don't think Reggie sensed my anger. 'Let's be clear about this. I can take you back to Hannesford and you can sit in your room for the rest of your life and never come out again for all I care. But I've been keeping your family company for a week now, which is something you don't seem to have the guts to do, and frankly I'm ready for a pint of beer. If you're not civil enough to join me, you can damned well wait in the car.'

Our faces were not far apart and I met Reggie's glare without flinching. The part of Reggie's face that was not scarred flushed to a dangerous, purplish red, and I thought he was going to explode with rage. When he reached for the car door handle, I had no doubt that he was quite capable of throwing himself out of the car. Quite capable of wriggling back to Hannesford on his stomach if it would make a point. But at that moment I didn't care. I'd have let Reggie crawl. Better men than Reginald Stansbury had suffered worse.

But then, in an instant, Reggie's anger was gone, replaced by a twisted smile.

'Well, well! Tom Allen, how very masterful! Have you left that tender heart of yours on the fields of France, Tom? Yes, we can go to Stonebridge if you like. Why not? Can't be worse than Hannesford. And I suppose I can still drink a pint of beer.'

We drove in silence. My anger, once roused, didn't die down as quickly as Reggie's, and I concentrated on the road ahead. Reggie appeared to be staring vacantly at the scenery.

'What about the mater and the rest of them?' he asked eventually. 'Won't they be expecting us?'

'I suppose so. But since you've given such strict instructions that your arrival is to be ignored, I can't see that it matters. Your mother is following them to the letter, by the way. When I left, she was explaining to the butler that the servants were to treat your return as if you'd never been away.'

'The butler? Is that still old Rowse? He used to have a weakness for the turf, you know.' Reggie seemed cheered by the memory. 'We used to swap information. Mad keen, he was. I wonder how he coped with no race meetings for the duration?'

The Falcon at Stonebridge was a dilapidated stone building on the edge of the moor, just above the village. It seemed deserted, but the arrival of the Daimler brought the landlord to the door. He was a man of fifty, stocky and phlegmatic with an impressive moustache, and he'd once known Reggie well. If his visitor's changed state shocked him, he barely showed it, registering no more than the faintest flicker of surprise. Between us, he and I moved Reggie indoors with minimal trouble and settled him in a corner of the snug near the fire. I saw Reggie flush at the indignity of it all but he made no complaint. And the landlord continued to prove himself a man of tact, bringing us beer and promising us food, then quietly withdrawing.

With a drink in front of him and game pie on its way, Reggie's spirits seemed to rise.

'So, Tom, what awaits me at Hannesford? What calendar of delights?'

'Nothing special tonight,' I assured him. 'Then

281

tomorrow . . .'

'Tomorrow my mother will have invited half the county to drink champagne and marvel at her fortitude, and possibly, for a shilling extra, to gaze upon her monstrous son.'

'If you don't want to attend the ball, you don't have to,' I told him, my tone still a little brittle. I'd not yet recovered my patience.

'Oh, I wouldn't miss it for the world!' There was a menace in Reggie's tone that would have made Freddie Masters shudder, and I found myself hoping that everything was indeed going to be all right.

'Tomorrow morning I might get Nurse Withers to wheel me around the grounds,' he declared. 'I don't think she'll take me as far as the Stansbury Arms, though. I suspect little Nurse Withers of puritanical tendencies.'

'Tomorrow morning there's Harry's memorial service,' I reminded him.

It seemed an innocuous remark, but it provoked a dramatic response. Part of Reggie's face flushed dark with rage and the hand holding his glass began to shake, his knuckles white.

'Of course,' he replied, struggling to maintain that tone of ironic detachment. 'The beatification of Harry! Mustn't miss that, must I? Cripples like me will be queuing up. Has he worked any miracles yet, do you know, Tom?' He raised his beer as if to drink but immediately slammed it back on to the table. 'It's a bloody *outrage*! How *dare* they? How fucking *dare* they?'

It was loud enough to bring the landlord's head peering over the bar. Reggie was shaking now, his eyes closed. I'd grown more accustomed to his

282

disfigurement by then, but seeing his face clenched with anger in that gloomy light, I felt guiltily aware how shocking those features could appear.

'It's a farce, Tom. I sit in a hole in Cullingford and *rot*, while they make sure the whole bloody county is paying homage to my angelic brother! Golden bloody Harry! It's a *farce*. The Stansburys of Hannesford! We're not a family, we're just a family name . . .'

He gasped as if struggling for breath, and I said nothing. I knew that for some time Reggie's continued exile in Cullingford had been self-imposed, but I felt no inclination to point it out.

'Anyway, I'm not going,' Reggie declared. 'I can tell you that now.'

'Very well, it's as you wish.' I said it to defuse his anger, but I knew it wasn't true. Reggie's absence at his brother's memorial service would certainly ruffle feathers.

'I'm sorry, Tom.' The red tide was passing now and Reggie even managed a twisted smile. He looked exhausted, and I wondered if bringing him to Stonebridge had been the wrong thing.

'I'm sorry,' he said again, and then, as if reading my mind: 'It was a good idea to come here. It's good to see the old place. I used to come this way often, you know. I suppose I thought I'd never see it again.'

The game pie arrived and we ate. When we'd finished, Reggie seemed calm again.

'You know, Tom, that first visit of yours, I told you something that wasn't true. I've been feeling uncomfortable about it. It was about your professor friend.'

This wasn't something I'd been expecting and my curiosity was piqued.

'Professor Schmidt? Go on.'

'You mentioned that row I had with him, and I played it down. Made out it was nothing. But you were right. I did call him all sorts of names. Actually it was all rather horrible. He collared me by the walled garden one day and accused me of something pretty shocking, and I lost my temper and said some fairly dreadful things. I know I shouldn't have. The man was a guest, after all. But in a way he was lucky it wasn't worse. I was tempted to lay him out cold.'

I remembered the vicar's description of the argument. I could imagine his shock at Reggie's invective.

'The thing is, Tom,' Reggie went on, 'at the time I thought he deserved it. But later, after he died, I found out he wasn't behaving quite as outrageously as I thought. I treated him very badly, I think.'

I waited, but Reggie seemed to have finished.

'So what was it he accused you of?' I prompted.

But Reggie only shook his head. 'Oh, it's nothing, Tom. It's all in the past now. I only mentioned it because I know you were fond of the professor and it was on my conscience a bit.'

I considered the state of Reggie's conscience. It would have been easy to say nothing, to leave that final stone unturned. I wasn't even sure I wanted to know what lay beneath. But the question, once formed in my brain, seemed to ask itself.

'That wasn't the only thing though, was it, Reggie?'

In response, Reggie looked up sharply, his gaze wary. 'What on earth do you mean?'

284

'I mean that Julia Woodward wasn't just a stranger to you, as you implied. She was rather more than that.'

Very slowly Reggie's face changed into an expression of pure fury, and his voice rose dangerously.

'What the *hell* are you insinuating?'

My courage wavered. 'I'm sorry. Perhaps it's none of my business.'

'*What?*' Reggie slammed his palm against the table so hard that the pint pots shifted. '*Tell me!*'

'It's nothing. I found a book you'd given Miss Woodward, that's all. One you'd inscribed. I know she was ... indisposed for a time after that. And I think you quarrelled with her, just before you left for London . . .'

'And you think . . . Just what *do* you think? That I abandoned her? That I seduced her then cast her aside? Is *that* what you're suggesting?' Again he slammed his hand against the table.

'I'm not suggesting anything, Reggie. I only know Miss Woodward had a bad time of things and died in a terrible way. But I know it's none of my business.'

'It's absolutely none of your business.' Reggie's face was working with anger. 'Is that what you're spending your time on up at Hannesford? Prying into Julia Woodward's secrets? How *dare* you? How dare you even mention her *name*?'

But now my blood was up too, and I met Reggie's eye without apology.

'Mrs Uttley says someone hit her, Reggie. Punched her, probably. In the face. Someone at Hannesford Court. Someone we know. You can't expect me to simply ignore something like that.'

And to my total surprise, Reggie crumbled. It was like watching a cliff of sand collapse into the sea. Anger had made him rigid but now he slumped forward, elbows on the table, his face in his hands. I could hear him repeating the words *Oh God, Oh God, Oh God* under his breath. When I reached forward and put a hand on his shoulder, he shook it off angrily without looking up. So I waited. Eventually I slipped away from the table and fetched more beer from the hatch. When I came back Reggie's shoulders had stopped shaking, and at the sound of the beer being placed in front of him he looked up, his face stained with misery.

He was ready to talk.

*   *   *

'I loved her, Tom. I just couldn't help but love her. None of the girls who came to Hannesford ever interested me. They were all the same—stupid, simpering things who flocked around Harry and were jealous of Margot. I couldn't bear their giggling and their flirting. And then one day I saw *her* in the woods. She wasn't like any of them. She was reserved and quiet and always on the brink of flight...'

Reggie snorted to himself and ran his hand through that prematurely grey hair.

'Just listen to me, Tom. Pathetic, isn't it? A brute like me who'd spent his whole life with a gun on his shoulder, suddenly rendered all poetical ... I might as well have set my heart on a wood nymph. She read romances and poetry and spent her days dreaming of God knows what, and there was I, this great hulking creature too tongue-tied to string a sentence together in her presence. Of course she wasn't in the least bit interested in me. I think I frightened her. I was too serious, too earnest. And I certainly wasn't the dashing knight of those tales of hers. I used to beg her to come out walking with me in the woods, and sometimes she did, just to stop me pestering her, I think. And each time I really thought that would be the day when I convinced her, when I made her fall in love with me. It was pitiful.'

Touched, I put down my beer. More people had arrived at the Falcon and there was a low hum of chatter coming from the other bar, but we had the snug all to ourselves.

'Do you know, Tom,' Reggie went on, 'I honestly thought I was the only one who had even noticed her. Oh, I know Margot used to invite her to things, but that crowd always ignored her. They were always perfectly charming at first, but then they'd just forget she existed.'

He touched the scarring on the side of his face. 'God, I used to hate those picnics! Always bloody picnics. All summer. Always the same. I didn't want her there. I didn't want her to be part of that circus. She was my own, private discovery. I wanted to keep her to myself, and the rest of the world could go hang. But she loved going, even if no one spoke to her. That's where she wanted to be.'

He took a sip of beer. He drank with a slightly odd motion, through one corner of his mouth.

'It was hopeless, Tom. I'd just about come to accept that nothing I could do would ever win her over. And then there came a day when she agreed to go walking with me. And right from the first that day was different.'

287

Reggie's voice began to soften and some of the pain seemed to drain from his face.

'It was as if that day everything I said seemed to be the right thing. It was a hot day and we walked right down to the water meadows, and she kept *looking* at me, Tom. I would look up and her eyes would be on my face, as if making up her mind. And I began to realise she was inviting me to look back, and suddenly the whole world seemed a different place...'

He looked up and smiled sadly.

'God, I was a fool, Tom. That day we ended up in the boathouse completely alone. Oh, don't worry, I didn't take advantage of her, or anything like that. The thought occurred to me, I admit it, but I didn't want it to be like that. I wanted ... perfection, I suppose. As it was, I allowed things to go further than I should have.' His eye met mine. 'I dare say you think less of me for that, don't you? I'm sure you'd have been a paragon of restraint.'

'No,' I told him quietly, 'I'm no paragon.'

'You know, Tom, I honestly thought that was the most wonderful afternoon in history. Who was the romantic that day, eh? Who was the dreamer then?'

His mention of the boathouse had set me thinking.

'So when exactly was this?' I asked.

'The 25th of June,' Reggie told me without hesitation. 'Risible, isn't it? I was sentimental enough to engrave the date on my heart.'

I tried to work it out in my head. That must have been the Thursday before the Rose Ball. Two days before I'd met the professor in the Rose Garden looking so perturbed.

Reggie's fingers had returned to his face. 'My

288

God, Tom, when I think of the young man I was then . . . Just look at me now.'

He shut his eyes for a fraction of a second and then went on.

'That day, in the boathouse, I remember kissing her and saying, *"Well, now you'll have to marry me,"* and she just smiled and said, *"Yes."* And I came away thinking myself the happiest man in the world. No, I *was* the happiest. Of course I knew my parents would kick up a fuss, but I wasn't bothered about that. They could go to the blazes. After all, Harry was bound to marry the heiress they always dreamed of, wasn't he? And then no one would care much what I did.'

'Did you tell them?'

'No.' He turned his face so that he was looking me in the eye. 'No, I told Harry.'

In the other bar someone laughed out loud. The sound rose above the rest of the hubbub, and Reggie waited patiently until the noise died down.

'I hadn't planned to tell him,' he went on quietly. 'It was a day or two later, the day everyone went off on that expedition to Bearhampton. Remember it? I didn't go because Julia and I had arranged to meet before lunch by the lake. I bumped into Harry some time that morning. He was on his way to play tennis with Anne Gregory but he seemed to sense something was up. He just kept worrying away at me, asking me why I hadn't gone to look at the horses. I thought he'd guessed.'

Reggie shook his head sadly.

'And perhaps I just wanted to tell someone. It didn't take long for Harry to get the whole thing out of me. I told him I intended to marry her. And you know what he did? He just laughed. *"What?*

Little Julia?" he said. *"Don't be ridiculous. You're not the first to dig that garden, you know. Your big brother beat you to it. On various occasions."* And he laughed again. Laughed in my face.'

Reggie twisted in his seat so that he faced the fire. Looking at him, misshapen and miserable, I felt a tightness in my throat.

'How did you reply?' I asked.

'Oh, I damned him to hell and told him I didn't believe a word of it. Told him he was jealous. But he just shook his head and said, *"Seriously, old boy, you need to watch out. She's trying to foist a bastard on you. Just ask her."* '

Of course. Even before Reggie had said it, it all made sense. Charming, dashing Harry . . . I found the fragments beginning to form shapes.

'So you met her as you'd planned?'

He nodded.

'In the boathouse?'

'No, down by the water on the other side of the lake. It was dreadful, Tom. Just dreadful.' He swallowed hard, then paused to gather himself. 'She was in love with him, of course. With Harry, I mean. I put the whole thing to her and she didn't deny a word. She simply nodded. It had been going on for months. They used to meet in the boathouse, or in that old chapel, the one in the woods above the river. I suppose Harry really *was* the shining knight she'd always dreamed about.'

I remembered the note in the margin of her book. How like Harry to have seen himself that way. And of course he must have known when he wrote it that Julia had been given the book by Reggie.

'So she *was* pregnant? And the child was

290

Harry's?'

Reggie nodded again.

'And he knew about it?'

'Yes. She told him as soon as she suspected.'

'What did he do?'

Reggie shrugged. 'What *would* Harry do? He washed his hands of the whole business. It was her problem, not his. That's what he told her. He told her to find a boy in the village to marry. Said he believed that was the traditional answer to the problem.'

'But she chose you?'

Reggie turned away from the fire. 'Of course.' He didn't sound bitter. 'I was the obvious choice.'

We were both silent for a few moments.

'What happened after she told you all this? What did you do?'

'I didn't hit her, if that's what you mean. I shouted. I raved. I think I threatened to break her neck. I told her that she had lied to me and cheated me and played me for a fool. That was the thing that really hurt, of course—that I'd dared to believe she might actually want me. And then I told her I would make sure I never set eyes on her again for the rest of my life. And she simply stood there with her eyes down and nodded at everything I said. I suppose I'd expected her to break down and beg forgiveness. I suppose that's what I wanted. But you know what, Tom? She didn't contradict a word I said. She just seemed relieved that she wouldn't have to go through with it.'

Reggie's second pint of beer was nearly finished and he spent a moment examining the last inch of liquid in his glass, swilling it around in careful circles.

'You know another pathetic thing, Tom? If she'd only told me the truth from the beginning—about Harry and the child—if she'd told me all that and asked for my help, I'd have married her anyway. Like a shot.'

It was time to be getting back to Hannesford. Busy though the household was with preparations for the ball, I knew that too long a delay in delivering Reggie would begin to cause anxiety. I waited until we were both back in the Daimler before returning to the subject.

'So you left Miss Woodward by the lake. Was that the last time you saw her?'

'That's right. I stayed around in Hannesford for the Rose Ball, just for the sake of appearances really, then I took a train up to London. In no time at all there was a war on.'

The road out of Stonebridge was a rough one and for a hundred yards or so I had to concentrate on keeping the Daimler straight.

'So what was it the professor said to you that made you so angry?' I asked when the worst potholes were behind us.

Reggie was busy lighting a cigarette. 'In his very polite, German way, he asked me if I was responsible for committing acts of violence against Miss Woodward's person. He said he wished to give me an opportunity to deny the charge. Well, you can imagine, I damned his eyes and told him to take himself off before I committed acts of violence against *his* person. Of course I said it less elegantly than that. I thought his impertinence staggering.'

'But you must have wondered why he thought such a thing? Surely you asked him?'

'He said he'd seen Miss Woodward running

back to her cottage the previous day in a state of considerable distress. He didn't give details. And as he'd overheard me shouting at her—issuing threats, he said—he wished to hear my assurances that I had not raised my hand against her in any way. So I told him where to get off, and that was that. To tell the truth, I thought he'd simply got the wrong end of the stick. And if I was surprised to hear that Julia had run off looking distressed, well, to be honest, I wasn't sorry. I *wanted* her to feel some distress.'

According to Reggie, he had kept his vow. After the scene by the lake he never saw Julia Woodward again. A few days after arriving in London he received a letter from her which he destroyed without opening. He blamed Julia and Harry equally and cursed them both equally. Reggie had always been good at holding a grudge.

After that, there were no more letters from Miss Woodward. Reggie avoided his brother, and when their paths did cross he made a point of cutting him. His anger carried him into the maelstrom of the trenches and dropped him there, the bitterness and the wounded pride eventually giving way to other, more pressing concerns. Viewed from the battlefields of France, the rest of the world appeared rather different, and there came a point when Reggie looked around him and realised his anger was gone. He was able to guess from occasional references in his mother's letters that Miss Woodward was still unmarried, and there had never been any mention of a scandal. That puzzled him slightly, because of course he'd heard nothing of the miscarriage that had taken Julia Woodward to Dr Thomson's. But it didn't deter him.

'So I wrote to her, Tom. I told her that any anger

I had ever felt for her had passed, leaving all my other feelings for her unchanged. I told her that, despite the time that had passed, I had no mind to be married to anyone but her. But, of course, I never sent the letter. I had some leave coming up, you see, and I thought I would post it just ahead of my arrival. But that leave was cancelled and the next delayed. I didn't get home for another eight months. And when I got there, they told me Julia was dead.'

The car rattled on for a few moments over the ruts and ridges, neither of us speaking.

'You know she killed herself, don't you, Tom?'

'I heard the rumour.'

'And do you know why?'

'They said something about a cousin of hers. But I imagine she was in a pretty poor state anyway, given what she'd been through . . .'

But Reggie shook his head impatiently. 'Think about it, Tom. Think about the timings. It wasn't a cousin she was mourning.'

As he spoke, his eyes seemed oddly lifeless, as though dulled by pain.

'She killed herself three days after news of Harry's death reached Hannesford. Of course, no one else saw the connection. Why would they? But I saw it at once.'

He attempted a rueful smile.

'So you see, Tom, there I was, still hoping to marry her, and once again my big brother got in the way. My *dead* brother. Always second to Harry, eh? The story of my life.'

'But you don't know for certain that's why she did it, Reggie,' I urged. 'It may have been coincidence. After all, given the way he'd treated her, she was more likely to hate him than love him.'

'No. She never stopped loving him.'

'You don't know that.'

Reggie turned and looked at me. 'As a matter of fact I do.'

But then, instead of saying more, he pointed to a spot at the side of the road.

'Pull over there, would you? I need to piss.'

I had to lift him down and help him on to the running board of the Daimler, then withdraw discreetly until he was ready to go on. Given the difficulties, I was surprised by Reggie's equanimity.

'That may have been humiliating,' he declared as the Daimler jolted forward, 'but on balance it was marginally less humiliating than little Nurse Withers and her bedpan.' He waved his hand at the wild expanse of the moor. 'Never underestimate the joy of pissing out of doors, Tom.'

'You were going to tell me something else,' I reminded him.

'Was I? I don't think so. I think I've done quite enough spilling of beans for one day, don't you?'

So we drove on in silence while I pondered the things he'd told me. I thought of asking how the professor's notebook came to be among his things; and the question of Julia Woodward's bruises had somehow been ducked. It was obvious Reggie must have more to tell. But on balance I was content to wait and pick my moment.

As we drew nearer to Hannesford, I sensed Reggie growing more restless, less comfortable with silence.

'So remind me, Tom, what's the plan now?' Ahead of us the chimneys of Hannesford were becoming visible above the trees.

'I thought you might prefer it if we pulled round to the back so you can slip in quietly. Everyone's under strict instructions to avoid any sort of fuss. I should think your mother will be looking out for us, but I expect she'll have made sure everyone else is occupied elsewhere.'

'Of course she will. She won't want to frighten the guests, will she?'

That was unfair. I pointed out that it was exactly what he'd asked for.

'Yes, yes, I know. The last thing I want is a welcoming committee. That's why I asked for you to fetch me, Tom, and why I wouldn't let the people at the sanatorium see me off. Less fuss. I've seen those farewells before and they disgust me. They're all sycophancy and false sentiment. I'm not having any of that. I tell you, Allen, I nearly didn't come back at all. There's nothing for me here. I hate this place.'

By now we'd come to the great gates at the end of the drive, and I slowed to pass the lodge. I knew there was a telephone there now, and I thought they'd probably ring ahead to warn Lady Stansbury of our arrival. A bend in the avenue meant the house was still hidden from view, but before we'd gone another fifty yards we saw two figures on the drive ahead of us and I recognised Susan and Lady Stansbury. I heard Reggie groan.

'Bloody hell. It's the welcoming party.'

I pulled the Daimler to a halt beside the two women and leapt out to open the doors for them. It was impossible not to notice how pale Lady Stansbury looked, and I found myself regretting my unannounced diversion to Stonebridge.

'Hello, Reggie. Tom.' The tension in her voice

was audible too. 'We were expecting you much earlier. Is everything all right?'

'Hello, Mama.' Reggie's face was a mask of indifference, all emotion vanished. 'I thought I said I wanted no fuss.'

'We know that, Reggie.' Susan spoke light-heartedly, but I could tell that she too had found the waiting difficult. 'It's just that we were sitting around all morning and finally we thought we'd come out for a walk to see where you'd got to.'

'We stopped for lunch,' I explained, as I handed her into the Daimler. 'It was my idea. I'm sorry if it made you anxious.'

'Don't be an idiot, Tom.' Reggie sounded fractious. 'They're fine. No one ever died from waiting.' He twisted to face his mother. 'I hope everybody else knows not to come out and meet me.'

'Yes, of course, Reggie dear.' Lady Stansbury was peering out over the park. 'I've told all the guests they'll see you at dinner, and I told Rowse to explain to the servants that you wanted no fuss. You remember Rowse, dear?'

'Ah, Rowse! Rambling Rowse, the loyal retainer!' Reggie's voice dripped with sarcasm, then suddenly turned cold. 'Yes, of course I remember him. Don't patronise me, Mother. It's my face I've lost, not my brain.'

By now I'd restarted the car and I heard Susan say with forced cheerfulness that she thought it was about to rain. Then we turned the corner and Hannesford Court lay in front of us.

'My word,' I exclaimed. 'Look at that.'

There was a moment of silence, then Reggie swore under his breath.

'What the hell is that?' he demanded, turning towards his mother. 'What *is* this? What the *hell* do you think this is? I won't have it, damn it! I won't have it!'

'But, Reggie, I told them . . .' Lady Stansbury's voice was little more than a whisper.

And then, just when I thought Reggie was going to lose all control of his temper, Susan laughed.

'It's the revolution!' she exclaimed, half amused, half in wonder. 'The revolution has come to Hannesford! The servants are out of control!'

Because in front of the house, inscrutable, arranged in two neat lines, the staff of Hannesford Court had come out to welcome Reginald Stansbury home.

In the moments that followed, no one in the car said anything at all, apparently robbed of words by sheer astonishment. At a loss, I brought the Daimler to a halt on the gravel sweep where the butler and two footmen were waiting beside an empty wheelchair. When the car stopped, they hurried forward to open the doors.

'What is all this, Rowse?' Reggie demanded, his voice hoarse, slightly choked. 'I made it very clear I wanted no welcome.'

But the old man simply bowed impassively. He was someone who in the course of his lifetime had perfected the art of being utterly unobtrusive. Yet now, in this extraordinary situation, he appeared quite calm, as if certain actions were clearly dictated by codes of honour and respect far more powerful than the whim of any individual.

'I regret to say, sir, I have been unable to prevail upon the staff to respect your wishes in this matter. The sacrifices made by the family during the recent conflict are a matter of a great deal of pride here at Hannesford, sir, and feelings ran very high on the subject. Your return means a great deal to us all. Now, if I may be permitted . . .'

I waited for a curse or a violent retort from Reggie, or for Lady Stansbury to take control of the situation with a blast of cold fury. But Lady Stansbury seemed in shock, nonplussed by fear of Reggie's anger, and for an excruciating moment the silence resembled the implausible climax of a melodrama. Then, very slowly, Reggie nodded his head.

'Very well, Rowse,' he said and quietly allowed himself to be lifted into the waiting chair.

It was only when the butler turned to wheel him towards the house that I noticed the tears on Reggie's cheeks, and suddenly it was no longer melodrama I was witnessing, but something raw and painful and moving. Reggie made no attempt to acknowledge any of those who had come out to greet him. He simply stared straight ahead while the tears fell. No one in those two lines spoke. There was no ceremony or speeches. The whole thing took place in silence and lasted a minute or less. And when Reggie had disappeared inside the house, the two lines dispersed with a low murmur. But to me it seemed they left something intangible behind them. A sense of dignity, perhaps. The heir of Hannesford had come home from the war.

*   *   *

That afternoon the sun cast long shadows as I walked into the village. Anne welcomed me at the vicarage with a smile.

299

'Your note sounded very formal, Tom. Is everything all right?' She gestured me into the hallway but no further. 'Mrs Uttley is sleeping and Miss Walker is happy to sit with her, so I thought you and I could walk out towards the Shepherds. We've another half-hour or so before it gets dark.'

She chattered on while she readied herself, and when we stepped outside she asked about Reggie, so I told her about our conversation at the Falcon and about his return to Hannesford Court. Reggie's story seemed to touch her profoundly. When I glanced across at her she was looking down, her face full of feeling.

'A pretty sorry business all round,' I concluded, 'especially for Julia Woodward. Is it really possible that she still loved Harry that much, even then? It seems hard to believe.'

'I can believe it.' Anne looked ahead, where the footpath twisted upwards. 'Not the real Harry, of course. The Harry she thought he was, the one who seemed like all her dreams come true. Poor thing. While he was alive she could still believe that one day he would come back for her.'

'You really think he could have meant that much to her?'

'Yes, I'm sure he could.' She hesitated, then pulled her coat closer to her. 'So Reggie admits losing his temper with Julia Woodward that day, but nothing more?'

'That's right. But I think there's something he hasn't told me. He was getting tired so I let him alone.'

For a time we discussed Reggie's return and Freddie Masters's concerns that he was going to cause a scene: both the memorial service and the ball were rife with opportunities for him to wreak havoc if he wished. Then we fell to talking more generally about the New Year Ball.

'I'm looking forward to it,' Anne declared. 'It's the first one where I won't be in some way *on duty*. And I intend to make the most of it. I shall dance all night!'

'Do you like to dance, Anne?' In my memory she had not been a frequent dancer.

'I do. With the right partners. The infirm husbands of Lady Stansbury's elderly friends don't count.'

'There may be few other options this time, you know. There's a shortage of young men.'

'Then you'll have to dance with me, Tom.' She turned towards me, her face bright. 'Do you know, you and I have only danced together a dozen times in all these years. It seems strange, doesn't it? These last few days, it's seemed as though I've known you for ever.'

I knew what she meant. In Hannesford she was my only firm ground.

We had left the village by a path that led steeply up the flank of the moor and had come to a point where the houses lay beneath us. The narrowness of the path brought us close together as we walked, and now she paused and placed her palms flat on the lapels of my coat.

'So tell me you agree to dance with me tomorrow, Tom. And stop looking so solemn.'

But I couldn't smile back. I felt nervous and slightly sick.

'I should like nothing better . . .'

Where was I to start? Looking at Anne I felt a terrible sense of hopelessness engulf me. I didn't want to keep secrets from her. I was certain of that. I couldn't think of anyone else in the world I could talk to. I wanted more than anything to be honest with her. It was all too ghastly for words.

And when the words came, they were halting and clumsy and awkward. I told her how much, since returning to Hannesford, I'd enjoyed her company. I told her how good it was, after a day at Hannesford Court, to come away and talk to her. I told her that I couldn't imagine being at Hannesford without her being there too. I explained that all my life I'd never really known what I wanted, but now I was beginning to understand.

And through it all, through all the words I could only hear the rumble of the approaching thunder. As it drew nearer, I could see her beginning to tense. I placed my hands over hers and pressed them, but they were tight, rigid, not soft as they should have been.

And then, when it was too late to stop, I faltered. Those eyes . . . I hadn't expected to see such pain in them.

'There's something else,' she said.

'It's nothing. It's really nothing.' And I meant it. I finally felt free of the past.

But she was still looking at me.

'It's Margot, isn't it?' It was unnerving how quickly she went straight to it. 'You always liked Margot, Tom. Everyone knew that. You didn't really want to like her, but you couldn't help it. And I saw the way she looked at you at dinner the other night. Tell me.'

I flushed. 'Honestly, Anne. I'm finally free of Margot. At last. It feels like a weight off my

302

shoulders.'

I felt her remove her hands from under mine.

'Please tell me.'

It would have been very simple to evade. To lie. A part of me wanted to snatch at the chance. I *was* free of Margot. That was the truth. What did the rest of it matter? But when I looked at Anne's face outlined against the monochrome sweep of the fields, I couldn't do it. And so I told her about Margot, about the night before; things I felt sure I should not have spoken of. Every word felt like a disaster, and yet almost a relief too. I didn't want to keep secrets from Anne.

When I finished, she was looking out over the village, her eyes a little glassy, her collar turned up against the wind.

'Thank you, Tom,' she said. 'You've been very honest. I think we should go back now.'

'Anne, I'm sorry. I'm truly sorry...'

But she didn't want to talk. When we reached the vicarage, I asked if I would still see her at the ball.

'Of course,' she replied. 'Why not?'

But her voice was flat and impersonal, and she didn't meet my eye.

*   *   *

I wasn't in the mood to sit up late that night. I felt too drained, too unsettled. Too wretched. Instead I lay in bed, convinced I could still smell Margot's scent upon my pillow. It occurred to me more than once that to venture to Margot's room might not be forbidden, might even be welcomed. I couldn't pretend that in the lonely hours of the night the

303

thought of Margot's body, Margot's touch, were not temptations. But I found them surprisingly easy to resist. To repeat our night together would be to turn it into something different. A snare instead of a liberation. A new trap closing. I had spent too much of my life ensnared at Hannesford to relinquish my freedom so easily.

Besides, I had something else to consider that night, something more immediate than the mess I was making of my own existence. That evening Reggie had refused to come to dinner, and when I'd looked in on him he'd seemed tired and a little morose. Then, as I was retiring for the night, I'd been surprised by a visit from the unobtrusive Rowse, who had asked for a quiet word. In unpacking Reggie's things, it seemed, one of the servants had come across a service revolver. Not an uncommon thing, of course, as many an ex-serviceman liked to keep a souvenir. But Reggie, apparently, had made a point of insisting his was placed somewhere he could easily reach it. There had been ammunition too, Rowse asserted, also to be left in a low and convenient drawer. It was not his place to report such things, he told me soberly, but as I was such a particular friend of the young gentleman . . .

I had nodded and thanked him, and was relieved to be left alone. So Reggie had a loaded revolver by his bedside. Should I be concerned? On balance, I thought not. Habits die hard. Every officer had grown used to reaching for his gun on waking suddenly. I knew of others who could not sleep without their old revolver close at hand.

Even so, I rather wished Rowse had kept it to himself.

12

At breakfast, all the talk was of that evening's entertainment. It would be the first such gathering at Hannesford since the professor's death. Violet Eccleston said she was looking forward to it as a *ritual*. Bill Stansbury and Denny Houghton considered it a capital lark. Neil Maclean said he looked forward to seeing the thing done in the traditional English way. Lucy Flinders was worried about her dress. And judging by his furrowed brow, Freddie Masters was still worrying about Reggie, who hadn't appeared for breakfast.

But before the ball there was the memorial service to negotiate, and I was feeling an unpleasant and growing sense of unease. I'd done little to prepare for it. In my old pocket book I'd found some notes I'd made at the time of Harry's death, notes I'd used to compose my letter of condolence. They were the nearest thing to a eulogy for Harry I'd ever managed. But as the moment drew closer I could see they didn't amount to much.

My plan had always been to spend an hour or two before the service drafting something that would pass muster, something suitable and uncontroversial and short. But that morning found me in the grip of some sort of paralysis. At the thought of what lay ahead I could feel a tickling sensation of panic begin to stir in my stomach. It was a sensation I'd learned to control by ignoring it until the moment the danger had to be faced, a technique that worked well enough in the trenches, preparing for an infantry charge, but less well with a speech to prepare. As the hour approached, I forced myself to add one or two lines to the notes in my pocket book, jotting down any helpful phrases that occurred to me. It was an outline, nothing more. I would have to add the rest when I got to my feet.

When Lady Stansbury asked me to look in on Reggie, it was almost a welcome distraction. He was, she told me, refusing to attend the service.

'And he *must* go, Tom. Just think how it will look if he doesn't! His own brother!'

But on this particular subject I had my own views. I felt pretty sure that Reggie staying away was no bad thing. The possibility of him causing a scandal if he *did* attend was far greater than if he did not.

'Everyone knows what he's been through,' I assured her. 'And everyone here knows he was too knocked up last night even to come in to dinner. We simply need to explain that he is conserving his strength. His absence will only appear shocking if we consider it so.'

But despite those soothing words, when I went to visit Reggie I was uncertain what to expect. The new, downstairs bedroom was a quiet spot that the bustle of preparations for the evening festivities did not reach, and I found him in his chair, silently contemplating the view from the window.

'It looks so cold out there, doesn't it, Tom?' The lawns were still encrusted with frost. 'Hard to imagine we used to spend so much of the summer out in the meadows.'

He spoke as if warm days would never return.

'I'm not going to the service,' he added, 'if that's what you've come about.'

'I know. That's what I just told your mother. She'll cope. What will you do instead? It would be a good chance to get out, get some air.'

'Perhaps.' Reggie shrugged, then twisted in his chair to face me. 'Tell me, Tom, do you think me wrong to hate Harry as much as I do?'

It was, perhaps, a question that had hung over him for many years. It was certainly one I didn't know how to answer. I moved to the window and looked out. The sky was grey as slate.

'Everything was always *easy* for Harry, you know, Reggie. And when that's the case I suppose it's inevitable someone grows up thinking the world is theirs for the taking.' I paused. 'But he was still a young man when he died. If he'd lived through the war, he might have changed. Like the rest of us.'

Reggie sat in silence for a time.

'Generous words, Tom,' he said at last. 'I wish I could find it in me to say them. But I know something about Harry you don't.'

I felt myself tense a little, but I said nothing, just waited.

'That time I came back here on leave . . .' Reggie had turned back to the window. 'The time I came back and found out Julia was dead, it was Harry that I blamed. I knew his death had driven her to it. You see, Julia *needed* someone like Harry. I don't mean his money or anything like that. She needed that spark Harry had—his life force, I suppose you'd say. She was so afraid of life, really, and Harry was the opposite.'

A muscle twitched on one side of his face, while the other remained immobile, as it always would.

'Anyway, even though he was dead, I blamed him. So I went to his room and I went through his things. Yes, that's right, I desecrated the shrine. I wanted to see if there was anything in there of her, you see. Anything he'd kept.'

'And was there?'

'There were letters. She'd written to him at the front every month or so, saying the same things— that she loved him, that she'd been revisiting the places where they used to meet. That's how I know about the old chapel, you see. It's where they would go to . . . to be intimate with each other. She never mentioned me, of course. Not once. And it was obvious from what she wrote that he never replied. But *he kept the letters*. He brought them home with him when he was here on leave. You see what that means, Tom? You see what that says about Harry? He may have wanted nothing to do with her, but he didn't mind being reminded of it all. Those letters were like trophies. He could have destroyed them, but he liked to be reminded of all that adoration. And that wasn't the only thing I found . . .'

He broke off and seemed to hesitate, but I already knew what he was going to say.

'The professor's notebook?'

Reggie looked round, surprised.

'So you know about that? Someone must have been looking for it, I suppose.'

'Anne Gregory. When she was collecting the professor's things.'

'She'd never have found it. Harry had this hiding place beneath a loose floorboard. He used to keep his treasures there when we were children. I never let on that I knew about it. He wasn't nearly so discreet with Julia's letters, you notice.'

I took out my cigarette case and offered it to Reggie. 'What did the notebook tell you?'

'Everything. It told me everything. All the things the professor knew that I had no idea about. That's how I found out the truth about what happened to Julia.'

He selected a cigarette but made no effort to light it. Instead his eyes remained fixed on mine. Cool. Appraising.

'You and I, Tom, we've both killed people. It's what happens in war. But have you ever *wanted* to kill someone? Deliberately, I mean. Have you ever wanted to go and end someone's life simply for the pleasure of watching that person die? No, of course you haven't. But I have. Before finding that notebook I thought killing someone in cold blood would be beyond me. And do you know what? I discovered that day that I could look murder in the eye and not blink for an instant.'

He shut his eyes, as if remembering. 'Mrs Uttley was right, you see, about what had been done to Julia. Only worse than that. The last day I saw her . . . That afternoon . . . After seeing me . . . She met someone in the boathouse.'

His voice wavered. For three or four seconds he said nothing, just took deep breaths until he was able to continue.

'That afternoon, my beautiful, foolish Julia had arranged a secret assignation in the boathouse with Julian Trevelyan. When she resisted his advances, he hit her. Then he held her down and took her by force. And that's why he had to die. I wanted him to feel my fingers on his throat and to know how much I hated him. I wanted him to feel the horror he made her feel. I wanted him to hear exactly why I was killing him, and then I wanted to watch him die.'

'Everything. It told me everything. All the things
the professor knew that I had no idea about. That's
how I found out the truth about what happened to

*   *   *

Reggie told the rest of the story in a voice that
was strangely detached. According to Professor
Schmidt's notebook, the professor had heard Julia
sobbing as he passed the boathouse. On peering
through a window, he'd seen her sprawled on the
floor, bleeding at the mouth, her skirts disordered.
He'd called out to her, but when she heard his voice
she fled, the professor stumbling after her into the
woods.

But the professor was a good-hearted man and
what he'd seen had disturbed him greatly. From
his notes, it seemed he'd never been in any doubt
about the sexual nature of the assault; what he
had seen had filled him with horror. For two days
he tried to speak to her but was turned away by
her mother, and for those two days his notebook
showed he was in turmoil. Small objects he found in
the boathouse when he returned there—a torn-off
button, a broken cufflink—were meaningless in
themselves, although he tucked them into the pages
of his book. Without Miss Woodward's testimony
nothing could be done, yet to do nothing was
intolerable. It was during those two days that the
professor approached Reggie. Having overheard
the young man raging at Julia, it was perhaps
understandable that the professor's suspicions had
led him in that direction.

As the story unfolded I wondered why the
professor had kept his concerns to himself. Had
he chosen to share them, I would surely have been
able to offer some sort of advice. But of course I
had been preoccupied with my own all-consuming

310

suffering; in my selfishness, I'd left him all alone.

On the day before the Rose Ball, he'd called at White Cottage again and this time he found Mrs Woodward absent. Somehow, without her mother to ward him off, he persuaded Julia Woodward to speak to him. In his notebook, he reproduced her account of events in almost painful detail.

By this point in his narrative Reggie was smoking grimly, his eyes rarely moving away from the window.

'Tom, do you remember what I told you about meeting Julia that day? Remember I said she seemed relieved when I broke it all off? It seems she'd come up with another plan. The fool! The stupid fool. She had no idea what she was doing. I could have warned her—anyone could have warned her—that you didn't play games with Julian Trevelyan. But it seems she'd bumped into him at some point and he had been terribly charming and kind . . . My guess is that he already knew about her and Harry, and wanted his own share of the fun. It would be just like Harry to blab to his friend. And Julian would have liked the idea of getting a share of something that was Harry's. But Julia didn't know any of that. So she sent Julian a note asking him to meet her in secret somewhere that afternoon.'

Reggie ground his cigarette hard into the ashtray and turned to face me.

'What on earth was she thinking, Tom? Did she really think Trevelyan was going to take her side against Harry? Or did she hope he would prove as susceptible as I had? He was certainly a better catch. But for Julian Trevelyan that note would have meant only one thing, and he went there that

311

day determined to get it. He was used to getting what he wanted, wasn't he? He was that sort of man.'

'And Julia told the professor all this?' I remembered the professor's kind eyes, his quiet way of putting you at ease. It wasn't, perhaps, as unlikely as it sounded.

'That's right. About Harry, about Julian, everything. And you know what the professor did then, Tom? He went to see Harry. My honourable brother. He found him on the terrace that afternoon and told him exactly what Trevelyan had done. He said he expected Harry to do the honourable thing by Julia, and he insisted that Trevelyan should be publicly disgraced. And of course Harry lost his temper and told the professor he was an interfering foreigner who'd better watch his step.'

I remembered the argument I'd overheard on the terrace, the raised voices, the sound of someone stamping away in fury. I hadn't been sure if it was Reggie or Harry losing his temper. When I joined him, the professor had looked shaken, upset...

'And, of course,' Reggie continued, 'Harry told the professor that anyone making criminal accusations against an English gentleman should do so to his face.'

'And did he? Did the professor confront Julian?'

But Reggie simply shrugged. 'I don't know. He was planning to. But that's where his notes stopped, the night before the Rose Ball. The following day he was dead.'

The confrontation on the donkey bridge, an old man slapped in the face, scrabbling in the dirt for his spectacles... Yes, he had confronted Julian.

I realised that Reggie was looking at me intently.

'You do see the point I'm making here, don't you, Tom? About Harry?'

But I must have looked blank because Reggie rolled his eyes.

'The point is, Tom, *Harry knew*. Harry knew exactly what Julian had done. The professor told him. And he chose to do nothing.'

Reggie shook his head.

'No, actually that's not true. He *did* do something. When the professor died, he went and hid his notebook. It must have been the first thing he did after the professor's death. Imagine it! Stealing from a dead man's things.'

His face was pale with disgust.

'He *knew*, Tom! He knew what his friend had done to Julia. And what was his response? He hid the diary! He was complicit. His own sister was going to marry that man and he did nothing. Brilliant, beautiful Harry! Mustn't let any unpleasantness get in the way of his perfect existence, must he? He could have broken with Trevelyan, warned him off, but that would have been messy, there would have been a scandal, and Harry was too fastidious for that. Much easier to pretend he knew nothing and to hope it would all go away.'

'And Trevelyan?' I was almost afraid to ask.

In reply, Reggie ran a hand over his injured face. He looked incredibly weary.

'I knew instantly I was going to kill him. The night I found the notebook, I made up my mind. I wasn't going to wait. I felt very calm about it, actually.'

He stubbed out a cigarette and, feeling

313

automatically for his case, began to light another.

'I knew Julian was in London, you see. Invalided out. I'd heard he'd been hit and I'd heard it was quite bad, but I didn't care. So long as he was still alive. So long as I could be the one who made him die. I left for town the next morning. I still had another couple of days of leave. I took some pages of the notebook with me, along with Julia's letters, just in case he tried to deny it all. When I called at the Trevelyans' house, his family were out. There was no one in except Julian and the nurse. I was shown up straight away, of course.'

He took a puff or two of his cigarette. Tired he might have been, but he was not uncomfortable with this part of his account. He looked strangely at peace.

'The nurse tried to explain to me how ill he was, but I wasn't really listening. To tell the truth, I was just terribly impatient. The more she told me Julian was in a bad state, the more I was gripped by a sort of panic that he might suddenly die, there and then, before I could get at him. And then she showed me into his sickroom and left me alone with him.'

Reggie's eyes met mine.

'It was pitiful, Tom. Truly. I had no idea. He was just propped up there, staring ahead, breathing in this hideous, rasping way as though every breath hurt. He didn't turn round when I came in, but even then I didn't really realise. I even started talking to him. It wasn't until I passed my hand backwards and forwards in front of his face that I understood. There was just nothing there, Tom. He was breathing, but that was all. I sat there for a little and watched him, thinking about what he'd done to Julia. Making myself imagine it. Then I placed

314

my hands around his throat. I could feel the pulse beneath my fingers as I squeezed. As my hold grew tighter I heard the rasping sound stop and I knew he was moments from dying. And then it struck me. By killing him I'd be doing him a favour. What was the point of that?'

Reggie's eyes didn't leave mine for an instant. They were calm, neutral.

'It was the cruellest thing I've ever done, Tom. Deliberate, calculated cruelty. Much worse than murder. I let him live because I wanted him to go on suffering. When I let go, the breathing started again. I just sat there for a little after that, looking at him, thinking of Julia. And then I got up and walked away.'

He laughed, a dry, mocking chuckle. 'You know, it only occurred to me afterwards that I should have killed him for Margot's sake, to save her that interminable wait. But it was too late by then. The big push was on, and it was my turn to be carried home in bits. The pages from the professor's notebook went the same way as my legs, so even if I wanted to I could never prove a word of any of it.'

I watched him slump back in his chair. He let out a long, low breath, then turned his wheelchair away from the window and rolled over towards the bed. I remained by the glass, looking out. Through the outline of my own reflection I could see a woman with a child hurrying along the path across the water meadows. Rushing to Harry Stansbury's memorial service, perhaps.

'And you never said anything to Margot?' I asked.

Reggie shook his head. 'What was the point?'

I waited till the woman had disappeared into the

trees, then reached down to stub out my cigarette.

'I'd better go,' I said. 'I'm supposed to be in church.'

*   *   *

I found Freddie Masters waiting for me outside the church door. We were two of the last to go in.

'For God's sake, man, you look dreadful,' he whispered as I joined him. 'I thought for a moment you were going to funk it. Just remember, *the most capital fellow who ever lived*. Keep it short. Then we can all go home.'

Inside, the church was full. As well as the contingent from Hannesford Court, a great many of those who were to attend the ball that night had travelled to be there; and from Hannesford village itself there was a substantial turn-out. Out of love for Harry? I wondered. Out of respect for the Stansbury family? Or simply out of that general sense that the fallen, whoever they were, ought to be honoured? Looking around from my pew at the front, I saw Anne a few rows behind me. She wasn't looking in my direction.

It quickly became apparent that Sir Robert had chosen the hymns. If I hadn't felt so sick, I might have laughed: 'Onward, Christian Soldiers', then 'Soldiers of Christ, Arise'. In between there were prayers for the glorious dead and a short address by the vicar about the value and virtues of youth. It worked rather well both as a tribute to Harry *and* as a veiled plea on behalf of the village school. Then, as the congregation worked its way through 'He Who Would Valiant Be', the vicar signalled me to approach the lectern.

316

I had no neat sheets of foolscap to take up with me. I had nothing to look at but my old pocket book, so I placed that carefully open on the Bible, turned to the page where I'd jotted down some lines about Harry. Opposite them, on the facing page, was scrawled a scrap of verse I'd found in the pocket of one of my dying men.

> *When the silence falls, forget us.*
> *We did not die to make you sad,*
> *We don't regret the life we've had.*
> *We grow forgetful with the grass,*
> *We let the trees grow over us,*
> *Forget us all, forget the past,*
> *As we forget you.*

In desperation I tried to conjure up a positive memory of Harry Stansbury. But it wasn't easy. Harry rowing on the lake, Harry playing tennis, Harry smiling as he set about the seduction of Julia Woodward . . . And then the music came to an end and all eyes were on me.

After the service I waited by the church door but he didn't appear with the others. When I went to investigate, I found him still in his pew, half in shadow. Beyond him the altar was lit up by a crescent of coloured light thrown by the stained glass. Part of Tom's face was silhouetted against it.

He looks so tired, I thought, and with a pang I remembered how, in that other time, I used to love his vitality, the sense he gave of someone embracing life, curious about it, interested in everything. Interested in me, even, when no one else had been. He had been free of doubts then, assured in a way I was not, and just the proximity of all his confidence had been a comfort.

But seeing him there in that shadowy church, I finally understood. The Tom I remembered had not come home from the war. I'd been so eager to have him back that I hadn't wanted to believe it. I'd wanted him, for my sake, to be exactly the man I remembered. Oh, I'd seen he was a little more serious than before, that his presence no longer seemed to have that infectious way of raising everyone's spirits. But I thought those changes temporary. He needed a bit of time to recover, of course he did. Time to adjust. But he would be all right. Tom was one of the lucky ones.

And it wasn't just me who'd been desperate to believe it. They all wanted Tom unchanged, I could see that now. Lady Stansbury, Margot, even young Bill Stansbury. Tom was dependable, Tom was a rock. Tom was their link to the past, something that had survived, something solid to build on. No one wanted to believe there were any cracks.

318

How lonely he must be. How lonely to be away so long, and to discover on coming home that no one wants to know who you are.

And now he was sitting in the shadows, alone with his thoughts. Five years of memories. Five years of things unspoken, all dammed up inside him.

It would have been very natural to go to him then, very natural to sit beside him and rest my hand on his. But the hurt of the day before was still there inside me, dull and numbing, and I didn't know what to do with it. I didn't know if it would ever go away.

When he finally rose to leave, he found me still hesitating near the door. I don't think he saw the tenderness in my face, only the uncertainty.

She was standing in the deep shadow at the back of the church, little more than an outline in the gloom. When I saw her I paused, and she stepped forward, into better light. She wasn't smiling, if anything she looked troubled, but somehow just seeing her there, just seeing her face, made the world feel a little warmer.

'I waited outside,' she said, 'but you didn't come.'

'I suppose I was ashamed.'

'Of your speech?'

'Ashamed of everything.'

'Come out.' She moved towards the door. 'It's much too cold to sit here.'

We followed the path from the church out towards Winnard's Farm, both of us shivering in the winter air. It was the route we'd walked that other time, when I'd only just returned to Hannesford. I'd seen Anne every day since then, I realised, and in her company I felt none of the dizzy ecstasy I'd once felt when walking with Margot Stansbury. But I felt no barriers either, no tangle of anxiety or pretence. No awkward distance. There were those who had gone and those who had stayed behind; until the fighting stopped, I hadn't fully understood how deep the gulf between them.

But Anne was on the same side of the barrier. And of course she always had been. Arranging flowers with those clear, grey eyes of hers, she was always there, the only one on my side of the divide. And I'd never really noticed. I had a great deal to be ashamed of.

'You said all the right things, Tom. About Harry, I mean.' She wasn't looking at me. Her eyes were

320

roaming across the fields.

'Did I?' I wasn't so sure.

'Freddie Masters was sure you were going to say something inappropriate.'

'I should have done. But I hadn't the courage.'

The rooks that had previously gathered in such numbers in those fields were absent, but very high up a lone buzzard was circling. In the silence beneath it, I told Anne all the things Reggie had said that morning—about Julia, about Julian Trevelyan and about Harry. At first I wasn't even sure she was listening, but as I went on the furrow in her brow began to deepen.

'It's a bleak enough tale, isn't it?' I concluded.

She seemed to struggle for words. 'It's appalling. Horrible. Julian Trevelyan . . . How could he? How dare he think . . .' She tailed off, shaking her head. 'And yet . . . there was something about him, wasn't there? He thought he had a right to anything he wanted.'

'And what about Harry? Covering for him. That's pretty shocking too.'

She looked up at me then and shook her head. 'No, Tom. I'm not surprised by that. I could have told you Harry was weak.'

'Then you knew him better than I did. I never really took to him, I know, but I thought him better than that.'

I paused, uncertain whether or not to go on.

'Do you know, Anne, when I was standing there in church just now reading through the list of Harry's war service—all the dates and the places he'd been stationed—I couldn't get over how incredibly short it was. I don't think it had ever occurred to me how little of the war Harry ever saw. He died before it had really got going, back in the days when it was still almost possible to think of it as an adventure.'

'You sound bitter, Tom.'

'I suppose I am. It's ridiculous, isn't it? But when I remember how jingoistic he was, the way he urged everyone to follow him out there, as though it were all a great lark . . .' I shook my head. 'How typical of Harry not to see the thing through. He was always doing that. Never staying around when things got serious. The rest of us got years of grinding hopelessness. Harry barely even got his knees dirty.'

Anne glanced across at me. 'Yet you stood there in church and said what everyone expected to hear.'

I nodded and turned away from her.

'I almost didn't. I went there this morning planning to tell them that Harry wasn't the hero they took him for. That none of us was. I was going to make them understand that the dead died shaking with fear. But you know what? Freddie Masters is right. There's no point telling the truth. I looked down at all those faces, all of them looking up at me, all so solemn and expectant. Waiting for me to make sense of it for them. Waiting for me to show them why Harry's death had value and meaning and was all for the best.'

I lowered my eyes.

'Did you notice all those photographs, Anne? When we went around the village on Christmas Day? A picture on every mantelpiece, the same in every village around the moor, like a thousand tiny lights still burning. I might have stood there in church and said it had all been wretched and futile and barbaric, but I couldn't. I had to tell them what they needed to hear, that Harry Stansbury died in the most noble cause in our history, and how proud we should be that England had raised such men as Harry.'

We had reached the middle of one of the wide fields that sloped up, away from Hannesford, two small figures in an empty landscape.

'Was that wrong of me? Tell me what you're thinking, Anne.'

But Anne shook her head. It was her turn to look away.

'Do you remember when you asked me about that Saturday, Tom? The one before the Rose Ball? And I told you I couldn't really remember much about it. Well, that morning I played tennis with Harry.'

I nodded, unsure where she was leading.

'Do you remember how certain I was that Harry hadn't been in the boathouse with Julia Woodward that afternoon?' She studied my face as if looking for something. 'Did you not wonder how I could have been so sure? Did you not think it strange? I was with him, you see. That afternoon. All afternoon.' She paused. 'In my room, up at the top of the house.'

'I see.' I looked ahead, up the path, not sure what to do with my eyes. In the next field a pair of lapwings were flapping to a halt.

'You were honest with me, so I thought you should know . . .'

'I see,' I said again. 'I'd no idea.' Harry and Anne. Harry and *Anne* . . .

'It happened that summer. I was . . . discontented. Unsettled. I was thinking it was time to leave Hannesford. I don't think Harry had ever really noticed me before then. Not *really* noticed me. But when he came home that year our eyes were always meeting. For a week or so we hardly spoke to each other, but I knew something was happening. He had a way of making you feel *complicit*, you see, as if you and he were sharing some special secret. Soon we started meeting in the gardens after dark . . .'

As she talked, I could imagine it all too well. Harry's charm at full power, the gardens at dusk, full of the scent of flowers. How often I had stood in a crowded drawing room and heard someone exclaim with laughter, *Oh, no one can resist Harry!*

'It was a sort of madness, I suppose. Intoxicating.' Anne shook her head. 'I never stopped to think. I didn't want to. And besides, it all happened too quickly for that. I knew I wasn't in love with Harry. That sounds shocking, doesn't it? But it didn't seem to matter. I felt so confident suddenly, I just didn't care. Invincible, almost. That was the effect Harry had. A few weeks before I'd been a nobody, and suddenly I felt I could do anything in the world. When he first proposed going out to the old chapel one afternoon . . . Well, I knew what might happen if I said yes, but I went with him all the same.'

She paused and I felt her looking at me, but I was scanning the edge of the moor, not sure what I thought, not sure I wanted to hear more.

'I felt certain everyone must guess,' she went on. 'It seemed impossible that no one had noticed. But I suppose that was part of the excitement. He would come to my room at night—I never knew when to expect him. He'd pretend to be smoking in the schoolroom. Or during the day we'd sometimes go back to the old chapel. The professor almost caught us there once.'

She stopped, and when I looked to see why, I saw she was pinched and shivering.

I offered her my arm.

'Come on. We should keep moving.' We started walking again, slowly, in the direction from which we'd come. 'When did you find out about Harry and Julia?' I asked.

'I didn't. Of course, I see it now. There were a couple of times when I noticed her in places that surprised me. But I was floating too high above the ground to notice anything.' She flushed as she said it. 'It's embarrassing to think of it now, Tom, but just then I honestly didn't care about what happened to the rest of the world.'

Now she too seemed to be studying the distant fields.

'Then, the night before the Rose Ball, I couldn't sleep for hoping Harry would come. It was so hot. After a little I decided I'd go down and surprise him. I'd never done that before. It was the middle of the night, and when I got there I found his room empty.'

She shook her head. 'Believe it or not, I actually thought he must still be downstairs drinking with his friends. So I waited, growing more and more anxious the longer I was there, feeling sure I'd be caught. Then eventually I heard a noise in the corridor, so I peeped out. And there was Harry. He was coming out of Laura Finch-Taylor's bedroom.'

I remembered the banging door, the sound of footsteps running away. The fragments were locking together.

'At the Rose Ball, Anne, when the professor collapsed . . . There were tears in your eyes. Tears in your eyes *before* he collapsed. I never understood why.'

'I watched him dance all night. With everyone except me. My punishment, you see.'

The path narrowed where it dropped down to the churchyard and we descended in silence for a little, Anne a few paces ahead.

'I suppose we've both been fools,' she said as we emerged among the gravestones. It was a statement that invited no reply. It certainly wasn't forgiveness. We seemed to be looking everywhere but at each other.

'It was easy to get caught up in it all,' I said. 'I know that better than anyone.' I glanced across at her. 'Are you still coming to the ball?'

She shrugged. 'I still don't know what to make of these last few days, Tom. I feel ... let down, I suppose. Which is absurd, because I have no right to expect anything of you. I thought I was angry, but I think I'm just too tired to be angry now. Things that should matter don't seem as important as they used to. And somehow ...' She looked up at me as though genuinely puzzled. 'Somehow I find you quite hard to hate.'

*   *   *

The New Year Ball at Hannesford: gay, brilliant, teeming, and characterised by an almost palpable sense of relief. It had been an uneasy year. War, it was discovered, did not end neatly. Men came home only gradually. The shops did not instantly fill with food. The dead stayed where they were buried, or were moved to lie in long, orderly rows, neatly labelled. There had been strikes, protests, even a mutiny; and long after the fighting stopped, the casualty lists continued to appear. The wounds were still open. But 1920 would be different, surely. In 1920 people would once again be allowed to be happy. And so the cars rolled up to the steps at Hannesford Court and disgorged party after party of people grimly intent on enjoyment. Not every invitation had been accepted, but those who came brought with them a sense that, after a difficult year, an old-fashioned ball was precisely what was needed to cheer up those around them.

They were welcomed into the Great Hall by Sir Robert and Lady Stansbury, and by Reggie, who insisted that he wanted to get the worst of it over. I watched him shaking hands in perfect evening dress, sustaining a display of graciousness and good manners in a way I hadn't thought him capable. There was something almost exaggerated about the performance, as if Reggie were laying down a challenge to those he greeted: *my behaviour is impeccable, so if you flinch it must be my face*. From time to time Lady Stansbury would look down at him, pleased and very slightly puzzled.

As the rooms filled, the air of excitement grew. Listening to the chatter around me, I couldn't help but think it sounded different. At the last ball, Hannesford had been full of hope and expectation. People celebrated as though the future promised them everything. Now, however loud the orchestra played, it could not entirely mask a gritty determination to make the best of things.

And also, of course, there was the shortage of young men. I'd almost begun to accept it now, and certainly Lady Stansbury had done her utmost to ensure there would be ample dancing partners for the young ladies. Callow youths abounded, as did grizzled bachelors of later years, pressed into service because still capable of a passable waltz.

Anne was one of the last to arrive, accompanied by the vicar and wearing a simple green dress that made her look neat and trim and lovely. She greeted me with a smile and a nod but the press of so many acquaintances gave us little opportunity to speak.

When I look back on that evening, I always imagine myself an observer, moving from room to room, letting the sights and sounds wash over me. Yet I danced a good deal: with Susan, with the doctor's daughter, with innumerable young ladies introduced to me by Lady Stansbury. I danced with Margot, too, but I was very aware of Anne's presence and felt ill at ease. I think Margot found me poor company. I even danced with Violet Eccleston, who was not often seen on the dance floor, and who danced with watchful seriousness, as though somehow mistrustful of the music.

Gradually, as the champagne continued to flow, the evening grew louder and the rooms busy to the point of awkwardness. I noticed Reggie, freed from his duties by the door, drinking freely in one corner, usually in the company of a Hannesford stalwart— the vicar, the doctor, even Colonel Rolleston. At first I made a point of joining them from time to time, but never for long. Reggie was drinking more than was sensible and growing acerbic with it.

It was around eleven o'clock when the word began to circulate that Freddie Masters had proposed to Susan Stansbury. That rumour was treated with a certain amount of scepticism in some quarters, and when it was confirmed by Lady

Stansbury herself that an engagement would shortly be announced, many were clearly taken by surprise. A week earlier the match would have struck me as astonishing, but since then I'd changed my view of Freddie; I rather liked the man. It was a surprising thought.

Bill Stansbury seemed pleased about it too. When he collared me between the Great Hall and the Orangery, he was flushed with champagne and speaking a little too loudly. 'Have you heard, Tom? About Susie? Isn't it capital?'

There could be no doubt that he found the prospect of having Freddie Masters and his DSO in the family an extremely gratifying one. I noticed that he was taking great care not to look at where Laura Finch-Taylor was dancing with her husband. To Bill the sight was clearly irksome. Eventually he pottered off in the other direction. The Stansbury boys had never been the best at holding their drink.

When I thought no one would notice my absence, I slipped out on to the terrace at the back of the house. It was freezing out there and I had the place to myself, so I stood for a few moments near the spot where the professor had died. Hoping for what? Some sort of release from my regrets? But there was nothing there, only an empty terrace in winter. It was too cold to linger, and too late to say a proper farewell.

When I returned to the warmth of the Orangery, Freddie Masters caught my eye and advanced to shake my hand.

'I hear you're to be congratulated, Freddie?'

'That's right, old man. Thought it was time to give matrimony a shot. Happiest fellow alive, and all that.'

329

We both watched the crowds, unsure what else to say. When Freddie spoke again his voice was quieter.

'You know, Tom, I never thought it could happen. Never thought I'd come through the fighting, for a start. I'm damned if I know how I did. And all that time I thought Susan was lost to me anyway. Now it seems unforgivable, when so many people are still suffering, to be so damnably happy.'

Watching him, sensing the joy bubbling inside him, I had the urge to reach out and put my hand on his shoulder, to tell him with all the words at my command that I wished him every possible happiness. But there were conventions, codes we'd both grown up by; so I simply raised my glass in acknowledgement, and we drank in friendly silence, watching the dancers, until Freddie's presence was demanded elsewhere.

It was not long afterwards that I learned Reggie's revolver was missing from its drawer. Old Evans had noticed its absence, apparently, and had informed Rowse, who felt it necessary to tell me. Tracking me to a quiet corner of the Orangery, he had seized his moment.

'Evans's suspicion, sir, is that Mr Reginald must have taken the revolver with him when he left his room this evening. Mr Reginald has been out of spirits, and I have noticed that he is drinking heavily, sir. One sincerely hopes that he is in no danger.' His voice was quite tranquil, as if warning a guest that the weather threatened to be inclement.

The thought of a drunken Reggie in possession of a loaded revolver was certainly an unsettling one, but the thought of confronting him about

330

it in public was not a great deal more palatable. I considered the options.

'I wondered, sir, whether Sir Robert ought to be informed?'

I shook my head at that. I had a strong suspicion that Sir Robert was not the man to deal with the situation.

'No, Rowse. Not just yet. Leave it with me for a while.'

I'd have a word with Reggie somewhere quiet, I decided. But when I went in search of him, he was nowhere to be found. I rather hoped he'd retired early, to sleep off the evening's excesses; if not, I would speak to him on his return.

*   *   *

There comes a point at any ball when everyone present knows whether or not the event is a success. By half past eleven, no one at Hannesford was in any doubt: Lady Stansbury's ball was a triumph. The music, the flowers, the food, the wine—all were superb; and the old building itself was magnificent, decked in the glory of another age. Everywhere I looked, fresh-faced young men perspired freely between dances but were tireless in their efforts. The bachelors of fifty held the line with sturdy fortitude, moving from waltz to foxtrot with barely a thought of escape to the smoking room. The dark colours of the war years were forgotten as yellows and blues and emerald greens filled the dance floor. And when Violet Eccleston cornered me by a pillar and asked if I agreed that dancing was really nothing but a continuation of ancient courtship rituals, Freddie Masters appeared miraculously and

331

magicked her away to dance.

Neil Maclean seemed in good humour too. I noticed him dancing frequently with Margot, and there was something in the American's expression as he danced, a brightness to his smile, that I recognised. I'd seen many men in love with Margot. What I'd not seen, I thought, was the look in Margot's eye. No coquetry there, no teasing, no triumph, no sense of a conqueror displaying a captive. Not even passion or laughter or fire. She looked *content*. At ease. Happy to be where she was, not thinking beyond the moment.

Lady Stansbury had seen it too. I came across her on the staircase that led to the gallery. She was looking out over the heads of her guests, watching her daughter dance.

'Off duty?' I asked cheerfully, in a tone more friendly and familiar than had ever existed between us in the past.

'A hostess, Tom, is never off duty. Relax for an instant and there is always a disaster with the meringues.' I laughed and Lady Stansbury's eyes returned to Margot and Maclean. 'They make a handsome couple, do they not?'

I couldn't deny it.

'His family is a very distinguished one in American circles,' she went on. 'I confess I had my doubts for a while, but we must move with the times, mustn't we, Tom?'

She turned to me, her eyes gentle. I saw in them something of the dreaminess I remembered from before the war, before grief had surprised in her that unsuspected kernel of determination.

'I haven't yet thanked you properly for your kind words about Harry this morning. Sir Robert was so

332

adamant that it should be you. I know Harry wasn't really your sort of person, Tom, but I knew you would say the right things.'

I began to demur, but she would have none of it.

'You don't have to deny it, Tom. I know Harry had his faults. He was a dear boy, and as a mother I was incredibly proud of him. But he was just a boy. He wasn't a saint. We both know that.' She looked out over the dancers again. 'I like to think, had he lived, he might have grown up and learned a few lessons and become someone rather fine. But of course every mother hopes that. It is not knowing that I find so very hard. Much harder than I expected.'

I left her still watching Margot dance.

It was about a quarter to midnight when I next saw Reggie. I had retreated to the gallery to recover my breath and from there had a perfect view of the Great Hall and of the doors leading off it. Reggie was sitting very still not far from the main door, alone, apparently watching the dancing. Something in his posture or in his face made me instantly wary. His expression was morose, but the way he held himself in his chair suggested he was poised for some sort of action.

My instinct was to go to him, but before I could move he had begun to propel himself forwards, towards the dance floor. Guests, taken by surprise, apologised and made way for him. When his chair reached the point where the dancing began, he made no attempt to slow down; he rolled straight on, so that the dancing couples had to check to avoid him. Many didn't see him until almost too late and came juddering to a halt, but the majority of those present in the Great Hall noticed nothing.

333

Strangely, the nearer Reggie came to the centre of the room, the less disruption he caused. The dancers began to flow around him more naturally, until he had become the fixed point at the centre of their vortex. It was then he reached beneath the blanket that covered his lap.

It seemed impossible that the couples dancing so close to him noticed nothing, but if they did they showed no sign of it. Perhaps they simply thought it was something planned, some part of the entertainment. Or perhaps I really was the only person there that night who saw Reggie produce the revolver; the only one who saw him raise his arm and point the barrel directly at the ceiling. My first reaction was a surge of relief. Reggie was going to fire into the air. He wanted to do no more than make a scene. But almost straight away he began to lower his arm, slowly and deliberately, and I could almost sense the finger tightening on the trigger. Through it all, I was absurdly aware that the orchestra was playing a two-step.

Then came the moment when I realised Reggie was aiming directly at me. The revolver was level with the gallery where I stood, and looking down the line of the barrel, I could see Reggie narrowing his eyes in concentration. Even then I don't think I moved, but I felt my body begin to tense. It all seemed too absurd, too bizarre. It was a mistake, surely. *Not me. Not me. Reggie can't mean me.* My eyes must have flickered shut because when I opened them again, I realised Reggie's arm was still moving, picking his spot, apparently focusing on something a fraction above me and a little to my left. And then, just as I turned to look, a shot rang out and I heard something shattering into pieces. As the room fell silent, the remains of an old chamberpot tumbled to the floor, smashing into fragments on the flagstones below. To my left, not very far away, the stuffed head of a bear, once decorated so flamboyantly by Harry Stansbury, had lost its absurd, fancy-dress crown.

Without question Reggie was now the centre of attention. Every head was turned towards him, and the doorways of the Great Hall were jammed with people trying to peer through. The orchestra was silent. One or two screams had followed the gunshot but now a hush had descended. For the most part faces were startled rather than scared.

'Ladies and gentlemen!' Reggie's voice rang out in the silence. He didn't sound drunk. He sounded exhausted.

'Ladies and gentlemen, I apologise for this unforgivable interruption. Unfortunately I found myself unable to remain here tonight without first performing a slight alteration to the décor. There is absolutely no reason to be alarmed. The mess shall be removed presently. Now, I want to dance. Where's Susan? My sister Susan? Music, please, orchestra! I intend to dance.'

No one moved. The silence had changed from surprise to one of excruciating awkwardness and I saw glances being exchanged: the exquisite, silent embarrassment of the English.

'Where's Susan?' Reggie roared, louder this time, and then turned to the orchestra and shouted for music at the top of his voice.

This had the effect of galvanising the conductor, who raised his baton with alacrity, but those closest to Reggie remained motionless. Then I heard a stirring in the crowd and saw Susan Stansbury

335

threading her way towards the dance floor.

'Susan!' Reggie exclaimed when he saw her, and suddenly his voice was that of a frightened child. 'Susan, I want to dance.'

She didn't speak, but she exuded perfect calm. Very carefully she took her position behind Reggie's chair, and as the music began, started to rock him backwards and forwards to its movement. I saw Reggie shut his eyes, and as the motion increased he rested his head against the back of the chair. When the music grew faster, the movement of the chair became more pronounced—a foot or two forward, a foot or two back. As if there were no one else in the room, brother and sister danced.

Later I heard it said that the dancing around them resumed spontaneously, but from where I was I saw exactly what happened. I saw Freddie Masters grab a startled Lucy Flinders and launch into motion, aiming at a gap in the crowds. Only then, with that example to follow, did the other dancers begin to move, and suddenly the room was full of the babble of voices, and the dance floor was once again a spiral of motion.

Amid all the confusion, I didn't see what happened to Reggie at the end of the dance. Freddie told me later that Susan had wheeled him quietly away and helped put him to bed. It was said there were tears on both their faces. But I saw none of it; by then Anne had joined me in the gallery.

'You know, Tom . . .' She leaned against the balustrade, her arms only an inch or two from my own. 'I always hated that chamberpot.'

I nodded. It represented something I was pleased to see brought to an end. 'So that's what Reggie was up to. I wonder how long he's been plotting it?'

But Anne only shrugged. Below us, the orchestra was preparing to begin another piece.

'Shall we dance?' I asked.

She didn't nod. She didn't even smile. But she did dance. And if her eyes didn't meet mine as we picked our way around the crowded floor, at least I felt her close to me again, moving to the same rhythm. And when the dance was over, finding ourselves near the French windows with the crowd very dense, it seemed natural to drift outside on to the terrace. There we stood in the cold, looking out over the dark lawns, waiting to hear the church clock chime midnight.

'What now?' I asked.

'We'll see,' she replied.

And I didn't argue. It was enough.